THE GOOD

DELIVERY

THE GOOD

DELIVERY

Nine Men. A Perfect Crime.

SEAN CURRIE

Dedicated to the people of Battersea, especially those who lived through the challenging times depicted in this novel.

As always, for Jaruwan.

CONTENTS

ACKNOWLEDGEMENTS

THIS IS MY FIRST NOVEL, and I'm fairly satisfied with the result. Whether readers will accept it, I don't know, but since I'm going to express my gratitude herein, thank you for arriving this far. I formulated the basic concept many years ago while standing a lonely bridge watch on a vast, dark forgotten ocean. Once I sat down to write, the story evolved beyond all recognition from my original idea, and it's better for that.

First, I should be grateful for three special friends; Judy Solivan, Lina Maria Donoso-Reyes and Puja Shrestha for their exuberant enthusiasm in my writing. With them in mind, I have tried consciously to add deeper characters. If nothing else, they have encouraged me to write a more accessible story. Thank you to the enterprise latecomer, Alanna Vishnudat, who worked studiously to assist me so much with the formatting.

I was comfortable with the authenticity of the original idea, but as I delved into areas in which I lacked knowledge, I knew not where to turn for advice. I have never been a proponent of that ephemeral concept called 'social media,' but this endeavor has changed my mind. I'm not revealing too much to announce the story contains a train— it's on the cover—and what do I know of trains? As it turns out, if you ever need to understand English trains, there is a wonderful place called RailUKForums, where I spent many hours learning from a dozen or so friendly, anonymous people who taught me so much. I genuinely came away with not just a greater awareness, but a new-found enthusiasm for everything on rails. As it turned out, the forum members also contributed significantly to such diverse subjects as pigeon fancying, Wandsworth ales and the common sugary sweets (candy) of early 1960s Britain.

A second forum came to my assistance when I needed to learn of England's 1963 road system? Sabre-Roads explained to me some routes crucial to the story and the general status of Britain's Motorways (Freeways).

Ah, these last two acknowledgements highlight a problem that I encountered early on. I'm an American living in Washington, D.C., where the book will be printed, and probably the majority of readers will reside. Accordingly, I bought a copy of the exceedingly large (and expensive) *Chicago Manual of Style*. It taught me how to write American. But the story, quite obviously, is unswervingly English. I churned this around in my head for a while, and eventually made a decision. As always, I compromised, so the result will doubtless annoy everyone. The punctuation and spelling are all *Chicago*, as best I could, but proper nouns and colloquial speech are English. You'll figure it out. I hope it doesn't distract.

My gratitude to the British Merchant Navy forum and my old friend Doc Vernon. This site is essential to understand anything first-hand about real, working ships. Additionally, the Facebook site; My British Merchant Navy. For each question, dozens of experienced posters jumped in and assisted. Thank you all so much. When not seeking nautical information, I was assisted by Jon Stagg, a railway enthusiast, but all-round knower of things, who read the whole book and contributed to a vast range of subjects, from jet engines, early 1960s Ford cars, the English legal system and London pubs.

Thank you to Martin McKay of the British Transport Police History Group who, if he didn't have a riposte, had the acquaintances to answer all police-focused questions. Again, the internet can be used for good.

Much appreciation to Neil Morris, (who calls himself a "reader," but offered so much more), who I 'met' through a mutual acquaintance, Steve Harris. Neil read the whole book and gave me much encouragement (and counseled when I became bogged down). He saw my lack of knowledge on the English nobility.

Much credit goes to Roger Thornton FICS, who along with another gentleman whose permission I failed to obtain, explained to me the peculiarities of the import/export system of what used to be called HM Customs & Excise. I've incorporated these details, because, let's face it, the men involved would have had to as well.

Thank you to the supportive Paul Hadley who contributed so much authenticity that I couldn't imagine the book without him. It was he, at the last moment, who advised of the severity of the 1962/3 English winter, of which I was unaware. Many changes were made to the story to incorporate Paul's ideas.

From the outset I made it my goal to avoid professionals. Eventually, I did employ Susan Carson (who I have known for many years) to contribute her artistic skills to the excellent front cover. If you want to see Susan's art, visit her website at carsonartmusic—it's filled with brilliant paintings. For the back cover I used a free image by Cristian Ruberti.

Finally, there are two ladies I could not have completed this process without. Jackie Westcott, my informal "copy editor" who, after first struggling with my American English, finally found her way through the book and discovered so many errors that required correction. With her Etonian friend and consultation of Debrett's, she explained to me the intricacies of the English nobility. And so much more.

And Kathleen Benzon, my splendid new friend that lived through those troubled times in Battersea and became my "content editor", clarifying decidedly what books and the internet couldn't fully explain. She was one of a hundred friendly—real people—on the Facebook post, Battersea Memories. I've read, what seems, an endless pile of books, web pages and posts (and enjoyed doing so); learning is the hidden gem of writing.

I owe all the above, and many more, a thousand thanks of gratitude. I'm forever in your debt. Having said that, let me be clear; I'm responsible for the undoubted errors, plot holes and your lack of enjoyment. If you want to discuss it, here's my email address:
seanjcurrie@outlook.com

November 2020

Prologue

THE RAND

July 1886 - Pretoria, The South African Republic

THE MINERALS PROSPECT MANAGER, his name lost to the winds of time, sat behind his small wooden desk in a wicker chair, and waived George into the room, "Sit down, Mr. Harrison." The manager had stern eyes, more gray than blue. He had not only had an awful day, but a dreadful month, so the eyes perfectly reflected his general demeanor. He didn't want to contemplate his troubles right now. This, before him, seemed a compelling development, but he knew how not to reveal excitement, and anyway, it was just a rumor. He stood, lifted the window sash, and a gentle, warm breeze stirred into the room. He liked winters here in this bite-sized town. Sitting back down, chair squeaking as he adjusted to his regular, formal position, he gathered the papers and read the top one to himself again while his visitor sat still and quiet:

Affidavit: "My name is George Harrison, and I come from the newly discovered goldfields Kliprivier, especially from a farm owned by a certain Gert Oosthuizen. I have a long experience as an Australian gold digger, and I think it is a payable goldfield."

George Harrison inhaled a long draw from the pipe he clenched between his stained teeth and exhaled thoughtfully. He wore his comfortable jacket, a shapeless brown tweed, frayed at the elbows. He parted his brown hair on the left, and a long forelock fell over one eye. He had arrived two days earlier and cleaned up in the rudimentary hotel, but his beard remained long and messy. He saw no point in shaving. His voice was loud, honking, and carried far, but he thought it better to allow the other man to initiate the conversation. The manager stretched his chin forward and adjusted his high collar and constricting tie, peered at his desk and tidied the two pens thoughtfully. Stroking the hair bordering his empty scalp, he looked George in the eye, placed down his statement, and pronounced, in a strong Afrikaans accent, "Now, Mr. Harrison, I'm told you believe you've found some gold here in the Zuid Afrikaansche Republiek of the Transvaal?"

George frowned, "Sorry, mate, the 'zood' what?" He could hardly comprehend these strange Dutch accents of the white people here.

The manager stared, "The South African Republic. The Transvaal, Mr. Harrison."

"Yes, I found some gold, and I say it's payable. I'm asserting a discoverer's claim," replied George straightforwardly. He didn't come to waste time; he had a distance yet to travel.

"Well, slow down, please, Mr. Harrison. First, I need some further information. Why don't you tell me your story? From the beginning," suggested the manager.

George had taken twelve weeks to walk here, to Pretoria, so he reconsidered; a few more wasted minutes did not impose, and anyway, he saw value in the uncompleted paperwork lying at the edge of the manager's desk. Clearing his throat, he began, "Well, let's see. I arrived in Cape Town on a lovely summer's day in January…"

"From where?" The manager interrupted.

"On a boat from Perth, Australia." The manager asked if that is where he originated. "Nah, I'm from Bong Bong, New South Wales, same place as Joseph Wild lived." The manager was unfamiliar with the name, so asked George to continue his story.

He explained how he had departed Cape Town a few months after arriving, because although the town was spectacular, it lacked any enticements for him. "I'm a prospector by trade, and made good moolah in the outback, but I heard the gold here was found different. I can now attest to that fact. Anyhow, I walked north from Cape Town, heading for Kimberly where I heard there were diamonds." He had climbed out of the Cape Fold Mountains that protect the Cape, and the weather became sub-tropical and it rained. "Dear God—and he's no friend of mine—I wished it had rained later on, but this is as dry as a nun's nasty country you got here." The low-lying narrow coastal zone soon gave way to a mountainous escarpment separating the coast from the high inland plateau. George walked and walked in a north-east direction.

"I stopped along the Karoo and got into some ostrich farming. They were as big as a boomer, some of them, but good leather and lean, tasty meat."

"Boomer?" enquired the manager.

"Boomers! Big roos!" he explained, and the manager nodded knowingly without understanding. As George had walked on, the landscape hardly changed; no wind, no rain, just stale raw air. Inconceivable formations of canyons and immense rock structures sat in the distance, circling the desert like a tremendous empty stadium, with red, rocky stands that he knew existed, but remained remote and out of reach. Each time his eyes wandered back to study the distant landscape, it seemed only a projection on the horizon. "I worked my way north as a handyman, a no-money prospector, sometimes digging for diamonds.

"I tell you," George continued, "I saw animals I never sawed before; elephants, for Christ's sake! Rhino, buffalo, lions, the zebra, and diff'rent antelopes. I got a little malaria fever; damn mozzies everywhere. I stayed for a while in a town called Prieschap on the Orange River." The South African central plateau contains only two major rivers: the Limpopo, and the Orange, which flow east to west, emptying into the Atlantic Ocean. "I had to stop there for a while, 'cos I had no way of crossing. Eventually, an Englishman called John Smith came along. He's an outstanding man. He had wagons, and he was going to Kimberly. We crossed the river; you know that takes you into the Orange Free State, headed for Kimberly."

The manager interrupted, "I thought you were a gold prospector?"

"Right, I am, but you can't walk past Kimberly without looking for diamonds," replied Harrison, as if the manager had either not been listening or didn't understand the business of prospecting.

"Please continue, Mr. Harrison."

"Well, the landscape got flatter and harsher, but nothing I couldn't handle. Cactuses, tumbleweeds. Dust devils, dead grass. Some nice desert flowers after the rain, but then flash flooding. I'd never sawed that before. Do you know what I remember most?" The manager, listening carefully, slowly shook his head.

"The sensations." George seemed to hesitate, reluctant to recall, perhaps, but then continued, "The wind; whistling and howling. So many birds I saw. And sometimes the sound of my own footsteps, the heavy silence. And yapping wild dogs." Harrison seemed to drift away with contemplation of the walk. He continued, nodding, "And the arid air, dust. My sweat, my dry mouth, bloody warm canteen water, the bitter taste of insects. And thirst and hunger." There was a brief silence, except for the baying of a horse outside.

Grassland had dominated George's walk, particularly on the Highveld. There were few trees, but a high level of plant diversity, especially on the escarpments. He consumed succulents to slate his thirst while saving water. Further northeast, the grass and thorn turned slowly into bush savannah, with denser growth.

The sunburnt, barren land became an eternal desert stretching for miles, and George admitted he had misjudged the distance and hardship. The intense sun blazed down on this harsh, yet ethereal, wilderness of red rocks, imbuing the lonely walker with the feeling of isolation in a giant, empty land. He believed himself the only man within many miles. When the sun set, the last rays of light scorched the desert gold, and the final beams of crepuscular sunlight perforated the horizon, like an arrow pointing him northeast. The incredible landscape changed into a vast, freezing cold nothingness.

The manager felt the story was colorful and truthful, but led nowhere. He felt he needed to interrupt, "And Kimberly?"

George smiled the knowing smile of the hardened professional. "Thousands of men have already blunted their picks and spades there. And came back cleaned out, backs aching, finding nothing. And the British are there," he warned, "financing everything, digging deep, expensive mines. I had a look round for a month, but there's nothing in the way of diamonds for the average bloke to find."

The manager knew that during the recent years of the Kimberley rush they found some gold in the Transvaal, primarily at Barberton.

It was never enough to tempt the diamond men of Kimberley. Yet this did not discourage prospectors. The problem being they were seeking gold as it had appeared in California and Australia before. They stumbled about like blindfolded men, groping their way towards what they believed would be the "mother lode," from which had sprung the traces of gold they had found so far.

Harrison detected the manager's keen interest, so he carried on, "So, I moved on. Heaps of people said there were gold and diamonds north of the Free State, so I headed there. You see, if there's gold or diamonds, I will find them. I just can't compete with big moolah. People said I couldn't walk a long distance. Some said I would die hiking north of Bloemfontein and others said I would die of hunger or be eaten by lions. But I don't die easy, Mr. Manager."

The listening man nodded perceptively, while George went on, "Half way there it was my good fortune to run across the Oosthuizen family. They have the Highvelt farm of scrubland in Langlaagte, which I guess you know means Long Shallow Valley. Which it is."

It was May by then, and a warm, scented wind, full with the hot oily smell of pancakes and sausage cooking on the stove by the roadside, drew him towards the farm. "They gave me work fixing a cabin roof on Langlaagte for a Boer widow, Petronella Oosthuizen. After a while I signed a contract with the family, letting me prospect for gold."

Harrison found fleeting interest on the farm. He already understood the work intimately. He knew the long hours, the sweaty, stinking, heavy clothing, the dry heat, the way it feels to drag yourself in at twilight after a day in the field, sitting on the doorstep and pulling his boots from his aching feet before eating the simple evening meal. The manager unsettled him from his account with the question, "Do you know a man named George Walker?"

The question took Harrison by surprise, but he hid the emotion, "Sure. He had a contract to look for gold too. But I found it."

"And Fred and Harry Struben?" The manager quizzed again. "They say they found gold in streams and quartzes."

"I met George Walker further south. It was a long walk, so we broke the journey on the Witwatersrand to earn some money. The Struben brothers offered Walker a job and pointed me toward the Oosthuizen family, a few miles away. I left Walker, but we agreed to meet up once the work was done and we would head north again," he explained.

"All these people say they found gold," declared the manager, a little indignantly.

George sat and smiled again. "Maybe they did, but not enough to bother panning for." Then he added his masterstroke, "The payable gold is underground."

The manager, confused, added, "I don't understand. How do you know that?"

"Witwatersrand means…" began George.

"A Ridge of White Water, yes, I know,"

"Oh, yeah. Keep forgetting. The ridges have sharp crests and are eight or nine hundred feet high. They rise out of low, rolling hills and valleys. Believe me, I looked. At the escarpment, like a long ridge,"— George held his arm out straight and slowly swept it to the right—"I could see the different layers, layers put down long before time began." The manager leaned forward slightly, recognizing a man who understood his business. George went on, "The sedimentary rock, you know, from an ocean, is a conglom'rate, with tiny, almost invisible specks of gold between the pebbles. I saw the reefs of rock going into the ground at an angle."

George sat back, and slowly shifted his head from side to side, "They might find some alluvial gold while panning around, but the main reef is underground." Prospectors find alluvial gold by scooping the beds of rivers or streams and panning for dust. George explained how the quality of the rock he'd stumbled upon had fascinated him, and realizing that it was ancient, he broke off a piece, took it back to the farm and crushed it. He later panned the rock in a borrowed frying pan and noticed a gleam of gold. Tiny amounts. "To get the gold, you must dig and dig. Huge quantities of rock, I reck'n."

The manager slowly exhaled, "Fascinating, Mr. Harrison. But if you can't get the gold, why do you need a discoverer's claim?"

"So I can sell it." Another brief silence, as if the two of them were completely misunderstanding each other. George continued, "Then move on north where I hope to find El dorado. It's north of here."

"We're not ready to release this information yet, Mr. Harrison. You understand the politics of the situation?" explained the manager.

George replied, smiling, as if to a young child, "The British will find out, eventually. And you know what? You're gonna need their money to dig on that kind of scale."

The manager stood, stretched, and gazed out the window at the dusty view, pondering the alternatives. What if this man was correct? Gold might be a lifeline for his young nation, but the British would know. How could they stop them? For now, his instructions were explicit. Returning to his desk, he picked up the file, "Mr. Harrison. If I give you the claim, will you seek to sell it right away? And for how much?"

Harrison already had his number; "Ten pounds. That's what I'll need to resupply with tucker and head to the eastern Transvaal."

The manager reached inside the folder and handed him the exact amount. "You've sold your claim Mr. Harrison. What will you do next?"

"You know, Mr. Manager, we think we're in charge of our lives... but we're not."

George Harrison headed north for the unproven goldfields of the eastern Transvaal. In October the government made a formal proclamation of the monumental find of the Witwatersrand, declaring it a public goldfield. The discovery completely eclipsed Kimberly, and the new settlement of Johannesburg grew up alongside it to become the nineteenth century's last great boomtown. Fortune hunters from Australia and California joined skilled Cornish and Welsh miners to dig. Africans from every corner of the southern subcontinent migrated to the city. The control obsession of both the Boers and the British led to the Second Anglo-Boer War of 1899-1902, which spread to the whole of South Africa. The Boers lost and South Africa became a British colony while the business of minerals became ever more the concern of Consolidated Diamond Mines and De Beers.

When George Harrison passed through, he could not have grasped he was on top of the richest gold field the world would ever find. How could he understand the eccentric geology of the huge Witwatersrand Basin in which the gold-bearing reefs (containing flecks of gold so fine they are mostly unseen to the human eye), outcropped briefly on the surface, then plunged down underground, sloping inward towards the center. The gold-bearing sides of the basin have never "bottomed out."

Today, we know the Witwatersrand comprised part of the "golden arc," an ancient inland lake containing abundant deposits of gold stretching sixty miles long and twelve thousand feet deep. It is the reason the South African currency became the "Rand" in 1961.

Harrison, who had experienced the Australian goldfields, recognized the rock as a gold-bearing formation which, if crushed, might yield an ounce or two of gold from every ton of ore. This is the essence of the South African gold mines. No one picks up nuggets. There is an unfathomable body of low-grade ore stretching in a wide arc from forty miles east of Johannesburg to ninety miles west, then swinging down southwest into the Orange Free State. The gold-bearing reefs, laid down two thousand million years ago, vary in thickness from one tenth of an inch to one hundred feet but, on the average, are only one foot wide. Thus, although the news of gold on Langlaagte farm brought men rushing to the fledgling city of Johannesburg, it was only those with capital who could participate. The diamond men from Kimberley quickly established control.

And when they dug and dug, they found so much more gold in the Witwatersrand elephant than anyone might have imagined. Gold is not like any other commodity; it's never consumed. It's always there, a mighty store of value. This curious yellow metal became money a long, long time ago and has outlasted all the other monies they have invented since. There is a universal acceptance of its value, regardless of any fiat money. Uniquely, gold, when it changes hands, is a payment; all other money is just a promise to pay.

Although legends of a South African "El Dorado" existed among the natives of the area, it was not until George Harrison staked the first claim that the vast riches of the Rand were discovered. By 1962, when our story begins, the Witwatersrand had produced about ninety percent of all the gold that humans had ever found.

And nobody ever heard of George Harrison again.

THE GARDEN

There is no honest man—not one—that can resist the attraction of gold.

- Aristophanes

Late July 1962 - Kent, England

FEW PEOPLE KNEW Billy Tumbler well, and fewer still imagined he might be heroic. His mother had named him after William Slim, commander of the "forgotten army" in Burma, she claimed. When she heard the traitor Lord Haw-Haw—with his distinctive nasal enunciation of "Germany calling, Germany calling"—was named William Joyce, she refashioned his name to Billy. He stood about five feet, five inches and walked with a forlorn but agile gait, like a slim, young man who had lost his dog. Some deemed him undernourished, but he reflected the time and place of his origin. His auburn hair was too long on top, in that new fashion, and cut too short at the sides. His irregular teeth were consistent with the age. His body itched with the scratchy, white shirt under the black standard issue battledress jacket worn one size too big, while his haunting blue eyes moved about the evil surroundings. Since the lunch break today he had roamed the somber confines, shunning the feared, girding himself for what he recognized would be the awful, inevitable encounter. Pausing midway along the clanking iron landing, having found an inconspicuous spot beside a pillar, he leaned against the rail, withdrew into the angle, and gazed down at the floor below comprising the cunning, the weary and the grim.

His anxious mind strayed, as it often did. After his father abandoned the family, and work on the river became forever unattainable, he had sailed with the South Seas Shipping Line out of London. As a serving deck boy, he joined the lucky generation that had been spared National Service after the War. On his second voyage to Australia, the captain had promoted him to ordinary seaman because he had enthusiasm, toiled hard and absorbed the craft of the ocean. His compatriots considered him a natural seafarer, one comfortable with the peculiarities of that business. He sent money home every month to his now single mother, experienced weather conditions he never dreamed possible, became intoxicated with alcohol for the first and only time, and had the chance—but shunned the opportunity with respect for his longtime girl—of an amorous liaison. He had a life and career ahead of him, and the opportunity to see the world.

Then, on recent leave, he stepped out one evening with two school friends, the irresponsible but entertaining Baker brothers, with the youthful intention of mischief. The rest, as they say, is history. But the legend compels to be told, or the world would never know.

While half-concealed beside the pillar, Billy recalled that dreadful first day of his recent life, six weeks before, standing alone before the omnipotent magistrate, fearful of eye contact with the gallery spectators. "This is nothing but a tawdry, petty crime driven by greed," thundered the voice of justice from the bench above. "There's nothing romantic about it. I sentence you to eight months. Take him down."

The brothers got fourteen months apiece, but that afforded minimal consolation. He didn't realize it then, but Billy would never see them again. He had rid himself of a noble career and joined the criminal class. Life wasn't fair, he appreciated, but he couldn't shake the devastating sense he had become a casualty of circumstance, as they led him away into another world where a hollow God allowed monsters to live.

Sign this paper, sign that paper, not recognizing and not choosing. His legal aid solicitor suggested he could be free in six months, while they moved him west to Wormwood Scrubs; the place of all nightmares. They took his clothes, odds and ends, and any remnants of dignity. That first night passed in a whirlwind of brick walls, in and out of Black Marias, the stench of decay, disinfectant and urine, dirty cream-above-green colored passages and one sleepless night with the other innocents. Then, they transferred Billy to this other Victorian internment in the county known as the Garden of England, with its wealth of fruit, hops and beautiful, green, chalky downs. The guards delivered him through the front gate and up two tiers to where other inmates waited.

The rituals of intake had been depressingly alien. Standing in line, he had stripped, squatted, and coughed in reply to the bellowed instructions still ringing in his ears. It was humiliating and degrading. They gave each prisoner a dirty bath, and the alacrity of the exercise hardly wetted him. The prison furnished him with a paltry collection of toiletries, blanket and sheets, clothing, two rolls of paper and a cheap bar of Sunlight soap. But all he had was his name. Now you're in it, Billy! One silly night of playfulness with a pair of old schoolmates and your life has gone. Now twenty, the Young Offender Wing being full, they assigned Billy to the general population. He found it harrowing to imagine eight months of unrelenting misery in the insidious seeping gloom.

Since entering, he sought a veneer of maturity, carrying his head high, but he couldn't conceal his compact frame or his beautiful, large-eyed face, broken with the scant teenage remnants of inflammation. He recalled how they displayed him when entering the wing, more grist for the mill of the vast charm vacuum of Her Majesty's Prison Maidstone, her hard, ragstone walls built to grind down the will of the six hundred men living at her pleasure; a lumbering public service advertisement for breaking the human spirit. When an inmate arrived, he was friendless. If young, he is alone and afraid. The factions and gangs scrutinized, like wolves readying their assault, perceiving the time he spent alone, with whom he ate, how he socialized, like an abandoned young wildebeest on the veldt. They packed prison with stupid, manipulative and pugnacious people, who day after day, year after year, had no space to claim their own, no choice with whom to associate, what to eat, or where to go. Threat and suspicion were everywhere, a relentless struggle for survival. Companionship, or even a gentle human ear, would be hard to find in here; no succor in the dark recesses of the caged male.

The prison smells swamped the senses, like a dead creature housing the lost souls of rejected men, along with a century of neglect and decay blended with fear, oppression and alienation that comes with incarceration. The reek of sin and shame oozed from the pores of trapped animals in search of redemption. Whether it came from the sweat and tears that stained the moldy mattresses and uniforms, or the filth that lingered on the edge of the grated walkways, no one could escape the foulness manifested in the sorry lives of those inside. In this surreal place, no measure of bleach could make it clean again, forever suffused with that nameless stench living beneath your fingernails and in your hair. It would linger in Billy's psyche forever.

He recognized the onlookers who paid particular scrutiny when a young innocent entered the mansion of purgatory. In the first days, they had threatened him. One belligerent had defined, "If you snitch on us, we'll kill you." His routine field of movement dwindled as each day passed. The persecuted were first timers, youngsters lacking strength and allies, appearing solitary and fearful. Rapists see these details. He was a target, and Maidstone was full of men desperate to quench their surfeit of testosterone.

His cellmate, Oliver "Peter" Mann, was an unsuccessful safecracker, and cordial enough. They spoke of their families and the crimes that had incarcerated them. Oliver cautioned of the law of captivity; "Out there in the common area it's struggle and conflict, in here just do your time." With a bunk bed and chamber pot wedged into an eight-foot by twelve-foot cell, the relationship with your cellmate could turn a rough experience into a dreadful one. Cockroaches crawled in the realm of his thoughts, tapping into the deep crevices of memory suppressed and distant for a while now. Sleep became elusive. When it arrived, Billy dreamed of terrifying monsters, but at night someone was always screaming, shouting, liberating their minds from the awful truth inside—no thoughts, feelings, or words; just howling. He yearned to lie down and hibernate for eight months, but this remained a place where elusive silence became his best, but unobtainable friend. He lived his life in the cell, three feet from the chamber pot. Forced by necessity to urinate and defecate before Oliver, the stink lingered all night. Unless they were brave and the weather allowed, then they could toss the contents out the barred window. As he lay in bed reliving every action of the recent past, the disgust and dimly lit horrors that lived in the bleak shadows of his worst nightmares returned. Above all else, Billy, as any inmate would declare, suffered the frightful insecurity of being enclosed in a room which locks from the outside.

"This is your cellmate. This is the man you get along with or there'll be trouble," admonished the officer, pushing him inside. Oliver smoked on his bed. He'd been inside before. This was his home, his singular territory.

The older man advised: "Share stuff with others; food and fags. Eat fast and say nothing to strangers. Walk away from fights. Never get involved. There are some right hard bastards in here."

* * * *

In the middle of the twentieth century, England—fifty million, overwhelmingly indigenous people—was an unremarkable place upon the cusp of a permissive and hedonistic age rapidly approaching. Much of the despair of the previous decade had derived from winning two World Wars. On the home front, communities and families had dispersed, the Blitz had piled terror upon terror, houses disappeared in an instant, and rationing made everyone hungry. Then, in one glorious moment in 1945, the British people overturned the status quo by chucking out Churchill and his Conservatives, electing a socialist government who understood they won the War, not for the nobility and gentry of England, but for the ordinary men and women who had suffered globally and at home.

The nation's frame of reference had dwindled since then, delivering austerity and stifling the dreams of young London men. They had steeped the previous generation in empire, and now couldn't tolerate a world unraveling faster than they, or anyone, might comprehend. The empire and thoughts of adventure were fading. The 1950s—back in the hands of the Conservatives—were years of shame; a nightmare of failed budgets, canceled glories, and embarrassments like the Suez debacle. There might have been a Cold War, a heartbeat from disaster, but the main combatants ignored the British, and the ordinary people just got on with their lives.

But by 1962, economic advances were spreading like the crocuses of spring, as the country aspired to catch up with an American-based, explosive euphoria of the future. An openly realized class system held the nation back, but the barriers were collapsing and friendships were possible between anyone, when they surrendered their prejudices. England remained monochrome and bleak, but skirts were slowly climbing higher, awaiting the cultural and social revolution just about to arrive.

Many of those young men had been children during the War and, now, having lived through austerity, they wanted a bright, rich future. Some of them were prepared to do more than others to achieve that goal.

* * * *

On a cloudy day, the building's skylight transformed into a grim and foreboding spider's web covering a virus of inmates, its hard, stone walls blinding those inside to the quaint surroundings of the bucolic county of Kent beyond. When it rained, the skies turned heavy, pressing down upon the inmates, squashing their psyches deeper, slowing time and grinding low any thoughts of a future. The days, rigidly rotating about the three-meal routine, stagnated the mind, other than the relentless defense of the self against the predators. Everyone, especially the young and tender, were in danger, unless you had friends, and Billy—young, vibrant and promising—had none. The inherent animal instincts of men never subside. Maidstone was nothing special, no different or worse than a few dozen similar hotels in service of the Crown.

The first visiting day morphed into the nadir of Billy's life. His mother had grown old so quickly. Sally, his best friend and lover, accompanied her on the train from Victoria, but the aching void of their absence distressed him. He had prepared a speech to confess his guilt, but when confronted with his mother, his mind became blank. All he wanted to say remained trapped inside by the searing pain in his throat. He recognized his responsibility to support them, and he had failed. Billy had always sought to make his parents proud, but he could feel the sadness slipping from his mother sitting opposite. It was all he could do to stop himself breaking down and crying for forgiveness, and relief washed over him when the meeting reached its time-stipulated conclusion. *Be a man, Billy*, he reflected angrily to himself. Endure this and begin again. For a moment, after returning to his cell, he became filled with a fearless, perhaps unrelenting desire, to secure his family's financial future. Whatever it took.

Billy jolted from his traumatic thoughts leaning against the pillar on the second floor, to the awfulness of the day, recognizing he lacked a route to survival. He understood that people in jail reverted to a more primitive behavior; the animal requiring a pack. He vowed to discover those that might preserve a level of dignity, although he couldn't then see how.

He gazed down through the netting covering the first floor, like viewing the same fetid insects in a cage, surmising that ninety percent were bloody idiots. He beheld Tommy, the "smiling con" they called him, flitting about in his naïve and gullible manner. But Billy knew, like everyone else, it was a fake smile. It only made his character sadder, like an invalided cousin, but at least no one abused him. He studied the old men, like Clive; nearing the point of surrender, or committing a dreadful act upon themselves. There was Smelly, who everyone avoided. Then, to his right, he saw them sitting at a table, attended by two fresh-faced men—one only a boy, really. He disliked Bishop the most; a stout, greasy man, the type who found satisfaction in the misfortune of others. Nobody liked him, but he kept an entourage based on fear and coercion. His second, a northern, bearded beast named Lyman, followed like a pet poodle, an evil compatriot to an evil man. He was guilty too, culpable of the worst crimes. They chatted, smoked, relaxed, seeking the carrion of fresh youngsters. Officially, the rules forbid prisoners from visiting other cells, but the screws frequently turned away for a price. The abusers would cover the tiny window with a cloth. Then, twisting to his left, Billy considered the daunting men on the far landing who nobody inconvenienced. They were the "faces," the hardcore "blaggers" (violent robbers), prisoners with profiles and reputations.

The prisoners cemented within these walls a rigid hierarchy of the interned. They revered the "old lags" (recurrent prisoners) because they had survived. But they reserved most esteem for the heavy-duty armed robbers, the men of action, the men with a trade. Then there were the "bellmen" (alarms), "screwsmen" (key copiers), "cutters" (acetylene), getaway drivers and "petermen" (safecrackers), like his cell mate Oliver. Lower down lived the tea-leaves (thieves), handbag snatchers and lowlifes. Below the abject and unconcerned were the manipulators, conning inmates and screws out of money and cigarettes. Bottom of the ladder were the homosexuals and molesters.

Moving on casually, so as not to attract attention, he arrived to the end of the second floor. He spotted some rat droppings in the corner as he swung to descend to level one, passing the young Jamaican with a swollen eye. Billy held out a hand in consolation, but the black man now shunned human interaction. There were those who believed they would thrive by acquiescing, but as soon as they did, they would have everyone asking for favors, and Billy had none to give voluntarily. He'd formed a simple plan; avoid everyone.

The following morning, on his now familiar routine of evasion, savoring the rarity of a prison day devoid of dramatic tension, Billy descended, paused, then turned to the fixed, small table near the center of the atrium and stood before Clive and his chess game. The old man gazed up, lifted his National Health glasses, shrugged and invited him to sit. Billy stared down at the board, ready to learn, to lose himself in the pastime of reason. Sitting down, he sensed the elder man stand and turn away as a dark cloud engulf him, blocking the dreary skylights. He stared up in alarm to behold a well-shaped man accept the chair opposite. Billy stared into the funeral black eyes, the center of a fine, rugged, square face; prodigious and strong with a scarred chin below a slim Panatela cigar. An elegant, black mustache covered the upper lip, the hair on his head slicked back. He had something about his eyes that made him appear capable of real violence. He leaned forward; the tunic stretching as his muscles filled and adapted to the new posture, his expression serious, but not unkind. Billy felt abandoned and uneasy.

The man grinned, slightly tilted his head, softening his eyes, "Do you know who I am?" He spoke with an easy, clipped voice. Billy, startled, shook his head. There was a resolve about Billy that faded into shyness the moment he opened his mouth. Though short, slim and vigorous, his voice was soft, high and wheezy, often falling short of breath during long sentences, so he talked in concise, self-conscious bursts. He'd seen the man, examined the innate elegance about him, but never drew near. How can you approach anyone in here? Then another man, lankier, imposing, sat next to them, adjusting his frame, his legs opening wide and bumping against him, unable to fit comfortably beneath the small table. Billy shifted his frantic gaze to see his large, straight nose on a confident face, his languishing eyes disinterested as he lit—not a roll up like most prisoners—a Player cigarette with a stylish Ronson lighter.

"The word is, young man, you've been to sea?" said the first one.

Billy, taken aback and ignorant of the conversation's purpose, frowned and nodded, tensing next to so much muscularity.

"Where are you from?" came the second query.

Finally, Billy found his voice: "South… southwest eleven." Why was he being questioned?

"Battersea? I've earned some respect in that manor. Whereabouts?" came the third question.

Caught unawares, he spluttered, "Grant…Road," and belatedly thought better of it. The man with the mustache swung his eyes to the left. The fair-haired one glared down and thought, "Grant Road? Up near the Junction."

"How long are you in for, Billy?" the man opposite searched again.

"Eight months…out in Jan…'ow do ya know me name?"

"I'm John Russell. This is Daniel Geddes. Heard of us?" came the formal reply.

Billy nodded. They had familiar reputations in the Metropolitan Borough of Battersea, the bogeymen of the local underworld, accused of so much more than anyone believed possible. His mind reeled. His eyes darted between them. Why were they talking to him?

"You can't trust anybody in here, Billy" said Russell with a knowing, father-like tone. "And I have an issue with trust. I don't trust anybody." Then, pausing, he changed the subject, "No previous right?" Before Billy could answer, he added, "…and you served in the Merchant Navy?" as if to confirm the previous answer.

How does he know that, thought Billy? "I…still do."

Russell sucked through his teeth, "Might be a little tricky now with a record sheet."

Billy remained silent, his mind in turmoil, nibbling on his lower lip. He had never thought that far ahead, just trusting he would return to the sea when this nightmare concluded. Fighting and receiving a misconduct ticket would lead to "chokey" (isolation cells). And what was the point? A third man appeared to his left, standing, gazing away in disinterest, his face below a bald head, apparently molded from beaten plasticine, his head squeezed down into his neck, the features rounded and blended into each other as if to avoid compromise. He was enormous, with a gaze in his menacing eyes that negated having to use violence. His otherness appeared unnerving.

"The first few months of a sentence are the worst; the mind half in, half out." Russell continued as if to reassure, "I can offer you work when you get out, Billy. Do you know the Prince Albert, across from the park, near the bridge?" Billy nodded, still trying to grasp the context of the discussion, "It's an opportunity, young man, an odd bit of skullduggery and a chance to say goodbye to the drab existence of your parents and grandparents. You can be inside pissing out for a change." He appeared to reflect before continuing, "You know, the worst crime a man can commit is to bring up his family in poverty. Daniel here owns the pub. Drop by, you'll find one of us there most days." John Russell spoke intently, "Good work, good money, Billy."

Billy's brief life at sea had hardened his resolve. Confused and inundated with the information and presence of the three men, he wavered, then said, "Wot do ya want? Are you in wiv' Bishop and Lyman?" instantly fearing he had used the wrong words.

Russell guffawed a quiet howl and leaned his head back, while Geddes removed the Player from his mouth with a pink, shovel-like hand and leaned in close to Billy, "We're not pansies, son, we're armed fucking bank robbers."

Billy sat wide-eyed. John Russell smiled, leaned back, and blew the smoke from his Panatela. "Life is shit, I know. We've all had our first nights. Bishop," he shook his head, "has he started walking upright yet?"

He turned to his companion who responded in the same manner, "I'm sick and tired of those two scamps slapping boys around," and they smiled in some long-shared, knowing awareness.

"Time to punch in, Daniel?" winked Russell with gusto.

"Oh! We're going there, are we?" He thought for a moment, "Well, I'll need a spare day," they both bellowed again, "and I might need to stretch first." They sounded a hearty cackle at that, but Billy remained uncomfortable.

They stood, clattering the clumsy chairs to leave, and John Russell turned, "The Prince Albert, Billy. Battersea Park. A man must do what he has to." Then smiling, "Then he can do what he wants." The abruptness of the conversation struck Billy. He favored more time to consider their words. He didn't feel scared as they walked away, since there was nothing cold or impersonal about them. Billy could never be sure if this was the start of another terrifying decent, or a turn to a new direction. How could he guess that these men were the instigators and organizers of all that might happen? An inkling of an idea grew in his mind and the truth became obvious; money was the only thing that cured the stigma of being born poor.

* * * *

There were eight showerheads in the cramped, anemic off-white tiled room, reeking of the fearful. Keeping clean was a necessity, though; an administrative policy, yes, and essential to avoid offending others. Gripping the towel tightly around his waist until the last moment, not lingering for the water to warm, Billy scrubbed his hair and joints rapidly, soaping and rinsing, then dressed without allowing the time to dry. The shower was not a place to loiter. Oliver had advised; "Don't look scared, the dogs smell fear. Don't make eye contact."

He cultivated a strategy to evade confrontation, along with which Oliver willingly complied. On days when they completed work early, they would proceed directly to the showers alone, before the afternoon shift ended, shunning the mass of naked bodies jostling for the water, before the prison locked down and nobody could move. Billy despised the thick press of bodies, smelling of sweat and panic.

On Thursday the two of them began their regular plan, covering each other in the bi-weekly perilous act. He loathed showering, but it was essential. He had never touched the pleasure of hot, running, clean water until at eighteen, he had joined the oceangoing MV *South Easter* to support his mother and girlfriend. But a shower on a ship was a relaxing indulgence after a hard day's labor, while here it was a journey into the darkness of man. Some days the occasion had been as banal as it should always be, others he had abandoned, gathering his clothes and hastily dressing, from fear of the possibility rather than the actuality of assault.

The cellmates showered across from each other, but when Billy finished, the wet, squalid room was unexpectedly vacant. As he stepped naked towards the changing room, he recognized the usual absence of a screw who should have been attending. And where had Oliver gone? A well-defined uneasiness swept upon Billy. He hurried to the bench where he'd placed his clothes and began dressing, a mad struggle to cover himself. And then it happened. The sudden violence wrestling him forcefully against the wall, pinning his body. A heavy, sour breath drenched his neck. Billy twisted and struggled. But someone had jammed his frame with the bulk of fifteen stones, allowing scant chance of escape as the powerful men forced themselves upon him. He had smelled before he heard the two of them; Bishop and Lyman. His voice, high-pitched, loaded with terror, tried to scream. Spittle sprayed his neck. He wanted to cry and howl out in pain. "I've been watching this tight little arse for weeks," breathed the appalling Bishop.

"Let me go, let me go, ya bastards." He felt the bear-like, hairy hand delve into the back of his belt, yanking it down, each nauseating moment filling him with revulsion. He squirmed, flailed his arms and kicked his feet, but they overpowered, pinning him against the wet brick wall. Then he suffered the punch into his right midriff, and with it the immense pain and humiliation of the defenseless situation enveloping him. His vocal cords froze and his stomach tightened, almost causing him to vomit. His brain reeled in the incongruence and fear of his frail position while his eyes welled with the pain.

Then…he was free, yet petrified to the slippery wall, his mind blurred for a moment, hearing in horror the thud of flesh upon flesh and the agonizing groans of another human suffering affliction, the shredding of tendons, twisted entrails and fractured bones. Billy, once the leading actor of the piece, now became a passive participant in circumstances beyond his control, as the wrenchingly intense and brutally powerful act concluded.

Falling to his knees, Billy drew a deep breath and slowly exhaled. His body hurt and his head swam. He gradually turned to regard Bishop, vacant eyed, his face askew on his shoulders, grotesque, lying prone and blood trickling from his head to the floor, his body slowly soaking in urine. Lyman, wide mouthed, bug-eyed and simpering, was bent over on his knees, his head to the floor as he groaned with pain, breath gasping. Billy staggered to his feet, fortifying his legs, collecting his clothes to cover his naked buttocks, staring at their ghoulish figures, the men from nightmares. Lyman's face fascinated him in its agony. Bishop seemed confused and suddenly wretched, turning gray, like death. Billy focused again, clutched his jacket and departed the showers, feeling the press of eyes upon him as he staggered briskly back the twenty yards to the safety of his cell, where he came upon Oliver, sitting on the chair, smoking nervously. He glanced up sheepishly at Billy, whose eyes were seeking an answer to what had transpired.

After a few seconds of silence, Oliver explained, "Looks like you've made some new friends, young lad. Really big ones." And for the first time in this place, Billy's adrenaline diminished and his adolescent face burst into a wide-eyed, beaming grin.

THE PUB

Gold makes monsters of men.

- Erin Bowman

October 1962 - Battersea, South London

THE GOVERNMENT RELEASED John Russell and Daniel Geddes from Her Majesty's Prison, Maidstone, on the last day of September 1962. They bid farewell to their friend and protector—a redundant layer of security—the enormous, and amiable, Wally Sparks; a rock against which the seas of hostility might crash with futility. They palmed the proper hands to have Billy transferred to Wally's cell, but he was secure now for the rest of his term. The entire prison understood what befell those who menaced Billy Tumbler.

Two weeks before their release, John's wife Emily—an attractive young lady, wiser than her age, perhaps—had visited and replied in the negative to the expected question; "Have the police been knocking?" She then, as was their usual routine, stealthily passed him a small piece of paper containing the words; "Winston leaves in February." He devoured the words in deep thought, then the piece of paper, and advised Emily to call a man named Razor—from her sister's house—who needed to be ready in mid-January; about three and a half months' time. Understanding no details, or even the general concept behind the assignment, she was discreet enough not to ask. She knew to obey John. She needed him and loved him. They had the baby now, attractive and healthy, and John adored them both. She understood a caper was being planned, but she knew he would never involve her, so why bother asking? If it foundered and they had to run, then she would be his dearest partner again. He could have the occasional dalliance. All that mattered was the baby, and John would provide for her. She knew of John Russell's profession long before they married, he being one of an unlawful faction supplying rumors for the borough's consumption. She acknowledged that his sensual combination of rugged, vigorous good looks, gentle smile and steely, penetrating eyes had overcome her alarm of his business dealings. He had not served a lengthy stretch since they wed, but coming out soon, she preferred he found a new direction. He said the next job would be the last one and, although skeptical, she wished it too.

They lived in a spacious and elegant mansion block of flats on Prince of Wales Drive, overlooking Battersea Park, with its children's zoo, boating lake, mini golf, and acres of nature trails to explore, minutes away from the delightful Albert Bridge and Chelsea. She embraced her marriage of three years with a new, healthy baby to fawn, protect and cherish, and the easy possession of nearly anything she reasonably coveted. Like every young lady of the age, she had grown up in a sexist economy, with a lack of contraception and a defined place in society. John Russell was her way out.

A thousand yards across the park, they constructed the Prince Albert during the golden age of pub building eighty years earlier. Established on the corner of Albert Bridge Road and Parkgate Road, just south of the river, it stood guard over the western edge of Battersea Park, one of only a few green spaces in the borough. It was Victorian in both appearance and name, built a year after her consort passed away, when the sadness hung heavy upon the nation. The distant view from the front door revealed—when the leaves fell—Battersea Power Station's robust, towering chimneys atop the brick-cathedral style building, dominating the skyline. Behind the salubrious setting, and always close by in Battersea, Parkgate Road led into an industrial past of warehouses, granaries, engineering works and vacant bomb sites of the Albert Wharf and Ransome's Dock.

Pubs were the English social retreat other nations seemed to have overlooked. In London, as in all British cities, there were pubs for all men (and often only men), regardless of economic, theological or cultural background. The public house was the heart of the people's England, where many generations found their respite from work with a home away from home. England's classic pubs offered traditional value and a rich history, not to mention excellent beer and a generous spirit selection; society's acceptable drugs—up to an undefined limit.

The pub functioned like a cornerstone, joining the grand and ornate four-story terraces of Albert Bridge Road, and some ordinary terraced houses of the side street. They built the ground floor of three—accessible from the road on the corner—with glazed red brick, topped with white wooden signage proclaiming the name. The locals considered it a quintessential spot for a refreshing pint on a parched summer's day. Battersea wasn't short of pubs, but this was one of the more discerning establishments.

Daniel Geddes had acquired the building a few years earlier, largely from his share of a Midland Bank robbery in Wimbledon. The pub and building were an investment in a charming area, and it made a little money as a bonus. The Metropolitan Police knew that he, Russell and a few others had committed the crime, but lacked sufficient evidence, nor the opportunity to plant any. The pub had suited him and he, the pub. Originally, he struggled to appreciate how the concept of publican appealed. But he liked the area, the peaceful park, and the bridge nearby giving trouble free access to Chelsea and the West End, perfect to fraternize with the wealthy locals. But he imagined that, with just a tad more money, he could own a worthier, sunnier place, on a Mediterranean beach, perhaps. A female licensee named Swoozie Popkin—with whom he had a strictly platonic relationship—held title to the building and handled most of the work; cash flow, parties, weddings, restocking and accounting, allowing Geddes the freedom to come and go as his alternative business dictated. He lived above the pub, on a floor with abundant space. Miss Popkin lived there in another flat. It was the focus of his life, and the men who shared his occupation. The police were mindful of this, and Geddes and Russell knew they were, like opposing teams of a human-sized board game.

The pub was traditional, and better for it. The bar counters were worn, and well-wiped mahogany, where people drank, smoked, thought, talked and occasionally laughed, forgetting their melancholy lives. In post-War Britain, much of the drinking occurred in pubs. It was mainly men that drank, and usually beer. It would be a few years before British drinking culture shifted in more fundamental ways. This is where you came to catch a sense of the public house as it was a century ago, the walls a rich, sulfurous yellow, shafts of late-autumn sunshine highlighting the smoke and dust in the air, the light picking out the optics, stacked glasses and beer pump handles. It had an ornate Victorian interior with lavish tiling and grand mirrors. This place, and a thousand equivalents, represented a limited, male-dominated Britain, a boozy place where businessman and bricklayers might mingle. Romanticism was essential to the pub's pungent atmosphere, along with drip trays, pokey urinals down a spiral staircase and swirling, sticky carpets. Despite its name and ubiquity, the public house was, in fact, not always a house for all the public. It mirrored the nation, with all its attractive and awful qualities. Though often venerated as a place of classless conviviality, they replicated the divisions of British society with ludicrous conformity.

There were three bars, plus an office at the rear where they were plotting the most audacious robbery of their time; a crime that would change all their lives.

The public bar—enter the main door and turn left—represented the inexpensive side of the house. It lacked upgrades. Pictures didn't enliven the walls, save for a few beer posters. The seats were hard stools and benches. The room's colors had a pale hue and the whole ambiance screamed restrained masculinity with a down-to-earth character. The regulars were noisier, short of formality and pretension, and often called out across the bar; restrictions on behavior being less stringent, and an experienced barmaid was essential. The conversation topics included horse and dog racing, football and the lack of money. A rawer form of humor lived there because typically the public bar encountered scant women. However, a requirement to participate was the customary London wit, for which individuals accepted a part of the greater whole. Otherwise, one stood alone at the counter, or parked themselves in the corner. It wasn't unknown to scorch the bar with a cigarette, or spit on the floor, and the public bar always involved that one essential working class, afterhours exercise; the dartboard. And the price of a pint was a few pennies cheaper than the alternative.

The saloon bar, for men of more prosperous means, or those who aspired to such heights, allowed them to drink in a more refined setting, in a mix of colorful and subdued lighting. Once inside, a customer would encounter a cluttered assembly of portraits, bric-à-brac, pewter mugs, curiosities, and Bass beer on draft. There was rich flock wallpaper, acid-etched glass, sporting prints, brass foot rails and plush red carpeting. Comfort, superiority, and elegance characterized the atmosphere. Well-mannered customers flirted with the barmaids.

The preference of bar depended on how you dressed and with whom you kept company. At the back, near the office, sat a small snug, no longer open to the public, but ideal for those stopping to converse upon Geddes's familiar line of business. When needing to ruminate—having recovered his freedom—the renowned South London face, who feared no man and had already risked so much, did sometimes step inside, sit quietly by himself and reflect on their detailed plans. This is where it all began. Some months after release from Wandsworth Prison a few years earlier, an old cell mate named Gerry Jansen dropped by the newly acquired establishment for a catching-up drink. Gerry—was he Dutch or African or something? —had struggled in prison, but Daniel resolved the situation once he trusted him. John Russell joined in their intimate celebration and conversation that day, assessing the visitor, while focusing on the story he recounted. It suggested such a fantastical idea, but it would demand extensive planning, the sort he specialized in, and within which he found so much satisfaction. The idea was half dismissed some time later when a gangster called George Smith gave them a good tip—easy, reliable work—for a Dagenham wages job. Had they now thought this latest work through sufficiently? A few details remained outstanding, but it was always the details, wasn't it?

Local life had continued without Geddes and Russell while in Maidstone, driven by their friend, Peter Badger, and the always reliable Salter brothers, though the work had been sparse apparently, usually of the smash, grab and opportunistic type. They needed Russell to organize the project crimes; that's what he did. The ring of felons, nearly all Battersea born and bred, considered themselves an extended family, where prospective work passed through occasionally. But John, Daniel and Peter were cautious of any work offered because the chief priority was always to avoid incarceration. They could always pass on unaccepted work for the right price. Information was everything.

The English pub possessed another important function besides drinking—a meeting spot, somewhere to converse with scant fear of a reckoning. Unsurprisingly, in all societies, places where people can come together on neutral territory form an important role of the social fabric. This aspect of the pub, in particular the London pub, played a key role in the unlawful trade that Daniel participated in. George Smith, provider of the Dagenham wages work, lived across the river, in Fulham. It was a good tip, and well within his outfit's ability. Quick in, a truncheon to a reluctant guard, then out, fast Jaguars heading west, then south over the river. They had successfully acquired the money and fled, except four men went to prison, and two would be there for a few years yet. But the earnings were now available to fund the next enterprise.

Smith, a sizeable man with a slow swagger and an impassive expression you didn't want to lock eyes with, had cropped, glossy black hair, and a serious demeanor. The lines on his pockmarked, blotchy face sank to reflect the pressure on someone leading a criminal enterprise for longer than he had once planned. He held grudges. Many coughed and slinked away when his anger grew. He had the same steely glare of anyone who had spent too much time in prison with the determination never to return. He said he had worked for Jack Spot and knew Billy Hill well, but life north of the river had encouraged him to gather up the aitches he used to drop. In his mock, old-school tie, he remained the rotting heart, and leader, of the Fulham gang.

He crossed the threshold of the Prince Albert behind a sad giant of a man filling the doorway. They called him "Daddy" Dave Walker, and he seemed and sounded a page behind. He was a well-renowned persuader from Streatham, and not a good first-impression sort of man. He still lived there, but drove over the bridge every day to attend the office, like two million others. His thick set, heavily muscled frame epitomized a violent, threatening man with the corrugated nose and scarred eyelids of his trade. Peering into his eyes was like glimpsing back in time. The last man to enter, Brian Spicer, at first glance, appeared ordinary alongside him, gazing around the saloon bar for business, like a provincial undertaker with a sideline in menacing intimidation, while full of nervous energy. But he too inhabited a world crammed with knuckle-dusters, knives, flying fists and pain. No one liked him, not even Dave Walker, but Smith paid him well. He owned a sense of complete self-possession, with a hidden anger ready to erupt at a moment's notice. The three of them exuded a disturbing, unsophisticated study of depravity, often confusing conviction with sociopathy.

Geddes observed disdainfully as they stepped inside his pub, his home, seeming for all the world like an unhinged three-man fight team. He didn't know Spicer, but he resonated an any-dirty-job-type-of-thug attitude, with an angry, irregular face hardened by bony cheeks suggesting laughs were unlikely. Geddes loathed these heavy gangsters in his place of business, but today it was a necessary evil. He had served time with Dave and felt he could handle him if he had to. Violence was an everyday commodity for sale. It hung like a detached entity in the room. Geddes nodded to Smith, attired in his dark blue Turnbull & Asser suit and suede shoes, and waved him over. He steered him into the back office, as the other two loitered, then inched towards the bar where Swoozie the barmaid withdrew her hand from something under the counter.

Russell and Smith shook hands with casual familiarity. It was a greeting of respect rather than friendship. Their association had been long and difficult. They had once been in competition, squarely and not too friendly, but the Fulham man had crossed the river to a more violent and diverse profession. Naturally, he didn't partake himself—although he could if required—but employed enough sycophants to delegate these days. They had both risen above their roots without ever forgetting them; the dark duplicity, betrayal and grubby ambition that ran through life in South London.

"Can we have a quiet chat in the office, George, without the scary soldiers?" John invited him in with the familiarity of their childhood, hunting for opportunities on the street. Smith followed, and they sat on each side of the wide, wooden, well-beaten desk. A teakettle brewed on duty all morning.

"This place is still a dump," Smith groaned with the tone of some-one who lived on the better side of town, glancing around at the leaning filing cabinets, mismatched drawers, empty beer kegs, broken cupboard door and a carpet that required changing years ago. The buzzing fluorescent bathed everything in a sickly yellow luminosity. The BBC Light Program played on a crackling radio. Smith sat resting with a face of utter nonchalance. He wasn't slumped, because his body was clearly too muscular for that. No one got to be a leader without the lowest morals. He expected loyalty or gave savagery in return. Anything good for Smith was bad for someone else.

"Yeah, that's the look we were aiming for." Russell pulled out a bottle of cognac and dispensed a shot into each snifter, fully aware of the background smell of cigarettes and stale beer.

"How's Emily?" asked Smith with a mirthless, razor blade smile while Russell ignored him and switched off the radio. He spoke oddly slowly, without affectation. He was quixotic, overweight because he rarely worked in the field, self-absorbed, violent and determined. Then, disconnectedly, "How've you been?"

"I was in the nick," drawing his lips back, to which Smith shrugged his broad shoulders as if to say, *that's the name of the game, Mate.*

"Do you know what your problem is?" asked Russell.

"Questions like that," he glared. "Was it bad?" like a man without charisma.

"No, I loved it," came the obvious, sarcastic reply. "How's the casino life in the West End, the drugs and the pimps?"

Smith waited a few seconds while his expression dulled, "I did my apprenticeship, John. I grafted my way there. You could do the same, get out of Battersea." As children in the War they had shared a rich, communal experience. Then they evacuated them, each with a gas mask and oversized label hung around the neck. Upon their return they played on the ruined buildings, and they ran about the streets thieving small stuff from shops, then selling the goods on the black market. They had played together on the bombsites, making their own amusements. Was it the War or a simple escape? In the slums of London, the only ways out were football, boxing, the military or crime. Then they had experienced prison; missed birthdays, weddings, funerals, children growing up. Their "getting on" betrayed so many others. Like their compatriots, they drank too much; maybe so they wouldn't hate themselves for getting this far.

He continued, "I'm loyal to the culture, to the people I've drunk with since school, to the people I've ate and shit with, know what I mean?" Smith treated women like they had an expiry date. And now the sixties. People had money for the first time, and with that came ambition. Smith, like many others, had dreams of becoming rich and powerful, replacing his heart with a cash register. Now, they had lived through the end of deference and the beginning of the permissive society. It was a knot they could never untie, like all the lost dreams and missed chances.

"You don't know me, George. Too much water under too many bridges." said Russell. Then, brightening his demeanor, he added, "Anyway, I feel I owe you some information."

Smith lightened his expression, just a little, "For the Dagenham job? Not my fault you got banged up for that," his voice dripping with disdain. He was no longer the man John Russell knew so long ago.

"Do you always disappoint people, George? Yeah, we made a pig's ear of that. It got violent, but nobody went to hospital. Well, maybe one. A day in my career upon which I do not wish to dwell." Changing the subject and his tone, "No, far from it, George. But I appreciated the information." He leaned forward as if to aid confidentially. Smith took a sip of cognac and his mighty, fleshy, but once-broken hand, delicately placed the glass upon the desk and leaned in, almost imperceptibly.

"Some serious foul play, George. Gold bars." He mouthed silently, "A million quid." Then, regaining his voice, added, "Maybe more. Interested?"

Smith, without modifying his expression, slightly shrugged his square shoulders and voiced each syllable of his reply, "Poss–ib–ly." They sat silent for a moment, then he added as if being awoken from a nap, "Seriously?"

"You've heard of gold coming from South Africa on ships?" Russell asked.

"Mmm," he nodded scornfully. "We all know the Union-Castle ships coming in every week. Guarded by armed soldiers. Impossible to blag."

"Not referring to those. That bullion goes to the Bank of England, and, as you say, rather heavily protected. This is different. Private sale of bullion going to the Johnson Matthey refinery in Wembley. I can tell you when and where." The silence dragged. Smith leaned back, staring at John Russell, and swallowed another sip of brandy. Russell could see his mind churning through the options, so he added reassuringly, "That's coming from me. Know what I mean?"

"What's the matter? Too big for you this one?" probed Smith, raising one eyebrow.

"I'm all for dreaming, but we put stopping trains in the too-hard box. Fix that and we'd be laughing," was the cheerful, but measured retort.

"We can stop trains," interjected Smith, narrowing his eyes.

"…and I don't have the easy muscle you have. Nor do I want or need the possibility of shooters. This is serious stuff, and we don't use guns," explained Russell.

The bulky man lit a cigar and took another sip of brandy. "You're turning down El Dorado?"

"Armed robbery is a serious crime, George, and it's a Royal Mail train. There are consequences. You understand how the law might reflect on it?" warned Russell.

"Better to be caught with the gun when you don't need it and not have one when you do. Who's your source?" he said skeptically. John Russell slowly shook his head and declared that the gold was coming in the spring. He could give the port, the ship name, the railway stations and the timing later. Smith nodded, blew another cloud of smoke, deep in thought. Then, reflectively, he went on. "I've been in this business too long, John. Banks and post offices used to be easy. Not anymore. I want out. Out of blagging, out of London maybe. I don't want to be doing this in my fifties. I just want enough to go straight." Smash and grab required nerve and poor security. It needed intimidation and surprise. Bank robberies often resulted in petty cash for the effort and a possible twelve years of your life. He had a terrible suspicion of not being able to cope with the future in a world changing so rapidly.

"You always were good at school, George. You need the big one. Here it is. I'm offering it to you. All I need…" said Russell hopefully.

Smith recovered from his reflection of another life and smiled. His voice had changed. He was doing something with his face. It took a while for Russell to digest what had happened—he was being nice?

"When I was young, I used to dream of being like Robin Hood," he reminisced. "When you see what you have, you see what you stand to lose." John Russell eyed intently toward his once young friend. "What do you need, John?" he finally asked.

Glad of the chance to explain, John Russell made his best pitch, "I just need a small prepayment. While you get the gold, I have a little sideline set up. I need some cash. An advance of ten grand on a five percent finder's fee when it's all over."

"Are you behind with the rent? Not sure I have that to hand..." Smith chuckled, uncharacteristically.

"Well, you can always sell one of your Botticelli's, can't you?" resuming their London wit.

"I'll think about it. Only a few firms in London can handle this," said Smith.

"I'll wait until...Thursday. I know those firms too," said Russell.

John Russell had pondered long and hard about disclosing this information, but he knew he had to spread the attention their own work might invite. Keeping information tight was necessary; essential, in fact, but another means to hide something was to invite those who were searching to seek another direction; the classic subterfuge. A feint. It was subtle; it was sneaky and intelligent. It was all that George Smith would never have seen. He had become lazy, overfed on easy money shoveled in his direction by vicious men and the alcohol-ridden entertainment area of the West End, where, somehow, all the avarice, hard-drinking, violence and competitiveness had filled the void in his soul. John Russell disdained the whole despicable profession, whether it be the drug-addled, hideous cockney twins of the East End, or the sadistic brothers from Peckham with their 'unpleasant methods.' He abhorred the implication of extending protection to clientele who never wanted it. Yes, he could show an inclination for physical force himself, but only—only—when necessary, and only to preserve the caper. He, like Daniel, had grown to find satisfaction in the thoughtful project crime. He liked to plan. He had made it his specialty.

The socializing deteriorated as Smith sought to analyze the larger situation while feigning conversation. Eventually, the air went out of the room and they parted, Smith deep in thought, out into the saloon bar to find Daniel and Dave reminiscing, as he pondered to himself; *Johnson Matthey?*

* * * *

In 1817, Percival Johnson opened a gold assaying business in London. Thirty-five years later, George Matthey joined him and, predictably, the company became Johnson Matthey. The following year the company gained the prestigious title of Official Assayer and Refiner for the Bank of England, ensuring its reputation ever since. They were the company that made bullion for the bank at the heart of the most powerful empire in the world. They began manufacturing jewelry, silverware and cutlery; all the sidelines associated with precious metals and artisanship. They produced the top value items at the company's refinery in the Hatton Garden district of Central London. As its gold refineries in the United Kingdom provided so many bars for the international gold market, those historical items remain widely held and traded around the world today.

The soft, yellow element is a heavy, dense metal. It's also the most malleable and ductile. An artisan can beat a single ounce into a sheet measuring roughly fifteen feet on each side. One associates gold with extravagance, glamor, wealth, riches and excess. It's unrivaled in its brilliant luster and glossy shine. Investors love Johnson Matthey bars because of the trusted name and longevity of purpose. As George Smith made discreet enquiries, it seemed wholly appropriate they would buy gold to manufacture the growing interest in smaller, distinct and decorative bars that the company had become famous for.

* * * *

Once their visitors had withdrawn, a feeling of relief crept through the pub, sweeping away the tensions and extraordinariness the three men had bought along with them. The mood of their native haunt returned to regularity and normalcy. Rarely did anyone challenge Geddes and Russell in the Prince Albert, and they hadn't today, but they wrinkled the atmosphere enough that no one desired a repeat performance soon. John Russell turned to Geddes, "Well, deed done. Bear strategically poked," and a smug grin of satisfaction passed over his face.

Geddes sighed and studied his friend, "I hope you're not messing with fire, John. They could be…" searching for the correct word, "…difficult."

A few moments later, a man, unofficial number three in the firm, strode into the office to chat with the two of them, now sitting, lighting up their smokes.

"Hey, Peter, welcome back. How was the holiday?" said Geddes with a hearty chuckle.

"Blimey!" began Peter loudly, as he usually did. "George Smith and his plug-uglies sitting at the bar. I've been stood standing out there all knuckle-duster'd up and ready for some aggro. The holiday? I thoroughly enjoyed it, thank you. Absolutely beautiful. A solid fortnight working on the boat in a heated house. I'm not going to lie to you, the new Armstrong engine looks and sounds gorgeous, like a Swiss watch. Well, it's a bit noisy, but I'll sort that out," he explained with his typical overuse of superlatives. He never finished and never quite got the right level.

Peter, like an old family retainer, had one of those endlessly fascinating faces, all wrinkled, creased, and continually interesting. His frame, on first sight, appeared gaunt, but it sprung with powerful muscles. His Adam's apple stuck out hard, and he possessed wide, sad eyes that had seen a hundred things in the army you were glad you hadn't. He possessed solid, high cheekbones, and had gained a squirrely unpredictability that could seriously personify threat. People jokingly described him as potato-faced, sparingly truthful, and blissfully funny. He had renounced the British Army beret for a jaunty pork-pie hat after National Service. He had an earthy cheekiness and a gleaming maniacal quality, too. Woe betide anyone who lacked conviction or deceived him concerning the work at hand.

Contrary to his tough, etched features and raspy voice (the result of a lifelong cigarette addiction), he had a gentler side and a glint of humor in his eyes that belonged almost entirely to his wife, Maria, although he kept a little for the John Russell crew when a generous caper was in development. As a craggy-faced, homely sort of man, he could turn from sweet sentimentality to acid menace in a moment. You wanted Peter on your side.

His Romany name had been Petsha Babik, but his mother changed it to Peter Badger just after his birth, when his parents carried him to London. But he could never be mistaken for anyone else, which was good and, from time to time, troubling. He had a face suggesting an unearthly, uncanny difference from the norm—beyond mere unattractiveness. He had negligible chance in a lineup and knew it. His accent and origin were unknown, but the word gypsy spread on the street, although not to his face, since people quickly learned he didn't let go of an insult easily. Always ready for the front line, they often relegated him to the important role of operational support and administration. Russell and Geddes recognized his allegiance and comrade-ship; the respect was mutual. He appeared indestructible; that was the factor about Peter. He became the shop steward of the gang, always representing the members, helping and educating the younger ones in the fundamentals of respect and thievery. He made the wheels go round. As a team they had reached the stage where they could provide most of the skills required, and so disliked using anyone from outside their known sphere of reference. The three of them fed off each other, trusting, when taking the time to reflect, that they were decent enough people who had, perhaps, made the wrong decisions.

As usual, he chatted too much, like people did when they had once stopped him from doing so. He dived back into his clichés; "I won't even go into the details. The boat looks marvelous. Bringing it back to originality bit by bit and I can't wait for the spring, but they say it's gonna be a crappy winter. Anyway, I digress. I don't need to keep going on about it. Absolutely impeccable for its age." He took out two black & white photographs to lay before the others. "Very, very, very simple. Sixty-footer. That's how I like to spend my evenings." Everything about him was happily self-contained and replete.

"You're on the Thames, right?" Russell broke in to change the subject.

"No," he frowned, disappointingly. *Didn't they ever pay attention?* "Grand Union Canal. Performance is bang on, no doubt about it. You know what I mean? Bits and bobs to tidy up, naturally, but it's almost ready to go back in the water. Obviously, I'll make a really nice job of it. Unlike the modern youth. Nobody wants to work anymore. Everybody wanting something for nothing," he regretted, not signifying amusement, "I'm sure you can both get the gist of what I'm saying. Anyway, I'm waffling."

"Yeah, a little bit," confirmed Geddes.

He had concluded long ago that the youth of the country lacked the resolve of his generation and lamented the government's decision to discontinue National Service. As his treasured Armed Forces declined in the wake of volunteerism, he reasoned; why toil in the working class when livable wages were within reach for some out-of-the box thinking and enthusiastic work?

"So, are we going ahead with this…" lowering his voice, "…gold bullion work? It sounds good, but maybe better start explaining the details? I'm gonna call the boat *The Golden Goose*. Gold is my happy place."

"That might not be the best idea, Peter," groaned Russell despairingly, "can we avoid the word 'gold' for now."

"You're the Gaffer," agreed Peter. "Oh, by the way, there's a flat-foot in the bar watching all the comings and goings." He used a common, if outdated, synonym for a policeman. John Russell's brow furrowed with interest, "Anyone we know?" Peter puckered and slowly shook his head.

"The Sweeney? He saw Smith and his muscle?" Russell asked.

"I don't think he's Sweeney, but he saw everything," verified Peter.

Daniel Geddes strode out and quickly returned after reconnoitering the bar, "My guess is C11" (Scotland Yard Intelligence Division).

Russell clapped the air, tossed back the dregs of the cognac and grinned, "Things are looking up today. I don't know what they do to them at Hendon," he guffawed almost excitely, "it's exhausting being right all the time." Organizing the caper required not only planning your own moves but also the moves of your opponents.

Interestingly, Peter had met a young lady named Sally Dawkins occasionally, but he had not yet met her boyfriend, the young protagonist Russell hoped would join the team when released from Maidstone.

"Right, I gotta go, chaps. Day job and all that," said Peter, moving towards the door.

"Bigger fish to fry?"

"A blue whale!" And with a wave, he was gone.

THE DETECTIVE

Gold makes the ugly beautiful.

- Moliere

Boxing Day, 1962 - New Scotland Yard, London

CHARLIE RIDDLE HAD WORKED with John Russell and Daniel Geddes for a few years now. He admired them. For the preceding two projects in which they had enlisted his services, he hadn't secured a full share, but he accepted a solid wage. It was a fair wage. He liked their professionalism, the way they planned every aspect—or at least all they could—and they were entertaining to be around and to learn from. If something goes wrong, John Russell stays on his feet. He covers every angle until everything is back on the straight and narrow. Then he stands back and never mentions the crisis again. Although Charlie dabbled in safe blowing, he did not as yet, regard himself a specialist, but he had apprenticed to the notorious George Godwin. He preferred the work of small explosives and maintained a short, but essential network of suppliers. He considered himself a competent pavement artist, but Russell had not used those specific capabilities yet, choosing instead to source other professionals.

That was John Russell all over—his attitude being that if the work jeopardized their freedoms, then use only the best. But Russell, like all talented leaders, put unmatched stead in knowing who he worked with. He disliked reaching beyond his small cabal.

Riddle, who the unfriendly called Jimmy, was a felon, and known to be, so that had made it easier for them to use him. Reputation was everything. Russell would use no one with a name for talking. He had a history, but mercifully a short one. What worried Charlie now was there had been no work since the Dagenham wages job—with which he played a minor role—and he was running low on cash. He wasn't the wasteful type, but he had a wife, children and rent—it all required money. He lived a little east of Battersea in Stockwell, where he worked in the maintenance department of the giant bus garage, from where routes went out all over London. It was steady work, but there remained some slack to take up. He could manage the safe, predictable drudgery, but it all went to the staples of life. What he needed was "off the books," work with cash quickly in hand. Cash, unmarked, easy to move into the stream of society and lost forever, cash that nobody knew the provenance of. He expected Russell and Geddes to make tracks out of prison, ready to work, ready for activity. Even if they didn't employ him, he would have heard something. But the gossip mill remained suspiciously dead. Nothing appeared to be in the planning stages and no auditions were being held for employment. He had dropped by the Prince Albert twice recently, where Daniel Geddes treated him to a beer. It had been a friendly, reassuring chat, and naturally, Charlie had touched on the subject of employment. But Geddes had adamantly replied they were planning nothing, although he'd heard George Smith might be seeking people. Work in Battersea had dried up.

And now this curious new rumor from his neighbor, Bob Cooke, who knew a bloke who knew a bloke in Southampton. "Cookie" said that this bloke's colleague, a dock warehouseman, had been approached by a big man, a "known London face." Inexplicably, he didn't reveal a name, but maybe he had been warned not to. The man wanted knowledge regarding gold imports into the Port of Southampton. He offered him three hundred pounds for the information. The friend of a friend said he'd been searching around the docks and the nearby railway station. Riddle didn't know there were other stations in Southampton. The two of them had discussed it over a beer in the pub one evening, both short of work, struggling to figure out what it meant. They didn't work with anyone else, well, not unless the money was right. They had chuckled at that one and ordered a couple more pints. As Charlie Riddle's mind whirled with the possibilities, he should have remembered the adage; a professional thief cannot flourish once he's known as an informer.

Charlie lived south of the River Thames, along with two and a half million others in a vast swathe of industrial land stretching from Wandsworth in the west to Woolwich in the east. Everyone north of the river thought there was something basically wrong with South London; a city with no artistic, scientific, intellectual or literary center. It had no center at all. The tourists rarely ventured south, if ever. There were no landmarks, other than Battersea Power Station, just endless rows of sooty brick houses laid out in unbroken straight lines, frequently adjacent to the inexhaustible factories and warehouses. The dirty river had cleft the mighty city into two communities. One was abundant, attractive and prosperous, the other, isolated by its northern flowing border, a desert of bricks, a monument to mediocrity and poor taste. There was a purposelessness, and widespread frustration rooted in the emptiness and pointlessness of South London life. Aesthetically bankrupt, it was a neglected space, where the people felt life could improve only by traveling halfway to Brighton.

Detective Inspector Thomas Halliwell, a first-rate policeman, lived north of the river. Everyone knew he was a member of the elite, including his peers, some of whom had tried, unsuccessfully, to induce him in some manner of corruption. *Something for all those extra hours, Tom.* But Halliwell was one of the good ones, and rejected the offers out of hand. He had been a policeman since the Second World War. Others might become entangled with the slippery side of police work, but not Halliwell. It had taken him six years to become a detective, posted to the West End Central Police Station in Savile Row, at the junction with Boyle Street, just a block from Regent Street, Soho and Piccadilly Circus. The Met., as the city-wide police force was often referred to, segmented the grand metropolitan city of London—some seven hundred and thirty-six square miles and eight and a half million souls—into seventeen police divisions. They had a group of geographically small sectors near the crowded center, diverging into larger districts in the sparser outer suburbs. West End Central opened in 1940 to house the headquarters staff of C division, covering Soho and Mayfair, geographically one of the smallest, but always full of people; some might say the more interesting character types. He felt comfortable in the neighborhood because of the challenge it posed, the constant interaction with those on the other side of the law and those walking the fine line between the two, savoring an entertaining night in the West End. This is how the forces of law and the law breakers understood it; two sides of a game, a game with unwritten, but recognizable, rules. West End Central established a notoriety for policemen walking along that line, but Halliwell believed himself comfortably above it.

Four years after becoming a detective, Halliwell achieved his next ambition by joining the Metropolitan Police Flying Squad, though still working from West End Central, but also New Scotland Yard, whose offices they called the "Factory." His reputation was of a hard, but honest man. Like everyone in the Flying Squad, he relied substantially on informants and information. A good police officer nurtured them, and Halliwell knew many villains personally. Charlie Riddle was one of those informants; a grass. He had a sort of henpecked expression, and his shoulders hunched a little, as if he were trying to hide inside himself. Although Riddell was a criminal, and everyone knew it, they didn't know he liked to gossip, especially when he lacked conviction, or something to do, or a job.

* * * *

The first Police Commissioner's headquarters in London existed at 4 Whitehall Place, a few yards south of Trafalgar Square, with a rear entrance on Great Scotland Yard. They've lost the source of the name to the mist of history, but it may derive from buildings that sheltered the diplomatic representatives of Scottish kings when they visited English royalty. The Great Scotland Yard side of the building held the public entrance and became synonymous with the police force of London (except the tiny City of London, which has its own constabulary). But by 1887 the police service had ballooned and accumulated a multitude of addresses in and around Whitehall Place, including Great Scotland Yard and several nearby stables.

Deciding they required larger headquarters, they built a new one on vacant Victoria Embankment land, overlooking the River Thames, a stone's throw from the original. The police moved late in the nineteenth century, and since the original name had become synonymous with law and order, they called it New Scotland Yard. It lay between Westminster Pier and the Air Ministry on Parliament Street, right next to Cannon Row Police Station. Designed by famed architect Richard Norman Shaw, the distinctive Romanesque edifice appeared resilient and castle-like, in banded red brick and white Portland stone on a granite base. The building was eccentric, lacking in bureaucratic efficiency with the impractical features of a medieval fortress. Many cursed the layout, so they corrected the intolerable position in the early twentieth century by building a virtual pastiche of the original next door, with stylized follies of turrets and spires. A bridge linked the two over the then public road. The buildings represented and symbolized the Metropolitan Police which existed originally, and by late 1962 continued, as a large force under central control.

* * * *

Charlie Riddle called Tom Halliwell one day, frustrated, needing somehow to release the pent-up annoyance of not working. The buses were insufficient, and the wife fretted about the absence of incoming funds. How could chatting to Halliwell improve the situation? He concluded that it probably wouldn't, but he needed to talk, and Halliwell might pass him a tenner, although a grass could never be sure of income nor, in this case, if he really had any intelligence. It was just all "strange stuff," he called it. They met, neither of them enthusiastically, over a beer in the Marquis of Lorne pub in Brixton. Halliwell, a resolute man, had the sort of face quickly forgotten. His heavy eyelids gave him a sleepy mien that only an interesting investigation could awaken. He wore a gray suit to match his gray, receding hair and gray spectacles; he blended in. He sat and listened to the willowy crook with the bony face and hollow cheeks across a small table. He had heard some other information, and this aroused his interest. And when Tom Halliwell got a notion in his head, he liked to run it down. He trusted he read the criminal fraternity of London well, and what he liked better than anything—other than his wife of fifteen years—was delivering them to the Central Criminal Court on a small street off Ludgate Hill, called Old Bailey. After hearing the description of a tall, fair-haired man, there was one point that Halliwell had to clarify. "Did your friend of a friend say 'known South London face', or just 'known London face'?"

Charlie Riddle was too experienced not to recognize when his audience required an encore. He always thought it was just lazy to tell the truth, and he also knew how to please the punters; "Oh! No. South London, Mr. Halliwell, definitely South London. You know I never lie." Straight away, Riddle realized who he had now implicated, and a deep uneasiness flooded over him.

Halliwell thought to himself; *not sure I should trust a grass who never lies.*

"What do you make of this, Charlie?"

Riddle took the last gulp of his beer, and gave a befuddled answer, "I don't know as well as you don't know, Mr. Halliwell."

"Glad to have witnessed your peerless powers of deduction, Charlie," he replied acerbically, not wishing to reveal his thoughts.

That this report pointed to the clientele of a certain Prince Albert pub in Battersea previewed what might happen next. Halliwell lived his life for these days. Many thought he had a charisma deficit. His wife, who he loved in that sad, dutiful manner, had borne him no children, and he exercised his mind with no pastimes or amusements; the criminal was everything to him.

* * * *

The early 1960s were the era in which the Flying Squad's close ties with the criminal fraternity, which had always been a necessary part of its strategy, were being exposed to public criticism. Flying Squad officers wore plain civilian attire and could carry firearms concealed in a belt or shoulder holster. Originally called the Experimental Mobile Patrol, it comprised elite, hardcore detectives selected for their capacity to apprehend "the most audacious" criminals, to wreck the careers of villains, big and small. Crucially, they were given approval to conduct their duties anywhere in the Metropolitan Police area, meaning that its officers could cross divisional and borough boundaries, giving rise to the name of the Flying Squad. They apprehended bad villains anywhere throughout the large city. With the expansion in organized crime after the Second World War, the city became a villain's paradise, so the Flying Squad's purpose narrowed to investigating serious crimes, in particular, armed robberies.

There were about one hundred and seventy officers in the Flying Squad, based in four London branch offices, and at New Scotland Yard. They had eight "squads" there, each headed by a detective inspector, like Tom Halliwell, who led No. 2 squad. Each squad comprised two detective sergeants (First Class), three detective sergeants (Second Class), three detective constables and three drivers of the highest quality, typically with a professional racing background. The Flying Squad had an unmatched reputation of excellence in policing, working hard, drinking hard, and taking hard criminals off the street. They remained the only dedicated mainland detective unit in England that investigated armed robberies from start to finish, with officers qualified in weapons and covert surveillance roles.

The Flying Squad had always operated closely with external partners and specialist units, principally the Criminal Records Office, Fingerprint and Photography Sections, the Fraud Squad, the Police Laboratory and C11 Intelligence. Given the Squad's experience of organized crime, understanding of operational activity across the neighborhood, and high-quality training of its officers, it used this ensemble of methods to study crimes and apprehend criminals. They brought to justice the capital's most violent offenders, and became almost universally known as "The Sweeney," a byword for fortitude, hard work and integrity, although by the 1960s a few cracks were starting to show.

* * * *

On Boxing Day, 1962, three days after drinking with Riddle, Detective Inspector Halliwell had other matters on his mind, but he was effective enough to promptly return his focus to the circumstances presented before him. He attended the standard weekly meeting that, if necessary, could occur more frequently. Today, he had something to say; ideas that had been brewing inside of him for months, since the day they had sentenced John Russell and Daniel Geddes to a desultory three months for their part in the Dagenham wage job. It was common knowledge they had led the gang, but had somehow—with dexterous legal maneuvering—been exonerated of most responsibility. Tom Halliwell, professionally, admired them. He nursed a grudging respect, but he wanted them back inside. He saw them as a challenge that required defeating, and Dagenham was the ultimate injustice. He recalled the manner in which they had smirked as they were taken down, recognizing they each deserved more than the sentence they had negotiated. Had they seen him, most decidedly, the two felons would have grinned up at him in the gallery. It hadn't made him angry, just more determined. Maybe he was old-fashioned, but he believed in public service. He had seen so many bad things, too much death and it had tested his faith in humanity. He saw everything as right or wrong. Just beyond his horizon he knew something mischievous was playing out, and after twelve years as a detective, he knew his instincts were correct.

The room was stuffy and needed fresh paint which, in 1963, could have characterized most spaces in New Scotland Yard. With Detective Chief Inspector Walker seated at the head of the table, six detectives sat around, half of them smoking. Eight telephone lines dangled from the ceiling to the apparatuses on the long, threadbare, brown table. The chief, a terse and serious, ex-army man with a crisp, sharp mustache, had a blackboard to his side summing up the operational plans of the previous occupants. They had painted the walls dull cream above shiny green long ago, interrupted by tall windows hung with pitch black curtains commanding the red-bricked courtyard. A portrait of the Queen was suspended behind his head. Six ashtrays overflowed on the table, more evidence of the preceding inhabitants. Going round the group, the chief finally reached Tom Halliwell. "Right, Tom, let's hear your thinking this week."

"I think somebody's planning a big job…possibly gold bullion. Most likely south of the river." Halliwell opened, eyeing down at his notes, gaining everyone's attention.

After a brief pause for everyone to take in the idea, "Any idea what job they might be planning?" asked the chief dubiously.

"Well, gold in a bank is generally considered impossible. Certainly, the Bank of England, anyway," responded Tom. "I can make some enquiries to see who else stores it."

"I agree, so give us some background. Where are you getting these ideas?" demanded the chief with a typical scowl of disbelief.

"We've been working on something and certain information is beginning to align in a manner we rarely see," proposed Halliwell, rather too obscurely for everyone listening.

"Go on…"

"Well, number one, a meeting occurred a few months ago between John Russell and George Smith…" began Halliwell.

"You're joking!" interjected the chief, "those two hate each other. I can't imagine they would somehow work together," he added incredulously.

"I know, Sir, I'm skeptical too, but C11 witnessed the meeting. Sergeant Jones, good man, reliable. No details, but I think it's worth keeping an eye on them."

C11 gathered intelligence on career criminals in the entire southeast of England. Their target was the criminal, not the crime, and the Met. gave them high electability as to who fitted the requirements. They identified their targets as "C11 nominals" with a dossier compiled of individual histories and activities. Once labeled, they remained of interest to the police for the rest of their lives. Criminals might retire, or be confined for years, but nothing showed they would change their ways once back in society. C11, who often gleaned information from the Flying Squad, lived on the first floor of New Scotland Yard.

"What else?" The chief's voice boomed. He admired Halliwell, and if he thought a crime was being planned, then it needed following up. He saw the theatrical game being performed, but he had too much respect for the detective's intellect not to let him to play it out.

"The John Russell gang, Sir. We all know they pulled the Dagenham job earlier this year. Two are in jail for seven years. They got away with nearly twenty thousand, but interestingly, no one is spending any money."

"Alright, Tom, I sense you have one more piece of this puzzle," said the chief.

Halliwell shuffled his papers to heighten the excitement, "A tall, fair-haired man referred to as a 'known South London face' has been seen in Southampton asking questions about gold." He stopped to view the reaction.

"Geddes? Doesn't sound possible," another detective voiced the uncertain attitude of the room.

"I have to say, Tom," added the chief, "I'm a little skeptical myself. I don't want to commit too much time and money to hunches, but facts are facts. Keep an eye on the situation and keep us updated." He turned to another detective, "Brian, what's happening at the airport?"

"Well, looks like it's going to be closed tonight. Big storm coming in, the weatherman says." And it did. Beginning late that night, and continuing into the following morning, two feet of snow settled on London. Frigid temperatures they had not seen for some time accompanied it. The winter of 1962/3 turned out to be one of the coldest on record, with the Thames freezing over upriver at Hampton Court, and even some smaller ports in Kent icing solid.

Tom Halliwell skipped the airport conversation and thought deeply to himself. He was determined to understand what was being planned south of the river. He could hear the faint sound of ticking, but, as his experience had often shown, the story might seem clear from a distance, but the closer you look, the murkier it becomes.

THE SEAMAN

Gold will never fill an empty heart.

- Dorothy Clarke Wilson

Early January 1963 - Battersea, South London

BILLY TUMBLER FINALLY AWOKE from an unsettling sleep at five-thirty, and beheld the warm, welcoming figure of Sally beside him. He could barely believe his splendid fortune of the moment. Breathing in her scent, he contemplated his slumbering girl, his only reflection to provide her with a better life. But the dreaded thoughts that had ruined his sleep lingered, even as his hand slipped over the silky skin of his lover, caressing the firm breast and erect nipple, hearing her soft, discreet purr of pleasure. She twisted her face to him, flicked some auburn hair from her smooth skin and rolled close in a cuddle, advising, with her yielding, plushy lips, she needed to work. Her face was not beautiful in the conventional sense, but Billy had been magically drawn to those lighthearted and talkative features long ago. Above the cutest freckle-sprinkled, daisy-bud nose, she had eyes that never lied. They changed color corresponding to her mood, but every man or women who saw her smile felt the irresistible impulse to beam in return. He treasured her lack of makeup, along with her always messy hairstyles, but the adult world had become a realm of responsibility; they required money. Whatever passion he might have—and she felt it too—expired with the realization of their financial situation, and the moment succumbed to the economics of reality.

Stepping from the bed, her body shivering in the cold, Sally revealed the story of how a man with a funny face had visited two weeks earlier with funds to cover the rent, but she had spent that on a tallyman debt for her friend Joany. The prison had released Billy barely a week earlier, and he didn't recognize the man she described, but he suspected the origin of the money. Someone had arranged the snow clearance of the pavement out front, and there had been a mysterious delivery of a paraffin heater, described Sally as she quickly layered clothing over her naked body. Billy, viewing her small peaked breasts from a crack in the covers, professed ignorance, but Sally spotted the half lie; people didn't donate money to strangers. In silence they both contemplated the other question; what were they going to do?

They were young, still full with the exuberance of youth, but they were no longer children and never would be again. The previous night had been so cold, even with the additional source of heat. Over a simple meal of bread and dripping, Billy had announced his plan to return seaward on the first available ship. It was a succinct and effective plan; the obvious plan. Neither of them liked it.

There were jobs in England in 1963; on the Tube, on the buses, at the river factories, although unemployment had spiked again during the cold winter. Molly, their neighbor, said there were jobs at the Hovis flour mill and the Nine Elms brewery; hourly wages for two and five pence. None of those options heartened Billy enough to apply, but like a juggler, he kept all the possibilities spinning in his mind. Working in Nine Elms would only perpetuate the current situation: stuck in Battersea, unable to escape, like insects frozen in amber. He had set aside the hidden third option, but then Sally had broached the subject of money from the mystery man again. Billy denied any knowledge, which was half true, since John Russell had expressed no financial arrangement. But he held his thoughts inside, full of darkness and foreboding. People with something to hide never have much to say.

Sally made herself ready, donning her working clothes, woolen hat and scarf, ungainly rubber boots and heavy coat. Hanging a handbag on her arm, she set out into the winter towards Battersea Bridge, snow crumpling under foot, plumes of breath reaching through her scarf, to clean the same houses Billy's mother had for so many years. Billy sat, finished his tea with a slice of bread and butter, and noticed Sally had left her gloves behind. He stepped outside himself, the long sunny days of the Indian Ocean lingering in his memory as the clouds lost their delicate, frozen freight again. He temporarily walked away from the poverty, noise and emotion of Clapham Junction.

* * * *

And what was this place? They say it used to be famous for its fragrant lavender fields. Later the railway brought a new kind of wealth to the narrow wagon-rutted byways of rural Battersea, nestled along the south bank of the River Thames, about three miles upstream of Westminster. Then, in the second year of Victoria's reign, Battersea changed when The London and Southampton Railway Company drove their first line from west to east, terminating at Nine Elms in the northeast corner of the borough. Industrial buildings appeared, and vast railway sheds and sidings, and slum housing for workers. The population exploded to 170,000 in the nation's blossom of late nineteenth century manufacturing growth. The Tumbler family had flourished here for generations; working, drinking, falling in love, fighting and struggling at the industrial riverbank, or on the river itself.

The establishment of the railways hastened the suburbanization of London. The earlier, open land south of the river became overbuilt as the railway companies consumed the old riverside windmills and quaint, wooden wharves. New industries replaced them; Price's Candles, Morgan's Crucible Company, Garton's Glucose factory, numerous flour mills, breweries and the stunningly ugly Nine Elms Gas Works, the view only relieved by the majestic power station some years later. The rail junction at the center of everything; industry, houses and people, had seventeen platforms vomiting flame, smoke, metallic vapors, and the soot from coal-burning steam engines joining with factory smoke in a black plume that settled on the backyard washing lines, streets and people. They added ever more sidings, yards, sheds and workshops which they once labeled the "Battersea Tangle." Despite its official name, the enormous sprawling intersection of routes from London's south and southwest termini—Victoria and Waterloo—funneling through the junction is not in Clapham, but serves as the commercial center of Battersea. London has many famous railway stations. It is said that all Londoners eventually meet under the clock at Charing Cross, but they also assume everyone will, eventually, pass through Clapham Junction. The name, stolen from the fashionable village to the southeast, has contributed to the long-lasting geographic misunderstanding ever since. In total contrast, the reality remained that social conditions in the borough's north were severely impoverished. The decision to create Battersea Park happened just in time to spare the whole of Thames-side Battersea from being engulfed by industrial bleakness. In truth, the area, the dark backside of the giant city, seemed incapable of ever prettifying its past.

Battersea life in 1963, however, was inextricably bound to what had transpired twenty years before, and during the intervening period since. As the bombs had rained down early in the War, Britain at first adopted the defiant slogan of "London can take it." But by the waning months of that conflict, it had become, in reality, a city gasping, hanging on desperately while looking forward, with forlorn hope, to a newer, better, peacetime future. Nearer the struggle's conclusion, the mood had evolved as German long-range V-weapons fell indiscriminately. The front line reached Battersea, like it had earlier been to the East End, when flying bombs hit Price's Candle factory, producing a blaze that took weeks to quench. At the opposite end of Grant Road to where a midwife delivered Billy, an old man, alone and traumatized, turned on the gas and left a note declaring, "This war is too much for me." The people of Battersea lived through the air raids, giving birth, hanging on, waking up to discover a neighbor had gone. When a bomb landed on Plough Road, the locals spoke of human flesh hanging from the electrical wires nearby. Contrary to the overtly enthusiastic Churchillian defiance, London could not have taken much more.

When the War concluded, insolvency befell the country. The fighting had ruined the infrastructure and tax base, while the nation, notwithstanding, had enormous commitments to an empire most people never wanted. When the urban working-class emerged from the rubble and ruin, the new government felt obliged to make a promise of something utopian. They committed to, and the people supported, unemployment welfare programs, a National Health Service, raising the school-leaving age, and the expansion of social housing construction. They pledged, and put into motion, the nationalization of the railways, along with the coal, steel and electricity industries. But that didn't leave much foreign exchange to import luxuries like food and cotton, for those who had fought and suffered on the front lines and at home.

In the 1950s immigrants began arriving in Battersea because poverty was terrifying where they came from. They harmonized well in a city where everyone was an individual, an eccentric or an oddity, boosting the teeming mix of colorful communities, adding generations of families embodying the passions, struggles and verve of the sublime city. After the earlier uniform society, a change began, as London matured into a conglomeration of strange peoples. Did the new arrivals believe they paved the streets with gold? In Mayfair or Piccadilly, perhaps, but here in Battersea, poverty was the same, just without the color and sunshine, oozing from the dirty-snow-covered streets, permeating the air with the sickly smell of candle wax and sugar.

Despite the promises, life in much of South London, amongst the familiar faces and places, continued in hardship. The aged, Victorian terraced housing estates built to populate the new rail networks and river industries, now had multiple families squeezed inside, often living in one or two rooms. Many parts of Battersea mirrored and felt like they did during the War, although now devoid of the deafening bombs and indiscriminate death. Clothing, in the years after the War, was secondhand and repeatedly repaired, bought at the Sunday morning street market or the rag shop. It was common to see children without shoes, and the impoverished ones often owned no underwear at all. Billy's mother queued for meat; horsemeat. Food in the immediate post-War period was often more strictly regulated than during the actual War, culminating in the average adult eating only two eggs a month. Sweets for children were mostly a result of charity.

But Londoners perceived, mostly, the rationing system as fair. They knew the lawmakers rationed the King and Queen too. There were those who took advantage of the system, and a significant black market prevailed, but few people wanted that. Since a decade earlier, the people had been growing more and more disillusioned with capitalism, so without the onset of war, the rumors of revolution might have materialized. Concern for civilian morale forced the government, this time, to take heed of its citizens, to recognize their hopes in a way it never had before. Wartime social welfare programs established the foundation for a unique postwar state, one in which government took a more active role in such areas as health care and housing.

Under pressure, class distinctions eroded. But there was no turning away from the romance of the West End, the oversized houses employing cleaners, the well-lit, expensive restaurants north of the black river. To the south there remained vacant bomb sites, unrepaired dwellings and prefabricated housing. The reliance on coal for the industries and domestic use led to chronic atmospheric pollution. It had been some time since Battersea had that new city smell.

Billy was born during the War at home, in a house lit by gas mantles. They had two rooms, a scullery and a shared toilet out back with gaps at the top and bottom of the door. The Harris family lived above and the landlord had declared the basement unfit for habitation because of water ingress. The running water was icy cold, except for an Ascot heater in the scullery. The rattling, rumbling noises from Clapham Junction a few feet behind the house constantly traumatized day and night. As he matured, Billy discovered, as many young men did, that not everyone was poor, and it angered him that few people had so much, while the vast majority had insufficient.

Just after Billy's twelfth birthday, Sally Dawkins stood outside their front door one day holding a large canvas duffle bag before her in two hands, having arrived from her foster parents one block north on Speke Road. Hers had been a troublesome childhood, losing her parents in the last month of the War. Then there were rumors regarding the foster father, and suddenly Sally—the girl everyone in the neighborhood knew and loved—moved in with the Tumblers. They agreed she could remain a few days. But she lingered a while longer, sleeping with Billy platonically, until people just assumed, they were all one family. The two children walked the thirty minutes to Battersea County School together every day. Billy's father first took him into the Essex Arms pub down the street for a shandy when he left school, by which time his relationship with Sally had grown more affectionate.

These were poor streets, but a spirit of togetherness still prevailed, if only just. Those who survived all knew each other. Grant Road remained a street where you could keep the front door key on a string in the letter box. Crime was of the occasional and petty sort; shoplifting and street gambling, which disappeared when, in 1961, the government legalized betting shops and no one had to use Charley the street bookmaker again. The gaps in housing generated by bombs persisted, and now they were planning the demolition of entire areas to build Le Corbusier's sterile, new city in the sky. Where Billy's family had endured for so long, were, after 1963, to be replaced by high rise modern flats, the architect's brave new world, where everyone became friendless and remote.

As they made ready development of the new concrete Winstanley Estate, some people began moving out to the suburbs. Families, friends and communities separated and a time of change began. The old terraced houses may not have been much, but they housed families with a noble spirit, while the whole road possessed a remarkable sense of community. The people lived in a society of relatives, friends and neighbors who could be relied on to help in times of need. To go elsewhere would be to move among strangers, far from the epic production mill of labor that was Battersea at its most homogenized and soulless. But Billy no longer wanted to remain in this street, this borough, or this city. He loathed the damp and cold, the black skies pressing down, triggering despair. And now the vilest winter he had ever experienced. The cold hurt deep inside, and he had been to warmer climates and experienced endless sunny days during his two years at sea.

While Billy had traveled the world, his extended family migrated east to Essex. When in Maidstone his mother had died of a coronary disease; the day he received the news became the worst of his life. Time had not crafted Wally Sparks to aid with grief, but the warden gave permission for Billy to attend the funeral at the Lambeth Cemetery in Tooting. He had not considered how Sally had financed the event. Afterwards, alone in his bunk bed, he understood how he had ruined the dreams of the woman whose love had kept him warm throughout all their hardships. But he had never fully appreciated the burden placed on Sally. She had inadequate time for introspection. Life went on; all she had was the silence of privation and solitude to enfold her every night. Yes, she habitually met her friends, but no one really knew what lay inside her mind. She would attend appointments; she would show up. She gathered with Kitty, Mags, and Joany; women who had spent their young lives in the shadows of fathers and brothers, being dutiful and raising their siblings. Each of them didn't understand how they were to build the lives they dreamed of. She continued with the daily duties, like collecting yesterday's newspaper from the lady in Chelsea and cutting it into toilet paper squares. And at night, she would lay alone crying, holding her hot water bottle with no one to even hear her tears. Now, out of prison, Billy and Sally were left with the three-pound weekly rent for rooms they no longer wanted. At least he had the women that now meant everything to him.

They could make livable wages, as long as living meant paying rent for two rooms and eating the bare essentials and not taking holidays. It meant accepting life as the world had dumped it upon them, even though there was a fresh feeling in the nation, of getting ahead, of escaping the past, of a new economic miracle. Secretly, Sally and Billy couldn't quite envisage how they might join the new paradigm. He craved to do all the trivial things that ordinary couples did with a little more money. And then, only once did she declare, as if an aside, the word "marriage." She saw Billy as the man she would walk down the aisle for. But Billy had heard it, and marriage now joined the other spinning plates in his head. He knew that a seafarer could never have a regular life. If he and Sally died one night from the cold in this damp, noisy place—or just disappeared—who would know or care?

* * * *

Albert Tumbler, Billy's father, served intermittently on the Thames barges, a member of the Company of Watermen and Lightermen. As a child he had suffered from diphtheria and measles; the ailments of the age. Billy had idolized him. Although only a baby, he had learned afterwards of his father's heroic work during the Blitz, moving dangerous cargoes while the city and docks burned. Many lightermen had died. Albert was a melancholy man, bearing within him some dark, mysterious past he never illuminated. Although a fully licensed lighterman, union man and member of the guild, many days he avoided work, sat alone at home, or visited the pub. That's how he dealt with the painful scars, the haunting memories and the lasting grief. He found relief and salvation, like so many others, in beer and whiskey, but never in violence. He wasn't an alcoholic, but immersed himself in the dead moments of alcohol on the merciless days when his memories allowed him no peace. Like his son, he was compact and lissome. He was the opposite of ordinary; capricious perhaps, unreliable maybe, and sadly for Billy, completely unknowable.

From the age of thirteen, when he could, Billy accompanied his father at weekends and school holidays, onto the river. "You gotta get a trade, Billy," he had told him, and at fifteen, against his mother's wishes, and to the surprise of Albert and Sally, he had left school. Not because he lacked potential. Indeed, his teacher had championed him to accomplish much, but Billy felt inhibited by the rigidity of it all, and he yearned to accompany his father. Initially, Albert denied his son's enthusiasm, but he soon saw in Billy a youthful man with possibilities; effervescent and irrepressible, a junior man learning the language of the cold, gray and threatening river, growing as his protégé.

No one could serve on the river though, without being licensed, which required serving under a master while unlicensed. The lightermen, in their heavy, unwieldy, flat-bottomed barges, were highly skilled men who conducted the unpowered vessels behind tugs on the river. Sometimes they manipulated eight feet oars, called sweeps, and exploited the tides without tugs. They were a charismatic group, their work intense, physical and dangerous. There were periods of boredom when they could relax for a while, clustered together, smoking and chatting about the river and their lives. On sunny days, windy days, or days choking with smog, they always worked. Lightering took place all day every day, an almost impossibly hard workload in all weathers with the constant threat of death, the river exuding a distinct mood, every hour, every minute. They worked on the heaving, reeking river—too dirty to remain alive in if you fell overboard. Lightermen required an intimate knowledge of the river's foibles, rewards and vicissitudes. The late fifties and early sixties were the Port of London's second glory time, with the docks full all the time. Every berth had a ship going or coming from some far-off exotic place, and the work and the atmosphere created for Billy, the best memories of his early working years.

He prized the outdoor life, the handling of ropes, the leaping between barges, docks and tugs, working with the Turnkeys, the Colyers, the Lees and the Morrells; the illustrious family names of the river. There were perhaps a hundred lighterage companies and five thousand lightermen to man their floating properties. Albert worked for Braithwaite & Dean Ltd., being picked up each morning to work somewhere on the river. The barges operated from Battersea in the west to Gravesend in the east. Ships anchored or secured to buoys and transferred goods to or from lighters. Lightermen then took the goods to their eventual destination, to a hundred different quays. Billy's body, once an ill-nourished frame, grew to a slim but hardy specimen. The men of the river, mostly from the East End, became his family of workers, with their rituals, their slang, their hardiness and professionalism.

Billy learned from his father and studied hard. He absorbed the teachings of life, while all the time believing he understood him.

When doing wrong, his father would gently admonish him in his soft, and knowing voice, but could then remain silent for hours. His silence was powerful. Those were the lonely days, when his father declined to speak, his eyes wondering in some far-off place at the back of his memory. Then one day, his father caught him handling stolen goods; two bottles of whiskey purloined from a ship in the King George V Dock; "I'm gonna sell them and give the money to Mum," Billy protested.

"That's bollocks," his father barked, uncharacteristically. "You're not gonna do nufink like that. I'll tell you what you're gonna do! You can't do this work forever, Billy. You're clever. You're gonna get a proper little job that some poor man from Battersea can do, like shov'ling coal or cleaning toilets. And you're gonna 'old on to that job like it's gold, 'cos it is gold!" Billy stood silently before his father and accepted the rant, although he had never experienced the like before. His father rarely talked, and this outburst perplexed Billy as to why he was not encouraging a river career?

"Let me tell you, Billy. That is gold. You listening to me?" he continued.

"Yes, Sir," replied Billy fearfully.

His father continued, "And when the guvnor walks in at the end of the day…and he comes to see what you done, you ain't gonna look in his eyes. You're gonna look at the floor 'cos you don't wanna see that fear in his eyes when you grab his face and 'it 'im to the floor and make him scream for his life."

Billy stood trembling before his father, wide-eyed, unknowing the man reprimanding him.

"So, you look right at the floor, Billy. Pay attention to this, boy! And then the guvnor looks around the room to see what you've done.

And 'e's gonna say, 'Oh, you missed a little spot over there. What about this little spot, 'ere?' And you're gonna suck all that pain inside you…and you're gonna clean that spot. And you're gonna clean that spot until you get it shining clean. And on Friday, you'll pick up your wages. And if you can do that, you can be chairman of the Bank of England. If you can do that," he finished.

Billy stood trembling before him until he said, "Yes, Sir."

"Could you do that kind of stuff, son?" His father restated.

"Yes, dad. I can do it."

The episode astonished him. Billy continued working on the river and enjoyed the occasional long passage when he could interact with his father. They played football in the empty barges, or staged mock boxing bouts. All the while they ran goods to mills, factories, iron and chemical works, food workshops and warehouses everywhere; the river the "Larder of London," employing twenty-five thousand dockers and clerks, along with police officers, landlords, customs men, café owners, crane drivers and newsagents. But nearing seventeen, Billy no longer recognized his father. He loved him, but he could sense the transformation materializing, realized in those quiet, aloof times without interaction that something had changed. Just prior to visiting Watermen's Hall to obtain his apprenticeship lighterman license, his world fell apart.

One Saturday, Albert, the quiet man, donned his best suit. His wife casually asked his intentions, but he produced no reply, just stepped out the front door, softly closed it behind and disappeared, as ephemeral as the river mist. A neighbor claimed he had seen him later that day at Waterloo Station. However the circumstances, Billy and his mother endured the mental disintegration of their father's disappearance, while the psychological scar left Billy searching for a father figure. Facing the anguish of his mother's predicament, and with Sally still at home, he bravely joined the Merchant Navy as an alternative to the river. Upon returning from his first voyage, his happiness spilled over, discovering Sally had crowded her personality into the void left in the compact house with her wonderful laugh and infectious warmth. Years before, on the street playing football, marbles, hop-scotch or conkers, Sally was confident, practiced and curious, while Billy seemed lost and vulnerable. Her round eyes and tiny figure made her seem childish, but the waif-like vulnerability was deceptive. Whenever he saw her it always reminded him of watching her dancing barefoot in the street, or scampering away from a game of knock down ginger. She was sociable, amiable, chatty and in need of attention, with a gentle, practical, forgiving character. Billy fell head over heels in love, and she reciprocated. Their relationship became intense and exceptional. She preferred to say he was her lover, not just a boyfriend. But the brief emotion of the moment could not disguise the truth Billy saw within it. He saw her life as a grim, Dickensian tale without hope, with no husband. She left school with a good mark in needle-work and became imprisoned within her own tiny life. She regarded him, not handsome, but mesmerizing. She wanted more than money—she wanted a trusting, loving relationship and a family. And she envisaged it right here, in Grant Road, a block from where she was born.

Billy left for the open ocean and had loved his two years at sea, better even than the river barges. He could forget all the troubles at home. He never dreamed he would leave Battersea, but once at sea and settled down, the routine, the breeze on his face, the sun on his skin, the cleanliness of the air made it all worthwhile. On his first ship, the *South Easter*, he witnessed, for the first time, an abundance of scorching water flowing from a tap. He experienced the sky full of stars like he had never seen before. He had enlisted as a deck boy in London on his seventeenth birthday, joining a run-of-the-mill cargo ship owned by the South Seas Shipping Line, with a full crew and two deck boys. The accommodation and food were basic, but the boys had a cabin to themselves and a tiny messroom. The duties included cleaning the head, carrying food to the mess rooms, and all the other menial and dirty jobs. The crew were rough and ready, but with a splendid sense of humor. He was determined to excel at seamanship and learned all he could, soaking up the activities of the trade. He did every kind of work that came his way; a splicer, rope coiler, tool carrier, mast climber and brass polisher. And when there was no more work, there was always painting.

The *South Easter* sailed with a general cargo for Australia. After four months on the Australian coast, they returned to London via India. It was all entirely new to him; one a vast, hot and sunny continent of English people, the other an almost impossibly colorful and riotous place, both of empire. The sights, sounds and colors of another world in the brilliant sunshine were a delight and an amazement to Billy. His pay was sixteen pounds a month, so he deposited an allotment of twelve pounds to his mother. On his second ship, the MV *South Fiji*, the captain encouraged him to continue the outstanding effort while knuckling down and studying to become an officer. He elevated him to junior ordinary seaman and advised he could one day wear a white uniform guiding the ship from the bridge, a dream of which his father would never understand. All his life it had just been geography in his father's atlas, but now he had seen the world, or at least some part of it. He had once believed there was nothing the world could offer that was not available in London, but what did the empire profit the people of Battersea, where the children played in the streets under gloomy skies and freezing winters?

* * * *

Now nineteen, a week out of Maidstone Prison, his hope of a career on the river gone, he headed east, back to the area known as Dock Street, in the teaming mix of colorful communities they call the East End of London. Billy fitted in well and, like others, the industrial inner city imbued him with wonder; the largest port in the world, central to the economy of London since the founding of the city two millennia before. It lays east of the Tower, as far as the River Lea, and covered the districts of Stepney, Whitechapel, Bethnal Green, Bow, Wapping, Limehouse, Poplar and Shadwell. Billy had visited many times and understood the area was more an attitude rather than a place. Throughout the nineteenth century they developed a series of enclosed dock systems surrounded by high walls to secure cargoes from shoreside piracy. The world of commerce knew the names: The West India Docks, the East India Docks, the London Docks, Surrey Commercial Docks, St. Katherine Docks, the Royal Victoria Dock, Millwall Docks, the Royal Albert Dock and, the furthest east, Tilbury Docks. In early 1963, apart from these, they lined the river with continuous quays running for miles along both banks, fifteen hundred cranes and hundreds of ships moored in the river or alongside the quays. For as long as it has existed, they have regarded the East End as the tough end of London, a place of extreme overcrowding and a high concentration of immigrants, synonymous with poverty, disease and crime. Billy didn't deem Battersea much better, but at least it didn't have Jack the Ripper.

As the new ships appeared, they were a modicum larger and a knot faster, but otherwise they had barely changed from their predecessors of an earlier generation. There was no higher cultural aspiration other than the architectures of profit and utility. Before the containers came.

This day in early January 1963, Billy rode the Tube to Aldgate East, exiting into a grim winter day in the East End. He wandered down the freezing slush of Leman Street into Whitechapel, then passed under the railway line to Ensign Street, hearing the nearby mournful hoots of ships and tugs dissociated from their source. Before reaching East Smithfield and the dock wall, he arrived to the Mercantile Marine Office, a three story and basement Georgian building like so many others in London, near the Red Ensign Club and the Sir Sydney Smith pub. From streets away what one couldn't miss were the warehouses, erect jibs of cranes, the funnels and superstructures of so many ships, crowded into the adjacent docks.

On his last ship, absentmindedly, he had washed his Seaman's Discharge Book in the laundry. It remained readable, but since the day's journey had taken him to the docks, he sought his mentor, the jolly, affable and full-bearded Mr. Edwards of the Marine Office. He was some ways from reaching the grade of able seaman, but now he realized his entire career, such as it was, might be in abeyance. Billy arrived, shined his dirty toecaps on the back of his trouser leg, and stepped inside the ground floor frontage, characterized by its polished granite and Doric pilasters flanking each of the four entrances. When called to the first floor, at the counter, he met his friend, Mr. Edwards. He recognized Billy too, which was encouraging. "That was a long voyage, Billy. Where have you been?" He explained truthfully that he had spent eight months in Maidstone Prison while Mr. Edwards scrutinized his book, not at first hearing Billy's report. Then he quizzically perused the young man before him. His expression turned surly, uncomprehending and, as Billy knew all too well, disappointing. "Prison?" It was as if he couldn't understand how a young man he had championed—maybe one day officer material—had fallen into such disrespect. Crestfallen, Billy accepted the scowl, feeling it shoot deep inside him, like a red-hot poker. He suffered the sensation of failure, now official; dark, like the sky over the narrow streets of Whitechapel, the sun dead, like all the other souls of this place. Billy considered what his father might say but that wasn't possible, because he was dead too.

"Well, this is not good, Mr. Tumbler. You're unestablished, right? They might offer you a 'pierhead jump' at the Pool, something last minute, singling up as we speak, but they won't like it." He marked a notation on a piece of paper and stapled it into Billy's disfigured-but-still-serviceable Discharge Book.

Billy traipsed outside dejected, and headed back north to Leman Street, through the melting snow piles amid the tinkling rivulets of water. He crossed the small interchange where a large red-brick pillar, nicknamed "Shark Island" supported the railway line overhead, comprising public toilets, surrounded by stone steps on which sat groups of men waiting for jobs or pierhead jumps; last minute, desperate employment on whatever became available.

His next destination, 20-22 Prescot Street, housed the British Shipping Federation, the "Pool," as everyone knew it, next to the Empress of Prussia pub. A dozen sailors sat around the bare, linoleum-floored room seeking employment. The front desk from where the ships were allotted was the supreme province of a certain Mr. Williams, who had his preferential shipping companies. Although he offered work to seafarers, his obligation was to guarantee the respectable

British shipping lines received the finest labor. The large blackboard across one wall didn't seem to possess enough ships to employ the men sitting there. Billy wanted a Foreign-Going ship, not Home Trade where he could hear the same news as Sally every day. Mr. Williams, a gray-haired man with pink cheeks and a permanent scowl, sat behind the counter. He was less than impressed with Billy's documents, proposing he might try again tomorrow or the next day—perhaps there might be a pierhead jump, or "something else." Billy assumed a "death ship," a grimy, forlorn hulk making ready to sail from one of the nearby docks, probably foreign and making sure it had more than adequate insurance coverage over all other concerns.

Plenty of men loitered in the area when unemployed; in the pubs, shivering on the street, or the hostel on Dock Street. But Billy returned to Sally. He had brought no gear anyway, and he wasn't about to leave her in a rush, or without a long farewell. This was not going as he hoped. It was as if he stank of prison, or wore a starry, yellow badge of a perceived subgroup. There was no such person as an ex-convict. The prison system stigmatizes. He felt the eyes pursuing him, although no one else really cared. He supposed it straightforward to resume a young career, pick up where he had desisted. Maybe he had just happened upon a quiet week in the Pool, but he suddenly feared the lack of prospects; no career and permanently broke. He felt worthless. His ship, whatever its name, would sail away without him. It didn't need him, a worthless ex-ordinary seaman losing all his dreams of an ocean-going career. The sea had cracked open the door to an entire world of which he wanted so much more. Now the hated words overcame him; too late.

Disillusioned, he wasted another fourpence on the Underground back to Clapham Common which was nowhere near his destination, but the Tube didn't service South London like it did the north. During the ride, the self-loathing reeled inside his head, oblivious to the stops and the people. On the longer walk back to Battersea afterwards, shivering through the snow and ice, he undertook the self-discussion of his options. Having been denied work of which he was reluctant anyway, the same answer popped up in his mind again and again.

He was back on Grant Road before Sally, to find the milk bottles had popped their tops on the doorstep. He sat alone, lit a fire, made a cup of tea, and deliberated. The more he studied the situation, the more his young, analytical brain summarized the problem into four solutions. He could return tomorrow to the Pool and accept whichever ship finally came his way; rust boat, death ship, or anything else they might offer. Or, and he was leaning toward the possibility, find alternative employment at one of the Battersea factories. His priority encompassed only Sally. The other alternatives were them both plunging off Battersea Bridge at flood tide, holding hands all the way down. Unfortunately, Billy was a naturally adept swimmer and the thought of drowning while gripping her hand didn't really seem credible. That left the last selection, the one he struggled not to acknowledge with much soul and brain-churning mental effort, and the one he had yet to reveal to Sally.

The following day, Billy strode out without fully explaining to her. He said he might try the factories. The scullery window rattled and whistled in the icy January wind, but the rent controls dissuaded the landlord repairing much. It was a lengthy walk from Grant Road, next to the roaring, rumbling interchange. Britain was a small country, geographically, but crammed with industry. Because of this, and because of the fifty million people who inhabited every hectare, because all those people were constantly on the move, her railways were the busiest in the world. It seemed to Billy that all those trains passed through the immense Clapham Junction. The grid of streets ran north-south and east-west in orientation, with buildings fronting onto them. The construction of the railway imposed a barrier to the north-south movement, with Falcon Road being one of the few routes leading towards the river. He walked at his easy pace, slipping now and again, passing the rag and bone man struggling with the icy wheels of his cart and the snorting, baying old horse. Billy recognized that his left shoe had broken. London is overlarge, but can feel so small sometimes. The sky was all pearly gray and shot thru with sun rays creating the morning's long shadows. An old man on a bicycle shakily zig-zagged past, his knees wide to avoid the chain.

His complex route resulted from the rail lines crisscrossing the area. He passed an off-license where his father would buy drink to consume at home, and a grocer's shop where his mother had their ration books registered. They had a license for ales too, but not spirits. At the top of the street where Winstanley Road crossed, was a paper and cigarette shop and on the other side the Winstanley Arms, where his father could drink without confronting the family.

He continued north on Falcon Road, east on Battersea Park Road (under the West London Extension Railway). Then north along the Albert Bridge Road towards the river, just as his mother had a thousand times before, walking two miles to clean the mansions of Chelsea. He dreamed of his mother as he went, dead a few months now, and his eyes swelled and watered again, remembering her warmth in the icy wind. No matter what Sally said again and again, he knew, through the pain of wrecking his mother's dreams, that the truth was she had passed because of his imprisonment. She had given him everything possible, a poor, two-room part-house, common scullery and outside toilet may be, but the house was always warm, the food was always good and filling, and she was always there when he needed her.

Now he had failed her, in a manner he had killed her, as sure as if he had twisted the knife between her shoulder blades. She had given him life, and he had taken hers away. He kept reliving the pain of watching her sitting across the shaky prison table, the tears spilling from her unknowing eyes, quizzing him in silence. Why? Why? Wretchedness described how he felt. There was something callous and morally questionable about his situation. His childhood had lied to him. All those who had encouraged him; "run free and find the future." But it seemed the despair and restrictions of his childhood had now progressed into early adulthood. Only now there was a seriousness and almost hopelessness to the situation. Inside continued to brew an anxious and despairing melancholy. He now knew that life would be a fight to the death, a conveyor belt of work to his eventual slaughter. At the end of it was the same fate as his father, uncle, and every other man he had ever known.

But there resided within Billy Tumbler an inherent toughness, waiting for that one break, that one asset to boost him onward. *This winter I'm gonna win*, thought Billy. His heart warmed with memories like a fire burning inside. These last few days had been grim, like the weather biting into his exposed skin, but he was going to dig in, determined to make life better for Sally and himself together.

Walking north towards the river, he could see the Victorian folly of a bridge slowly growing ahead of him. The grass of the park remained covered in soft, untouched snow. As a child, he had never seen grass until the family went to the park. His mind recalled the sounds, sights and smells; freshness and the joyful noise of the fairgrounds where his mother had taken him in her net hat and sturdy arms. Sally came too, when they rode the spectacular Big Dipper, along with swings, roundabouts and the luxurious smell of candy floss. To the east he saw the towering red-brick power station that defined the borough, yelling out, "look how mighty we are, see how much power we need."

Victorian mansions and four-story houses, now subdivided into luxury flats, led to the Prince Albert public house. Billy, drained from indecision just minutes earlier, began now to form a nebulous plan in his mind. He knew not where it would end, or even how it might begin, but he understood the next step was through the doorway of the Prince Albert. He summoned the memory of the shower rescue, the removal of Bishop and Lyman from the prison, never to be seen again. Others had stepped aside to avoid him, fearing the consequences of a perceived slight. Billy hated violence, but in prison he had reveled in its protection. It wasn't a place for compromise.

He stepped into the warmth of the public bar, confronted by the familiar smell of stale beer and ashtrays, while the darkness contrasted with the outside icy glare. He absorbed the scene, devoid of customers, and stepped to the bar to meet the contemptuous face of a youngish, middle-aged woman, trim-bodied, her shoulders slightly rounded. She yawned like she'd seen it all before, comfortable in her place and motions, passive in a macabre manner. Billy eyed the draft pulls, nibbled on his lip and uttered, "IPA, please."

She expertly looked him up and down with her smokey eyes, appraising his age; "One and nine pence, dear," she said, filling the glass.

Then, from behind, the recognizable, booming, deep voice, "It's on the house, Swoozie."

Billy swung round on the stool to see the towering physique and smiling face of Daniel Geddes, his enormous hand outstretched in greeting. "Hello young 'un, you made it," and a feeling of relief and liberation swept over Billy. He owed these men, and possessed a secret longing to become one of them, to earn some respect for once.

Carrying his beer into the office, he met John Russell again, and was glad to see him. "You're a little day-brightener, aren't you? Glad to be out? It was grim, wasn't it?" he asked.

"So happy, and I'll never go back," answered Billy.

"Rightly so," agreed Russell, shaking his hand enthusiastically.

Turning to Daniel, "We all say that at one time or another, don't we?" The atmosphere was jolly, congenial and friendly. They had shared an experience that only they understood, like soldiers back from the front line. They chatted amiably, about prison, without using the adjectives "scarring," "horrible" or "terrifying." They talked of his welcome home to Sally and his failing search for the only employment he thought he wanted or could do. Everyone smiled. They brayed at the easy jokes, like an old team getting back together again.

They spoke of Bishop: "He's not feeling too clever."

Billy, although alien to the geography and the situation, felt warm and wholesome in their company. He could never explain—although these two men well knew—that prison had changed him. It was strange, almost impossible to reconcile that he might have appeared the same, but Billy Tumbler was now a different man. The institution hadn't helped him in any manner; it might just have made another criminal.

John Russell explained, as he sometimes did, how society never did him any good. How, with his upbringing, he should have had a "shit life," but had made a conscious decision to amend those circumstances. Living and dying with nothing to show for it scared him.

"Well, thrilled to see you, Billy," Russell smiled, then paused, his forehead furrowing, "looking for work?" Billy explained his experience at the Pool, now forever tainted with the stain of Maidstone Prison. He thanked them for taking care of his mother's funeral and the fortnightly stipend for Sally while he completed his time inside.

Geddes broke in, "You don't owe us anything, lad. We take care of our own."

"And now I'm one of you?" asked Billy, quite perceptibly. He knew they were negotiating.

A lengthy silence followed, broken by Russell. "Look, Billy. We have important work coming in a few months and you're just what we need, but it's not a fancy dress party. Are you interested? Think seriously, this is a once in a lifetime event. With this, we all retire, but we need a man we can trust."

The two robbers declined to disclose any further details, advising the utter importance of secrecy and the unbelievable shares upon the work's conclusion. He regarded neither of them lacking in confidence. There was no discussion of failure. They had been planning the perfect crime for a year and this was their one and last chance, perhaps, of eluding the dreariness of Battersea on a gray, bitter day like this.

Billy drank in their words along with his beer. It was all too much. Why did they want him? Again, they answered he met their desired physical characteristics and experience capabilities, but no details were forthcoming. He liked them; he felt safe in their company; he wanted to know more; he wanted to join in, as if their company were cathartic. *More money than he would ever need?* They agreed to reconvene the following morning in the park for a decision. When Billy departed, he thought for the first time in his life, he had a choice. Stepping into the street, the winter donned a temporary fresh coat as the yellow sun broke through the clouds like a passing, golden smile.

Money was the only thing that eased the stigma of being born poor.

THE AGENT

Gold is so heavy it settles down upon the lowest souls.

- Austin O'Malley

September 1962 - Durban, South Africa

WITHOUT KNOWING IT, Joseph Minghella finally had a prodigious stroke of good fortune, bought about, perhaps, by the naked wooden lady on the bow (which he hadn't seen for many years). Or maybe it was the smashing of a champagne bottle, or the dolphins swimming alongside or the tattoos on his arms. Alas, none of those superstitions had rallied around, until a man of dubious history and character walked into his ship's office one day. Gerhardus Jansen and Joseph Minghella had a strange relationship. Earlier, any affiliation would have been inconceivable, but much had happened in this corner of the world during the previous months. Auspiciously for the two of them, nobody knew what they were contemplating, or were to discuss.

Gerhardus—who everyone called Gerry—for an ample man had a light, jaunty stride. He was six foot or slightly taller, with a hairless head and a black mustache that turned into a narrow beard beneath his chin. His voice rumbled with a strange mixed accent, somehow incorporating London-English and Afrikaans. He was garrulous, self-absorbed, yes, but humorous and some kind of raconteur when required. He had street smarts, ambition and sufficient reading to rise above his station. He had met Captain Joseph Minghella, a man lacking an ounce of charisma, of the good ship MV *Aphrodite May*, three times before. The ship, an honest, fine and robust vessel, was first rate from bilge to mast, but she appeared humble and nondescript with her gray hull and beige superstructures. She stopped in Durban, South Africa, on an irregular schedule every few months in a western extension of her core business centered on Singapore, typically in the exotic timber trade. Occasionally, the ship brought a small cargo of palm oil.

Gerry didn't like him much when they first met and thought, perhaps, few others could. However, during his occasional chats with officers aboard, their guarded consensus was he kept out of the way and drank too often. Keeping out of the way was what all seafarers wished of the Old Man. They had scant choice; Minghella might have been insensitive and cantankerous, but there were far worse ship captains sailing the oceans.

The political moment caught both white men in its grasp, while they mostly ignored it. Since the previous year, tensions had risen in Durban, on the east coast of South Africa. The government strengthened methods of enforcing their preferred constitutional system characterized by an imperious political culture based on white supremacy. That system ensured that South Africa was dominated politically, socially, and economically by the nation's minority population. Gerry despised the politics, but could not envisage how he might change the structure.

Gerry worked as an agent of the Grindrod Shipping Company, attending ships in the Port of Durban most days, including the occasional visiting vessel of the London & Oriental Shipping Line. Grindrod had been operating in southern Africa for a long time, providing specialized services in port and for ships en route. They also acted as a clearing and forwarding agency. The captains liked Gerry, because he appeared diligent, hardworking, gregarious and approachable. His black lover probably adored him and he reciprocated, which was a problem in South Africa. The Immorality Acts prevented people of different races engaging in extramarital sex, and the Group Areas Act prohibited distinct races from even living in the same neighborhood, let alone the same house. But Gerry cared little, although there was the possibility of prison. His Grindrod runners enjoyed working for him, because they thought he was trustworthy. They could not have been more mistaken, because Gerry Jansen harbored a dark, criminal secret.

For a year or more Gerry had visited Minghella each time he brought in the *Aphrodite May*, easing the bureaucracy of customs and immigration and receivers and freight forwarders, ordering the correct (and finest) longshoremen, arranging local transport for the crew, or expatriation for those going home. He learned the eccentricities of a captain and arranged a token for each visit; a modest gift or invitation. As far as he could fathom, Captain Minghella required only alcohol, so he brought along a decent bottle of whiskey. The captain was sixty now, devoid of retirement savings and still some career ahead of him, but Gerry could sense the lack of enthusiasm. All he possessed were a bunch of yesterdays and fewer and fewer tomorrows.

After the men in uniform who attend a vessel's arrival in any port had departed, and the chief mate was actively organizing the cargo operations, Gerry sat for a chat and a glass of whiskey. He soon discerned that Captain Minghella required something recently missing from his life. Now, prematurely aging, the smaller man in his fraying white uniform, sailing in a career he no longer coveted, was left sending money to wives in self-imposed shameful support of children he didn't know. Gerry sat and listened every time to Minghella telling his pitiful story of losing all his life savings, and the ignominy of the Admiralty Court, and the despair of being away from his new lover and life in Singapore.

As the whiskey slowly disappeared, a brief silence ensued, as if Captain Minghella was reflecting on another life beyond this one. Gerry understood he hankered after retirement, back to the sleepy life in the sun. Gerry had an exceptional attribute, the ability to see an opportunity missed by others.

The captain, in a reflective mood amid the haze of whiskey, spoke the thoughts he kept inside: "You haven't really lived until you have a lot to regret. I have some regrets, Gerry." He remained silent for some minutes until Gerry thought, perhaps, he should say something. But then, the captain changed the subject and the mood and set Gerry daydreaming. "Did you know, the ship has been nominated to lift another of those gold bullion cargoes in the spring?" he said. He still thought of the calendar in that English, northern hemisphere perspective.

And Gerry kept his cool. "You mean the one in the coming autumn, loading in March (1963), Joseph?" He wanted to discuss, but not now. They had drunk too much, and he needed to be alone to reason this through. The two of them parted as the ship continued to deliver some canned fruit and rubber. After hearing all the sad stories unfold, Gerry, back in his office ashore, scrutinized the shipping schedules, paying extra attention for one specific reason; he'd spent time within the notorious, filthy brown walls of Her Majesty's Prison, Wandsworth, with a certain South London face named Daniel Geddes.

* * * *

The emotions of Joseph Minghella hid behind his world-weary, cadaverous face, reflecting the darker feelings he held inside. He suffered with a substantial deficit of self-image because he stood shorter than the average man and he stooped slightly. His career had been long and mediocre—with one significant setback—and he now coveted its conclusion. Relationships with the opposite sex had been taxing, which he blamed on his perceived physical inadequacies, or when being candid with himself, on his sullen disposition. Few people liked Joseph. He possessed an unconscious attitude, which, with reflection he believed warded off his exasperating sense of powerlessness. Fortunately, his employment provided him with that heightened sense of control that made each day livable. His occupation behaved every bit as extreme as a drug. If he could create a physical distance between himself and the person or situation that triggered his anger, he could manage the space required to calm down and move forward. But life had shackled Joseph with the literal opposite. In this work, everything seemed laborious and humdrum. Insignificant issues that didn't use to bother him now caused anger, so he lashed out at those around him. His moods affected about thirty people in his proximity, because Joseph Minghella was a captain in the British Merchant Navy.

Had one not known him, they might have considered his career impressive, but in reality, it had been a protracted, mostly uneventful and yet once, controversial. It depended entirely on how he spun the stories. Joseph had been born the same day Queen Victoria died in

1901, after his Italian immigrant parents had moved to England at the conclusion of the nineteenth century. They raised the children in the northeastern industrial city of Newcastle, having arrived from the impoverished, mountainous, northern Italian region around Parma. In Britain, many Italians worked as statuette makers, or mosaic and terrazzo workers, whereas the Minghella family toiled in the ice cream trade, with which history has lumbered them with a certain caricature ever since. Their language, Catholic faith and extended family structure readily distinguished them from the local population.

Newcastle and its eastern neighborhoods; Wallsend, Hebburn, Jarrow and South Shields—stretching out along the River Tyne—were the cornerstones of the British shipbuilding industry that had constructed the dreadnoughts and merchant fleets of the era. Young Joseph (his parents had given their children English names), had suffered like many others for not being native in that manner in which the English feel superior to others. They did not, however, experience the complete hostility then encountered by other migrants, like the Jews and the Irish. It was a time when they equated cruelty and bullying with character building, so Joseph accepted it, not understanding the psychological repercussions. Somehow, again not grasping how, he took part in, and grew to love, the customs and rituals of his nation of adoption. As a teenager working in the family business, he soaked up the propaganda of the liberal empire amongst his school friends. Reading the daily lists of dead on the Western Front had not diminished his enthusiasm for Kitchener's recruitment demands, so in 1917 he joined the Royal Navy to fight the great fight. Despite his family history and name, or perhaps because of it, he thought of himself as absolutely English.

He had married his first wife, a young English girl named Vanessa, in 1925, leaving the Royal Navy as a lieutenant. But he had soon tired of routine life in northern England and initiatcd a new career as a third mate with Clan Line, where he grew to love the Merchant Navy and the relative independence imparted to its officers. He toured the world, worked relentlessly, fell in love a half dozen times and abandoned Vanessa. He then married an Irish woman after a protracted stay in Cork one summer. It was a messy, superficial affair, and, by the attitude of her family, he knew early on it was a mistake. He'd worked himself up the career ladder until he became chief mate on a Liberty ship during the Second World War. It was a war that had seen unremitting death and loss in the Atlantic theater, while Joseph spent most of his time moored alongside in Gibraltar.

Nearly seventeen years later, he had been everywhere and done everything a seafarer could. An English and an Irish wife had each suffered his sporadic visits, but in all his travels around the world, the one place he loved was what his generation called the Far East. Joseph Minghella had thought long and hard about what drew him to eastern Asia. Yes, the women—and some men—were petite, exquisite, hypersexual, dutiful and mysterious. As customary, Joseph had seen the situation through the jaundiced eyes of the European colonialist without bothering to learn the alternatives. But, eventually, having traveled so far, he couldn't face the monotony of ever returning to the England he had once called home. He had long lost his religion and the Italian propensity for family. After the second separation, having fathered three children, he moved east, where, professionally, things went downhill.

After the War came promotion to captain, and a captivating enthusiasm for drinking. But in 1955 he committed the one crime for which the master of a ship would find a challenge to return from. He lost a ship aground on the insignificant speck of land named Roughton Island in the Balabac Strait, just south of the Philippines, which made nobody happy. They had all survived readily enough in the warm, caressing seas, but it was a sloppy affair, culminating in salvage, general average and unhealthy economics. He promptly blamed the youthful third mate on watch that night, a man, who he believed, couldn't cross a desert without bumping into something. That was how the Admiralty Court (a subsection of the Queen's Bench Division of the High Court) saw it too. They disciplined the officer accordingly. But the captain is the captain, and maritime lore dies hard. Joseph Minghella had kept his license, but rumors circulated far and wide. He had been fortunate, after a long idle period, to find alternative employment with the nascent London and Oriental Line, a British company operating almost only in the Far East, following the imperial routes of empire where they discovered their niche. As a captain, Minghella was temperamental and reckless with each officer of the watch, often stumbling onto the bridge and unnecessarily supplanting control. This led to resentment and disdain from others on board. His skin these days had grown slightly older with new indentations and markings, but his mind stubbornly refused the wisdom that should have matured with age. Though sensitive to slights, he lacked the self-awareness to know what others thought of him, so nights in the bars contained much amusement and repugnance of their leader sitting in his cabin alone, drinking whiskey. He was brittle and defensive; a gruff, outcast, and solitary man.

Like most Europeans in the east, he initially socialized with his Caucasian peers. In a protracted, interminable night of drinking in Hong Kong at the Neptune Bar, he had fallen in with two Australian fraudsters. They drew him into a financial scam, providing desalinated water to Darwin in the Northern Territories. The information sounded reliable, following the revolution in membrane technology, making reverse osmosis economically viable. He invested his life savings—eight thousand pounds—in the enterprise. Soon after they had completed the investment, he uncovered the hoax and began a more than common slide downhill with alcohol.

*   *   *   *

Joseph Minghella took the *Aphrodite May* back east, still indignant with life, while the year before, he had found a new wife, named Grace, in Singapore, although the state had not officially endorsed the relationship. She was his longed-for "nice girl from somewhere else." She had a Chinese name, but Joseph knew her as Grace. He adored her Oriental beauty and the affection she showed him. They rented a delightfully ramshackle, cramped apartment behind the bars on the Sembawang Strip, to the north of the island, near the Johor Strait and the causeway to Malaya. He woke up one day and sensed that time had slipped away. England now seemed antique and irrelevant, so he disinclined to return. He loved the rudimentary, slumberous life in sleepy Sembawang, a disheveled backwater of the island, where the poor lived on fried tofu and soy sauce. While on leave, the village fulfilled all his needs. There were a men's tailors, and the barber had baths. There was a noodle seller nearby who sent a child walking along the strip knocking two short bamboo sticks calling for orders. And there was an old lady who wore a pointed straw hat and carried two immense pots of soup on the ends of a long bamboo pole. The shops were simple wooden tables and makeshift stands displaying goods. There were Indian stalls selling their food as an alternative. He could walk the entire stretch, hand in hand with Grace, of an early evening lit by hurricane lamps immersing themselves in the spirit, sounds and tastes of the unassuming, unhurried environment of the Orient without pretense.

Singapore had gained self-governance a few years earlier, and now a new Prime Minister—Lee Kwan Yew—would make a big statement. But Joseph had no problem with that. Sembawang, once a rubber plantation, would be the last area to focus his attention. It now housed the giant British dockyard offering employment and sustenance with seafarers frequenting the bars of the Sembawang Strip. For Joseph, a worthy Englishman at heart, their intoxicated conversation provided occasional alternatives to the embrace of his Asian lover.

He no longer aspired to the sea. This sleepy backwater was now the only home he needed. He longed to be back in Grace's clammy embrace, drinking cold Tiger beer on the deck of the apartment behind the bars that serviced the vast shipyard. Placating the customers, they named the open-fronted saloons: the Melbourne Bar, the Avondale Bar, the Golden Hind Bar, the New Ocean Bar and the Nelson Bar. After a night of alcoholic relaxation, one could move onto the local fast-food restaurant for Bobby's Egg Banjo, a sandwich of runny fried egg, inserted between two fat slices of bread. Alternatively, they offered chili crab, fried rice and onion omelets. Or satay sticks and nasi goring, all to eat on the stroll home, while avoiding the storm drains and enormous rats. Or he could sit on the flimsy chairs and chat and drink with the visiting seafarers, but more often than not, Joseph just relaxed with Grace, sipping a fine whiskey. She was his own "Grace Kelly," smaller, less refined but more liberal in bed, he assured himself. For the first time in his long life he felt satisfied with the company of another, but as many other people recognized, to be free, one needed money, and Joseph had lost his.

* * * *

The *Aphrodite May* returned to Durban two months later, in late August 1962. What had made the ship so fascinating to Gerry in June was the news from Minghella he waited for so long to confirm; she would lift another bullion cargo in March 1963 (the coming southern early autumn). The preceding gold lift had proved an eventful occasion for the port, the shipping company and her designated master of the day, Joseph Minghella. And everything had gone well, despite nobody on board knowing exactly what to do. There had been some concern since the vessel did not possess a purpose-built specie room, like the usual Union-Castle ships.

But the London & Oriental Shipping Line had secured these occasional special cargoes and felt positive they could manage again. With no specie room, what they had was a deep tank in No. 3 hold. The deep tank—part of the ship's original design—could carry the occasional liquid cargo, such as vegetable oils or even low grade unexotic chemicals. They rarely carried such, but the tank could also carry any small, dry cargo, being ideally suited for mail. The tank was about fifteen feet by fifteen feet, with a height of thirty-five feet from the tween deck floor to the bottom of the hold. The top comprised a large steel plate secured with ninety-six bolts. For the random liquid cargo, there was a small manhole through which they could feed a hose and monitor the liquid height and temperature.

On this visit, Gerry had sat and drank with Captain Minghella again amongst the hustle and bustle of visitors; immigration, customs, port inspection, chandlers and others. Back in his own office ashore, Gerry began seriously to reconstruct the story he had heard long ago, to remember what he'd heard over a strong coffee.

* * * *

Time for some sober reflection. On a peaceful Sunday afternoon, Gerry sat and thought deeply while the first basic elements of a plan he had picked up from a seaman in Wandsworth prison formed in his head. He'd forgotten his name as time passed, now it came back to him; John "Tiddly" Winks. The story he told sounded incredible. Gerry's first reaction was to dismiss it as absurd; it couldn't possibly be real. Tiddly Winks said he had discovered the perfect crime, as if it were there for all to see, and yet no one had. Like most big crimes, it had begun with a meeting and an idea.

Gerry thought back to that time in Wandsworth, serving a four-year sentence for embezzlement when he had the fortune to be sharing a cell with a notorious bank robber named Daniel Geddes. Prison in winter meant frigid cold, isolation and hunger. Geddes had obtained plum jobs in the library and the laundry, which at least offered warmth and something to do. Neither of these benefits improved the smell of shit and perspiration, like a toothache that wouldn't go away. Gerry would never forget the smell of an English prison and supposed their South African counterparts possessed similar curses. Prison for Gerry would never be behind him. It was the first time his guile had not been enough; he came to need Daniel Geddes.

When he walked out of prison on license—parole—he found a country shabbier than when he had entered, with no petrol, no food, no money, facing ruin. The fortitude of men had surprised him inside. Especially the strong ones, the men who had seen it before but carried on with a never-eroding ability to endure, get it done, do it again and again until they met their goal. He heard the stories of organization, brute force and criminal cunning. They were men with presence, cold courage, larger than life-sized men who never rolled over. He had sat and discussed the plan he'd been told with Geddes in a pub called the

Prince Albert, and he had been warned; "For a job like that to be successful, it needed completion without detection."

Gerry moved on to another life, where he could begin again, avoiding the constant lies, deceptions and half-truths that had permeated his last few years in the business of ducking and diving. An associate of Geddes—John Russell—had provided Gerry with one of those old, white, twelve month passports.

"You'll never see the lights of Harrods again, Gerry," Russell had told him, but Gerry wanted to live another life. He was heading south and quietly slipped into obscurity.

* * * *

The following day, in September 1962, Gerry and Captain Minghella opened a fresh bottle of Teachers Highland Cream. Sluggishly, Gerry coaxed out the same stories of Grace in Sembawang, the lost eight thousand pounds, the disillusionment of the sea and the anger inside. For these two months now—when he first heard of the next gold shipment—he had been pondering, almost daily, Captain's Minghella's position in life and what he required from it. Gerry could read people. And few people pass up the chance to make their lives more comfortable, so eventually Gerry posited the idea; "Joseph, I have some friends in London who might help retrieve your eight thousand pounds. Call it ten thousand."

Minghella, having only drunk a quarter bottle, was perfectly aware what Gerry had said, but took some time to appreciate the full implication. Involuntarily, one of his unruly eyebrows lifted. "How do you mean, Gerry?"

"If you were prepared to do something for them…rather, to *not* do something, they would be very grateful. You get the gist, Joseph?" To state the obvious, but to make sure Minghella understood, he added,

"I'm referring to the cargo coming up in March." Captain Minghella, with furrowed brow, eased himself up from his comfortable chair and took a brief walk around the modest office. Gerry felt the subtle shift in disposition. Joseph was a little unnerved and undoubtably taken aback. He needed to think this through. The silence juddered.

Joseph Minghella suspected some details and knew—absolutely—the coming voyage that Gerry was referring to. "I know its perplexing, Captain. These are not small-time crooks. Ten thousand pounds is a very good deal." Captain Minghella returned to his seat, notably free of histrionics, because Gerry had seen his weakness and judged the situation correctly. He asked for more details and felt the gravitational pull into a darker space.

The plan he had ruminated on for years now finally coalesced in his mind. In theory it should work, but he would need Geddes and Russell. They were men who got things done. They might also have the money and knowledge to follow this through. They would know everything. He needed to talk to Daniel Geddes—now! When he had first called London, he got hold of Geddes and Russell in the final planning stages for the Dagenham wage heist and there was no enthusiasm for discussing speculative business so far out.

That was then, but this was now. When he called Geddes, he was told he was unavailable. He called again the next day only to discover that the two of them were in Maidstone Prison serving a term for section 33 of The Larceny Act, Receiving Stolen Goods. He knew Alice, Russell's wife, so wished her and the baby well, and asked her to pass a message to John; "Winston leaves in February."

THE MECHANIC

The desire of gold is not for gold. It is for the means of freedom and benefit.

- Ralph Waldo Emerson.

January 08, 1963 - Battersea, South London

I T HAD BEEN A LONG, cold, contentious night, with scant sleep for either of them. Billy couldn't remember when they had been in such disagreement. He thought back to before she moved in. When playing in the street as children, he could not imagine the two of them ever being in dispute during the lives within which they existed. Sally was part of the city; unafraid, bold and interactive, always there for everybody, and more and more, for Billy. But last night, they had argued—Sally vociferously—into the early hours of the morning. She carried on talking, while Billy mostly listened. It was as if she believed with sufficient repetition, he would understand her concerns. "I know you're private, Billy, but we need to talk. You can't put me in a box," she declared.

He tried to moderate the exchanges, occasionally holding her tight, but unusually the affection had not eased her protest. How much he wanted for her to attend a hairdresser when she desired to placate her flamboyant tresses; she would look so radiant. She coveted a baby, and he concurred, but that would require money. Ultimately, Billy, without losing his composure, was more determined than her to not allow his dreams to evaporate. Not this time.

Just before dawn, Billy awoke to find Sally in a better frame of mind, "I'm making tea, Billy. Get dressed and make the fire. It's freezing!" she shouted from the scullery and he heard and felt the more upbeat tone. It being a Saturday she didn't clean houses in Chelsea, but planned on helping at the Battersea General Hospital; what she and everybody else called the "Antiviv." Billy was so proud of her. She never stopped giving and he keenly believed the world owed Sally Dawkins something worthier, not just her modest dreams, but more than the essentials of life, the same lives their parents had become trapped in. All this talk of getting on, the nation "never having it so good." What did it mean to a young couple living in a damp house in Battersea paying controlled rent to someone they didn't know? Some neighbors were readying themselves for the coming move to the brand-new towers called The Winstanley Estate, a stone's throw from where the two of them sat huddled before the fire, drinking mugs of steaming hot tea. But, the previous night, Billy pointed out—confidently, he thought—that the new accommodations would, at least initially, be for families and those with children. If his mother were alive, they might have a chance, and it would have gladdened him to see her living in a new flat with standards of comfort she could only imagine. Hot and cold running water, indoor toilets, radiators, full kitchens and perhaps a view of the river. What chance would a young, unmarried couple have? If he returned to sea, where would she live all alone? A few days earlier, the Pool had made Billy's decision for him.

Sally had listened, intermittently, to his reasoned perspective on life, but she kept returning to the key issue, his idea of working with—what she called—the "'orrible John Russell." He was a known villain, once a black-marketeer and all the antisocial status he brought with it. Not too long ago, he'd been selling stolen food to old ladies to make money for himself. How could Billy possibly consider working for him? And that other man, Geddes, she considered him a well-known "thug." She wouldn't or couldn't, reveal her sources, but "everyone knew it," which was more than enough evidence for Sally. But she hid her emotions, finally. She loved him too much. If this was his dream, then she would stand by his side. She envisaged him getting older without his temperament developing beyond adolescence, and that suited her fine. She would take care of her Billy.

He waited for the perfect time. When she began donning her worn, blue overcoat with the torn sleeve, pulling on the ugly boots, he stepped closer and they embraced. They had grown into a young couple who considered themselves a team, ready to take on the world together. Pulling her close, he whispered into her ear, "Sal, sweetheart, I wanna marry ya soon, start a family together."

She pulled slightly apart, smiled that wonderful smile, studied him and kissed her lover. But before she could answer, he added, "I'm gonna see Mr. Russell today. This morning. I jus' wanna 'ear what 'e 'as for me." His approach had been to confuse her with the tempting proposal of marriage—which he had identified as her one consideration above all—and the dreaded thought of John Russell. "You'll see, Sal. 'E's treated me really well. I'm just gonna 'ear 'is story, to see what 'e's off'ring." That was a lie, of course. Russell and Geddes had clarified that once he heard of their plans, there would be no turning back. But Billy wasn't about to disclose that.

She stared back disconcertedly, "Please, Billy, be careful. I love you."

"I will. I love you, Sal," he reassured, a little unconvincingly, but he understood that being a father meant earning a wage, and he felt what he was doing for her meant even more than marriage. He was also exhausted with life, beginning each day knowing it wouldn't match his dreams. She didn't want to argue anymore, so she buttoned up the coat and stepped out into the frigid morning air, avoiding the hanging icicles, as the snow fell dirty to the ground. Billy sat back at the table and placed his head in his hands and hated himself for lying. His only solace was that he knew, deep down, it would be the best for her, that soon she would understand. Sally walked eastward along Grant Road, drifting into the middle of the street, avoiding the piles of dirty snow and a giant snowman the children had built with black coal eyes, and daydreamed she walked all alone in the darkness.

Half an hour later, Billy followed her out into the street and took the same treacherous route she had towards the Albert Bridge Road, passing the hospital where she worked and he felt the tears well in his bitterly cold eyes. He rationalized his decision making; he had no career; no prospects and they were permanently broke. Inside, he felt an unshakable menace lingering, a tale of guilt for his mother's demise and a regret that burrowed its way under his skin. His father had once told him, just under Tower Bridge, "Don't seek shelter in the majority, son."

A hundred yards further, looking east into the sun, the snow radiated that eerie sound of nothingness. He imagined for a moment he heard the distant tolling of Big Ben. As he turned and walked through the wrought-iron gates of the park, he saw the two men sitting on a bench twenty yards inside. Their greeting was cheery and familiar, like co-workers beginning a day's work on every other day. Billy sat on the brushed-clean bench, hands in pockets, hunched over against the cold, while Geddes stepped away and lit the obligatory Player cigarette, glancing about to affirm their solitude.

"Well, Billy? Do you want to work with us?" John Russell asked. And Billy knew that would be the first question, and yet he had believed there might be more time to consider. But then he realized there was no time, and all last night and this morning he had spent considerable energy advocating for just this one answer. He said nothing, but examined Russell in the eyes and gently nodded in agreement.

"All right, Billy. I really think you've done the right thing. Now, I'll explain your part in the scheme. No turning back. No talking to anyone, right?"

Billy nodded again, and then sat and listened to John Russell's fantastic tale of conspiracy, plot and escapade. Occasionally he interrupted his story to ask Billy a question of the sea, and Billy did his best to illuminate, based on the bare facts as he understood them. He strove for detail, but said all would become clearer once they had finished here. Then he completed with the usual London question, "What d'ya think?"

"Are you serious, Mr. Russell?" replied Billy with an air of incredulity and suspicion.

Russell moved his head slowly up and down, "Deadly serious. Can you do it?"

"Um, well, it's a bit daunting, but yeah, I fink so. We might need…"

"Don't worry, anything you need. Anything. We get it. You're in!"

Had he overcommitted himself to a group of people he hardly knew? He felt he was entering a labyrinth, emptied all the pockets of his mind, and who knew where it would end? Geddes had returned, having smoked two cigarettes. Smiling at Billy, he added, "Glad you're on board, Billy. It'll be a grand adventure. Ever been to Woolwich?"

They agreed Geddes should take Billy to see the Mechanic, whose legitimate business existed in Woolwich, on the other side of London. The Mechanic, a long-term affiliate of the gang, worked and played under the name of George "Razor" Wilkinson. He regularly furnished them with cars, stolen within two days of use, then burned afterwards. He supplied minor items like hidden bludgeons, and large appliances such as acetylene, drilling gear and other tools of the trade. The two of them climbed inside the new Ford Zodiac Mark III, where Geddes quickly lit another Player. Handing the packet to his diminutive passenger, he asked; "Do you really not know what we're doing?"

Billy shook his head at the cigarettes, and replied, "I know what's involved, and I know 'ow much Mr. Russell 'as said I might get. He told me 'imself," reflecting the confused tides of opportunity and ambition overtaking him.

"But it can be done?" reiterated Geddes firmly.

"Yeah, I fink so. You know...depending." But Billy was overawed by the pleasing luxury feeling of the car's fabric interior and soft seats.

He surveyed beyond the car window in deep reflection as they slipped their way onto a twenty-mile collection of signposts connecting urban thoroughfares, purporting to be a primary road. The zigzagging highway, mimicking the Zodiac's waywardness on the icy roads, had the unenviable task of being the notorious South Circular Road. Its counterpart, the North Circular, strode purposefully around the growing suburbs north of the Thames, pushing aside anything getting in its way, carving through twenty-five miles of residential London, one of the city's major routes. The one thing most people had to say about the North Circular was that it was a lot better than the South Circular. England in the 1960s defined the onset of progress, as more roads, more cars, grand buildings—commonly make with large slabs of concrete—had just begun construction. The North Circular seemed better than its southern counterpart because North London, with all its pretty neighborhoods, West End, Westminster and leafy suburbs outclassed the endless rows of South London terraces, inhabited by the millions of people who kept the dirtier and seedier aspects of the giant city turning. It was an incoherent primary road facing plenty of criticism, but it was one way to Woolwich from Battersea.

Billy sensed a connection with the driver. "Daniel. Why do ya do this? I mean, being a thief?"

After a brief pause, "Putting aside the need to make a living?" he responded.

"Yeah. Why be a thief?" Billy genuinely wanted to understand.

He thought for a minute and then, "Just started. I was very young when I was born. Bit of this, bit of that. Ended up at the West London Magistrate's Court. They sent me to Stamford House Remand Center. I learned to fight when I was young, 'cause I had to. You see, when I understood I was a big man I hit another man and it horrified me. I thought I could never do that again. But the next day I found out I was still me. I was bullied at school. It's my turn now."

Then Billy asked more questions about Daniel's earlier life, pushing the need to find out why he had taken this life route. Geddes had never married. He boasted of an assemblage of willing young ladies whose acquaintance he rotated. Billy knowingly took this to be an exaggeration, but only to a certain extent. Peeking sideways at Daniel, it was easy to believe his deep voice would attract women, his charming manner (until angry), immense frame and garrulous, but controlling behavior. Billy could imagine that when Daniel entered a room all the ladies would gawk appreciatingly, but also men would turn their heads in respect, or alarm. His size made him resemble an immortal god, a liar perhaps, but a charmer and a gangster. He was both funny and terrifying.

Billy, furrowing his brow, "An' this work?"

Geddes continued, "They were different times, Billy. You keep climbing to get out of the shit. You get…institutionalized. It becomes a way of life. The next time was a first-time magistrate, a woman. Lady Sybil Campbell. She sent me to prison. I got the birch there three times. It pierces the skin, but I could take it. I went to Portland Borstal sawing logs, for Christ's sake. I drifted into it. Just wanted enough to go straight. Know what I mean? To live in a pub, to drive a new Ford Zodiac." Billy saw the exciting, glamourous lifestyle of Daniel and John Russell. He thought of them as remarkable men who had a dream and lived it.

Daniel thought again, and reflected, "I've been looking for this one all my life, Billy. The chance to get out. Know what I mean?"

"Did you 'it Bishop, Daniel?" asked Billy, changing the subject with a genuine need to know.

"Anyone of a dozen men could have done that. It had to be nipped in the bud sooner or later," disclosed Geddes.

"But you?" Billy pushed as Geddes slewed away from yet another traffic light, the Ford's wheels losing traction again.

"You can draw your own conclusions, Billy," the extra-large man responded too vaguely for his liking.

And he considered it for a while as they bumped along the snow-packed road, and then reflected, "Well, if it was you…fank you, Daniel."

"Not everything in life is up to me, and I've made my peace with that. We may not have a moral code in the traditional sense, but there are rules. There should be respect." He thought for a few seconds, then added, shrugging his shoulders; "Then we either end up on a Caribbean beach or we die in prison."

Geddes had grown up in the War, playing on bombsites like all the other children, and became quickly hardened by the violence on display. After the war they recruited him to National Service, but he either avoided much of it, or had wasted his time "running over hills up north."

"Do you 'ave any advice for me, Daniel?" the young man enquired.

"Yeah, don't break the rules of the game," then, making sure not to sour the atmosphere, "And keep off the grass."

Billy roared at that. He appreciated the confident manner in which they talked, and thought this experience was wonderful, sitting leisurely on the wide, blue fabric bench, as the large car wafted along, Geddes guiding the slippery vehicle into corners, Billy rolling into the door, then back into the empty middle seat, laughing out loud in astonishment. It smelled new. So clean, soft and luxurious. He imagined that one day he might own such a vehicle.

"'Ow much did the car set ya back, Daniel?"

"Erm…about a grand, I think. You thinking of getting one?"

"Crikey! Ya spent a fousand quid on a car? I can't even drive." He had never learned, nor had anyone else in the family. It seemed a complete waste of time in Battersea. All the shops and pubs they might frequent were within walking distance and, on the rare occasions when they had had to travel further, they took the bus. Then Billy had an excellent idea. "Daniel, I wanna fank you two for all the 'elp with the money when I was inside, like." He meant it honestly, but couldn't form the correct words to explain his gratitude.

"Not a problem, Billy. You're one of us now."

"I'm really short of money, tho'. The rent's gone up t' free quid now! Is there any…" as he spoke Daniel had removed his wallet from his suit jacket and fumbled while holding on to the top of the wriggling steering wheel.

Taking out some notes, he offered them to Billy, "Here's a ton to keep you going. Buy your girl a present and take her out for dinner tonight. And get yerself some nice clobber."

"Wow, an 'undred quid? Fanks, Daniel."

They passed through the High Streets of Clapham, Dulwich and Catford, the southern heart of England's industrial darkness, past the suburban columns of smoke, as Billy viewed a bright, new-world culture of aspiration on a billboard with adverts for Shredded Wheat and a new movie about "an extraordinary gentleman spy." They heading in a sinuous fashion east, back to the south bank of the river, to the broken, disappointed and now rejected ward of Woolwich, an ancient trading place for wool. In the borough of Greenwich, it was famous for the now-dwindling Royal Arsenal, which manufactured armaments and researched explosives for the British Armed Forces. Then the empire dissolved and England just handed all the troubles over to the United Nations and began cutting the military budget.

There is a famous ferry and a foot tunnel crossing to North Woolwich and the Royal Docks. Woolwich, once, was an important military and industrial town. Then the demographic center shifted south in the 1800s, the area becoming a Victorian slum, stowed away in a hopeless corner of London where the important people didn't care. Some areas were notoriously overcrowded, and a desultory, shabby quality to the place endured near the river. It became one of London's worst corners. Later in the nineteenth century, they replaced more and more houses with industrial developments (coal wharves, a gas company and a power station). The post-War period brought changes to the town's fabric and infrastructure as they widened streets and demolished entire neighborhoods to make room for the new, fashionable, concrete tower blocks, where the occasional stranded tree brought an aura of end-of-the-world inevitability.

The Ford Zodiac passed through the doomed urban spaces, the notched shadows of rooflines, where many of the old industrial buildings remained. "There's Woolwich," said Geddes, pointing to the Dockyard chimney, a tapered, dark brown metaphor of the past. Between the Arsenal and the Dockyard lay an area that was once Old Woolwich, where he turned left, then right and skid to a halt next to a medium-sized warehouse displaying an old sign; "Tuff & Hoar Ltd."

He parked near a small door with "Wilkinson Warehousing" above the lintel, and explained that Razor was "a lovely man, good to everybody, straight as a die," ironically the greatest attribute of a gang member. Although they could see the water; the air lacked the smell of the sea. Geddes, high on testosterone and low on fashion sense, rang the bell. A man wearing a flamboyantly patterned tea cozy on his head opened the door a minute later. He instantly recognized Geddes and motioned them inside. From behind, another man approached, wiping his hands on an oily rag, so Geddes called out; "'ello Razor," and extended his hand.

But the other man showed him his greasy palms and shrugged apologetically. "Nice 'at, Daniel, are the Russians coming?" in his quiet cockney accent appraising the other man's sheepskin Cossack hat.

"It's called style," retorted Geddes dismissively.

"Congratulations on hiding it so well," rejoined the other man.

He introduced Billy, "Ah," said Razor, "the tip of the arrow, the vital element of the plan. Been looking forward to meeting you, young man." Billy savored their friendly conviviality as the two smiled reassuringly, while Daniel complained his new Ford might be leaking oil.

Razor dismissed his veiled request for assistance, "That's fine, the street needs lubricating as well. You've come to see what you've come to see?" as he led them to the tea urn.

"Have the law been rattling cages?" Daniel asked quietly as they walked. Razor gently shook his head.

Daniel looked at an old car, almost unrecognizable on jacks, "I got a hand job in one of those once."

"Sure it weren't a Barclays Bank?" said Billy, his confidence growing, tittering out loud.

This elicited the reply from Geddes, "You're a cheeky sod, aren't ya?" He already liked Razor, a meat and potatoes man like himself, with a face like an unmade bed. The large space reverberated the sharp, echoing noises of the copious activity of men working on the mundane and unrewarding tasks of their legal undertakings. Wealth was alien here in this oasis of chaos in the dying, tranquil town outside.

"I hear you still have two men in prison; Herman the German and Jimmy Jazz?" asked Razor.

Geddes nodded, "We're taking care of the families as best we can."

Mechanical noises proliferated, along with dust and the smell of chemicals. Two lorries and six cars, some in parts, occupied the building's interior. Grinding, welding, hammering and shouting rebounded from the walls.

Razor was continuing the tradition of his father, Alfred, who had opened the company fifty years earlier when Woolwich was the center of so much activity, the beating heart that had brought England kicking and screaming into the twentieth century. Alfred still worked with his son, who felt obliged to keep him updated with recent work, including the "off-the-books" enterprises. The two of them, father and son, had considerable training and experience in automobile repair and maintenance, mostly rebuilding salvage work, which was transient and readily moved on for a small profit. Additional work comprised collision repair, painting and restoring, along with lorry and diesel mechanics. But those in the trade—the illegal one—knew they could rely on the Wilkinsons supplying distinctive items. This specialized business now took more and more of their time. They maintained a low profile and believed a few more years would be enough. With the rapid advancement in technology during and since the War, the family realized their business was becoming less and less tenable in the present circumstances. And Razor became more and more concerned with his father's health.

The workshop was well-equipped, including three vehicle lifts. They carried out body repairs and worked on the oily and greasy parts of vehicles, while absorbing particulate dust from sanding and toxic chemical fumes from painting. It was a time before the health and safety of the employee were even acknowledged. As they walked, he shouted to another man, "Give it another welly, mate," and his words echoed with the dearth of soft furniture and carpets. Turning to his two guests, he added, "He thinks he works here, but we've got one more interview," and winked at the grinning Billy.

Razor had been a mechanic at Le Mans. Billy considered him and recognized a man comfortable in his manner and place, believing he knew his profession well. It etched his face with the lines of a happy life. His crow's feet spoke of laughter and the creases in his cheeks showed a man who smiled easily and cackled at life. He wore loose, dark blue dungarees and a gray sleeveless shirt, while his body reflected the struggle he engaged in; muscular arms were the benefit of sweat and grime.

Many mechanics specialized in a particular field, but the Wilkinsons were proud of their "jack-of-all-trades" flexibility. For the current operation, they would supply a lorry of certain specification and some engineering in a box. For security, they had agreed to call it the "Engine." Occasionally, Geddes had asked Razor to participate in the front office of their enterprise, but after the first experience, he had declined. He wanted to keep the family, and the business, low key, away from the busy eyes of C11 and the Flying Squad. He treated them to a mug of tea, then took them down a passage behind the main working space to a locked door. He opened it and switched on the lights. Little changed, other than the light, so dirt, grease, wood chips and the smell of oil confronted them, as before. A radio blared out an unidentifiable news program from an office in the corner. Razor took pleasure listening to the radio while he worked, but didn't live influenced by outside events.

"So, here it is. The box, sorry...the Engine. Actually, it's a crate." Boxes and crates are dissimilar. If the sheathing of the container (plywood in this case) can be removed, and a framed structure remains standing, the container would more likely be termed a crate.

"How big is it?" asked Geddes, stretching his neck to see more.

"For your purposes, ten foot long, five high, five wide. Approximately. Of course, it's somewhat smaller inside."

"Dovetail joints?" asked Geddes, as if he practiced carpentry on the weekends.

Wilkinson frowned, "Box wood joints with full cleated ends. We needed the size and rigidity. And it's a serious load. Actually, it's all very clever." He explained that the effectiveness of a wooden crate is based on the weight it can carry before the cap (top, ends, and sides) is installed. Skids, or thick bottom runners, were specified to allow forklift access for lifting. The specific design, type of wood, type of fasteners (nails, screws, bolts), and workmanship strongly influenced performance. The cleated box had six panels faced with wood strips. They had made the panels of plywood instead of solid or corrugated fiberboard. Wooden cleats reinforced the panels. The box was impressive, and he felt proud standing before it.

"What are all these metal bits?" queried Geddes, this time keeping the question general, while Billy looked on with extreme interest.

"Good news on that front. Anchor plates and corner straps. Let me show you around. We added rubbing strips at the bottom, like its palletized, in case they go the forklift route. See, the sheathing is supported by frame members, struts, diagonals…the inside is a complete aluminum tubular frame. This thing is so strong."

"I don't even know what that means," said Billy, who had been staring and listening.

"The whole thing is made of oak and beech. Hardwood plywood. The plywood is to make it look cheaper than it is, but it is also stronger than it looks. Excellent strength, stiffness, and it won't creep," he said. He stopped and stood back admiringly. Then he continued, "Inside it's sectional. Each section has a gusset plate with struts, diagonals and horizontal braces. Grade A and A/B plywood. Lag screws everywhere. It's lovely, isn't it?"

"You can't have done all this yourself!" noted Geddes suspiciously.

"Not to ruin it for you, Daniel, but no, I didn't," replied Wilkinson.

There was an uneasy silence. Billy stood still, shifting his wide eyes from one man to the other. "I contracted some of this out around Woolwich."

A shorter silence before Geddes quietly remarked, "The deal was to keep everything inhouse, George." Turning more serious, "We thought you were going to do everything yourself."

"We like to do things on the cheap, Daniel. You know me. I contracted different sections out. They had no idea. For example, who knows what a welded aluminum pipe frame is for? Only when it gets in 'ere, do I—and my Dad—put it together. Don't ask me if we can trust my old man. You can trust him." *Yeah, but I don't*, thought Geddes. "He's too old, too tired, and too talented to care about all this stuff," he clarified.

They were each Englishmen, but they had no deeper understanding of what that meant. Woolwich and Battersea might have been unknown to each other. "Up north" was another country, and the Watford Gap was the end of the world. Only Billy had seen the real outside, and only sparingly. Their lives might continue for decades and they might never meet again, yet they all understood they were free men. They represented the good of perseverance and hard work, or so they imagined. Any impiety lay with the obliviousness of a country towards a certain class of people just trying to get on. They mostly despised the past and the restrictive regimes of servitude and deference, but it bought each of them to this place, the guarantee of liberty if you followed the rules, and now the opportunity to take the one and only chance they might ever get.

They concentrated on the work before them.

"Now, come and look at the icing on the cake." Rather too dramatically, Razor stepped nearby and pulled a large cloth from an object worthy of contemplation. Geddes and Billy stared, both inspired and confused. "It's a jet engine."

They were taken aback, "Jet engine? Young Billy's a clever lad, but he's not a bloody jet pilot!" stated Geddes, rather obviously, but Billy was glad he had relaxed the irritated demeanor of a few minutes before.

They all joined in enthusiastic laughter, while Razor explained how they would use it. "To cover the length, we are suggesting the paperwork says two Goblin jet engines, but in fact, we've only got one. And, of course, we're not putting it all in. You see here, the widest part? These are called the cascade vanes. Just behind here,"—he pointed with his hand—"I'll cut it."

"When's it shipping out?" asked Daniel, seeming to lose interest.

"January twenty-eighth, from George the Fifth. Henry is working on the export documents for us," clarified Wilkinson.

Geddes, now glancing on incuriously, said; "Okay. I'll leave you two to chat about the Engine. I gotta put a tiger in me tank. Be back in a while," as he turned and walked outside.

"Off you go and I'll waffle on a bit," said Razor.

When Geddes had gone. "Can I ask ya a question, Razor?" said Billy, glad to be alone with the kind man with sad eyes and a loud, crackling laugh. Some people wear a smile, whereas this man was the smile. Everything about him was easy and unpretentious. Billy drank the tea, but took in so much more from this considerate man. Billy, for a moment, wished he had been his father.

"I think you'll be asking me plenty in the next few weeks, young lad."

Billy, as usual, had lots of questions, but in this case, without Geddes, he changed the subject, "Can ya tell me 'bout Daniel and Mr. Russell?"

"What do you wanna know?" he replied curiously.

"Am I doin' the right fing working with them?" asked Billy.

He finished his large mug of tea, and then comfortingly said, "I worked with them once. I was a so-called heavy. Not as much fun as I thought it would be. It's all adrenalin and alcohol. Being a robber requires amnesia, you know? I couldn't take it. I could see the muscle leading to shooters one day. But now this. A good plan. A chance to get out, like winning the pools. My old man fought in the War, and what did 'e get? A pension of twelve shillings a week. I grew up in the War. Death and carnage were common for me. I really don't know what made us so obedient," shaking his head. Without laughter, Billy saw a more sorrowful demeanor. His dark eyes became glossy and his face fell to the pressure of gravity contemplating his father. Billy understood him. His silver-flecked hair bore the telltale sign of familial distress. Perhaps his own contribution, thought Billy, might soften the desolation of this warmhearted man.

"Crime became the way. I just wanna better life. You can be like Russell. Party at the Astor or the Embassy, buy your shirts from Harvie & Hudson."

Nobody knew what they had with this caper. Secrecy—always such a precious commodity—was essential, so he kept a low profile. Some crimes were just for the buzz, some like this, were serious; and just for the money. He had no desire for glory, but he had grown up close enough to poverty for it to frighten him.

"Look at all the monkeys in prison, Billy. I like my door to lock from the inside. Know what I mean?"

Billy listened with his innate, almost childlike innocence, "Yeah, I know exactly wot ya mean. An' Mr. Russell?"

"Well, you stuck to your manor, that's good. Can I make a suggestion?" Billy nodded. "They're well known to the police, you're not. The Sweeney knows nufink of you. You have no C11 file. Just wait to see how intense the police will be afterwards. It will worry Daniel and John 'cos the Sweeney might start planting stuff. So, you keep a low profile, young lad. Understand?

Billy thought for a moment, then revealed, "I got it. Fanks, Razor."

"And remember. Put it this way, Billy. If you're gonna work with South London faces, these are the best two. I'm content with John Russell," his mind wondered elsewhere, but subconsciously, he understood that a search for positives could easily become a hunt for excuses.

THE GAMBLER

We have gold because we cannot trust governments.

- Herbert Hoover

January 15, 1963 - somewhere north of London

IN ENGLAND, BEFORE THE WAR, if you inhabited a large city and
sought an escape to the countryside, then most people boarded a
train, or rode a bicycle, or perhaps walked. Cost and time defined
the range of countryside you might view. By 1963 the rural scenery
had turned into not only a place which produced food—and a lot of
it because of the import restrictions of the 1940s—but also a place to
visit and experience, mirroring a nation slowly unearthing from the
economic depths of a world at war. England had mightily contributed
to that War, and the one before, and now came out of it with little to
boast of, except a rapidly evaporating empire and a moral sense of
pride in having done the right thing. But the nation had a young,
vibrant population tearing at the chains of her past. The Conservatives
were back in power, but the changes implemented immediately after
the War were now established, and the people were not turning back.
John Russell had survived that tumultuous political change and saw

now the economic regeneration of England unfolding without the restrictions of class. He needed—demanded—to be part of it.

He built his understanding and daydreams of the countryside with boyhood readings of *The Wind in the Willows* with Toad, Rat, Badger and crazed motorcars, *Alice's Adventures in Wonderland* with the White Rabbit, Cheshire Cat and March Hare. It was a dream world where beauty, adventure and peril derived from fascinating stories, something essentially English and decent. He still avidly read books. He well recalled the months he invested in the southwest during the War, the beauty and magic of the English countryside that could be found in Dorset, but not in London. Like most children of the city, they evacuated him and he experienced his first sighting of a cow.

He had cherished the isolation, and the distance from his intimidating father. Eventually, he had learned to admire the countryside and the differences it revealed with the city from which he had escaped; from the highly strung, fidgeting pale youth, lacking a sense of humor. He wished many moments of his traumatic childhood had never happened. Upon his return, it disheartened him to discover that his father—a working man who never worked—remained. He hadn't even been maimed or disabled. He still had the power to overwhelm his only son, John, and the anger to use that power at the slightest provocation. War made coarse beasts of every man, and with hindsight, he felt it had thrown away his childhood. John Russell had grown up lonely and unhappy, contemplating God to be cruel and arbitrary, while the world was a foul sty. His dislike of authority extended from the bloated owners of property to the politicians and the police.

Like most successful men in his profession, Russell devised a sideline disguised to launder money falling into his lap. The police were always observing known villains, and anyone overspending would have questions asked of them. He owned Chapman Motors in Stockwell, an area of Lambeth, but he told people it was in Vauxhall, near the Oval Cricket Ground. It sounded more respectable to his clients. The business specialized in upmarket motors, where they maintained, tuned and cleaned the cars. Sometimes they just stored them for the wealthy of Chelsea and Kensington, for the people he met in the clubs of the West End. And here he was, having borrowed someone's stunning Aston Martin DB4, a car with a compliant ride and desirous lines, in British racing green, weaving his muffled way through icy, idyllic country roads, the quintessential storybook England of meandering canals, frozen duck ponds and quaint slippery bridges. The snow added a Christmas card flourish and quieted the ride. Upon his return, they would rewind the Aston's milometer. The road was a swirl of dirty gray and brown in an expanse of soft white as they cut through pastures of occasional sheep and flashing images of hedges. England was an ideal country for a road trip in 1963. Starting at the Prince Albert, they drove, like knights of the road, northwest from the Edgware Road in London—once the long and straight Roman Watling Street—to the M10 motorway, a spur of the country's first such road, the M1.

In the never-ending rolling expanse of pure, snow-covered fields, the two city men settled into the intoxicating speed of the Aston Martin on a wide, flat, six-lane road without speed limits. The countryside rose and fell like an enormous, soft, white ocean swell. Occasionally, a copse separated the fields, or a farmhouse or barn stood out in their oppositeness. This world had become alien to the two of them. Here, the people rode horses and shot guns, raised pheasants and hunted foxes. Worst of all, if you hadn't been born here, they would regard you an outsider. People in the city ate and rarely thought of agriculture. If they did, they understood it as primarily a food factory, where a small fraction of the rural population works hard to make profits for an even smaller group of rich landowners. Most people lived in urban or industrial areas, whereas the country was predominantly rural and agricultural in character. The farming was a mix of arable and pastoral.

The initial delight of the clean air and unspoiled views soon soured. Now Daniel Geddes, who never liked a hastily rushed breakfast from which Russell had dragged him, hungered for the noise of the busy streets and craved his authentic life with friends in the pub. As soon as the bared-tree avenues of North London ended, he thought they had entered a terrifying provincial nothingness.

Near St. Albans they swung west on the A45 toward Daventry. At Southam, he turned left on Butt Hill toward the civil parish of Napton on the Hill, in rural Warwickshire. "So, who's the 'Man on the Hill'?" Geddes grunted, lighting another Player, horrified by the silence of the lands they drove through. Russell turned to Daniel, who had been suspiciously quiet until then, while turning into a road lined with traditionally rendered cottages. The village seemed intimate. At its center sat the Bull Hotel, a sixteenth century coaching inn painting a quaint canvas of a pre-industrial society. In many ways, England is a small country, but like a telescope, move it one degree and you're in another galaxy. He slipped the Aston silently past the twelfth century church and the King's Head pub to a small winding lane.

"I want to say something before we get there," voiced his passenger, having not received an answer. Russell slowed the car and pulled into a rustic gate beside a shallow rise that sloped down, lost in the hedgerow. He pulled out a small, thin Panatela and lit it with a lighter.

"It's not like you to hold back, Daniel, what's troubling you?" he asked.

Geddes considered the situation. He knew John Russell had committed some ruthless acts in his time. He could fight with fists, legs, head or anything that came to hand. But he had no physical fear of him; he had convinced himself of that. "I like him, but I'm worried about the kid."

"Yeah, I know, you said that. And I'm worried about..." countered Russell.

"...the customs man. Yes. But I think we can cope, and I have to trust you with the boy. But you know, right in front of us might be the weakest link." Geddes had laid out his fears.

"You mean Biggles? Well, you can size him up yourself in a few minutes," Russell responded.

Geddes nodded, "Yeah. Whatever his name. What if he can't handle it?"

"Why don't you push him a little, Daniel? See if he cracks," he replied.

They killed a few minutes smoking, staring out the cracked-opened windows of the Aston. They accepted the enormity of the challenge they were undertaking. It was larger than anything they had pursued before, but they also recognized that if successful, they would not have to struggle again. Their heads were full of the details of the operation, each running elements of it through their minds again and again, seeking desperately to ensure they had omitted nothing. And then there were the details of afterwards. The essential element was not to panic. If all went well, there might be suspicions, but there would be no evidence. No fingerprints, no eyewitnesses.

John Russell understood his friend's reluctance. He had never valued the upper class, and he wasn't about to now. Why should he show deference to people born into money? He disliked Harold MacMillan, and all he stood for; the hereditary privilege, the public schools and the old school tie relationships. John Russell firmly believed he had reached the height of his profession through bloody hard work and meritocracy, not wealth or social class.

Russell and Geddes had had many arguments over the years, big and small. But their shared experiences during the previous nearly ten years had melded them, with a few others, into a small, but devastatingly effective group of villains.

"Well," he said, "Let's go and see what he can do."

They drove into a graveled drive, where a sign hung, slightly lopsided, declaring "The Grange." Brown, dead weeds poked through the snow around the gate posts. The Aston Martin grumbled along the crunching drive, its sounds subdued by the snow, perhaps a hundred yards from the hedge and road. Russell had visited before, and each time, but especially today, it gave the impression of a Christmas storybook page, set on six acres of land, a shocking counterpoint to the paucity of day-to-day life in January Battersea. It was a property he might become comfortable with, especially with Alice and the baby. She would have clean air and space to flourish. Its dull red and pink bricked symmetrical facade typified late Georgian architecture. Apparently, it contained five bedrooms, four bathrooms and a spacious living room with double doors leading to a large farmhouse kitchen and dining area, all with wooden floors and chandeliers throughout. It was a chilly morning, but no smoke emerged from the chimneys.

A man appeared from an outbuilding, or garage, and moved towards the house. He noticed them, smiled, water vapor emanating from his mouth, and waved at the Aston.

"Tally-ho chaps, come on in." The car's occupants seemed out of place, but, as usual, confident.

"Hey Biggles! How are the howling dogs?" shouted Russell cheerfully as he brought the car to a stop alongside the front door of the house. Stepping out, he introduced Daniel, which elicited an outstretched gloved hand and the reply; "Wrigglesworth, but please call me Gonville, old bean."

Horrified, Daniel glanced at John, who smirked and pointed out, "I call him Biggles. He thinks he's some kind of Baron or something, but he's just a crook like us." The man they were scrutinizing was an inch or two shorter than Reardon, slighter, but straight-backed and vaguely imperious with an air of upper-class twittery. The gentry is a historical British social class comprising landowners living off rental income, or at least they had a country estate. His land was for occupation, not profit. Most of the landowning class had a coat of arms, but lacked titles of nobility. Daniel felt he sounded like the cynical upper-class waster in the sports car who gets the girl. Wrigglesworth looked back at Daniel, and saw a handsome, but contemptuous face, slightly flattened by too much drinking, and cigarettes and punching. A beguiling gangster he was not. *More unpleasant, less heroic*, he thought.

They had schooled Wrigglesworth at Eton and he graduated from Oxford with a first in something, or so he said. He was born in India, went to boarding school and took holidays on the continent. He once enjoyed hunting, and for relaxation studied every book he could find on spiritual and motivational self-improvement. He supposed himself a member of the lowest grade of the peerage in Great Britain. Russell had long lost interest when he first heard the conversation in Durham Prison. He epitomized a well-bred, narrow-chested and wild-bearded man, the sort who honored the Charge of the Light Brigade. He scorned the socialism of 1945, hated the nation's disasters of the 1950s and failed to grasp the new permissiveness, confused by the social changes taking place around him. He accepted privilege, whereas John Russell loathed it. Sadly, for him, he saw the world as orderly, deferential, nostalgic and hierarchal. He was a man rapidly running out of time, while a prodigious drinker of wine, port and the occasional cognac. He often wore sandals.

He used a pseudonym, Anthony Brightwell, when traveling and trading—a necessity, he declared ironically, given the shadowy, dangerous world he occasionally inhabited. His continuous requirement for more and more money was motivated by an addiction to gambling, usually in the West End of London. Sadly, that need drew him into the company of the likes of Russell and Geddes, whom he would much rather have avoided. He regarded them as men of modest backgrounds with inappropriate, expensively tailored Turnbull & Asser suits, while Geddes wore a silly fur hat.

Russell had met his Lordship five years earlier serving a two stretch for smuggling in Durham, in the northeast of England. He offered them refreshment, which they took to be alcohol, but advised they had driven all this way for an industrial demonstration. "We'll have a drink after that." The sky was mostly clear. Inside, the house was cold. The interior seemed neglected and frayed at the edges. There were spaces on the walls where pictures might have once hung. Display tables and the mantelpiece were devoid of ornamentation. Gonville Wrigglesworth had squandered much of the family fortune wagering a diminutive ivory ball losing momentum on a spinning wheel. And the horses had all gone.

Scanning around, Russell commented, "Down on your luck, Biggles?"

"Indeed, I am, old chap. Caught me on a foul day. Is it that noticeable? Cup of tea?" He took a few seconds to glance over at Geddes while they had shaken hands, thinking to himself, *my God, do all these people look so frightening?* Humbly, he pronounced, "I need this work, John." All he saw contained disgrace and decline. What were the alternatives?

"Well, look on the bright side, we're here," replied Russell with a wide smile, devoid of humor.

Ten minutes later, teacups in hand, they watched Wrigglesworth prepare a demonstration. Across the drive from the house stood a brick building with garage-style doors. Without opening them, a smaller door led into the Baron's ill-lit work room, walled in sepia-colored brick. On the steel floor, in the center, sat a tilting furnace and crucible. The disheveled room had junk stacked at one side, and two cluttered workbenches. Some bulbs were out, leaving a sickly, hesitant luminosity. The aura did not engender confidence.

"Okay, show us your wizardry and magicary, Biggles," requested Russell.

"Take a seat, chaps," he offered, but there were no chairs. Daniel glanced at Russell, sighed, and sought somewhere to lean. All three had a sense that a language barrier existed between them.

Clearing his throat, Wrigglesworth began: "This, gents, is how I sense it will go. Shoot me down in flames if I am inaccurate. You will deliver to me some amount of London Good Delivery bars..."

"What?" said Geddes, causing an immediate break in momentum. There was a short, painful silence, as if a child had made an unfortunate noise in polite society. "Bars! I assume the bullion is in the form of gold bars, yes?"

"What else would it be?" Geddes answered a little sarcastically, with a steady gaze, his eyes beginning to narrow.

"Well…coins, perhaps?"

There was another brief and difficult silence. Russell and Geddes glanced at each other, "We thought it would be in bars. 'Eavy ones."

Wrigglesworth waited, looking at them as if they were two schoolboys, "Yes, gold is heavy. Do you not know what you're getting? I thought you had a man in South Africa?" As soon as he spoke, he wished he hadn't; the two men stared back at him with intense, almost vicious eyes. He added, "That's probably the wrong phrase there."

Looking around, Russell asked, "What happens if the police do a swoop of this place?"

"If there's no gold bars, then we're fine. They can find a few scraps; I'm in the gold smelting business. I have a Refining & Smelting License."

"And if they find bars here?" enquired Russell.

"Then we are in deep trouble, gentlemen," replied Wrigglesworth, an uncertain smile on his face, again sensing the error in communication as soon as the words left his mouth. There followed another lengthy silence with both his audience members focusing intently back at him. "What?" he ventured quizzically.

"Allow me to enlighten you of your misguided notion…" advised Russell, drifting into a better standard of English in the Baron's presence. He stared back at Russell's face; still, intent, suddenly frightening. "Let us be absolutely clear, Lord Wrigglesworth. If anyone…anyone gets tugged by the Poe-leece,"—he said it slowly and deliberately—"then they never, ever name names. I don't care what they offer, no one will talk. That includes me and Daniel here. And it includes you!" he pointed a finger. Then, shockingly for Wrigglesworth, he added, "If you grass on us, I'll see you laid out in lavender."

The host, his eyes wide, turned to Geddes, perhaps to see if he had spoken in jest, but he added ominously, "Mr. Grim 'imself."

All Wrigglesworth could come up with was: "No…right, yes…I got it. Quite. No talking to the Police. I'm fully on board with that. A gentleman never kisses and tells." He smiled.

But Geddes felt the air thicken with tension, "So, what are these bars?"

Wrigglesworth, feeling prehistoric in their presence, breathed slowly, his eyes wearily glancing at Russell, then looking away, concentrating on Geddes; "Yes", he cleared his throat again, "Yes, the London Good Delivery bar. I'll try to keep this brief…"

The London Gold Market in 1963 was the largest in the world. Ninety-five percent of the gold traded in London was unallocated and part of a paper system of exchanging. Market members comprised investment banks, commodity trading companies, brokers, central banks, refiners, and mining companies; it was a wholesale market. Participants traded on a principal-to-principal basis, sometimes known as "Over-the-Counter." Like any worldwide, internationally accepted system, some measure of standardization was essential. Everyone involved required to know they participated at the equivalent level, with the same commodity as everyone else. To service this professed aim, the Bank of England, in 1750, set up the London Good Delivery List. The goal was to use standardized documents and only recognized refiners that could manufacture gold bars to the standard prescribed by the Bank.

All gold traded Loco London (i.e., actually in the Bank's vaults in London) embodied the accounts of the customers who owned title to specific bars. The Bank adopted a system of book entry transfers where a customer could transfer bars between other gold accounts within the Bank, without the need to move them. A physical delivery of a customer's bars in or out of the vault would credit or debit the customer's account. Otherwise, the bars remained in the storage positions where they already dwelt in the sub-basements of Threadneedle Street in the City. In 1963 there were thousands of tons of gold in the Bank, stored in eight to ten vaults on two levels.

Besides being the largest market in the world, London, a few years earlier, had been one of the largest physical gold refining centers, with companies like Johnson Matthey, the Royal Mint Refinery (owned by Rothschilds) and Engelhard being the main refiners. By the early sixties, however, various economic developments in the global market eroded this dominance. Competitors, like the Rand Refinery in Johannesburg, could now make London Good Delivery bars to the accepted standard.

What defines gold bullion is that its value derives entirely from its precious metal content. Unlike jewelry or coins, gold bullion has no artistic component of value. Refiners produce gold bars in many sizes, but the London Good Delivery bar is what most people understand as bullion. They weigh about four hundred troy ounces—about twenty-seven pounds—and are about eleven inches long. They stamp them on the top (the larger face) with the manufacturer's name, the weight, and the assayed purity. They lack an idealized, super-smooth finish. Gold of this purity is so soft that the bars are frequently scratched, and flattened on their edges and corners, so the surface may be dented where the bars have been stacked together. They were, and remain, the most important bullion product in the world.

London Good Delivery bullion fetches the best prices when sold. The rules established by the Bank ensure that investors were trading gold of a comparable fineness and weight, supporting market integrity and stability. However, bullion in this form is, effectively, inaccessible to private buyers, because the bars—so formidable and cumbersome—are exorbitant, and the vaults where they must be kept do not trade with the public. For criminals to possess a Good Delivery bar meant they needed to change its appearance, but without affecting its value.

Daniel, having focused on the explanation, concentrated on the original prize, and asked, "Can you make fake gold bars?"

"Yes. The best way, the most convincing method, is to use Tungsten," advised Wrigglesworth.

"What's that?" came the immediate reply.

"Sometimes called Wolfram…" he added.

"I say again, what the fuck is that?" Daniel was becoming irritated after the lengthy explanation of the Good Delivery bar.

"Tungsten is an element. It's a rare metal…what's wrong?" expressed Wrigglesworth, sensing danger.

"Nothing. Just fucking looking at you," glared Geddes, his hyped-up, edgy personality coming to the fore.

"You're annoyed," supposed Wrigglesworth.

"No, you're annoying," Geddes clarified. "I'm not the bloke in the orchestra who plays the triangle. Know what I mean?" he asked, along with the alpha glare directed back at Wrigglesworth, who could sense the danger oozing from every inch of Daniel's body. He grimaced, knowing he possessed the pain threshold of a six-year-old.

"No! Don't worry, we're not going to use Tungsten—the melting point is too high anyway. The wonderful thing about Tungsten is, it weighs exactly the same as gold. So, it would have been absolutely the very best…"

"Are you winding me up?" snarled Geddes.

"So, we will use…?" cut in Russell without empathy, but sensing Daniel could be about to step forward and ruin the day.

"Lead, of course," said Wrigglesworth, "Now, this is how I intend to handle the gold, chaps."

The manufacturing trial began relaxed and conditional, guiding his hand to the centerpiece of the operation, the tilting propane-fired furnace. He gestured to the pipeline exiting the building while securing the loose ends of a cowhide leather apron around his waist.

"I didn't have to consider this too long. Propane directly exposes the crucible to the heating source and provides a different level of heat," he said, feeling more comfortable, engaged in activity. "Obviously, any crucible selected must be able to withstand the heat the furnace can apply. So, I've chosen crucibles with high graphite content and high thermal conductivity for fast melting in a gas-fired furnace." He donned his face shield.

Geddes and Russell glanced at each other as if to say, *looks like he knows what he's talking about.* Lighting the flame—which all three appreciated—and adding his heat-resistant gloves, he continued, "I can charge the crucibles while outside or when installed in the furnace, but they don't have to be removed for pouring. This is a major convenience and adds speed and safety, and reduces losses. I never heat above the maximum temperature, of course, which could contribute to a crucible failure. Very dangerous." He moved the pieces of equipment with casual practice, placing pieces of lead inside. It became a therapeutic experience for him, standing, vampirically lit, before the furnace. He considered alchemy seductive.

"Crucibles for tilting furnaces require integral pouring spouts. They provide the reach and accuracy needed for the pour." The two men stood, silently impressed. "In addition, I make sure to never allow the metal to solidify in the crucible's bottom. I pre-heat them and the metal as the furnace heats up. Any moisture can cause the crucible to crack on heating, but that doesn't happen if you know what you're doing," and courageously, he winked in their direction.

Wrigglesworth explained how the Procast crucibles should be tempered before use, as the one in the furnace glowed a hot and dusty shade of burned sienna.

"How are you gonna cut the bars? Argon arc gun?" probed Daniel.

Wrigglesworth dismissed the idea as gently as he could. "No. Very expensive. I've been debating with myself the method of cutting—assuming they are bars," he clarified, a little boldly.

"Powered hacksaw?" volunteered Daniel.

"Yes, I considered that for a while. But I think the losses would be untenable. Dust and cuttings everywhere. I tried a cold chisel and I don't have a high-pressure press. So, in the end, I chose a propane torch. I've been using this set to cut manageable sizes, but I'm having a problem getting the right parts for it to work exactly the way I need it. It will be the same process for gold, but since they are thicker, it will take a while longer."

Geddes stepped in his presentation, "Pay the man and buy a new one." Expenses were available.

The melting point of gold is about 1,900 degrees Fahrenheit, which means he would require temperatures that hot to melt the cut bars. He made his burners from one-inch steel pipe, with a standard grill regulator. He had decided a high-pressure regulator to be unnecessary. "So, of course, I have a fan—Alcos, electric driven—which blows in the air and propane. They need not be at high pressure. At this standard, low-regulator pressure, the gas burns much more efficiently. Much less waste. Much cheaper gear. You know, I will need lots more propane. You can get that?"

They nodded, "Working on it."

"May I ask where?"

"I'm fairly sure you don't want to know," declared Russell.

"I thought you could cut a hole in a potato and place the gold in that?" said Geddes, perhaps testing the smelter. Wrigglesworth pretended not to hear the comment. He didn't wish to offend, and the man was thumpingly, frighteningly big. He continued working as the room temperature increased.

Russell shuffled his hands along a shelf. "You don't have much borax or sodium carbonate?"

"No, it's pure gold, so we shouldn't need that. There won't be any impurities. This is not refining. It's not even smelting, really," explained Wrigglesworth.

They had agreed already they would convert the gold into smaller bars, obliterating its identity, and move it through legitimate chains for cash via the public market. Gold never ages, never changes, doesn't care, never judges. It would not squander its value, only its shape. Small bars would be easier for Wrigglesworth to transport and market. If he had to, he could slip coins into the crucible to represent jewelry scrap, but pure gold is what they wanted to sell; the mathematics were just simpler.

"I'll also need a lot of lead." The visitors nodded in agreement. "I have a good collection of ingot molds. All graphite. And simple, so no special design like using a Delft Clay Method—too clumsy, too slow."

He demonstrated cleaning the mold before using, rubbing with a pumice stone, then wiping with an oily rag. This inhibited contact between the gold and the mold. "When I'm ready to pour, I arrange the mold on here," pointing to a stool standing about eighteen inches off the floor above an iron tray collecting any spillage. He then tilted the crucible and furnace so the lead (or gold) poured directly into the mold, rather quickly. He upturned the mold, tapped it a few times to remove the contents entirely. He pointed out there might be wastage here.

"Do you dip it in water?" asked Geddes.

"You can do," he nodded.

"So, we'll have small, minted bullion bars?" said Russell, perhaps hopefully.

"Noooo!" Wrigglesworth knew he had replied too abruptly. "I mean to say…minted bullion bars are cut with a die from a cast that has been rolled to a uniform thickness. All the surfaces are smooth and even. They stamp the markings onto the bar using a minting press. And company markings on minted bars will be "raised" because of this process. No, cast bullion bars—what we are producing—are made by pouring molten precious metal directly into a mold." His hand pointing to the mold. "Markings are usually stamped on the bar using a hammer or a press, if we wanted to, but I wouldn't recommend it. The surface of the bar can be uneven and have some small pits and grooves."

Wigglesworth continued with the demonstration.

"Where did you get the furnace?" asked Geddes.

"Legally," replied Wrigglesworth, "I can assure you. A. H. Wilkes, Birmingham. The best." The two men, becoming bored, were impressed with the large lead bar he made at the completion of the demonstration. "Voila." Wrigglesworth enjoyed the melting process. It felt magical watching the metal transform into a liquid and then cooling down into a distinct shape. It justified the sweltering heat, the intensity and the weird fetishing of the process. As he explained, he opened a drawer and pulled out a full gold-painted replica Good Delivery bar and placed it on the bench between them. Stepping back, he felt satisfied, and he could judge from their expressions they were too. Russell picked it up and held it, weighing it in his hands. "The genuine ones will be considerably heavier," remarked Wrigglesworth, removing his apron.

"Gentlemen, there is, of course, one rather large problem." That wasn't what his two visitors wanted to hear. "If I take, say, five bars at a time, where do you intend keeping the remainder? I'm thinking there must be hundreds…"

Russell cut in, "We were going to hide them all here. You're getting a full whack!"

"No. No, no, no, no. I'm happy to do the metallurgy and the fencing, but you cannot keep three tons of gold in the house!"

And they knew he was right. They had discussed it several times, but could not overcome the glaring hole in the plan. They couldn't— would not—keep it in Battersea, or in some unknown lockup in North London. It was too risky. They needed a safe location with easy eyes on the money.

Changing the subject, Russell asked, "Where are you expecting to move the gold?" Wrigglesworth agreed to explain with some background history.

Bordering on the western boundary of the City of London is the world's focus of jewelry and precious metals, both a manufacturing and retail center, with rows of shops displaying ribbons of precious metals. It had begun as a garden owned by a sixteenth century politician, named Hatton. But it emerged with the glorious titles one associated with jewelry, precious stones and rare metals; Johnson Matthey, Sharps Pixley, Rothschild and the Diamond Bourse. The catalyst for Hatton Garden becoming the jewelry center was De Beers, the diamond mining corporation, establishing their headquarters nearby at Holborn Viaduct in the 1870s. In prior days, its esoteric business rituals took place on the street or in the ethnic cafes which characterized the area. For much of the twentieth century, the jewelry business took place in an unwritten code of conduct between men who had dealt with each other for years. They often strolled around Charles Street, Leather Lane, Vine Street and Saffron Hill with a fortune in their jewelry pouches, conducting their business in the street every lunchtime.

However, with such a concentration of sought after, high value and easily transportable goods, Hatton Garden has had a murkier, transgressive history. Its darker side has ensured, reluctantly but unsurprisingly, it became loosely integrated with certain aspects of the criminal fraternity, as the public and traders exchanged millions of pounds every year. That crime segment was the upper-world commercial type—organized crime—not the smash-and-grab lowlifes abandoned to their ethnic composition, skill base, and geographical isolation. Did career criminals use skills attained through association with the Hatton Garden business community to innovate serious crime methodologies? Probably.

Russell and Geddes were part of that fluid, but highly effective era of "project criminals"—in this case thieves—who managed their social opportunity networks to gather intelligence and dispose of their takings. Jewelry and gold sealed the long marriage of convenience between The Garden's crooked dealers and inner-city working-class crime fraternities. Certain dealers straddling the legal/illegal divide were known to be fences who dealt in plundered goods. Dubious dealers provided tip-offs when to steal from an honest dealer or manufacturer's premises for best financial reward. Another of the fence's facilitation roles was to smelt stolen jewelry into scrap and then pass it onto the global legitimate bullion dealers, thereby laundering the proceeds. Over decades, large quantities of stolen jewelry had changed hands. Because of an integration of upper-world and underworld, Hatton Garden offered facilitators and skills for expanding acquisitive criminal practices. If they recast the gold into unmarked, unidentifiable ingots, then many dealers, legitimate or not, would buy it because it was gold; pure and simple. Once into the Garden area, the gold would be lost among the trade and daunting geography of miniature streets. Wrigglesworth felt confident he could move the gold in Hatton Garden, or alternatively, Antwerp. He lived on networks, rather than merit.

He impressed the two robbers with the demonstration. Wrigglesworth had melted some lead and formed it into a perfectly shaped Good Delivery bar, which they knew he had fabricated on the premises. They felt no need to mess with success. They could both envisage numerous ingots covered in two coats of gold paint, fully meeting their requirement. They needed to purloin some propane; but that was what they did. Peter had subcontracted a few youngsters to obtain a suitable quantity of roof lead. He would carry it here and work with Wrigglesworth to tidy the process, promote some efficiency with the propane torch system, and use his demonstrable handyman skills to shape suitable lead bars.

"Well, since you've been such get along, go along guests. Let's have a drink to skullduggery," offered Wrigglesworth.

"Well, just one. I'd like to eat while I'm still young and we've a way to go," responded John Russell.

Over drinks looking out on the generously scaled patio, under a bright and hollow sky, they chatted and considered the day a worthwhile process, except for the problem of where to stash the gold. Then Wrigglesworth, adding a touch of drama to the stillness of the afternoon, dropped the bombshell: "I was visited two days ago by a man named Foggy Meadows, along with a human-blood-drinking monster called Brian Spicer."

His visitors eyed each other. "Did Meadows mumble a lot?" asked Geddes.

"Yes, exactly. He said George Smith was seeking to do some smelting and asked if I was interested," clarified Wrigglesworth.

"And you declined, of course?" specified Russell.

"Of course. I'm on your team, John." They divulged the highlights of Spicer's record sheet details: wounding with intent, grievous bodily harm, blackmail and witness intimidation. Wrigglesworth suggested, and they agreed, Spicer was about as much fun as an orphanage fire.

Then, after a few seconds stillness as they considered the news, "It's not good," voiced Daniel.

Russell disagreed. "No, it's handy, 'cos its right on the plot. Now we know where Smith is in all this."

"What about where to hide the you-know-what?" asked Wrigglesworth.

"I think it's fair to say we're in a bit of a fix with that one," declared Russell, while taking another gulp of red wine.

"Not only that, John. We're gonna have to keep transporting it here to be worked on, and let's face it, there's gonna be eyes all over us when this goes down," exclaimed Geddes.

The three of them sat, shivered, and contemplated. Although, to be fair, Wrigglesworth thought he had done enough. It seemed as if their work today had been half done. "I have a suggestion, John." He then voiced his proposal on a separate subject than that which they had been discussing, considering the need to hide the gold as their problem. Russell listened with an open mind, but it was obvious the hiding of the gold was much more important right now. They could consider his novel idea later, but Geddes just stared at Wrigglesworth anyway, and slowly shook his head.

Russell had heard his proposal before, so answered indifferently: "It's an idea."

Wrigglesworth: "A good idea?"

Geddes, slowly shaking his head: "It's an idea."

"Well, I'll leave you to discuss the idea while I rustle up some more drinks," suggested Wrigglesworth, sensing it had been an agreeable day.

Daniel Geddes stood up and regarded the velvety, white lawn, following its gentle slope. Then, looking around the room, he remarked, "So, this is privilege and entitlement? Looks like he's hard up right now. Sold a lot of stuff. Won't be worth turning over afterwards," said

Daniel, his formidable nose losing feeling without heat, and they chuckled as one.

Wrigglesworth returned carrying a tray of drinks and saw them chuckling. He wondered to himself, what did people like that consider funny? But, as for this work, he was fully on board. He probably needed it more than any of them.

"Biggles," said Russell, "We're having a meeting on Thursday at Peter's place in Putney. It would be good if you can join us. We'll see how your proposal goes down."

"Like a lead balloon," muttered Geddes.

After a few more sips of alcohol, Russell knew it was getting time to go. But then Geddes, still viewing through the French windows, honestly quizzical, asked, "Is that a river at the bottom of your property, Biggles?"

"Yes. Erm, no, actually, it's a canal. The Oxford Canal." There was a lengthy delay while Geddes continued staring towards the water a few hundred yards away.

Then, finally turning around, he added, "Does it join the Grand Union Canal?"

"I believe it does, a few miles over there in the village."

Daniel Geddes gazed wide-eyed down to the sitting John Russell and, almost simultaneously, they had the same revelatory moment of inspiration.

THE MEETING

A person may not like someone else's religion, but he'll accept his gold.

– Robert Kiyosaki

January 20, 1963 - Putney, London

BILLY HAD RETURNED HOME FROM Woolwich with a palpable sense that he had now engaged in a tangible enterprise of substantial fiscal and personal magnitude. A few months earlier, the scenario would have been beyond his imagination. Sally had arrived home shortly afterwards, to feel the excitement so evident in his manner. It had been a while since Billy had been so animated and full of energy, but he quickly revealed he could not disclose any details. She could see he wanted to talk, to share his perceived good fortune, but those who suffer the most don't know what they want. Billy knew for certain now. She wasn't so sure, but his exhilaration somehow nourished her by osmosis. As customary, Sally, despite her fears, rejoiced with her lover, the one man she most needed to see happy again after so much misery.

Now, just possibly, he had a plan for them, for their marriage and for a way out of Grant Road, out of Battersea forever. Sally Dawkins had endured a demanding life. Hers was not remarkable, but everyone who met her—once they knew her story—had to admit that her sunny disposition was a glorious paradox. Everyone liked Sally, and many loved her, in the purest sense. She wasn't classically beautiful, nor the prettiest girl in Battersea. Her teeth were a little prominent, but that just made the smile appear more legitimate. Her auburn hair hung just below the collar line, surrounding a fine-planed, freckle-flawed face. She was five feet three, petite, but possessed the energy of a superwoman. She smiled often and laughed without restraint. But what no one could miss, apart from the eyes that glistened like golden antique jewelry, was the pure human energy she expressed towards all other men and women she encountered. She listened, she laughed along, she sympathized, she felt their pain. Loyalty was natural, enjoyable, and human to her. Just like now she became intoxicated by the happiness of Billy and it overjoyed her, if not really for the enterprise he could not speak of.

Sally's mother had been tiny and, unlike her daughter, had few teeth and two children. She had never seen a naked man, and had never visited the Tower of London, but possessed a compelling sense of place, of right and wrong, which she bestowed on her children. Her relationship with her husband might have been strained, but was not atypical of the time. Sally, the second child, was born on Speke Road in Battersea, a month before Billy Tumbler, although they remained heedless of the event for many years. Eighteen months after her unassuming birth—at home by midwife—a German V-2 rocket fell from the sky, unheard, unnoticed, and blew an immense hole, destroying three houses. Seventeen people died, the only survivor being the eighteen-month-old Sally Dawkins. By an enormous coincidence, she found foster parents in the same road where she had been born.

In the 1950s state nursery schools didn't exist so, like all the other children turning five years old, she attended an infant school. Having survived the initial pangs of separation, school life fell into a predictable routine, including the event she most anticipated, the daily ration of milk, a third of a pint supplied by the government to supplement a child's diet. Sally's foster father worked at Morgan Crucible Company near the river and never helped in the house because he worked all day. He came home at the same time every day for a hot meal, while Sally had grown into the daily routine of scrubbing and dusting, never questioning her duties or position in life. She had minor aspiration beyond being a wonderful homemaker.

School life for Sally mirrored that of many children in Battersea who lacked the specialized clothing for the gymnasium in primary school, so they just removed their outer clothes and exercised in their vests, underwear and bare feet, or the family bought canvas plimsolls from Woolworths on St. John's Road, near the Junction.

Visits from the school nurse would interrupt the routine, as the children lined up to have their hair raked carefully with a nit comb seeking infestation. There were routine eye and hearing tests and visits from the school dentist. Socialism had come to Battersea, and it averted much suffering. However rough it might have been, everyone agreed it bettered the standards of their parents. There was a palpable sense that life was improving slowly.

She received the polio vaccine, given to every child on a sugar lump. They didn't vaccinate against Measles nor Mumps because they considered them survivable. Class sizes were large, typically over thirty children to a room, as the "baby boomers" filled the cities. The limited teacher ratio meant strict discipline. A troublesome child commonly suffered rapped knuckles, caned buttocks or a ruler across the palm of the hand. Reading, writing and arithmetic (the "Three R's") were given prominence, as was learning by rote. The multiplication tables were chanted aloud in class, and they considered neat handwriting to be crucial and duly practiced daily. Her foster mother had once told her, "When you get engaged Sally, you know you've reached your goal." Sally knew no different and remained suspicious of countries the other side of the world. The furthest she'd ever traveled was the summer hop-picking in Kent.

At eleven, her foster mother died of tuberculosis. Her foster father, his hair yellowed by tobacco smoke, walked out a few weeks later, not having the ability or the disposition to continue supporting a girl. The general outline of her life had been a gently tragic tale of death and family dysfunction. The government had introduced a new tripartite system of schools based on meritocracy to facilitate social mobility. Her life in disarray again, she failed her eleven-plus, and attended the bulging Battersea County School, one of the earliest comprehensives in the country, somehow stuffed by the London County Council between the houses of Culvert Road and Dagnall Street. Almost homeless, at her new school she became reacquainted with Billy Tumbler, fondly remembering their days playing in the street. She joined the family for dinner one day and stayed for the next eight years, initially sleeping with Billy because they only had one bed. At eleven there was no concern of a sexual dalliance. A few years later the country slid into recession, and the area around Clapham Junction became a poverty-stricken bed of prostitution and crime. Sally proudly remained above it all, a flower in full bloom, wide-eyed and full of laughter, but her life never seemed to undergo the economic recovery that followed.

The following morning, after a cold night beside ice-covered windows painted by winter's frost-laden hand, she endeavored one more time to seek reason with Billy. Sally sat across from him at the kitchen table, having just completed a simple meal of sausage and beans. Billy, holding his hot mug of tea to keep warm, looked across at his lover, as she stared down at the floor seemingly deep in thought. "Are you sure about this, Billy?"

"Wot is our life, Sally? We 'ave to get out of 'ere. Look at us. Even if I get a ship, prob'ly a death ship, and even if I live to come back in nine months or a year, we'll still be in the same place. But without the money from Mr. Russell, 'ow we even going to pay the rent?" Then, changing the subject, "Let's go to Arding & 'Obbs, buy some clothes, then tonight we can jump the train to Victoria an' the West End an' 'ave some good food somewheres."

"Would we still be us?" she implored. "Stay 'ere, Billy. Take a job in the fact'ries, we can be together ev'ry day. We can get by."

"Yeah, that's all. Getting by is all we've ever done. This is our chance to get out, Sal. I don't want us to just get by anymore," he reasoned.

"I just don't like it. These are bad people, Billy," she pleaded.

"They saved me life in prison, Sal. This is our one lifeline."

They were both Londoners, the city a kingdom to itself, full of villages with their own unique character. London was a vast, splendid, gray place. "I belong to London and London belongs to me, Billy. An' to you." She was right. London's busy, full of people going somewhere, a place where people walked in a straight line, and a city where it rained in late July and the police sirens made that funny barking noise and the only condiment was the squeeze bottles of Tomato Sauce at the Wimpy Bar. Everyone drank that thick, milky tea, and every café had mothers with crying babies and lonely old men lingered in the J. Lyons Tea Room. They shared this majestic, sprawling, multicultural city with almost eight million small, human stories, all of which they could understand.

He knew, yes. They were Londoners, and proud of it. But he added, "I don't want you going back to an 'orrible squat, and these concrete tower blocks are not gonna be much better." London was the best place on Earth to be miserable, with the residents affecting a world-weary air suggesting they'd already done everything in town twice. The image that came to Billy, if he remained, was of a rain-lashed platform full of commuters jostling for space on a crowded train. It seemed to him there's nothing more to London than waiting at Clapham Junction for trains going to work and waiting for life to begin.

"I want to take you where the sun shines for weeks and weeks, Sal. Where there is space, fresh air, good food and warm sea water." He scrutinized her magical eyes and continued his reasoning. "All our friends and fam'lies are either gone to Essex, or goin' soon, or they're goin' to the 'igh rises and we won't get in, Sal." Then there was silence, except some quiet sobbing. They embraced, which soothed all problems.

* * * *

The meeting unfolded, as scheduled, at Peter Badger's flat in Putney, just behind Woolworths on the High Street. There had not been unanimous agreement to gather, but there was a consensus that people needed to understand their individual responsibilities and that of others within the grand scheme. Before opening, John Russell sought around to see the manner of men they were. He understood all too well that a leader's weakness is his army. He had all these people working for him, but hardly any direct power. He sometimes thought of them as a bunch of losers banding together for the big one, but a reasonably cautious gang, well prepared, low key, rarely socializing. Rank didn't matter, talent mattered. Prison had done little to deter them from crime, and Russell was betting everything on the future. He saw it as a military or political campaign. He was in this for the long run, all in for finishing the race. Good or not so good, there was a family atmosphere to the gang, and a curious feeling of sheltering because they were not the cream of the crop, just ordinary men prepared to go a degree further than most, and accept the consequences.

The plan was neither straightforward nor without a few yet unsolved problems. As expected, for most of them, the priority concerned the size and timing of the money distribution. He recognized his crew would not readily accept the waiting for their "whack." What convinced Russell, what he wanted people to know, was that if anyone talked, then everyone else would know who it was. He was serious about this. He wasn't sure who might gossip, although he had a few fears. With time on hand, he worried about things that might be of no concern.

The evening began agreeably enough in Peter's large, sprawling place. Above the garage he had a workshop/hobby room with three comfortable chairs and a few not so comfortable, many bearing the scars of cigarette burns. Everyone pressed together because of the lack of space. His wife provided the tea and biscuits. "Thank you for the custard creams, Maria. You're all in for another little treat tonight," announced John Russell as the small, but obviously dynamic lady headed for the door. Like the other wives and girlfriends, she knew something serious was afoot, and she had already had a long conversation with Alice Russell, who had come to the same conclusion. Russell momentarily stared at Peter's wife, imagining how much she might know, when Wrigglesworth elicited a general groan.

"Do you have any Bourbons, Maria?" Awkwardly, he responded, "What? I rather like them." Maria, a resourceful and kind human being, blessed with beauty wrapped in golden Latina skin, laughed loudly and left the room.

The firm, for want of a more convenient label, had centered on Russell and Geddes for nearly a decade now. For most of that time, Peter had also been a member. He'd known Daniel for a long time before. People liked Peter, and even more so when Maria was nearby, because he could be troublesome, with a certain paranoid ability to destabilize the situation. His emotions remained cool when alone or with her, but other men could produce an explosive chemical reaction, like dropping sodium in water. She made him seem human, with a clarity of purpose. He was a man who did what he wanted, with an ambition for his family, including a country residence. He had charm, but no grace about him, and a dirty laugh.

These three were the core of the group, but they knew dozens of other questionable characters, two of whom were serving sentences for the Dagenham wages job. They all felt the responsibility to support the families while they served their time—the tacit agreement being that they, or anyone else, would do the same for them. They had, in addition, provided legal support by employing a recognized barrister. It all cost money.

In the English legal system, solicitors traditionally dealt with any matter, including conducting proceedings in courts, although they were required to engage a barrister as an advocate in a higher court, since the profession had split in two. They presented minor criminal cases in the magistrate's courts, which make up, by far, most benches. More serious criminal cases might begin with a magistrate but would then be transferred up to the Crown Court, then to the Court of Appeal. The gang's solicitor, Henry Hale, was sitting amongst them that evening, munching on his second custard cream.

The group did occasionally work with others, but not collectively. If anyone came up with work, like a random breaking and entering, or a mailbag snatch, they understood they could earn some beer money. They didn't require permission, and there was no common pot. And work by yourself, or with others, did not earn you or your family a pension. However, they all understood that it was the big scores, the Dagenham wages snatch, for instance, where people could earn significant money, like an annual salary, which some might spend in a month. And the trouble with spending—especially if you lived in Battersea or Putney—was that everyone noticed, including the forces of law enforcement. The gang were people who worked together, trusted each other, but they were people the police monitored.

Every firm needs a leader. John Russell's manifest gifts of personality and intelligence could have carried him far if directed honestly. He had worked hard to pronounce his tee-aitches and use his vowels properly while improving his English. He liked to read books and genuinely loved the planning and plotting. And he was better at it than anyone else. The excitement began with the preparation, the surveillance and the secret meetings, all leading to the major event. Project crimes like this, based on organization and violence, had transpired because commercial safes had just become too good. They opened the old safes easily—many thieves had learned how in the army. The fifties were the era of safecrackers, but by the sixties it became too burdensome to open them quickly. Crooks realized that cash in transit was nowhere near as well protected, so it became an age of grabbing from security vans and trains. With less finessing of the money, it all became confrontational and violent. Blagging, as they called it, resulted in more people going to hospital.

They ran the gang on similar lines to a pirate ship; chaotic, ramshackle and slightly democratic. If anyone considered Russell or Geddes incapable of bringing in sufficient funds, then they would elect another leader or drift off to work with alternative criminal enterprises. It was a business; the only crime being to bring up your family in poverty. In the brief interlude before they began, Peter, with a captive audience, launched into a story concerning his boat, "Quite a lot of you might find this funny," he began, which prompted Russell to intervene.

"Right, thank you, Peter, let's get back to this crime thing." Standing before them, he continued, "We've all been doing this too long, just getting by, and we've been lucky. We used to do the easy targets, but there's no money in it anymore," as a few lead-lined puns crashed around him while the audience settled, furnishing a strong, lived-in feeling to the banter. With the typical unorthodox language that gave a voice to their marginal, misunderstood community, Battersea criminals shared the same accents, vocabulary and grammatical novelties as everyone else in the neighborhood. Their compactness would reduce the chance of informers as the wit broke out in their usual crime-filled clichés. The firm was word of mouth. They hadn't all attended the same school together.

"What are we going to do? Age gracefully?" he went on. "Before we get too old for this, I would like to commit a crime without blood and pain."

"Some people are reaching out into other work, John," chimed in Peter. He wanted to highlight the shortage of employment while the other two had been in Maidstone, and the slow response for needed additional money.

Russell nodded understandingly. He attempted to explain the style of transaction with which he had no interest. "We're not gonna do 'long-firm' fraud business. And do we really want to be in protection, like those thugs in Bethnal Green and Peckham? I'm not interested in bribery or gangsterism. Gangsters want the power. I want the money. I'm a thief. We are thieves! We're talking about a lot of poppy on this one," said Russell.

The repartee was like a ritual murmuring incantation, and all attendees agreed. They were here tonight because they subscribed to the bigger, better picture. If not, they would have already moved on.

"We've spent two years figuring this out. It's a serious piece of work," he continued.

"Do we need more people, John?" interrupted Razor, setting his teacup on a saucer. There were seven of them lounging around, when all heads turned in the front door bell's direction, out of sight on the floor below. After some muffled dialogue they listened to the ascending footsteps, and in walked Billy Tumbler, declaring modestly, "I've got some Bourbons."

"Ah! Employee of the month," cracked Wrigglesworth taking the plate.

A man named Arthur Treadway murmured, "He's too young!" which didn't go down well.

"Hey! Bang out of order," said Geddes, who understood that rule number one might be to never work with someone who is personally unknown to you, but he had grown fond of the young man.

"He works for us?" said the lawyer, suspecting, as most of them did, his lack of provenance.

The atmosphere ceased being funny as a steely-eyed glare from Geddes immediately confronted him. "We don't need threats, Daniel," he went on, then glanced down at his empty tea cup as if considering options while avoiding Geddes's scowl.

"It's not threatening, it's respect," he clarified, which most criminals understood and accepted.

John Russell cast a reproachful eye about, quickly taking offense. "None of that! You don't know what he's capable of, and you don't know what he will do. He comes with my personal recommendation." All were wary, since they knew they had only met last year in Maidstone. Taking a stool, Billy was surprised by the affirmation, but recognized immediately the change of mood in the room.

"Young Billy here is one of us," and Billy tentatively smiled and nodded to those observing him. Peter, sitting too close to Geddes for his own comfort, judged he'd never have the measure of him, so decided on the lighter touch.

"As long as he's not Irish," and everyone united in laughter.

"Now, to your original question; the fewer who know, the better it is for everyone. More people would be nice, I admit, but then there would be more risk of a leak. This is the big one, fellas, this is the last one I'm doing." This elicited a buzz of approval and mild surprise. Was he going to retire? This could be the defining chance for everyone in the room. "Once a big touch like this goes down, every thief and lowlife in London will come looking for a piece. Those living a 'charmed life' (informants) are inevitable." He considered the question sufficiently answered, so changed the subject.

"Right, Gonville…" everybody turned their heads quizzically, "…come up here and do some reckoning and sums for us on the blackboard."

"Gonville?" was the general resonance as Wrigglesworth stood and stepped to the board.

"Right chaps, here are the financials, which should brighten the evening for everyone," as he began writing on the board a complicated mathematical formula explaining the price of gold. All eyes followed the chalk as he wrote.

In 1919, the five leading gold bullion traders and refiners of the world met at the premises of Rothschild & Sons to perform the original London Gold Fixing, the daily setting of what they considered to be the price that day. Many believed that speculation, using international currencies during the Great Depression, had played a significant role in its expansive reach worldwide. To contain a repeat occurrence, in 1933, Franklin D. Roosevelt signed an executive order requiring American citizens to surrender their gold for a value of $20.67 per ounce. The following year, the American government set the price of gold at $35.00 per ounce. The price, thirty years later in 1963, remained "fixed," as it had been since 1934. Not fixed in a classical "gold standard" sense, but a pseudo version compelled by central planners. Private individuals could not participate in the convertibility of gold or currencies; only central banks. The American controlled Bretton Woods economic system had long sought to manage the price, while pegging the dollar to its value. Bretton Woods established the gold-dollar exchange rate system, which valued all currencies against this price of $35 per ounce, with the worthy goal of preventing the economic hostilities that fostered the Depression.

The London gold market closed during the War, but had eventually reopened in 1954. The benchmark began again, determining each business day a fixed price for settling contracts between members of the London bullion market. The annual flow of gold into London exceeded that required for industrial and speculative demands, so central banks bought the residual at the fixed price of $35. Therefore, the market price of Loco London gold depended on central banks, backed by the United States as buyer of last resort. Speculative trading, politics or war could modify the price, but only to a limited degree.

While Wrigglesworth continued scrawling on the board, confusing his audience, Razor finally voiced everyone's concern; "I still don't understand."

"It's written up there. That's the clue, init?" said Peter.

"Follow the arrows," advised the solicitor, Henry Hale.

"Arrows? I can't even see the Indians," declared Razor.

Sensing the confused atmosphere of the room, Wrigglesworth condensed the mathematics down to its basic level. "If the price of gold is about thirty-five dollars a troy ounce, then each gold bar…"

"A Good Delivery bar," interjected Peter, not because it furthered any understanding, but he felt he should add the information he already knew. Peter liked to contribute.

"… er, yes, exactly. They're called Good Delivery bars. Each bar will value at approximately £5,516. If, as we speculate, there will be about three hundred bars, then that would value the total haul at about £1.6 million, or £160,000 per…I believe the word is whack?"

A stillness infused the room momentarily, before Peter voiced, "Bloody 'ell. Wow!"

"Yes! I like it!" and a good-natured, self-congratulatory atmosphere permeated the conversation.

The mathematics pleased John Russell too, but he calmed the crowd, "What about fences?"

"Excellent point," continued Wrigglesworth, still standing and feeling comfortable before an audience, "we should all remember, gold is not like diamonds, pearls and other jewels. It has no artistic value. Gold is gold all over the world. If it is ten or twenty cents cheaper on the other side of the Atlantic, people will transport it just for the arbitrage."

"What?" voiced Peter on behalf of them all.

"Never mind. Once the original has been hidden—transformed, if you will—then it has the value 'fixed' in London every day. Usually about thirty-five dollars. Now, the only problem with gold is…"

"Hold the fun!" exclaimed Peter, like a bad penny, again a little too loud. They all turned to watch a developing confrontation. "Am I missing someone? I only count nine whacks, so why divide the total by ten?"

"Well spotted, Peter. Let's gloss over the price details for now and confine ourselves to the agenda," suggested Russell.

"I didn't know we had one!" And everyone laughed again.

John Russell felt it about time he began breaking the painful news, of which there was more than one piece. He raised his hands, "Settle down." Once he achieved a reasonable level of noise, he continued, "The problem is…"—the room went quiet—"The problem is we can't just dump three tons of gold on the market, as big as it is. Not only will the market go haywire, everyone will know its stolen, purloined or otherwise illegal. Then it will be impossible to move."

There was a concerned ambiance amongst the group. The smiles of a few minutes before now turned to frowns. Billy, meanwhile, felt overwhelmed with the sensations flowing through his brain. He wanted to be here, and the familiarity eased his anxiety as he glanced at each felon sitting in the room, trying to judge their character. He found the room antiquated, but tantalizing. And now this? *Did he just say 160,000 quid? Each?* He couldn't imagine a man making that much money in a lifetime. That was considerably more than Russell had suggested only a few days earlier. He felt he must have misheard, and he wanted to speak out, but he didn't intend to appear foolish. Why didn't he write it down? Some glanced at each other, asking without speaking. Peter jumped in again, speaking slowly, "So, that means...?"

Russell continued, "It's going to take some time before all the money will reach us."

This caused a slow grumble of surprise and concern in the room. "How long? When and where's the flop?" queried Peter on behalf of them all. All was well when he was speaking. Once he went quiet, the anger grew inside.

"Hot gold needs to cool down. Six to twelve months is our best guess," answered Russell. To keep his gang in a compliant mood, he related the numbers again, which Billy was grateful for.

"What's that all about?" Peter again voiced the general concern.

"Superstitious, Peter?" smiled Geddes.

"I'm not superstitious, just a little 'stitious," said Peter, sensing that, somehow, that was a reference to his origin.

"Can we just have the gold bars?" said the lawyer. "I want cash, John." Getting the eye roll he deserved.

"Yeah, and I wanna fuck Gina Lollobrigida," replied Geddes.

Wrigglesworth tried to be rational: "Experts know where most of the world's gold is. They'll notice when sizeable amounts blunder onto the market. Gold is essential but impracticable. Great to have, but hardly convenient for day to day use."

The lawyer, backed by Arthur Treadwell, voiced an alternative, "Can you just pay us a wage, John?"

There followed a protracted silence as people tried to digest the argument until John Russell slowly explained. "This is an antiestablishment crime. We pay pensions for families and barristers for defense. Sometimes we can nobble a jury, yes, but this is a criminal organization entailing risks not found in honest labor. Our work is antisocial." He stopped, looked slowly around the room. "This is the biggest payout any of us are ever gonna get, but we need to be patient and we need to play it safe."

Peter remained somewhat agitated, so Geddes rearranged himself on his chair, as if to say, *I'm here watching you.* "So, how many full whacks?" changing the subject.

"Good question. One, me, two, Daniel and three, Gerry in Africa," began Russell.

"Is he still dead?" said Arthur Treadway, trying to lighten the atmosphere.

"Number four. Peter gets a full whack. Peter will organize the transport and all other odds and sods. Peter, I need you to drive up and work with Biggles. Get the smelter all organized, along with the extra propane and the lead."

Peter, satisfied with a full share—never in doubt—nodded in agreement, sat back and smiled.

"Five. Arthur gets a full whack for the lorry work in Southampton. We have a lot of details to go through and we still need to maintain surveillance down there. Lots of work, but Daniel and Henry will help where they can." Turning to Wrigglesworth, he added, "Biggles here gets two whacks for…"

"Whoa!" "What?" cried a chorus of dissenters.

"Calm down, I'll explain in a moment," assured Russell. "Henry gets a whack for organizing all the paperwork in Southampton and for setting up the bank accounts in Switzerland."

"Switzerland?" Peter again, but only because he reacted faster than everyone else.

"One moment, everyone. Razor gets a full share for the Engine and work on the lorry and all the other stuff. Finally, young Billy here gets a full share for his specialized work."

"Which is what?" said Arthur Treadway, just beating Peter to the punch.

"…and the ship's captain gets a big drink. Ten thousand. That's it," ended Russell, triumphantly.

"I think you need to answer the questions, John," reminded Peter. Russell glared deep into Peter's eyes, and a quiet stillness permeated the room. Billy sat quietly, and self-consciously sheltered close to Daniel, just in case anything happened.

Most of them were already acquainted with Henry Hale. He had never earned a whole share, but with his contribution on this occasion they considered it justifiable. The solicitor, and sometime accountant—a man neither good nor truthful in either role—was gregarious and slightly rotund. He wished he didn't wear glasses, but his eyesight was so inadequate, he had no choice. He wore a rakish mustache to compensate and thought himself dashing. The opposite sex disagreed. He had met Russell long before and had organized the best barrister to avoid prison time in a post office robbery in Wimbledon. Hale still maintained a practicing certificate, but his chief priority for Russell, and a few others of his ilk, was providing legal advice while trying his best to avoid the law, as if leading a lawless double life.

Previously, he had been much more confident in legitimate business matters, such as contracts, conveyances, wills and inheritances. He dealt with all the paperwork and communication involved with his client's cases, such as writing documents, letters and contracts tailored to their needs; ensuring the accuracy of legal advice and preparing papers for court. Once a client's business took them beyond the magistrate's courts, he would find the appropriate, and typically costly, barrister to represent them in a higher court. Henry Hale had all the attributes of a bad solicitor; lack of communication with his clients, lack of enthusiasm, outrageous billing statements, unethical behavior, failing to meet deadlines, not returning calls and obvious conflicts of interest, and he had meandered into illegal work occasionally. He felt he shouldn't have put himself through all that hard work just to mop up the troubles of other people's own making. Not unless he was handsomely paid anyway. His once blue eyes had turned grey as if the humanity had somehow leaked out.

He had overcharged people, but no longer. He had fraudulently extorted money from a dead women's estate; he had created fake documents and policies, but all that had changed when he met Russell and Geddes, the first of several criminal clients he had been nurturing. If the police considered them racketeers, at least they had an excuse, but their solicitor was a racketeer in fact. On this occasion, Henry would earn his money. And John made sure he understood; he would return his calls, or else.

When they load a cargo onto a ship, the shipper will have created a bill of lading accurately describing the goods. The carrier (usually in the person of the ship's captain, or his agent) will sign the bill of lading, accepting responsibility for the safe carriage of the goods to the port of delivery. They forwarded one of the original bills by airmail to the receiver (consignee) of the goods at the delivery port. His presentation of the bill of lading to the carrier on arrival was proof of his ownership of the goods and his right to take possession.

Along with the bill of lading, the carrier would prepare a manifest detailing the cargoes on board with items like number of packages, description of goods, weight, measurements (freight is commonly based on the larger of the weight or the volume), freight prepaid or payable at destination and other sundry charges, if applicable. They also forwarded copies of the manifest to the carrier's office at the delivery port, to the port authority (British Transport Docks Board), HM Customs and Excise Landing Officer and the Dock Shed Foreman.

Concurrent with the physical transport of goods over a long sea passage lies the delicate subject of the international payment for them, whether plastic flip-flops, oranges or gold bullion. There is always a buyer and seller involved, and, unfortunately for everyone, perhaps, it means there will be banks involved. Banks act as trustworthy third parties to the sale contracts, and banks deal with documents and not with goods. This interface between the three worlds; money, credit and goods, requires that the documents involved must be accurate and in what common law describes as "strict compliance." There is no room for documents which are "almost the same," or which will do "just as well." The documents that the bank receives, as an intermediary, provide them with security if the buyer fails to reimburse them.

The gang had many workings with banks, but never through the customer's door. They did not understand the documents involved, nor the concept of "strict compliance." John Russell considered paperwork the wobbly mess of the well-structured caper. Therefore, Henry Hale would, for the first time, receive a full share.

In the 1960s, most ports had a Custom House, the head of which held the title of The Collector, and in a substantial port, such as Southampton, there would be Deputy Collectors. At each berth at the port would be based Her Majesty's Customs Landing Officer, who would examine import and export shipments as required. For commercial importations, they entered the principal customs declaration on a "107 (SALE)" form. In the event of a consignment with a value over five hundred pounds, the importer had to provide a signed and certified C105 Form to be attached to the Customs Entry, along with invoices and a packing note (if available). The C105 confirmed the value declared on the invoices was accurate and proved they were paying for the goods. This method prevented incorrect invoices and underpayments of duty and purchase tax. Henry Hale would play the central part in importing a special cargo, in this case "two de Haviland Goblin jet engines."

Hale would lodge the Customs entry, prepared by the forwarding agent, together with the attached papers, in the Custom House, and they would be subject to their satisfaction of correctness. The calculated duty and purchase tax would be paid to the cashier in the Long Room of the Custom House, and an Out-of-Charge Note issued and collected by the forwarding agent. The forwarding agent lodged a banker's bond with HM Customs and Excise so they would accept the cheque.

The forwarding agent then had to obtain a Release Note from the carrier after surrendering to them the original bill of lading, endorsed on the back by the Importer evidencing entitlement to the goods. The Release Note and Out-of-Charge Note were then taken to the berth and shed where the cargo was stored, and lodged with the Shed Clerk's Office. Once transport had been arranged, the collecting driver—in this case, Arthur Treadway—would approach the Shed Clerk's office for the consignment. They would give him a slip to hand to the British Transport Dock Police barrier at the Dock Gate exit.

This bureaucratic process applied to all imported goods.

Few understood these details or felt a need to know. Hale would take care of it, and he'd better get it right. At an individual level, each member of the firm either oversaw all the details (Russell and Geddes), got involved as much as possible (Peter), or just concentrated on their own work. Peter had sat through a tedious explanation by Hale—who he didn't like—but had not forgotten his original question, "And the situation with the double shares?"

Russell acknowledged that it required an explanation. Wrigglesworth had proposed the idea when they met, before the latter had spent time in Maidstone. Initially, Russell—under the strain of trying to figure where to hide the gold—had dismissed it, agreeing with Geddes's conclusion that it would not happen. However, now possibly relieved of the problem of where to hide the bullion, he thought through Wrigglesworth's idea, and it made sense.

Wrigglesworth would act as a banker. When they gave him five or six bars of gold, he would allocate to the ten shares an appropriate value; the weight multiplied by the price of gold that day. In this manner, everyone would know the exact value of each share received for each delivery to the smelter. Wrigglesworth's apparent extra share would cover losses in the smelting process (which everyone could see as a viable possibility), loss of value by dropping the fresh ingots on the market, cost of transport to London and Europe, cost of middlemen and any other expenses that might be involved with fencing the gold. There was the genuine possibility that Wrigglesworth might not receive much of his second share, or he might not even receive his full first share. Nobody was sure how it would play out in the coming months.

Peter didn't take it completely positively. "Okay, I get it and I kinda trust you. But, just for the record, he's getting an extra share, right? Just saying, it's never happened before."

"Well, let's move on…" declared Russell.

"Hold on," said Peter, never one to let anything go, "what about the kid?" Then, seeing Geddes's fierce expression added, "I mean Billy…er, what's Billy's job," and for good measure he added the weakest smile in Billy's direction.

So, John Russell began relating the plan that Billy would follow. The nonchalant audience slowly settled down in quiet attendance, listening to the long, detailed scheme. When he had completed, they looked at each other and at Billy. Peter was the first to speak again, "And 'e doesn't get a second share?"

"No, no, no…" Billy quickly interjected, but too quietly for anyone to hear.

"Pull the other one," declared Razor.

Russell smiled at the room. "If it was easy, everyone would do it."

But everyone, in their own manner, was now glad to understand their role, however small or large, in the grand scheme. Everyone felt better when, at last, they finally understood, like watching the magician and knowing how he did it.

"What if things turn to custard, John?" asked Razor.

John Russell was confident that nobody knew what they had. Keep a low profile. No glory. "I think so you chaps don't have to. Tom Halliwell, the CID, the Robbery Squad, the Intelligence Squad, the Railway Police, and the GPO won't figure this one out. They'll be talking about this one for years. But remember, we're not playing with mugs. We're talking about road blocks, car searches, house raids and shakedowns. They'll suspect who did it, but without the gold they can't prove anything. Let's make sure we're alibied up. Don't go around flashing money once it begins coming in. Stop doing weed. Now, it's my good maiden's birthday, so I have to go."

Now they all knew the prize, but not one of them even considered the price. Arthur Treadway, an actor by trade, began a speech in his best Olivier voice, "This story shall the good man teach his son, and Crispin Crispian shall never go by, from this day to the ending of the world, but we shall be remembered, we happy few, we band of brothers…"

But the gang were chatting, moving chairs, lighting smokes, shaking hands (including Billy's for the first time) and getting ready to head out into their own worlds and digest the information they had heard. Billy remained until only John Russell and Daniel Geddes remained. "You didn't mention George Smith, John," said Daniel.

Russell grimaced. Then, "You all right, Billy? They like you now."

Billy smiled and thanked them, then timorously added, "Can you do me a favor?"

"Sure," smiled Russell.

"My gel's downstairs yapping to Maria. She wants to meet the both a' ya.

THE AIRPLANE 9

Gold is money. Everything else is credit.

- J. P. Morgan

March 02, 1963 - London

UNCOMFORTABLY, SALLY KISSED BILLY goodbye at the front door, reluctant to let him go. He leaned close to her ear and whispered conspiratorially, that he would return soon and take the next steps to beginning together a bright and loving future. They had spent the previous five weeks discussing whether he should go. It had rarely been acrimonious; they were just too in love. Finally, Sally assented to his mandate to provide, and they parted tearfully. They had compelled the premise to her during the earliest days of childhood. Men worked, while woman cared for the house, with her primary role being the provider of a hot dinner when he returned. Since they were young and fertile, sex remained a distracting indulgence, and continued the expression of their relationship requiring no custom or guidance, just a barber visit to buy condoms, "the pill" not being available to unmarried women. Sally was much in love with her

Billy and she succumbed to his aspirations to work with known serious villains out of that emotion. "How afraid do I have to be, Billy?"

When the door finally closed on the second hefty thrust, she fell to her haunches against the dingy wall, her back pressed against its coldness, her hands shivering. She felt abandoned, her reason slipping away. Abandoned not by Billy, but to some new world he had entered. Her heart ached with missing his warmth radiating against her. Her head gently rested in the palms of her hands and she broke down in tears, irrevocably trying to grasp the metaphorical cliff they were leaping off together. She dreaded this new adventure they had drawn her man into.

However, if he wanted to give her a new life of sunshine on the other side of the world, then she would suffer with him, as long as she could keep her Billy. And for Billy, he promised himself that there would be no more beginning each day at the bottom of the hill.

It all seemed so ephemeral, illegal and perilous. It *was* illegal. Billy, in his woolen hat and donkey jacket, carrying his seaman's bag, crunched through the ice to the end of Grant Road. It wasn't a conscious display for the neighbors, but if anyone saw him, there he was, walking, then perhaps taking a bus down to the London docks. He was a man any bystander might not notice. But on this occasion, when he turned the corner onto Plough Road, there, under the railway overpass, was a black and maroon Rover P4, its engine ticking over, plumes of smoke escaping the exhaust in the cold air, with John Russell inside. With few words, they drove west together to a hamlet once known for a row of houses near a heath. They had built an airstrip there which became the Great West Aerodrome and, in 1944, they renamed it London Airport. Russell knew better than to talk, understanding the young man had his own thoughts. The plan he had been working on for years still contained a few brittle links, barely clutching it all together. This surely was one of the weakest; a youthful man departing the love of his life, being required to undertake some challenging work. But Russell had put all his trust in Billy, and no one seemed to know why. What if he now lost his nerve, lost his belief, just wanted—naturally—to lie in the arms of his lover? He must have been considering the repercussions of an extended stay in prison again if it all backfired. Surely it would be a longer sentence, whatever happened. Eventually, Russell felt he had to initiate a conversation, shake Billy from the quiet malaise of a seafarer leaving the sanctuary of his home.

"Here's your ticket," aware of the inner turmoil in Billy's head. He took it without examination. "We were feeling flush. At least you'll have a nice ride before the work begins." Billy peeked at the details. £227, first-class, one way to Johannesburg, and he chuckled and shook his head. How could someone pay such a foolish price for an airline ticket? How many months would he have to work at sea to make that? But did Billy understand the full price that the ticket might cost him? Then Russell handed over a brown envelope, "Five thousand pounds. You know what to do with it." Billy nodded.

The Rover droned over Chiswick on the new flyover, then back onto the Great West Road to Hounslow. Billy finally remarked, with a tone that Russell understood to be serious and perhaps slightly hostile, "Whatever 'appens, promise me you'll take care of my Sally, Mr. Russell? I don't wanna do summit if anyfink 'appens to 'er."

John Russell drove on, eyes ahead, churning inside at the implied threat while his knuckles turned white on the wheel. *Was he threatening me?* For a moment he had that animal instinct of wanting to cause violent harm. Maintaining his silence a moment longer, he rationalized the situation, and just how much had been invested—money and time—and how far out they were hanging without a safety line. Billy was the safety line. No, Billy was the *front* line. "That I guarantee. But just remember, in a few short months you'll be together on an Australian beach planning a new family," he replied, trying to lighten the atmosphere.

This young man had him—right now—like no one else ever had. John Russell didn't take threats lightly, and make no doubt about it, this was a threat. It needed the right response, but it could not be the usual one. He remained silent, driving west. An hour later, the Rover pulled casually into a vacant curbside space at London Airport as it rained gently, the street lights gleaming below the sad, overcast skies. Billy pulled his soft bag from the boot of the car outside the newly opened, glass-fronted Oceanic Terminal, recently built for long-haul flights. He hesitated, drew a deep breath and said, "You really need me for this, don't ya, Mr. Russell?"

"Yes, we do. But we're a firm, Billy, we all take care of each other. This is our one big chance. Do your best," as they shook hands. Before Billy turned away, he finally felt part of the team, the firm, the big league.

Then, smiling at the man beside him, he added ambiguously, "I ain't afraid of wot I'm capable of, Mr. Russell." The words hung in the wet air, echoing some fresh and vital fault line. He was going, and he would do as instructed, John Russell reasoned. But what he didn't know was just how close Billy had come in the last few weeks from walking away. The weather had finally warmed on some days. London believed the cold was nearly over, as Billy walked to the terminal through a one-way door.

Stepping inside the substantial, modern, two-level terminal atrium, he hesitated and took a few moments to observe another world; modern, antiseptic and dynamic, with several people roaming at random, confused by the onset of jet passenger travel. Billy stood and breathed in deep, admiring the natural light of steel and wide, glass sides of the space. All these people and he felt alone.

The luxury express trains and ocean liners inspired the designers, and it showed. As airplanes developed, the concept of traveling by air became something of potentially broader appeal, and the airlines acted to brand their new industry as more comfortable and more genteel, with one unique wonder of travel: speed. In 1963 it remained an adventure only a few could afford. Billy gazed around at the bland, futuristic interpretations of space and flight below the grim, visible outside skies, but his eyes focused on the slow chaos of movement before him. It smelled clean here, but he thought it lacked any warmth or comfort. He removed his heavy jacket and woolen hat and stuffed them into his soft bag.

He inspected an ultramodern scene with which he could hardly associate. The bright lights, the cleanliness, the signs from all over the world; KLM, Air France, Pan American, Lufthansa and Qantas. Billy thought himself "worldly" because he had traveled, but his wandering had been in another earthly domain. What he saw before him was sanitized and artificial, and he supposed the people were too. Then, smiling, building his confidence, he thought to himself, *not one of all these people could guess wot I will do.* And he was correct.

Billy sought around, then stumbled upon the BOAC check-in desk. After watching an older lady in a red pillbox hat and matching three-quarter length coat do the same, he hesitantly handed over his ticket. Inexperienced as he was, it seemed the appropriate action to take. The young lady, standing before a long map of the world in her uniform and military-like hat, beamed wide and disregarded his offered identification. She glanced at the ticket and smilingly directed him to passport control and departures. In 1963 there was, effectively, scarcely any documentation required to board an airplane, only the obligation to clear passport control. There, Billy, looking dapper for once in a cheap suit and tie, handed over his Seaman's Discharge Book and Identity Card, which the official readily accepted without question.

Clearing passport control, it surprised him to come across shops! Why would people shop at the airport? Billy couldn't wrap his head around the concept. Food, maybe. He understood people might buy food to eat, or a newspaper to read, but perfumes, crockery, clothing and a new watch? Leaving the shoppers behind, Billy found a quiet seat looking out over the apron and took time to contemplate. So much had happened. He had spent much time in Woolwich; he had new friends of the serious criminal fraternity, and he had spent many pleasing hours with Sally. He'd taken her to Martin Ford's, and Freeman, Hardy and Willis for shoes, and Walter's in Falcon Road and Marks and Spencer's to renovate her wardrobe, but as always Sally felt better being frugal. She balked at his largess and hoped this adventure wouldn't change her man. They'd rode the No. 19 bus to Piccadilly Circus and walked up Shaftsbury Avenue, then back down through Seven Dials, St. Martin's Lane and Leicester Square eating wherever they wanted. She was shocked when he pulled her into a black cab and they rode back to Battersea like royalty. She wouldn't allow him to drive into Grant Road, so they jumped out at Arding & Hobbs and walked home under the roaring, clattering Clapham Junction.

Sporadically, he touched his jacket to confirm the brown envelope remained safely in his pocket. Inside were over five times the annual wage of many people in Battersea. But what had that pretentious toff Wriggle-something said? 160,000 quid? For Billy, these numbers were as fantastical as this room was whimsical, this temple of spaciousness to the future. But he was done with considering the larger picture. They had decided and all would turn out well. A few weeks of work, then he could prepare Sally for Australia.

A while later, he heard his flight number—115—being called from somehow in the ether. He stood and followed an eager throng of attractive people, better dressed than himself, down a long, zig-zagging, sloping corridor, then out across the now wet, wide-open apron, to the waiting transport of the future, sitting poised, sleek and swift. The de Havilland Comet, so innovative compared to the propeller-driven airliners of the day, gave the impression of one mission only: swiftness. It conjured up every depiction of the future Billy had dreamed of, and others he might not have imagined.

He lacked the self-assurance of the other passengers striding forward as if boarding a red, double-decker bus. Before the airliner steps, some gathered for a photograph, while a man with a clipboard checked off each passenger's name. Billy thought it better not to indulge and climbed the steps alone, like the others, after the baggage and mail had been stowed. He felt like a movie star, because it required their salary to fly. And if this was the society he had—if only hesitantly—joined, then he had to free Sally from the emotional and economic shackles of her origin.

They had painted the revolutionary transport white over shiny, bare aluminum, and added a thick, dark-blue line running front to back, highlighting the windows and BOAC script above. Billy found himself caught between the dread of flying and the desire to experience a unique sensation. His youthfulness enticed him onwards, and the confidence of other passengers momentarily eased his fears as it drew him into a fantasy world which he could never have envisaged before. In 1963, pressurized airplane cabins remained relatively new to the industry. And a nonstop flight? Well, no—reaching South Africa would require multiple stops while flying at over eight miles per minute in between.

When the de Havilland Comet took to the sky in 1949, it changed aviation forever. Passenger airplanes of the time were low flying and uncomfortable, with unpressurized cabins and propellers powered by deafening piston engines which shook with noise and the paradox of exploding up and down in an effort to go round and round. They had to fly through, rather than above, the weather, and suffered the turbulence accordingly. It was undoubtedly flawed, but its far-reaching design, while flying higher, faster, smoother than any other airliner, rendering everything else obsolete. These airplanes were the elite of BOAC, with their own special call-sign: "Jet Speedbird." At speeds of up to five hundred miles per hour, passengers experienced the ride of their life, flying high above the weather. Air travel existed in its last days of being an affair for the rich only. Before the Comet, ocean liners were the primary mode of traveling interminable distances. With few other passenger jets in service, everyone envied the Comet, an airplane for the British Empire, just as the empire collapsed. The Comet exemplified British modernity, which remained an illusion. By this time, they had fixed all the early troubles that had plagued the airplane, but the Boeing 707 had arrived and they lost another suddenly vulnerable industry to international competition.

The airplane had a range of 2,500 miles, making it ideal for medium-haul trips. The all-aluminum, low-wing, cantilever monoplane derived its energy from four Rolls-Royce Avon turbojet engines buried in the wings. It had a four-man cockpit occupied by two pilots, a flight engineer, and a navigator. The clean, low-drag outline featured some uncommon design elements, like the swept-wing containing the fuel tanks, and four-wheel undercarriage units. Facilities included a galley serving hot meals, a bar, and separate toilets for men and women. The airplane had life rafts and individual life vests stowed under every seat.

Perhaps the most striking feature of the Comet experience was the relatively quiet, vibration-free flying, as widely promoted by BOAC. It mimicked a vision from the future, with a mirrored aluminum fuselage to afford passengers unprecedented views of the Earth from a cruising altitude of up to forty-thousand feet. This flight was scheduled with five stops to Johannesburg enduring twenty-one and a half hours.

He sat comfortably, but awkwardly, on the plush, wide, green fabric seat, unfamiliar with how he should act in this habitat and society. He toyed with the window curtains, then gently stretched out his legs in the first-class seat accompanied with complimentary deluxe cushions and blankets, the texture of which he had never experienced. Departure time arrived, although he was unaware without the advice from the cockpit. For some unknown reason, his mind drifted as the airplane taxied. He thought of Sally alone, the coal man coming tomorrow. At least she had Daniel's money to spend now. She would sweep clean the coal hole out front and heave the heavy bucket up from the cellar. There would be dust everywhere. He had left five gallons for the paraffin heater. He thought of her wonderful, but small body having to work so hard every day and he knew—one hundred percent—

that he would give her a better future. His mind wandered free of relevant thought, *Bom, Bom, Bom, Bom, Esso Blue.*

He had been daydreaming, the background white noise of the electrics, hydraulics and air-conditioning concealing the surrounding environment. He considered the taxiing an interesting sensation, viewing the terminal and other airplanes—machines of science fiction as far as he was concerned—jostling about the airport. Then the machine halted, and the reality came to Billy. He didn't like it, but he was not utterly terrified, just disconcerted. A brand-new phobia was joining the cultural psyche: the fear of flying, and Billy now suffered it too. Sitting there, ironically in such comfort, he was about to cede control of his life to some unknown force, a magnet of vulnerability; the fear of death.

He heard and felt the sensation of the powerful adjacent engines spooling up, roaring, and his chariot leaped forward. Unconsciously, he gripped the seat arms, closed his eyes and thought of Sally, with the sensation of falling back as the airplane rotated into the air. He was flying at last, and he didn't like it; the hanging in the air, and the phenomenon of enormous speed as the Comet roared higher. No turning back now.

"Are you all right, young man?" Billy remained quiet, his eyes closed, but nodded gently, as the stout man waved to the nearby stewardess, "Two Scotches, Sweety." He now became aware of his companion in the next seat. He manifested the aura of the successful businessman; every airlines' ideal traveler. Almost everybody wore their finest clothes to fly. They were the privileged few, so they dressed as if attending the theater. The men wore suits and somber ties, while the female passengers wore dresses, high heels, hats and pearls. It was glamorous and stylish. To fly meant you had arrived, you were part of the jet set. The girdled female stewardesses were part of the production; plastic smiles, perfectly dressed and charming. They were leggy, chatty, and wore their hair short enough so as not to touch the collar, while maintaining "high moral standards."

On the first flight segment to Rome, the stewardess served dinner. Billy saw the trolley approaching, and sensed the ensembled anticipation. His neighbor asked if he were hungry, wringing his hands, making sure everyone knew he was. Billy leaned closer and asked how much it cost. The stout businessman smiled, "No, young man, it's free, included in the ticket price."

Billy partook, while his companion wallowed in the meal, perplexed initially by the portable table laid out before him, as the pretty hostess—selected for her looks—leaned over to serve soup, roast beef, salad, vegetables and dessert, all on china, while the wine came served in fine glassware. The portly man complained at the lack of lobster, but Billy had never eaten lobster and wasn't about to. There were pictures on the walls, vases of fresh flowers, white tablecloths; they had spared no expense in decorating the cabin. The fresh-smelling airplane when he first boarded now swirled though, with clouds of cigarette, pipe and cigar smoke. But there were upsides too—like the ever-flowing drinks and an almost party spirit of camaraderie as passengers socialized in the cocktail bar with their fellow jet setters. Billy remained prudently reserved, and the whiskey bettered his fears.

And, once he's stared out the window, there was barely anything to occupy his mind. He soon forgot the adventure of flying in its monotony. Billy read a few magazines without the impression of movement or vibration until the alcohol subdued him and he fell asleep.

Flying was so utterly rare that other passengers felt compelled to document every moment on postcards with pictures of the plane or an in-flight meal, to show their less fortunate loved ones what the newfangled experience beheld.

The same hostess drifted silently about the cabin, asking if anyone wanted yet another drink. She reclined the seat for the dozing Billy, and the flight droned on and on. He lay half-awake dreaming of Sally in her well-worn routine of the day. She would clean the elegant houses of Chelsea, then return home, trying to warm her house. She might pour some scorching water from the Ascot heater and splash around in the tin bath, ready to dress for an evening with her friends; Joany, Mags and Kitty. She'd walk through Clapham Junction station, meet up with the girls, then stroll and chat incessantly up St. John's Hill, the four of them arm in arm, ready to take on the world together, to their favorite, curved brick building, the Granada Cinema. *What were they showing?* She had cash, now. He knew she would treat her friends to coffee and a knickerbocker glory at De Marcos, or pop into the Continental Café by Merrick Road. Then they might walk collectively, each talking without apparently listening, laughing and forgetting the dreary days, to the Windsor Castle pub up Lavender Hill.

The large man had tasted most of the drinks menu, as the first leg of the journey passed in a blur of luxury and alcohol. Billy used the men's toilet and became baffled at the ability to pour abundant streams of hot and cold water while this seemed so difficult in Battersea. Then he was landing in Rome.

After Rome they stopped in Khartoum, then Nairobi and Salisbury, drinking, eating and sleeping in between, as time zoomed by, without knowing their whereabouts. He sat, separated from another life below, in an effortless existence where everything became a whim of desire focused only on him. He saw some splendid sights over Africa; it seemed so vast, and devoid of cities. The sensation of taking off and landing had dimmed slightly, and his initial fears only jolted back into his consciousness in the giddy lurches of turbulence. In between, he soon learned the nonchalant, relaxing demeanor of the seasoned traveler. After Salisbury, the stewardess, who he had now learned to call Beverly, came and sat in the empty seat beside him, crossing her long legs and leaning in, clandestinely. Beverly liked to play her own game of pigeonholing each passenger in their own story. Over the years she had become proficient in her soothing pastime. She had watched him and could not discern his age. Without seeing his face, he might be anything from late teens to early thirties, but that remarkable, grinning expression revealing a somehow mischievous narrative she could not concoct a story for.

"Hello, Mr. Tumbler. Are you enjoying the flight?" Billy smiled and nodded, recognizing she's definitely from north of the river. She contemplated, before adding, "I have been a stewardess for nearly ten years. I have seen many passengers, but never one like you." He reflected her gaze and inside, grew concerned. "I've seen businessmen, diplomats, politicians, young, ill-mannered children of the wealthy and the pioneers of Africa, all flying south. But I've seen no one like you, Mr. Tumbler. Something tells me you don't quite belong here, but here you are. With a first-class ticket." She appraised his eyes while Billy feigned ambivalence. "You're like the young man who nobody sees coming, aren't you?" Again, Billy returned her gaze and tried to smile, breathing in her day-old perfume, but in his head remained a journal she couldn't read. She sat for a few moments, her eyes revealing the curiosity she laid before him. Then she said, "Whatever you are doing, Mr. Tumbler, I wish you the very best of luck." And she stood and slipped away.

Finally, nearly a day after departing London, they touched down in Johannesburg, South Africa. Apart from being tired, Billy felt he had not traveled at all, as if the airline had cheated him. Beverly gave him a conspiratorial finger-to-the-lips silence sign. He gave her the wide, Billy Tumbler smile and disembarked, feeling confused and slightly disorientated by the mild weather. Fortunately, geography separated London and Johannesburg by only two time zones, so he experienced minimal jet lag. He followed the crowd and passed immigration without mishap; "I'm joining the *Pendennis Castle*," and the officer viewed his documents and waved him through. Officials the world over appraised British seafarers of the time as ambassadors of liberty and trade, and they rarely encountered hindrance, especially if the local agent had advised them prior arrival.

Baggage claim was a confusing, apparent disorder he neither expected nor understood. Black porters organized the luggage by hand and travelers identified and requested their bags from the pile one after the other. Each passenger gave the handler a generous tip, but Billy had no local money. As he stood around feeling alien and awkward, a large, loud white man bundled his way into the melee and thrust out his hand, "Hello, I'm Gerry Jansen. Looking for me?"

"Oh, yeah! I fink so. I'm Billy. Wot's goin' on 'ere? 'Ow do I get me bag?"

"I'll sort it out." And in a few minutes, he had the bag and laid out some plentiful tips. Upon returning, Billy questioned him: "I 'ave a question for ya, Gerry. Security an' all."

"Fire away, young man," replied Gerry, apparently watchword ready, as they strolled towards the exit.

Billy thought deep, hoping he would understand, "Oo's the number one barmaid at the Prince Albert?" Gerry guffawed at the question. It was a joke Geddes and Russell would concoct. Finally, he answered with a broad smile. "You mean the wonderful Swoozie Popkin? She's quite a lady. Did you know she has a gun under the counter in the public bar?"

"No. Wow!" but he felt better and liked Gerry almost immediately. "Why are there so many sooties 'ere?"

"John didn't tell me you were a comedian," but Billy missed the irony. "It's as much their country as mine. Maybe more." Billy nodded in acknowledgement. He meant no disrespect; it was the language of his time and place.

"C'mon, Billy, we've got a long road ahead of us." They named the airport Jan Smuts International, after the former South African Prime Minister of the same name. They walked outside where Gerry had a Mercedes 220 SE waiting with a driver.

"Oo's this Jan Smuts?" asked Billy.

"He was the Prime Minister a couple of times," revealed Gerry.

"Oh, 'e was a bloke?" thought Billy out loud, and Gerry liked his combination of naivety and absurdity. Or perhaps it was just innocence.

South Africa was undergoing another tumultuous year, with internal and international resistance campaigns against the country's apartheid legislation. The government had sentenced Nelson Mandela to five years imprisonment upon returning after illegally leaving the country. Gerry asked about Battersea, "a place where the roofs leaks when the sun shines;" John Russell, "still micromanaging everyone?"

Daniel Geddes, "still thumping people?" and Peter, "still reading the tea leaves?"

Billy dozed on the ten-hour drive. He couldn't imagine a country could be this unbounded. Then, one moment, he woke up. "Oh, Gerry, I 'ave summit for ya." He handed over the envelope containing five thousand pounds, then napped again. On and on it went until he felt he didn't care anymore. They arrived at Gerry's place on the outskirts of Durban around midnight.

The next morning Billy awoke from a comfortable slumber in the best bed he had ever laid in. He wanted a bed like this; soft, clean and fluffy, for Sally. Breakfast was fruit, tea, toast and eggs, which they ate on the verandah surrounded by monkey thorn, acacia and coconut trees. Billy could hardly contain himself, "Wow! The weather's fantastic. It's so sunny." He inhaled the fresh, lush, morning air and found it more invigorating than grubby South London. He knew Sally would consider it wonderful too.

He met Gerry's black lover, Amahle—"It's pronounced ah-*mah*-she and means 'the beautiful one',"—which Billy thought appropriate. He eyed her during breakfast and agreed she was strikingly attractive. Gerry lived in Hillcrest, an area about twelve miles to the northwest of the city. A good area, he called it, and advised Billy he should avoid some obvious places, like Verulam. But the dangerous areas were few. "Use your common sense. If there are no people around, don't hang about; they're probably absent for a reason. Just like Battersea. Are there blacks in Battersea yet?" he asked Billy.

"Oh, yeah, a few." He had little experience of the new colored peoples of London. There were some by the time he left school, and the street bookmaker's runner was black, but they had closed now. The immigrants came for what? The streets paved with gold? Or just to get away. They were drastically different, yet shockingly similar, because poverty's the same in Battersea, just wetter and colder, he reasoned.

Gerry invited Billy to the best restaurant in Durban; Saltori's, on the first floor of the Trust Buildings on Gardiner Street. He appreciated the offer, but was ambivalent about the food, and did not like the uncomfortable atmosphere. Who eats minestrone soup voluntarily? He'd never seen a rotisserie chicken before, but it went down well. Why didn't Gerry bring Amahle? In the bar afterwards, alcohol made Gerry noisier, cruder and more abrasive.

"So, you're the man with no shadow, eh?" he asked Billy.

"Apparently," responded Billy. "Is that wot Mr. Russell said?"

"You're certainly not the heavy type that Russell and Geddes usually employ." Billy recollected what had happened in prison, and understood the community he now moved within. The evening became a long, messy and satisfying distraction at the bar. Billy didn't know what a martini was, and it just reminded him of what he didn't have, but that had honestly not been Gerry's intent. And Billy didn't hold a grudge. He was getting to like Gerry more and more. And Amahle. They swam together in the pool during Gerry's working absence. Billy stared at her swim-suited body, admiring her perfect ebony shape, while her intelligent eyes contemplated him, seeking an answer while coyly withholding the truth. Billy's conscience plagued him, but he always found it easy to remain silent. Not unlike his father, he believed if there were no appropriate words, then better to keep quiet.

On the third day, in downtown Durban, Billy stood regarding the bench before him. It was a regular wooden seat, the sort you might see in Battersea Park. It was an object he had seen before and understood.

It rarely caused the mind to consider and form an opinion. But this bench was distinctive. Gerry returned with two cold bottles of Coke Cola.

"Wot's this all about, then?" Billy asked.

"Oh, the benches. You understand the political situation here, right Billy?" he asked.

"Er, sort of," but he didn't really.

So, Gerry explained it in greater detail. "I don't want to overstate things, Billy, but the world is completely bloody awful," ventured Gerry, and he thought this young man agreed.

Later that day they drove past a gathering of black men standing and sitting around. The wall behind them said "Away with Verwoerd." Billy saw a storefront that read "Servants and boys' meat, only 20 cents." Gerry voiced his opinion that the nation may face a revolution. He loved the country, he liked the people, and he enjoyed living with Amahle, but he recognized that to continue here would be impossible, not if one had principles. And he meant it, despite the irony of a thief discussing principles.

He took Billy to a shoddy area where he might witness the bottomless depths of poverty. He looked and saw the dearth of money sought by the scared and suffering humans, and wished somehow his own free spirit might give hope to the oppressed. "There are no pensions here." Billy pondered, and hated the world.

Gerry disliked the political structure, and willingly flouted it, but not so openly as to draw attention from the forces of law. Whatever government did, it had nothing to do with him. Wages in the city for the majority black community were higher than on white farms outside. Many found employment on the docks, mostly at The Point, the northern promontory enclosing the harbor. After the completion of the railway from Johannesburg to Durban, and the dredging of the harbor entrance, shipping had flourished. The Point remained the principal center for general cargo movements. The most important, labor-intensive and skilled sector in the harbor were those handling break-bulk, or general cargo. It needed to be loaded and unloaded piece by piece, bag by bag, crate by crate. Just like it did in Southampton.

The South African Railways and Harbors Administration used shore workers. While stevedores, working inside the ship's cargo holds, required more skills and earned higher wages, dock laborers were among the largest groups of workers in the city, and were pivotal to the smooth operation of the port. The vast majority of these workers were casual and Zulu. They loaded and unloaded all cargo from nets attached to cranes or winched by hand.

Gerry had made it his business to become intimately associated with the Zulus and their gang leaders, known as *inDuna*, or headman; both sides adjoined, swimming in a sea of corruption and criminality. The headmen were quintessentially ambiguous characters who the workers required for employment. A relationship of mutual dependence developed between the workers and their immediate supervisors, replete with patronage, favoritism, bribery and victimization. Gerry worked both sides and felt comfortable that he could have a significant influence over the loading of the *Aphrodite May*.

The next day, Gerry took Billy to the beach. "Wow! Nice beach. Not like Margate," which was true. He looked upon miles of soft, flat sand, Durban's Golden Mile, running the length of the city. The towering, rolling waves swept in from the warm waters of the Indian Ocean, and upon the waves, it amazed Billy to see surfers. The city had tall, modern buildings. The weather was subtropical, warm and radiant. With a population of just over half a million residents, it appeared to be an agreeable, compact city. Could he live here? The only problem—something he could never abide—was the prospect of servants and segregation, so he dismissed South Africa from his retirement checklist.

Late in the day, Gerry drove Billy to the bustling port, where he gained effortless entrance, since he seemed to know everyone, and as a ship's agent, possessed the appropriate passes. Even people he had never met seemed to know him, the ample, loud white man on the docks. He steered past the ships with open stomachs, cranes dipping in and out. They came across a warehouse with a ribbed roof, full of bales and boxes, all anonymous amongst the multitude of their like. He pulled the Mercedes slowly inside and paused. He observed the warehouse interior and, seeing negligible movement, asked Billy to—unobtrusively—glance to his right. Billy turned and smiled. There was the Engine again, like an old, long-lost friend, which he had spent so much time inside and out in dreary Woolwich.

"It's been here a week now. The *Aphrodite May* arrives tomorrow. Time to buy some fresh fruit and vegetables?" suggested Gerry.

"Yeah. And toothpaste!" replied Billy.

"What do you think, Billy?" asked Gerry.

Billy turned his face back to the driver and smiled. "Time to go to work," before self-conscientiousness became a dizzying paralysis. Gerry snicked the lever back into drive, and they pulled out of the warehouse with an irrational feeling of hope.

* * * *

At the precise moment that Gerry and Billy sat in the Mercedes glancing surreptitiously at the Engine, the car's air-conditioning running to keep them comfortable in the heat, 5,900 miles away on a wet, cold morning in London, Detective Inspector Tom Halliwell sat at his desk in New Scotland Yard.

"Tom?" said another detective, sidling up to his desk.

"Hello Bill," he responded, wearily.

"Are you still working on a potential link between John Russell and George Smith?" Brian asked.

"I certainly am," replied Halliwell, opening his eyes wider. "Have you heard anything?" he asked with a hint of anticipation.

"Well, I might have something for you." Bill kept his voice low. "I have a grass in Tooting Bec who says that Brian Spicer has been out and about looking for a smelter." Halliwell's eyes widened slightly as he drew in his breath.

There was silence for perhaps ten seconds. "And?" asked Halliwell.

"That's it," responded Bill. It really wasn't much on its own, but it fit unerringly into place, like a missing jigsaw piece. So, it is a gold bullion job, he thought.

"Let's go and chat with the chief," suggested Halliwell.

They waited less than ten minutes to see Detective Chief Inspector Walker. His office wasn't as large as many thought it might be. It was also fairly sparse, but in front of his desk—which carried two telephones and some paper trays—were two uncomfortable chairs. He didn't expect visitors to settle and relax.

"Make this quick, detectives. I have a meeting to attend," he barked.

"Four pieces of information, Sir; George Smith overseen meeting John Russell by C11. That's solid. Something that would not happen casually. Second, Russell and Geddes are not spending any money from the Dagenham wages job. Third, Geddes has been spotted twice in Southampton." Halliwell had laid out the bare facts.

Bill completed the fourth part, "Smith is looking for a smelter!"

The two detectives sat, silently watching the chief digest the information, slowly stretching his neck, before coming to the obvious conclusion, "Bullion?"

Tom Halliwell smiled and slowly nodded. A secretary gently knocked on the door, opened it enough to squeeze her head inside and said, "Chief Inspector? You asked me to remind…"

"Tell them I'll be a few minutes late." Then turning to the men sat before him, "Bill, we need more information from Fulham. Get your squad onto that. Tom, we need more information from Battersea. Your men, right? I'll talk to the Transport Police…"

"May I suggest, Sir?" Halliwell asked, and the chief nodded, "Maybe we'd better take a closer look at those Union-Castle ships and the trains bringing gold for the Bank of England."

"Yes, do that. We'll have a full meeting tomorrow morning, while I try to get my head around this," the chief responded.

And right there and then, unknowingly, the police had committed their first and most serious error.

THE TRAIN

Like liberty, gold never stays were it is undervalued.

- John S. Morrill

March 27, 1963 - Southampton

IT HAD BEEN ONE OF THOSE DAYS unable to decide if it was late winter or early spring. It had been a protracted and severe season, devoid of a frost-free night from Christmas to early March. Low temperatures kept the snow lying around in some areas, refusing to wane. Sidney Wellmeadow considered himself a regular man and had no time for anyone who wasn't. His craggy, pockmarked face, partially hidden with scraggly mutton chops that clung to his face like ravaged ivy tendrils, grimaced at the cold. "Summer Comes Soonest in the South," the advert proclaimed. *Yeah, right*, he thought. *I live in the south and it's bloody freezing!*

He smoked heavily, as was usual with seventy percent of men, and kept repeating he couldn't afford it and would refrain, but never did. Sidney's hobbies included pigeon fancying, dog betting, darts, watching football, getting drunk in the pub, unsuccessfully flirting with barmaids and yelling at their slow service. He no longer had to fight with his bickering wife, now living in Peckham he heard, but most annoyingly, he had to provide maintenance to her and the two girls. Memories of the heady days when the marriage began were growing fainter recently.

He admitted he could be lethargic occasionally, but others knew him as a freeloading, belligerent, and confrontational man, especially in the last two weeks when news had broken of Dr. Richard Beeching, the Chairman of his employer, issuing a report calling for extensive cuts to the rail network, expecting the closure of over two thousand stations and losing sixty-eight thousand jobs. Sidney considered this *bloody unacceptable* and voiced that opinion at work. Although he had many ideas himself—and they hardly ever materialized—he knew when something wasn't right. Men of Sidney's occupation were often robust characters with a good deal of individuality; indeed, a lack of personality would have been considered eccentric, so he continued voicing his views. Everything was changing too quickly, and he didn't like it. Does anyone ever think about my problems? *The rulers of the country in their pin-striped suits, bowler hats and umbrellas could go and...*

It was a time when men wore hats or flat caps identifying their trade and class, while women wore headscarves. Sidney donned his customary navy-blue bib and braces, smock and grease top cap with a green and gold "British Railways" badge above the peak. He closed the front door of the rooms he rented on grim and seedy Thessaly Square, turned, and carrying his black, driver's bag, walked towards the vast, sprawling—and still bomb damaged—complex of the Nine Elms Locomotive Shed, just behind the house. Sidney earned twenty-one pounds, two-and-ninepence every week, which was a regular wage, but better than some. He thought of himself below the middle class, but not quite in the lowest class, one of perhaps twelve rungs between the top and bottom of that irritating British system beginning to show the first signs of crumbling. *Good riddance*, thought Sidney, as he walked towards the shed to board a train going south this morning.

The borough of Battersea, in which Nine Elms formed the northeast part alongside the river, comprised a large tide of dreary working-class people continually on the edge of wrongdoing, finding its highwater mark to the southwest around Lavender Hill, probably. Battersea's history told a gritty tale of the labor movement, the economics of greed, the seduction of capitalism, strikes, starvation and bloody toil. Sidney had done it all and accepted it was now too late to escape, but the odd morsel of successful wagering on his day off compensated. Nearly everyone knew someone engaged in a nefarious enterprise, or had been offered an introduction themselves. Small stuff, like selling suspiciously obtained domestic appliances on the black market, illegal gambling, off-sales drinking or passing on information to those who shouldn't know. Even people with steady work turned to crime to make ends meet or pay for luxuries, but the majority never had contact with organized crime. That was unusual. Since the War, beating the system was endemic and an accepted way of life, and Sidney's guidelines of right and wrong had long been blurred, the past and present filling him with cynicism.

Three days before, a most unexpected opportunity had fallen in his lap, and it lingered in the mind. He had been supping his customary pint of Youngs Ordinary in the Nag's Head public house on the Wandsworth Road, leering at the buxom barmaid, June, when a man innocently engaged him in conversation. Or so he initially believed. He had the habit of always wearing his cap, even when not working, so it readily identified him as a railway employee. The man was agreeable enough. Tall and muscular, but the intent behind the discussion developed and grew clearer to Sidney. His dress style was not quite new, not quite stylish, as if he carried something heavy hidden within. Sidney had that feeling you get when you observe a man and you know he can hurt you, and he thought, *there's always a big man telling a little man what to do.*

The exchange remained cordial as he feigned attention and willingness. The man bought him another beer, but he couldn't be sure of his cordiality. With the courage of alcohol, he cheered up and agreed to his offer of two hundred pounds for some innocuous information. Not his proudest day, admittedly, *but what harm could it do?* thought Sidney.

* * * *

The same morning that Sidney walked towards the Nine Elms Shed, in a world seemingly far from British Railways, a general cargo liner had entered the port of Southampton. The Union-Castle Line enjoyed an established reputation for sailing well-found ships into the port on a weekly basis, running goods, passengers and mail from South African ports. This celebrated British shipping company held together their homeland and South Africa with the "Cape Mail Express" service, leaving Southampton every Thursday afternoon. Their ocean liners called at Las Palmas or Madeira, followed by a lengthy, nonstop voyage to Cape Town, continuing to Port Elizabeth, East London and a turnaround at Durban. They were one of the shipping lines that held the empire, then the commonwealth, together, while helping Southampton grow comfortably large and prosperous over the years. The Harbor Master, acquainted with the planned appearance of their ships, typically directed them into 35 or 36 Berths where the River Test met the River Itchen, the most southern quays of the port, remote and secure out on a man-made peninsula. Along with a substantial quantity of corn, fruits, non-exotic metals and minerals, sugar and wool, some Union-Castle ships carried aboard a small, but heavy cargo of gold bullion, protected in the ship's specie room, heading for the Bank of England and the world-dominating London gold market.

Everyone concerned knew the name of the ship, it's assigned berth and its projected time of arrival. The dockers, the agent and chandlers, the ship's personnel, were all conversant with the comfortable procedure at Southampton. A ship arrived early on a Monday morning and the cargo moved from the docks to London Waterloo railway station on a dedicated bullion component of a scheduled train. The agenda ran well, and on time. Yet, what those who should have known better misunderstood, is that punctuality and regularity are concepts that often intrigue the dishonest mind.

This unobtrusive trade garnered a good number of interested groups, including the criminal fraternity of South London. They were conscious of the operation; individuals with a myopic, dedicated desire to accumulate wealth, making the argument that the law should get out of the hard-working man's way. On the Southern Region of British Railways, much thievery had already occurred, but it was usually of the grabbing-the-occasional-mailbag type. The gold was, surely, discussed in a sentimental form in pubs, snooker clubs and even fine restaurants from Wandsworth to Dartford. The Union-Castle Line bullion shipments lay, literally, like a glowing pot of gold unobtainable by those who believed they had some right—no, obligation—to take it. No matter how many gangs sat around drinking and planning the "big one," no one could conceive of a workable manner in which to obtain the prize, frustrating an undercurrent of illegal urgency while maintaining the meaning of their lives. There were several reasons the big one had never happened. First, the prize was moving; never a reassuring scenario for the larcenous fraternity. That's why they robbed banks; they weren't moving. Second, they knew police accompanied the bullion; anecdotally, armed. They couldn't be sure, but engaging in that business meant tooling up like cowboys—and twelve years banged up if it went awry. But third, and most importantly, gold is heavy! That left the felonious conundrum—how to move the gold quickly before overwhelming law enforcement arrived? Years before, "Tiddly" Winks, lying in his cell in Wandsworth Prison with nothing else to do, had figured that out. Perhaps he could never imagine that someone might actually implement his audacious idea.

* * * *

The motor vessel arriving that morning, on March 27—the *Aphrodite May*—was not a Union-Castle ship, and her arrival, although not unexplained, might be considered an irregular event. In 1963, the British Transport Docks Board assumed control of the port, and was glad to accommodate her business, booking her into 26 and 27 Berths of the old Empress Dock, much closer to the port entrances and the public roads of Southampton. The vessel's master, one Captain Joseph Minghella, had mailed copies of the cargo stowage plan to agents at Southampton, permitting the booking and reservation of dockers and equipment, as appropriate. Relevant details of cargo quantity, description of packages, pallets, etc., tonnage, identification marks and special features were included. Two days prior to arrival he had sent his instructions for discharge by wireless telegraphy. Naturally, the port authorities, agent, receivers and dockers had their input, suggestions and requirements, but, ultimately, the captain had the final say. Claiming the protection of the bullion as paramount, he advised everyone that on arrival, the vessel's hold No. 3 tweendeck (where they had stowed the gold in a deep tank) should be cleared of the three small cargoes it contained. Concurrently, they should inspect the deep tank as remaining closed from the load port. Specifically, he was intent on establishing both the inspection seals of the hold entrance doors (one forward and one aft at each hold), and of the security of the deep tank itself. Once his safekeeping responsibilities were established for any interested parties, then commencement, under strict supervision, of the protracted labor to remove the large plate cover of the deep tank could ensue. Meanwhile, they could deliver cargoes from other holds during daylight hours while work on No. 3 should be suspended. At the completion of daylight, discharge would then concentrate on the deep tank in hold No. 3 only, while under stringent security precautions.

The captain adjusted the vessel's arrival to 5:00 a.m. at the pilot station, allowing for an appearance at the berths of about 8:00 a.m. The forces of law, both the local Southampton constabulary and the British Transport Police had, as customary, undertook patrolling the docks and railways. Operations of these kinds were one of their core responsibilities. Those remaining after most of the dockers completed their shift at 5:00 p.m. on that first day, paid attention, watching a squat, USA-class steam shunting locomotive as it brought a sixty-four-foot-long, maroon-colored, windowless bullion van onto 26 Berth. The driver positioned the van adjacent to hold No. 3 of the *Aphrodite May* under one of the five dirty-gray Stothert & Pitt, thirty-five-ton electric cranes that ran on rails along the dock. The Southampton Police created a small cordon with portable barriers at the east and west limits adjacent to the vessel's bow and stern. A few officers carried visible side arms.

As darkness overcame the concrete and watery setting, and the trash-eating seagull squawking subsided, Southampton's docks remained busy like any other evening. Those alert at the Empress Dock could witness the familiar noisy hubbub; a shunter pulling a few open wagons, a Standard Class 5 hauling passenger stock somewhere, to westward lay the RMS *Queen Elizabeth* at the Ocean Terminal and beyond that, the massed ranks of cranes at the New Docks, water dripping from the steel skeletons in the humid air. A Light Pacific-class locomotive set off behind 26 Berth warehouses with luggage vans and a tender, visibly slipping. The air grew cold again.

The delivery of the bullion began as the evening set in. The procedure started by raising each pallet of wooden boxes from the deep tank in a wire net on the ship's derrick cable. These were the same nets provided at the load port. Supervised by the chief mate and the company port captain, hand-guided by a few selected dockers, they carefully directed each pallet through the plate cover opening into the tween deck. From there, they transferred the pallet hook to a dock crane, hoisted it from the hold and slowly deposited it adjacent to the waiting bullion van. The police assigned significantly singular attention as responsibility for each pallet crossed the ship's rail. There were the usual spectators too; the captain, the agent, and harbor master. In common law, when goods pass "across the rail," responsibility transfers to the receiver. The physical entity of the railing embodied in law, that fine line between one party and another. It was in everyone's interest for the operation to run smoothly and without incident. The area was well lit, and although events were occurring nearby, 26 Berth remained undisturbed with no other work undertaken. Each pallet held twelve or thirteen rope-handled wooden boxes collectively secured with steel BAND-IT fasteners. Dockers removed each box individually from the pallet and manhandled them inside the van. The weight of each required two men to carry, reducing the prospect of any single person absconding with a box. Two hours of earnest, but modest work later, they repositioned the boxes within the safety of the bullion van, and no one would steal a British Railways van, would they? They returned the wire nets onboard the *Aphrodite May*.

Once they verified the gold boxes secure aboard, the police decided the bullion van should remain on 26 Berth in the presence of officers until later in the evening. At 11:30 p.m. a "Ruston" diesel-driven shunter growled onto the north track of the Empress Dock. Its cyclopean, silver-eyed buffers bumped up to the bullion van, and coupled, while the entourage remained in vigilance. There was a general intermingling of men from the Harbor Master's Office as the Transport Police confirmed the security of the van and its contents again. The police rigged and tested a mobile radio base set, enclosed in a former military ammunition box, powered by a car battery. Two unarmed Transport Policemen would remain with the van until London, as the journey of the gold bullion began its next precious move. All involved had conducted the same procedure before and felt positive in its certitude. No one perceived the anomaly that had occurred before them.

The shunter ran up its engine, billowing dirty gray diesel fumes and the stench of modernity, to pull the bullion van slowly forward from in front of the warehouse on Brazil Road. Hauling the gold northwest along Central Road, passing the old Inner Dock to its right, the short, brawny locomotive exited the police-guarded port gates, crossed Canute Road while a mist licked around the streetlights. The locomotive powered slowly towards the adjacent Southampton Terminus Station, while a flagman and the local police held at bay the nonexistent traffic of the night. The Ruston clattered the bullion van across the ladder of slips and crossovers to stand on the Up Local line at Southampton Terminus. It then pushed it back south to noisily connect to a brake, three maroon mail vans with barred windows, and three passenger coaches waiting for the journey north to London.

* * * *

Sidney Wellmeadow had been a locomotive driver for a long time. He occupied a chapter of life where he could see retirement. He could also see the modern diesel locomotives coming, and he wanted no interaction with them. He had his pigeons and his gambling. He saw the fresh young men and the lazier older ones, pressing buttons and sitting in comfort. *All they had to do was bloody stay awake.* Sidney saw no happy involvement in the pending work coming with the rail revolution. The age of steam was nearing its conclusion, along with it the romance and a wealth of heritage being callously thrown away. At best subdued, at worst he felt a sense of foreboding.

Having arrived in Southampton earlier that day, he now strolled from the sweating pavement of Terminus Terrace across the short track sidings north of the terminus toward the Bullied-designed engine sitting alone, ready for another magic railway journey across the distances. She lay immobile but simmering alive, the tranquil breathing of the machine in repose. The "West Country" type locomotive, 34007 *Wadebridge* was a mechanical beast to be mastered by the driver, wrangling control of a hissing, smoking monster. Or, according to Dr. Beeching, an extravagant, resource consuming relic of a bygone age.

He'd driven the dark green machine before and was readily willing to handle her again this evening. He thought of *Wadebridge*, and her sisters, as powerful monsters unable to control themselves. But in the secure hands of Sidney Wellmeadow she became a domestic kitten, all happy and gratified. But, most importantly, he was about to head north, back to Waterloo, and then returning the engine to her, and his home, at the Nine Elms Shed behind his rooms in Battersea. He fingered the envelope in his pocket, smiled, and fantasized of the dog races tomorrow at White City.

On arrival, he climbed from the dark, stone ballast the five rungs into the dust-filled footplate light of the glowing cab, and felt that lower back twinge again. Pulling himself inside, the fireman, Oliver Wilson, habitually sucking on a black and white Everton Mint, coolly greeted him, while shoveling fuel to the firebox.

"Evening, Oily," as the fireman slammed the firebox door and stepped back. Sid knew he disliked the sobriquet.

Resting his shovel, Wilson responded, "Little late, aren't we? Where you was, Sid?"

None of your bloody business, he thought, "Oh, just seeing a man about some pigeons," meaning he didn't want to discuss the matter, and Wilson didn't pursue it. He had a pale face with thin red lips. His eyes had a way of peering out the corners, and Sidney was never sure if he could consider him a regular chap or not. How could he pass an eye test with eyes like that? Completing his mint, Oliver fished a Rizla from his pocket and rolled some tobacco.

"This Beeching thing will be the end of me, Sid," declared Oliver.

Well, at least I know someone with problems worse than mine, thought Sidney.

He agreed that he was likely to join the sixty-eight thousand, and the fireman suggested he needed an alternative source of economic return. *Silly bollocks*, thought Sidney. The two men, seasoned professionals, continued with routine procedures; "counting the parts," oiling around, refilling the lubricator, checking the bearings, and otherwise conducting an enormous amount of tinkering.

Another crew had driven the locomotive down from London earlier, and her fire remained alight. The blower was on just sufficient to keep the air moving. The fire door remained closed as they glanced intermittently toward the pressure gauge. The human and the mechanical worlds interacted more directly and dramatically on the footplate than just about any other industrial location. Sidney knew few strangers could subdue this fiery feline. He and Oily were a team that made steam with the minimum use of coal and were careful with the water. They were each accomplished in their profession.

They spent another hour shoveling coal, smoking and cleaning, as the steam pressure grew, conducting final preparations prior movement. The railway locomotive; forceful, strident, daunting, exciting; a focus of exhilaration and awe had redefined space and altered the concept of time since its introduction. Before their arrival the time kept by one place or person was often different to the next, but the railways had harmonized it for a universal timetable to function. "Train time" was the result. Sidney's instructions were for a 12:30 a.m. move back to Southampton Terminus, platform 6, to hook up—with his tender—a bullion van (with the two British Transport Police officers; unarmed). During the journey north it would be their role to provide location and situation updates to the Police Control Rooms along the route while protecting the cargo should there be an incident. Sidney would also connect to a Traveling Post Office (three maroon-colored vans with high, slit windows, interconnected with six sorters in the center van), three passenger coaches (interconnected), and a guard's van: collectively the barely known, financially noteworthy, 1:10 a.m. Southampton to Waterloo Up-Mail.

Right on schedule, a short, high-pitched whistle from Sidney and he slowly guided the ninety ton, sixty-seven-foot-long locomotive out of the siding onto the Up-Local. He brought the machine to a halt, then reversed to the waiting coaches, steam issuing and billowing, the familiar reek of oil, coal and fire filling his lungs, pistons slowly stroking, like a snorting bear waking from her hibernation. From his left-hand position in the cab, Sidney leaned over to monitor the boiler pressure, then back to satisfactorily establish the vacuum gauge of the exhauster. There had been a slight feeling of slip, typical of this design in the chilly night, but Sidney resolved that with a dose of sand. There was something thrilling about the size and power of *Wadebridge*, along with its use of the elemental forces of fire and water. To have control of such a machine, to have all its power and complexity obedient to your hand, Sidney felt, was a heroic endeavor. He never took this work less than seriously.

He liked the almost enclosed cabin of *Wadebridge*, sitting back, sliding open the window, and leaning out, then back in, balancing the regulator and reverser, he slowed and edged the sleek engine back toward the waiting mails and bullion van. The non-bullion elements of the Up-Mail had arrived at 12:44 a.m., after their trip east from Weymouth on a cool and dewy morning. The platform bustled with moderate activity; railway men, post office workers and police—more than Sidney thought appropriate. The guard walked forward and approached Sidney, who, seeing him coming, stepped down from the footplate. They shook hands, but had never met before. Although Sidney may have disagreed with the concept, the guard had ultimate responsibility for operation of the train. They had trained him in emergency protection duties. The guard explained to Sidney the train formation, the trailing weight, stopping patterns and confirmation they would conduct a brake test before and after departure. They exchanged names for the guard's journal.

Right on schedule, at 1:10 a.m., Sidney recognized, below the floating globes of incandescent yellow platform lights, his guard blow a whistle and swing a green light with the signal to depart. Melding the twin fogs of meteorology and morality, he provided a short, piercing whistle, then exercised his skill, allowing the steam to flow again. He allowed sufficient pressure for the rods to begin their familiar stroking back and forth. The train stirred slowly north, steam and smoke releasing in a soft, low cloud beneath the dark, leaden sky, the slow, caressing, hissing sound gathering momentum and rhythm. His feet and legs felt the scorch of the engine fire when Oliver shoveled in coal, but his shoulders felt the wild chill rush of air as *Wadebridge* lurched and shook and clattered—the engine, like some kind of tamed beast elicited no reaction from driver and fireman other than; business as usual.

Bang on time, thought Sidney proudly, then remembered briefly in a flash of perception, punctuality always benefits the criminal. He had realized earlier today, and again now, that the big man, the benefactor of his two-hundred-pound cash envelope, might, just might, be arranging an event tonight. Sidney had warned him they would make up the train of various components, but one of them was a Traveling

Post Office, and "the Royal Mail was greater than all of them", the unshakable Establishment.

Thick black smoke spewed up temporarily as she lugged her small consignment slowly forward, a sign the firebox wasn't burning efficiently, but they soon had it under control. Understandably, the sight, and no doubt the sound, would conjure up a vision of hell, the footplate being an alien, threatening environment like the time-machine from that H. G. Wells' novella. The observers, including the watchful eye of the signalman, saw and heard the wheels scraping on the lines, as Sidney moved north and plunged under Central Bridge. He listened to the locomotive compose its sounds, the rhythmic energy of trains, the engine's huffing resonance of smoke and exhaust gas being emitted through the stack, the hissing of the vacuum pump as he began working her up to fifteen miles per hour to conduct the break test. After that, he was alone with the white spirits which rage inside the belly of locomotives, a dynamic, self-adjusting system, never balanced and never restful.

Sidney loved the resonance of trains—proper steam trains—and could feel this potent engine warming up. Once on the run north the two men settled into their routine, monitoring pressures and watching for green lights as *Wadebridge* sauntered the brief run to Eastleigh. Leaving that station after a six-minute stop, they tested the brakes again and headed through villages and the spring countryside, increasing to "line speed" (the safe speed for the line), all other places inaudible while the locomotive's smoke and steam rose to blend with a sleeping low layer of dark, gray cloud.

The Train

But Sidney's mind wondered again as his actions slowly grew automatic. Why had that man needed to know the timing of his departure? Was that public bar conversation a sign of the menace to come? Why had he given him the arrival time and the approximate load lying in the bullion van? He understood why, naturally. But that was his business and the post office and whoever owned the gold. Sidney knew why; for two hundred pounds. Very nice, thank you.

Entering the countryside, *Wadebridge*, with its distinctive, air-smoothed body, made a compelling vision of three hundred tons hurtling through the night at sixty miles per hour, past "the thousands still asleep, dreaming of terrifying monsters." All the while Sidney looked intently forward to see the line of green lights leading into the distance. He shuddered to imagine what might happen at a red, but no one could make a green light red, right?

At these speeds the driver and fireman had no simple task, engaged in both precise and backbreaking work. The scene in the cab was elemental, tons of coal and thousands of gallons of water (and not a negligible quantity of lubricating oil) converted to energy, pulling the train from Southampton to London. The journey continued in its inconspicuous northeast direction, metrically stopping briefly at the predetermined stations. The next was Winchester. The platform was quiet; the mist thickened. Sidney leaned out and focused rearward, but could only hear some goings on with the mail. He crossed the cab, passed Oily and looked out the other side, back along the six-foot. Nothing. He wanted back, back to Nine Elms, to get this night over with. In the quietness he waited for his thoughts to catch up, then beheld Oliver inside, the open fire door highlighting his lined face appearing strangely inhuman, like a gargoyle. Sidney's anxiety felt pal-

208

pable. *Oh, my God! Maybe Oily's involved.* He could take over and drive. Stop the train and men with pickaxe handles and ammonia blinding gear would overwhelm them. What if he disabled Sid and stopped the train somewhere quiet? I mean, no one could stop *Wadebridge* at these speeds, but Oily could. *What about Safety detonators on the track?*

Then a green light and whistle from the guard, as Sidney moved the train forward again, towards Basingstoke, through a vast, yawning black infinity. Sidney, looking forward and out into the countryside, wanted only green lights now. And there was little else other than the pure, black greenery glowing ahead, pulling him on to London. They made Basingstoke without incident. At each station, Sidney gazed from the left window, assessing forward and back, awaiting some kind of encounter, perhaps, but it never came. Then Farnborough.

Between each station, the air carried a chorus of diverse, tonally rich sounds and complex rhythms—pounding pistons, hissing steam, syncopated clattering wheels on tracks and screeching whistles—the train transformed the outside world's sonic landscape. This immense hissing beast momentarily drowned out the sound of the night, projecting its expressive note to the population en route. Then, at Woking, Sidney felt certain he saw the man he drank with in the Nag's Head, standing in the shadows. Adrenaline streamed through him like a boxer before a fight. But nothing happened, and they were up to speed again. He began obsessing about something he couldn't see as they rushed forward faster than a racehorse can gallop, in bleak, foggy weather along embankments, and through shallow cuttings, where it was impossible to see the dark, foreboding night away from the reassuring glow of the fire. All the while the gold remained in the bullion van, effectively unprotected, Sidney supposed. The postal workers were in their own mindless, repetitive world sorting *"letters of thanks, letters from banks, letters of joy from girl and boy."*

The icy breeze passed Sidney's face, which made his skin grow cold, so he returned inside, slid the window closed and looked at Oily, all the while contemplating if or how something could happen. Then he was glancing forward to see the next green light, then to the right, but Oily was busy shoveling and sweeping. He didn't seem like he was about to overwhelm him, but they were now in the middle of nowhere.

Then they were near Surbiton, the next stop, not in, but not out of London. Sidney, aware and still keeping Oily in his eye, relaxed as he guided the train into the claustrophobic environs of suburbia, the houses crowding onto the track, the crossings and bridges growing more frequent and congested. The station had a moderately sized goods yard situated to the eastern side of the platforms. Two additional sidings were on the western "Up" side. Whatever Sidney believed might happen, it just would not happen in Surrey. All right, it wasn't London, but it was only ten or twelve miles from Charing Cross! An encounter now would be absurd! "The Smoke," the grand metropolis, reflected against the clouds with its luminous physical presence, as the train fell into the vortex of the exciting city and the brightly lit streets flashed by.

Out of Surbiton, throwing white steam over her shoulder, he drove *Wadebridge* the fifteen-minute run on the Up Main Through line as it elevated at Vauxhall, squeezing over Lambeth Road and Westminster Bridge Road, under the signal bridge into her destination for the morning, the gluttonous Waterloo Station at 3:45 a.m., its capacity devouring her smoky serpents. The terminus, the largest and busiest in England, a place for important arrivals and departures, like holiday makers escaping the mostly unacknowledged grimness that lay beneath the holiday cheer, or Epsom race goers, or the city commuters by the thousands every day. The immense terminus had twenty-one platforms with a wide concourse under a towering ridge-and-furrow roof, built like a cathedral, with cafes, dining rooms and cozy enclaves beyond the platforms. Widely praised for its architecture, the new curved building to the front of the station housed offices and facilities for passengers, including a large Georgian style booking hall, but it was quiet that morning. Sidney led *Wadebridge* across a few sets of points then alongside platform 11, between which and platform 12, lay an indoor street called "Cab Road", upon which mails would be unloaded, stopping at its end with a harsh and powerful wheeze at 3:48 a.m. He breathed a sigh of relief, like a poor joke without the punchline. Sidney wiped his brow and wiped away the distance. Had he missed something?

He'd driven the Up-Mail many times, but rarely had he seen the platform more crowded. As usual, there was a congregation of postal workers attending the coaches emblazoned with the royal coat of arms, along with their dollies and lorries. He had even seen the odd policeman before, but this was special. He counted eight, no, ten bobbies, then looking forward he saw three more before the concourse. Platforms 11 and 12, sometimes called the boat train platforms, had large, seven-foot wrought-iron gates, and the Cab Road that ran under the station clock between them had been barricaded.

Rag in hand, Sidney stepped down and stretched to see what they were all doing as he lit a cigarette, while Oliver said he would brew a cup of tea. There were postal workers disembarking from their coaches. Perhaps a half dozen travelers alighted from the passenger coaches and walked towards the police-manned exit. With the postal workers, railwaymen and police, there must have been over twenty men on the platform. Whatever that man who gave him the two hundred pounds might do; he was positive nothing had happened during the journey. How could it have? And now, there were just too many men (some armed) milling around the coaches as they unloaded the postal bags and bullion boxes. Lined up were four or five red Morris vans with their drooping faces.

Besides the Post Office vehicles, and startlingly obvious, were two dark-green two-ton Commer "Walk-Thru" vans, backed up to the railway bullion van swallowing the boxes one by one into their spacious interiors. On their sides were written "Security Express Limited."

Sidney Wellmeadow stood and watched while the convoy lined up after they secured the last boxes, then started out along the Cab Road, across the passenger concourse, under the lofty station clock and through the exit onto the Approach Road.

He didn't see it go down to enter the streets of London, crossing the River Thames a few minutes later on Westminster Bridge. Once north of the river, the convoy proceeded along The Mall, then to Buckingham Palace and Hyde Park Corner, to turn north along Park Lane to Wembley. The Commer vans, accompanied by two Wolseley 6/90 police cars, trundled on like heavy monsters, the drum brakes and asthmatic engines slower than ever with the enormous weights being carried.

* * * *

Like many people that habitually work at night, or early mornings, Detective Inspector Tom Halliwell hated that ringing bell. It was 5.00 a.m., which wasn't as bad as, say, 2.00 a.m. That was always the worst, but he knew this must be serious. And it was stunning news. All he momentarily recalled after replacing the telephone receiver were the words, "Park Lane," "fucking mess" and "bullion." A failed bullion robbery? His wife was so used to it she could sometimes sleep through the commotion, but this time Halliwell was too clumsy, too noisy, too enthusiastic—this he just had to get to. Through his mind flashed all the possibilities of what he might encounter. Strange that it should happen in North London. He stumbled and hit the floor pulling on his trousers and his wife aroused herself, clicking on the bedside light. "What is it, Tom?"

"I think I've got them: Russell and Geddes," he responded hopefully.

He apologized, then stumbled out the bedroom door, slipped on his shoes, grabbed his raincoat—not knowing what he would need—and opened the front door, leaving the comfort of his private life, his anodyne, friction-free marriage in the leafy suburb of Camden Town. A police Jaguar sat by the curb outside to take him through the rain-cleansed streets of London.

There is confusion concerning the details of what exactly had taken place. Less than ten minutes later, Halliwell arrived at Park Lane, nodding to the uniformed officers, showing his credentials, then shaking hands with Detective Sergeant Alan Humble, the first officer to arrive and the first person whose face he recognized. It was a starless morning and Halliwell was struck by how deserted the city felt. It was quite a scene, a combination of mayhem and viciousness, and he was glad of the two floodlights they had set up, revealing the panorama of disorder being swept by police. There were officers crouching over unseen objects, and a variety of official vehicles, their red and blue lights an assortment of smudgy illuminations eviscerated by the wet air. Park Lane had been closed by blue lights on three-foot tripods. The morning light was silently subverted, but there began just the slightest hint of dawn coming from the east, or perhaps it was London waking up, as usual.

"Morning Tom," greeted Humble in a dour, soft, fatherly demeanor he had gained over many years of night work, "thought you and your heavy mob might like to get close to this one. I called Johnny Brown to get your men up to date." He'd known Halliwell a long time and considered him an intellectual leader.

"Yes, good. Thanks for calling us, Alan. What's transpired to cause this mess?" said Halliwell, pulling his coat against the cold, speedily waking in the brisk breeze, finally attaining his bearings.

"Well, two bullion vans, under armed Met. escort, have been hijacked. Here's the result," began Humble, sweeping his arm in a broad semicircle across the roads, wet and slippery.

"Hold on," interjected Halliwell, now awake, "Bullion from where?"

"Waterloo. Before that Southampton, I think." He examined his notebook, "Yep, Southampton, came in yesterday on a ship. Didn't catch the name yet."

Confused from the news and his own lethargy, Halliwell thought, *what happened here?* "But…how can that be?" he said.

Humble continued the story instead of waiting, "The crooks took out one police car with a row of tire shredders—you can see it lying back over there. The first Security Express van took off without the escorts and swung round this corner." He gestured over the wide medium to Upper Brook Street. "So, I'm thinking, perhaps an inside man, but the driver's dead. Follow me, Tom." As they crossed the wide road he went on, "Anyway, bit of bad luck, he took the corner as if getting away with the gold and ran into that hole in the road that had only been dug yesterday by the council. Didn't see the flags, I guess. There were signs all around, but I s'pose he wasn't looking."

"Goodness, it's a mess..." uttered Halliwell

"The thing you and the squad need, of course—four arrests," Humble concluded triumphantly.

Halliwell's eyes, sleepy as they were, opened wide, "Who?"

"We have," again reading his notebook, "David Alan Walker, Brian Henry Spicer, Alfred King and Andrew Reginald Spencer." They arrived at a silver Jaguar Mark 2 squashed up against the corner building having been hit by a black police Wolseley.

Halliwell cut in, "No one from Battersea?" Humble shook his head.

They continued to walk to the Security Express bullion van lying on its side, "Er, no, Tom. Were you expecting someone in particular?"

"I just felt...for sure, somehow John Russell and that lot would be involved," he thought out loud.

They had arrived at the van. Halliwell peered inside and saw the mess of gold bars and wooden boxes piled up on the side of the vehicle lying in the road, and some kind of awareness inundated him; things were not quite what they seem here. *What's wrong with this picture?*

But he breathed his summation; "What a mess. Where was the gold going?"

"Johnson Matthey at Wembley. They're waiting for us to let them pick it up. Forensic boys still taking photos, and all that."

Alan Humble stepped to the van, stooped and lay his hand on a loose gold bar. He picked it up, but Halliwell observed inquisitively, "May I?"

Humble handed over the eleven-inch bar. As Halliwell took it, he knew right away something was amiss. He weighed it in one hand, took with his other a penknife from his pocket. The bar was lighter than he thought it should be. Detective Humble frowned as he watched him take the penknife and scratch the bar deeper, until the gold broke away revealing a dark, gray interior; "Oh, my God! This isn't gold. The bars are bloody lead!"

THE LORRY

The great merit of gold is precisely that it is scarce…it cannot be created by political fiat or caprice.

- Henry Hazlitt

March 27, 1963 - Southampton

JOHN RUSSELL HAD LONG IDENTIFIED the customs clearance as a fragile link in the entire plan. As much as Daniel worried about Billy, Russell knew it was the customs clearance. They could arrange just about everything else and expected, with some generous probability, to satisfy its desired conclusion. Russell believed in Billy. He knew he would prevail, but the customs clearance relied too much on the performance and behavior of others outside their influence. He understood the situation required closer attention.

In 1963, Her Majesty's Customs and Excise operated as a department of the British Government, having formed early in the twentieth century with the vital responsibility of collecting the direct and indirect taxes associated with the import and export of goods. Its officers functioned, among many less flamboyant tasks, in the detection and prevention of attempts to evade those revenue laws, most noticeably, through smuggling. They also performed other functions of administration, and the maintenance of law, order and justice. In places designated as customs areas, they had a wide range of legal latitude, often exceeding the police. They could seize goods or delay clearance merely on a document anomaly or their perception of suspicion. There were severe penalties for those who broke tax laws.

He saw the specific dilemma that customs might detain the Engine in bonded storage while processing. Safe, swift and anonymous handling were imperative. They couldn't tolerate slow treatment or scrutiny. Since one cannot avoid customs when entering a country, this made the perceived predicament non-excludable. He had to resolve this. He also knew that certain products might require specialized documentation or a physical examination to ensure the declarations were accurate. These general concepts were about as far as the gang leader's understanding went, which called for the expertise of the lawyer, Henry Hale. Neither Russell nor Geddes liked Hale, but they felt their physical threat compelled proficient work from him.

In every port, at every dock or wharf which handles international shipping, there are officers who inspect each ton of cargo arriving from a ship's hold, assessing the duty payable. Not only is it challenging to evaluate without hampering the consignment, the oldest trick in the book is to smuggle heavily dutiable articles concealed within those on which the duty is less burdensome. Many of these officers were in uniform, called the Waterguard. In their outfits, closely resembling naval officers, they boarded newly arriving ships seeking taxable transgressions by crew and passengers. They were the least liked people in the port. Additionally, HM Customs had its own Criminal Investigation Department, and their own plainclothes officers, called the Outdoor Service, who devoted considerable time on ships and in warehouses assessing dutiable goods and cargoes. To facilitate the process, compliant and exacting paperwork was essential. Substandard paperwork could draw unwelcome attention.

Henry Hale had found an amiable, cooperative and, some might judge, suspiciously loose freight forwarder who came highly endorsed by the people engaged in avoiding taxes. But what bothered Russell was the complexity involved in its own world and language. None of the core players would thoroughly grasp the academic uncertainties of "paperwork." They agreed the freight forwarder would handle the clearance for a small drink. Russell, Peter and Geddes debated whether to visit him, to make clear he understood the seriousness of their concerns. "Do you want me and Daniel to get more involved?" Eventually, they settled on a low-key approach.

One of a freight forwarder's primary functions is to arrange customs clearance of goods entering the country. They act as the respected middleman in the daily processing of thousands of documents. They can undertake this themselves, or subcontract to a company that specializes in customs brokering. To provide customs services, the freight forwarder requires sufficient funds to deal with the bonds and guarantees prescribed for duty and tax payments. The freight forwarder, Woolston Freight Forwarders, determined on the evidence submitted of an importation of two de Havilland jet engines ("used, destined for maintenance") would be roughly £158. Their cost for handling the paperwork would be £25. Through Henry Hale's firm of Fernsby & Hale, they willingly supplied the funds into the freight forwarders bank from their own bank in the City of London. Hale had quickly identified the peril involved to his own company if law enforcement were to scrutinize the paperwork chains too thoroughly. John Russell had summarily convinced him that others were taking plenty of risks. Well-ordered and accurate documents are essential for a freight forwarder, and required for a successful import clearance and receipt of payment for delivery. Efficient bureaucracy smooths the flow of commerce, and HM Customs—at their core—intended for business to flourish.

Information reviewed by a freight forwarder typically comprised the commercial invoice, shipper's export declaration, bill of lading and a few other documents prescribed by the carrier or country of import. The paperwork would verify that the de Havilland Engine Company were the importer of two "used" Goblin jet engines returning to England for maintenance and inspection. The freight forwarder had negotiated for British Haulage Services to collect the goods and transport them to their place of operations at Leavesden in Hertfordshire.

There persisted the problem of a zealous customs officer. The plan provided for a cursory inspection, but nothing more. Russell could foresee the entire operation disintegrating because of a customs man in a foul mood, or with time to spare, or a perceived aim to satisfy. They agreed that Arthur Treadway would play the role of the anonymous haulage driver, with his own character and corresponding makeup. He had to avoid possible later identification in a police lineup. They also spent the best part of a month watching the Port of Southampton and the operation of customs officers. This generated its own problems. First, the port security restricted entry (although there were techniques to bypass the obstacle), and second, the surveillance took place over eighty miles from Battersea. It all called for time, expense and manpower.

They debated the operation a few days before the Engine's expected arrival. Treadway spoke in a soft, comforting voice: "There are four customs officers rotating duty in the shed being used for imported goods on that berth," he informed those sitting before him in the Prince Albert snug.

"Are they vulnerable?" asked Russell.

"Not really, although they all have family in the area. I've had a chat with three of them and I think we're all right with the paperwork. It's my understanding that Henry believes the same." They each knew Arthur having worked with him before, but he was not of them. He had not grown up poor south of the river, and they were not entirely sure of his background.

"And what if one of them has a hard on? What do we do then?" asked Geddes. "He's not gonna come over all heroic, is he?"

Arthur shrugged his shoulders to suggest that would be outside his sphere of decision making. John Russell decided for him, "Yes, that's the crux of the problem. Anything they do has a consequence, and this is a headache waiting to happen. We need the Engine quickly." He waited a few seconds before deciding, "We go in subtle, with heavy backup. If violence is necessary, then it has to be." Geddes nodded in knowing agreement, while Arthur Treadway seemed puzzled.

As the two sizeable men walked out the room satisfied, Arthur turned questioningly to Peter who tried to explain, "It's within their...you know, that thing they do."

* * * *

Arthur Treadway sat alone in the cab of the Atkinson Mk I lorry, its engine below and beside him, with that rumbling Gardner grunt, coughing and hissing, ticking over. Behind was a mostly empty flat-bed. The heater of the lorry had malfunctioned, but the forecast was for a mild, partly cloudy day; the dreadful winter having almost concluded, although piles of snow lay around, becoming ever dirtier. The flatbed wasn't empty, but on the six-wheeled, twenty-three-foot platform, a small wooden frame covered with canvas nestled behind the fiberglass cab, presumably for carrying tires, rope lashings or tools. He stared about at the lines of Leyland, Foden, Dennis and Scammell lorries lined up, their exhausts emitting plumes of smoke.

So, this was the real working world? People drove lorries daily across the country; London to Birmingham, Liverpool to Norwich, Southampton to Leavesden. There were thousands of lorries, big and small, crisscrossing the nation day and night. The work of the lorry driver was incredibly hard, often putting in a hundred hours a week, with unhealthy food, dirty lay-bys, dropping cargoes in a town without a map, your wife turning away from the smell of five days on the road, the headaches at night. They lived a romanticized, but marginalized life, on tortuous roads with underpowered noisy engines and weak brakes. It was a hard life, but Arthur had tried to understand it, as if immersing himself in a new role.

This one Atkinson, perhaps once an aquamarine blue, with red trim at the lower levels and wraparound windows, appeared anonymous. The wheels were red. The sign above the light and uncluttered cabin said "Robinsons," apparently the owner of the transport company, part of the British Haulage Services conglomerate.

He had ridden through Gate 4 on Platform Road, right near the Admiralty Building, across from Queens Park. He passed the Custom House, a three-story red brick building with stone dressings in the Baroque revival style, where Henry Hale had made sure they had presented the accurate documents. The entrance contained a security gatehouse and customs fence that mark the boundary of the docks. A port official of unknown designation walked over and peered towards the sign in the cab window, handwritten with the name of the ship, *Aphrodite May*, and pointed him towards the East Docks, calling out; "Twenty-six Berth."

* * * *

Arthur Treadway had acted since childhood. He adored an audience, so the stage became his profession. As he grew older, he found steady employment in repertory work around the country, and then stumbled into minor parts in London. He had performed at The Arts Theatre, Windmill Theatre, Camden Theatre, The Adelphi Theatre, St. Martins Theatre and The New Theatre in Oxford. He knew Harry Secombe and Jimmy Edwards. He had dinner with George Melly, the jazz musician, every Christmas. He'd worked with Joan Plowright, Thelma Ruby and Clifford Evans. When the electronic age arrived, he had parts in *Variety Bandbox*, and *Educating Archie* shows, and *Variety Playhouse*. But, with his first leading role in *Blue Magic* at The Prince of Wales Theatre, critic Milton Shulman savaged him. Edward Goring in *The Daily Mail* labeled him "plodding." *Plays and Players* was worse, while another critic dubbed him "singularly graceless." It all hurt. It was a mistake, like everything else. He fell into a drunken stupor and his once-familiar and so-close friends melted away, which hurt more than the critics. No one appreciated his new intoxicated persona because they had all suffered the same themselves and held it together.

His unprepossessing features were difficult to describe, and he had an uncanny ability to morph from one personality to another, varying his age with a change of jacket and posture. He might have been forty or sixty. While drinking his face became drained with a gaunt, expressionless stare, because he had lost the will to perform. Without the sustenance of associates and friends, he realized he might wither, and he wasn't getting any younger. He saw the new theater and television of satire and irony barreling its way into the national psyche. Who can bear to feel himself forgotten by time? Depression and melancholy seized him. His face and voice, once so flexible and alive, became jaded and gray, like an old mayoral painting from Lewisham Town Hall. Only the eyes, medium and bright, occasionally showed any life. He had pressed his career too far; he had stretched himself beyond his comfort zone into a world not made for him, a world of star quality, which he never had. By the year's end, he had collected an unpayable tax demand and surrendered the urge to engage the brain or any other attributes.

When younger he had required the crowd, the adoration, but he had moved beyond that—now he needed money. And by a stroke of luck one late summer evening he had run into John Russell, and over too many drinks at the Astor, in Mayfair, he slipped, without looking back, into support roles, this time in criminality. Acting was lying, hiding the truth, and this new career rescued him from becoming gin-sodden. He had always cherished the theater and performance. Now in his late fifties, his whole air breathed of gentle eccentricity as he turned himself into a new character. He could pick up outfits at the costumiers Morris Angel on Shaftesbury Avenue, where he knew the proprietor well. Arthur had a singular ability to mimic others, special-izing in judicial types, doctors, Members of Parliament, and a clipped, dominating voice with a wavy sense of vulnerability. He had so many voices it was difficult to be himself, never quite uncovering the veil of illusion. Overall, his new career was an unsettling illustration of the compromises people can talk themselves into.

He enjoyed working with John Russell; he relished being near him. His gang were not wicked, he supposed, just foolish men flourishing in a dream that still, somehow, barely held together. He questioned if these people were worthy of his talent or sensitive soul, but it didn't take Arthur long to completely identify with the leading members, knowing the thrill of action and adrenalin. He thought them emotionally inadequate, but exciting, so led his recent life vicariously through what he thought they might do, or from the scraps of information they provided. Experience had taught him you never quite knew with women, and he little understood the silent mystery of the female experience. His longtime companion, Sebastian, learned of his relationship with the other face of the law and asked if his rationale was a glimpse of violence? Unconvincingly, Arthur denied this.

*   *   *   *

Struggling to select the character who might drive a long-distance haulage lorry, he had shunned the obvious cockney, and introduced his less-used Glaswegian working man. He maneuvered the lorry from Gate 4 into the port, bounced down Central Road, crossing tracks, then veered left over more rail tracks, having to linger for a shunter passing towards the Empress Dock. He had visited often in recent weeks, wearing such a diverse persona that the police and other officialdom would be unlikely to recognize him. He took on the character of the part he played, slipping his flat cap atop a few dusting wisps of gray hair on a face gashed from long-ago fights in the Gorbals and a Yosemite Sam mustache. The caper overcame the weariness of age. This would be his biggest first night.

He parked the Atkinson at the near edge of the warehouse, its vertical thirty-foot sides crowned with even archways and a grid of windows along the top. He stepped down and went searching for his next act, slipping deeper into character. Holding the Release Note and the Out of Charge Note Henry Hale had collected from the carrier and Custom House respectively, he walked out to locate the Shed Clerk's Office. They would have been notified if the Customs Landing Officer had any further interest in the landed goods. As he opened the office door, he heard a piercing train whistle somewhere distant within the port.

There were two men inside conversing loudly about football, one with his feet up on the table. Arthur interrupted; "Efternoon, gents. Ah hae some paperwork tae pick up a crate from th' *Aphrodite May*." He should have practiced more. His voice conjured up a picture of an Englishman hamming the accent, but the curtain was up now.

The men were amiable enough. The one with his feet on the table—he presumed the shed foreman—reviewed the papers, frowned and replied, "Oh, yeah, one of the customs men wants to have a look when you go. Pull the lorry into the second door down"—pointing toward the east, "we'll rustle up a forklift."

"Is thare a problem wi' customs?" asked Treadway.

The foreman shrugged his shoulders, "Not for us. Here's your exit slip. Once you've loaded the box, drive down to the far end of the shed, he's down there. He has to stamp and sign it. Then you're on your way."

Returning to the Atkinson, he clambered up into the cabin, gunned the engine, and said apparently to himself, "Some customs officer wants to look at the Engine after we get it on board." He pulled forward, along the side of the warehouse away from the dock, to the second large door, perhaps twenty feet wide, and turned inside, the dearth of light closing any color. He glanced to his right before the stacked boxes, containers, packages and assorted goods, and saw a large, red Coventry Climax forklift maneuvering, finally pausing before a wooden crate and sliding its forks underneath.

Arthur stepped down again from the lorry and guided the forklift driver to place the crate close to the cab and facing rearward. Saluting the forklift driver, he took his time—perhaps fifteen minutes—securing the crate, as he had studied in Woolwich with the nice man, Razor Wilkinson. Then, having fastened all the lashings and cargo straps, he returned to his cab. The Atkinson belched and grunted forward, as instructed, to the far doors of the warehouse, the engine echoing inside the shed. He judged the key to this role was to appear uninterested, but hurried, because it had been an interminable day and there was a ninety-mile journey still to make, including skirting London.

At the culmination of the extensive shed there stood a ten-foot long, wooden table in the open. He dragged the wheel over, turning to the left, parking as close as he could to the table, facing the exit ten yards ahead of him. He switched off the engine, peeked at a piece of paper and whispered into the opening at the rear of the cab, "Number one, number one on your sheet. I know the man; he's called Peter Jones. He has a wife, lives in the Maybush area. I'm out!"

Stepping down, he took his papers collection to the table, and waved to the below average stature, Officer of Customs and Excise walking towards him. He wore a cheap, ill-fitting dark gray suit, under which one could see his mustard colored cardigan and gloomy tie.

Weakly smiling, Arthur said, "Ah hae some papers need stamping."

"Ah, yes, the Goblin jet engine," cheerily grasping the papers. The customs officer stopped for a few seconds and scrutinized Arthur's eyes with that gaze of a man who supposes they'd met before. He adjusted his eyeglasses and studied the papers, "I worked on Gloucester Meteors while in National Service. 1955 in Linton-on-Ouse. Do you know Yorkshire?"

Arthur replied, "Ah take the lorry thro' it sometimes. This one's aff tae Leavesden." The two men shook hands. Arthur appeared comfortable, shrewdly understanding the key to any stage is confidence. Uncertainty would kill the performance, and he recognized the threat nearby. The moment he saw Jones, he understood the exchange would pass quickly and effortlessly. Customs Officer Jones began roving his eyes across the paperwork while recounting his brief history with de Havilland. It was a jaunty and positive conversation.

"The box has an inspection door. Let's open it up and have a peek inside," suggested Jones. This didn't catch Arthur by surprise, but he played along as Jones directed him to a small bolted door halfway up the front side of the crate, facing the rear of the Atkinson. "Do you have some spanners?"

Arthur said, "Och aye, sure," and picked up a small toolbox from the cab. Once he had unbolted the twelve-inch-squared-door, the customs man climbed aboard the bed and bent slightly, torch in hand, to peer within.

"Oh, yes, there she is, the ugly brute, a genuine Goblin all right, although the fuel lines and starter are missing. I guess they know what they're doing. Just look at that ugly face." He straightened and turned from the box as Arthur nodded disinterestedly and twisted the nuts back on the closed inspection door. As he stepped down from the flatbed, Jones said, "Thanks for letting me have a look. My Goodness, I must have worked on dozens of them things over the years. Let's get you on your way to Leavesden." Then he stopped mid-stride and appraised the paperwork again, "Oh, it says there's two engines in there." He smiled to Arthur in that manner of acquiescence and a shared in-joke, and bent over the table, picking up his customs seal. But he had already rendered the error, and Arthur feared the consequences.

In a thunderous, crashing outburst, all the monsters of his imagination came surging towards Peter Jones, the human. Two thickset men burst from the wood and canvas sanctuary behind the cab. The first masked man tumbled to the concrete. The second stepped across him, shoulders square. Officer Jones's nightmare of a tall, sinister, brutal weapon, the standard kit of the terrorist thug, approached. The black boilersuit crafting the man bulky, but dynamic and lithe, peerlessly blending the awkward movement with unrivaled, physical strength and precision. His menacing, military-style, 1950s army combat boots screamed violence, an allegorical view of masculinities destructive elements in a balaclava. Before Jones could react, he was on him—bloated and concealed, enclosing his mighty arm about his neck, effortlessly lifting him from the ground. Jones, taken aback by the alacrity of the assault, wrestled to defend himself, adding, to little avail, "No!"

Then the other, once-concealed thug, picked himself from the ground. He stepped towards Jones and lifted a large-bladed Gurkha Khukuri knife to his face. Snarling in a crude cockney accent in his lacerating, direct delivery as if a relentless, unhinged force: "Shut your cake'ole. Sign and stamp the *facking* paperwork, you *ka-hunt*, or you and the family in Maybush get it!"

Jones hung from Geddes's arm, his feet swinging in the air. It had all happened so fast. Arthur stood frozen at the moment, shocked by the swiftness and intimacy of the violence. His voice eluded him. He stood there preying the assailant wouldn't employ the gruesome blade, giving reign to his pity and fear, comparing the wan weariness of Jones with the hypertension masculinity of John Russell. He sought to step forward, try to impede them, but he remained petrified, watching wicked men being evil. The poor man, as Arthur thought, was released, unsteadily. He turned, stamped, and trembling, signed the paperwork. By the time the ink dried, the two military-dressed brutes had clambered ungainly back into their temporary hide, both men molded by their physically demanding chosen profession. Arthur, believing now that reality was more interesting than living happily ever after, finally aroused from his frozen thoughts. Stepping toward Jones, and with a compassionate expression, he offered him a brown envelope, "Finish your shift, Peter. Here's a drink for your trouble. Go home tonight to your family and never…never say a word! You don't want your family to meet them," as he pointed to their hide behind his cab.

"Sort it out!" growled Russell, staring at Arthur with penetrating eyes, laden with menace that gave him such a special feeling inside.

Climbing back aboard, extracting the Atkinson from the warehouse, Arthur turned back and shouted, "What is wrong with you two? He was gonna sign! Did you have to do that? He didn't do nothing wrong."

He heard a muffled reply, "I can get a lot worse, believe me," as the inhabitants were removing their balaclavas and feeling content with a job accomplished.

He would have had an amicable chat with the gateman, returning to his role of a Scottish long-distance lorry driver, but he recognized in the moments of post violence his character mask had lapsed, and his mustache had loosened. So, as soon as they gave him the all clear wave, he wrenched the wobbly gear lever forward, let out the clutch, and the Atkinson jolted onto Canute Road, passing the South Western Hotel and Southampton Terminus Station to their left. On his right stood the former White Star Line office, then slowing to turn left onto Crescent Road, he headed north, feeling the anxiety draining away and the overwhelming surge of relief. Taking a deep breath, he yelled back; "Hey! You back there, can you hear me? We're out! On our way to Britannia."

There was a muffled cheer from behind, mixed with the continuing gripe of discomfort. Arthur drove on, relishing the drive north along Marine Parade alongside the River Itchen to his right, into the dowdy, working district of Belvedere. Some berths here remained, working grain, timber, and cars. Shipbuilding and heavy engineering continued along both banks of the river, but the older docks had grown redundant. Where Marine Parade met the junction of Britannia Road, across from the gas tower, Arthur turned the Atkinson into the doors of a warehouse being opened by Peter Badger. The lorry crept in, facing towards the river, then stopped as the doors closed behind. Arthur jumped from the cab, as Geddes kicked open the plywood box side and slithered out, cursing the cramped conditions and his aching back. Russell followed and shouted: "C'mon, let's get to work!"

Razor Wilkinson jumped up onto the lorry bed, and banged on the front of the Engine, "Open up!" They heard the interior clasps being released, then the front three feet of the box shimmied slightly and the crate door containing the face of the Goblin engine swung slowly open, as if the occupant wasn't sure. Then the young man inside saw their waiting faces and pushed it wide, stepped out, arms raised in triumph, and jumped onto the waiting bulk of Danial Geddes, the nearest person standing there. Still being grasped by Geddes, his face a beaming smile, Billy Tumbler turned to John Russell, "Free 'undred, Mr. Russell! I got 'em all!"

And as Danial lowered him to the floor, he stepped to John Russell, who himself possessed a satisfying grin. They shook hands like the return of a long-lost friend, "Three hundred, Billy? Really?"

"Yes, sir! I got 'em all!"

Russell hugged him, while everyone looked on hyped and excited, reveling in his success. After all that work, so many months of slog and heartburn, was this really it? They had been in the cold for so long, without a ray of hope, but now the young hero had returned. The days were slowly growing longer, and the spirits of the gang rose on the return of Billy, an ordinary young man, not like the heroes of literature. Each one there shook his hand and congratulated the junior man—he had done what so many had thought to themselves impossible.

THE SHIP

Poor is the man who can boast of nothing more than gold.

- William Scott Downey

March 08, 1963 - Durban, South Africa

BILLY TUMBLER HAD A DREADFUL, tangible dream. He ran through the night, scurrying in the darkness, running away from the last memory he had of Bishop's tormented face, like a crawling, creeping horror, an object of terrible fascination from which he couldn't rip his gaze. The windows he ran past were dark. He banged on doors, but nobody answered. He twisted locked handles to no avail. He screamed out for help, but only a bleak silence sprang from his wide, open mouth. No one in the world heard him. Then, in that strange place between sleep and waking, he swapped the dream sensations with that perplexing sense of proceeding without the faculty of sight, a shift of surroundings into which he was somehow familiar. The eccentric movement replaced the nameless and faceless dread that had temporarily taken him from the genuine world into a realm of sinister imagination. It felt soothing now, just a gentle, relaxing, oscillating transfer from side to side. He was dreamy and half asleep, but the firm bed felt alien and that bought his awareness to the fore.

He lay in the blackness, recounting the previous twenty-four hours. It began with lassitude; the darkness wrapping closer about him, enveloping him in denuded sensation, suffocating his dreams. He had deferred, rejected scrutiny of the clock tacked to the wall. Then the sudden, unnerving sensation of soaring through the air, but without seeing. He felt better not seeing, feeling himself floating sideways high above everything, just like the Comet. Then a rapid plunge, abruptly slowing, and a gentle thud as the crane driver settled the Engine on the wooden tween deck hatch boards of the *Aphrodite May*. The movements had shaken his mind awake, turning to his attention the enormity of the place he had brought himself to.

The previous six days; the jet setting, the relaxing Durban beach, the clean, vivid air, the sedentary dark crate had now all come to this. Like a coffin buried underground, it was a circumstance without exit. He stood, steadied himself, his neck bent, leaned towards the crate side, unscrewed the upper aperture stopper and squinted outside into the sunshine-flooded tween deck hold, only to see a faded-red forklift truck rumbling towards him, smoke issuing behind.

The forklift gently collided with his new home and elevated one side as Billy held on and maintained his balance. There was much clamor and hollering outside, as the box slid towards what he supposed, the wooden planking protecting the steel hull. He sat quietly back down as the Durban dockers secured the box with turnbuckles. He heard their casual chitchat of another language. They laughed; the last intimate human sounds he would experience for eighteen days. Billy remained noiseless for the next few hours, occasionally peeking out to see an abundance of mail bags being thrown into a caged, secure area directly across from him. More shouting and random commotion followed as they removed the deep tank hatch bolts, while he peered through his partially obscured view, hearing only muffled sounds. He watched as they lifted the hatch clear with a wire from above—either a crane or a derrick, he couldn't see. Once swung clear, some officials entered the tween deck, along with two green-attired military men carrying guns, their camouflage strangely incongruous in this dark, gray world. They all stood around reconnoitering the space below, like council workers staring into a hole. A while later a pallet entered on a wire net from above, with what appeared ordinary and unimportant boxes snuggled on top. They manhandled the pallet towards the deep tank opening and lowered it down inside. As far as Billy could see from his disadvantaged view, they followed this with three more.

Reaching full realization, he was here, the furtive amongst the recognized, the criminal amongst the legally occupied. This was not the time to consider the wrongs and rights of life; they had all decided, except now he was intensely alone and vulnerable again, fully engaged in what Daniel would have called the "sport of thievery." His eyes cleared slightly, but the miniature and cramped space was in near complete darkness. He lay down, and focused his mind on the comforting movement, like sleeping in his mother's arms, and the soothing thrum of the giant machinery, the new soundtrack of his life.

Billy lay on his narrow bed and idly put his mind to another world called Battersea.

* * * *

General cargo encompassed a vast diversity of goods; bagged and baled stuffs, cases and crates, drums and barrels, food, furniture, timber, rolls of paper, motor vehicles, articles of machinery and an untold enormous assortment of individual, unimportant things. Prior to the transformative introduction of containerization, they carried general cargoes on ships equipped with derrick booms and other mechanisms to load and unload them in ports large and small worldwide. They were the mainstay of international trade, left to tramp the globe in their own, sometimes distinctive manner. A ship's master (or captain; the terms are objectively synonymous for our purposes) would be given orders to reach a port and load a specific cargo, or multiple cargoes, then take them to another port next door, or on the other side of the world. The owners and ship-managers then permitted him to navigate, run and tend his ship however he saw fit to fulfill the contract of carriage. That's why they paid him. His primary obligations were the safety of his officers and crew, security of the ship and the cargo. He could run his ship as he pleased, in his own curious manner—a conduit for eccentric moments—and many did. They constrained him only, perhaps, by tradition. The business bore a breed of competent, but sometimes idiosyncratic men. They were always men.

The *Aphrodite May* was a conventional, three-island cargo ship, like so many others, a design evolved since they first installed an engine. She was one of three owned by the London & Oriental Shipping Line, and, like her sisters, had been built in 1955 by John Brown Company on the Clyde. She met the annual commitment to carry occasional bullion cargoes from Durban to Southampton, while diverted from her regular area of trade, the Far East. They had won the charter purely on an economic level. On the four prior shipments of gold, the shippers and receivers had pronounced themselves pleased with the freight. Since, besides bullion, they carried mail under contract, it entitled them to fly the pennant of the Royal Mail during this passage, along with a rarely-used classification, "RMMV," for Royal Mail Motor Vessel.

She was a tweendecker, a ship with two decks. They called the upper one the weather, or freeboard deck, because that's where the seas landed. The lower one created a space above the hold called the tween deck. Smaller or lighter cargoes, such as bales, bags or drums, could be stacked in the tween deck space. Beneath this was the hold, which, because of the tween deck, had a reduced column of space to stow general cargo, thus avoiding compression from over stowage. Tween deck hatches were often flush fitting to allow the use of forklift trucks.

She had three holds forward of the accommodation house, which itself sat above the engine room. There were two holds aft, through which a shaft tunnel ran to the propeller. The builder designated hold No. 3 to carry bullion, since it had a deep tank—a tank from the floor of the tween deck to the bottom of the hold (confusingly called the tank top of the hold), used to carry occasional specialized liquid cargoes, such as palm oil, or molasses. Situated at the aft end of No. 3 hold placed it next to the engine room, from which they could generate heat, if required. To tolerate the additional higher pressures of a liquid head, the tank had added stiffening, which, to encourage delivery of liquid cargoes and ease of cleaning, was affixed to the outside of the tank. It seemed like a large, square, well-supported white can, built as part of the vessel's original structure.

The tween deck could be a gloomy place once closed up. It was about nine or ten feet high—enough to accommodate the forklift truck. The main hatch, the ceiling of the tween deck, comprised rolling steel leaves on wheels connected by chains. It covered, or uncovered, roughly eighty percent of the hatch. Directly below it, the entrance to the hold below, the tween deck floor comprised heavy, manhandled wooden hatch boards resting on steel cross beams, for which they required a derrick boom to extricate. There were two vertical access ladders to the hold, one forward, one aft.

Cargo holds had to operate anywhere in the world, and apart from loading or discharging, and occasional cleaning, they were closed up and watertight; a primary prerequisite of a watertight hull and reserve buoyancy. Since mildew can have an adverse effect on certain cargoes, ventilation was vital to remove heat, dissipate gas, help prevent condensation and remove taint. Proper ventilation, therefore, was indispensable for satisfactory carriage, and would also prevent rust on the ship itself. Natural ventilation, like that on the *Aphrodite May*, used cowls which they trimmed into the wind to intake outside air and trimmed back to the wind to allow air circulation and extraction from the hold.

* * * *

The *Aphrodite May* had arrived to Durban from Mombasa, carrying a part cargo of hardwood for final delivery at Southampton. These were the facts confirmed by the Post Office and the Metropolitan, British Transport and Southampton Police departments upon the conclusion of the voyage.

When Billy had accepted a commitment to the John Russell crew, it was because he brought along several specialized skills that met the demands of the planned unlawful caper. First, he physically fit the specification; short and slim. His anonymity appealed too; he was unknown to the police. Russell had asked Geddes, "How are we going to find someone from our manor with an alibi while the police are watching?" But best of all, Billy had been to sea, so had experience of ships, the fashion in which they moved, the smell, sound and resonances, the innate recognition of endless movement. He had celebrated the ocean; he had sought to visit Valparaiso, Van Diemen's Land and Timbuktu. He had learned that sense seafarers have of handling physical objects, of being comfortable working on a moving platform where the passions of the sea could be, occasionally, breathtakingly amplified.

Expediency created the position of ordinary seaman. It allowed a seafarer to gain the experience of an able seaman; a man well acquainted with his duty. Russell understood an OS would have had some experience with splicing wire and rope, rigging, overhauling, and stowing gear. The OS would know how to work safely aloft and below, to conduct general maintenance, repair, and upkeep material and equipment. He could handle tools and paint. In short, an ordinary seaman was an all-round sensible man capable with his mind and hands. He knew this would be a key provision of a gang member to accomplish the intended work, and the hope of acquiring a man like that seemed problematic. Peter had a narrowboat, but Russell didn't believe the skills were comparable, and he was correct in that assumption. That meant seeking a member of another gang with maritime experience, which appeared unthinkable without arousing attention. Billy understood how much time, money and work had gone into this adventure. He had heard the entreaty; "Nothing stands between us and the prize," from the new people in his life. He understood how important he was to these men, and he aspired to be one of them, to belong. Going to South Africa had demanded a heart-stopping determination from Billy. Somewhere in the past few weeks he had crossed a significant, but unidentifiable line.

* * * *

The expectation might be that safeguarding highly valued goods on a ship—bars, coin, or other treasure—would require the vigilance of many men. This, however, is not generally the case, since once they stow the assets in the rooms set apart for that purpose, and the vessel is out to sea, guards are superfluous. When carrying bullion, typically a ship will place it in a specie, or strong, room. The walls, roof and floor might be lined with two-inch steel plate. The locks could be of the double variety, made more secure by steel hasps covering the keyholes, and they provide them with hefty padlocks. There were usually two sets of keys, one of which remained with the captain, typically in his safe. Naturally, the padlocked room would be placed in the most frequented section of a vessel, or alternatively, low down in the hull where it might be over-stowed with cargo to deter the rare immoral act. The major liability comprised crew members believing they could help themselves to the bullion, for which the carrier would be responsible. The room usually carried a government wax seal from the port of loading, the impression being broken only when an official, and receiver, at the destination arrived to take possession. Some ships, including the *Aphrodite May*, spot welded closed the two hold entry doors while at sea.

Anything carried in the room under a bill of lading will, by common law, have the benefit of some protection. The carrier has an implied duty of care to make the room reasonably strong enough to resist thievery and not be broken into during the voyage. There was minimal threat of anyone stealing gold in transit on a ship. It would be necessary that the pirate should shoulder a sturdy box weighing some 150 pounds and vanish with it without being seen. Shipmasters declare gold among the safest cargo of any to handle. There was no discussion of attempted thievery being made from outside his ship. How could that happen? The trade was considered so safe that shippers often insured the cargo at its full value.

* * * *

In May 1961, South Africa became a Republic. This date served as the starting point of the nation's golden age, at least economically. Prosperity became noticeable in many spheres of life, and its rate of growth was unsurpassed. With the burgeoning economy, by 1963 the government introduced diesel locomotives on a large scale, so on March 8, a faded maroon, South African Railways bullion van, had traveled eight hours from Johannesburg to arrive onto the dock at Durban. The boxes of gold were unloaded, placed on wooden pallets and hoisted into hold No. 3 of the *Aphrodite May*, as Billy had spied them from his situation in the Engine.

Gerry Jansen had witnessed the gold being loaded from a safe distance, and later monitored the *Aphrodite May* departing, waving to Captain Joseph Minghella standing on the bridge wing. He acknowledged to himself that he had done all he could do. He had handed over the £5,000 in a brown envelope, with the promise that an associate would present the balance in Southampton. He had initiated the plan from the outset when he recalled the fantastic story of John Winks all that time ago in a cold, Wandsworth prison. He had paid the dockyard Zulu headman a substantial bonus to make sure they placed the Engine in the correct position in hold No. 3. As the ship disappeared beyond the North Pier of Durban Point, he reflected; *Good luck, young Billy.*

He had about him a quiet contentment of duty well done. He had accomplished as much as he could. In telephone calls with Russell, he understood most of the work in which others were engaged. He felt comfortable in his part. He had enjoyed meeting Billy enormously. "Sharp as a tack," the Londoners would say. The young man had about him a credulous, but not simple, likability; youthful, but not juvenile. Gerry thought he just might be as perceptive and shrewd as John Russell himself, and felt positive that as an ordinary young man he would become, briefly, extraordinary. He would seek the newspapers in a few weeks, wherever he might be. He had already decided that he would leave South Africa tomorrow, never to return. The voyage from Durban to Southampton measured 6,724 nautical miles and, without stopping, would typically take seventeen-and-a-half days at the *Aphrodite May*'s sixteen knot conventional speed. Almost everyone on board expected a leisurely, refreshing voyage through warm, sunlit seas, once having rounded the Cape of Good Hope. Everyone, except one young man, that is.

* * * *

The day before, Billy had monitored the time, rather than the view. And time dragged. Initially, he had regretted not bringing a book or a small game to distract himself, but he soon realized he had time to reflect and a lot to consider. He had sat, or laid, mostly in the dark, but occasionally brightening his world with a torch to peruse the wall of equipment and supplies before him. In the early evening, he became hungry and restless, so searched the cans of food for something he could eat without cooking. Just as he found the desired corned beef can, he was assailed from above by the thunderous jolt of the steel hatch beginning to close, shattering again and again, shaking the existence of his home, as each heavy steel leaf extricated itself from its stowage position and landed on the coaming, following the preceding one until covering the entire hatch. He heard the familiar banging and mechanical work as the crew turned the running wheels upon their cams, lowering the slabs of steel and then securing the cleats, ensuring a watertight seal. Silence fell upon Billy's world as he entered his own mind-warping new existence. When Gerry had sat and discussed the terms of Captain Joseph Minghella's ten-thousand-pound payment, the first stipulation dictated that he would ensure hatch No. 3 would not be opened on the voyage. Captain Minghella thought to himself, *why would we open the hatch?* He did not envisage any reason they should do so. With the light from the torch Billy made his sandwich, peeled a sophisticated orange treat, ate, and lay down to hear and feel the ship's departure from Durban, ready to burn off the coursing, nervous energy within him.

Once Billy felt, as he supposed, the engine maneuvering under pilotage, he examined the clock. Five-thirty in the afternoon; less than an hour to sunset. He judged that sufficient time to engage in some preparatory work. Attaching a torch to his belt, he stepped toward the thirty-six inches of Goblin engine face and unclipped the six heavy-duty toggle latches holding the front door—effectively the front three-feet of the crate—including the engine facade. He pushed it slowly open, jammed two wooden retainers in place to prevent it closing upon himself, and stepped outside, his eyes dilating in the darkness. He opened the torch and left his hideaway; hard, safe and peaceful. There he was, sylph-like, the ultimate stowaway.

He stood, stretched a bit, and beheld the sound of the hold beyond the gaze of the world above. The darkness was utterly confusing for a short while, as he absorbed the tones, smells and the touch of surfaces. He stepped tentatively away from his solitary confinement and moved into his own playground, the entire tween deck. Like prison, there was no life, no color and a dearth of texture. Donning his gloves and sweeping the torch around, he seized a can of low viscosity penetrating oil and a paint scraper, stepped carefully across the steel floor, passing the wooden hatch boards and on to the white-painted deep tank. The bright paint glowed as if the cargo inside was somehow escaping the steel cocoon within which it lay. Looking around, the torch opened the world to his eyes. It was familiar to his experience, but new and unaccustomed in this instant. Toward the forward part of the tween deck the torch revealed some secured barrels and pipes, and to port, a cage crammed with mailbags. He kneeled down and scraped the thick paint from each of the twenty, one-and-a-half-inch steel hex nuts, affixing the access plate to the larger, deep tank cover plate. Once accomplished, he fed penetrating oil around each, then recalled Peter's words, "Make sure it's one hundred percent." He smiled at the memory, then returned to the crate for the night. No need to rush. He had plenty of time.

He awoke from an insubstantial sleep about midnight, feeling the movement and the deep thrum of the engine nearby as the *Aphrodite May* departed Durban, headed to Southampton. He saw no point in working. It had been a long day, not fruitless, but slightly frustrating, and working with lights at night had been agreed by all to be tempting fate. Security was imperative. The lights, or their reflections, might readily be seen exiting the air vents by the bridge lookout. That was a risk they didn't need.

Billy awoke from a healthy sleep at 6.00 a.m., but then realized in his bewilderment he had lay in the wrong direction. He made a note to amend that tonight. He skipped breakfast to reconnoiter his surroundings again. Behind the Goblin engine-front he unclipped the six clasps retaining the door, swung the whole rig open and stepped into the darkened hold. He considered the door position, and decided to leave it ajar from now on, unless the ship encountered heavy seas. The Engine had limited ventilation at its top, so an increased airflow would improve the conditions. It wasn't dark. He had heard the hatch being secured yesterday, but there were now two thin blades of light; the dim, drab world of the tween deck becoming dusty-filled yellow from the two forward air vents.

Familiarizing himself, he returned to his home and pulled out a long electrical power line. He walked it over to the socket outlet behind the deep tank on the aft bulkhead and plugged it in. The next step was vital. Shaking it loose back to the box, he connected the electrical element of his small cooking range and saw it slowly changing to orange. He had power. Planning a long day, he fried up some eggs and corned beef while brewing a small pot of tea. Surrounded by so much food, it felt extravagant. The second condition of Captain Minghella's ten-thousand-pound payment depended upon him guaranteeing that power remained to the holds during the voyage. It would have been routine for the chief mate to close it, but Captain Minghella made a casual remark about the electrician having to conduct some testing, so it remained on, and the matter was not discussed again.

Billy next erected lights near the deep tank and took a while removing the twenty bolts of the fifteen by twenty-three-inch manway hatch with a hand spanner—the penetrating oil having performed its work overnight. Once levered open, like prizing unlocked a dusty tomb, he shone the torch inside and was confronted, unexpectedly, with excess mail bags that could not be stowed in the cage. They had flung them into the deep tank above the bullion. It meant additional work, but Billy felt capable if he organized meticulously.

With the additional mailbags temporarily dismissed from his mind, he set about hauling an array of hollow aluminum shear legs from his timber and tubular-framed home and awkwardly set it above the manway. Shear legs are unwieldy, but Billy had rehearsed thoroughly with this set. Razor had fitted each leg of the tripod with safety chains and a large eyebolt from the apex for the suspension of a lifting apparatus. He had also added rubber lined feet. The value of shear legs is they ensure the leg bracing does not impede the access to the confined opening below, while the unit remains free standing. He had spent days working in Woolwich, trying distinct setups of the equipment. Shear legs can be stubborn, and rarely used, but after three days and many modifications and adjustments in Woolwich, Billy was comfortable with this setup. "Perfect working order," Peter called it. Finally, they had an aluminum, fully adjustable tripod set, at what they believed to be the best elevation for the purpose.

He stood on a stool, and to the suspension point above the small manway, he connected a modified Land Rover wire winch powered by the ship's electric supply. Razor suggested it could hoist five hundred pounds; more than enough. The electric wire had been pre-made to connect with the ship's power, simple to run out, with two extensions, one for the winch, the other for lighting and cooking. Gauging the dimensions and appraising the workload, Billy felt he could accomplish the tasks without electricity, but it would be long and arduous. However, peering down into the deep tank for the second time, seeing the vertical ladder, with power he felt confident of success. The hatchway would be a tight squeeze for a larger man.

Billy set to work: he descended the ladder into the tank, dragging the slack winch wire and hook. He attached one, or frequently two mail bags, clambered back to the tween deck and electrically hauled the bags, cramming them through the manway. He threw them into a loose pile on the side. Nearer the base of the pile, he came across the pallets holding the boxes within which should be the bullion. Once cleared, he saw each pallet held six strong boxes. When he examined closer, he saw two of the pallets had an extra box, therefore counting fifty boxes in total. The dockers in Durban had fastened each layer of boxes in position with two or three stainless steel 5/8" BAND-IT straps. He made a cup of tea, so he could sit and plan the process. It was risky, but far from hopeless; he felt sure of that. He recognized that climbing would be the greatest exertion of the entire enterprise, like ascending the chimneys of Battersea Power Station. From a small bag of hand tools, he selected a pair of cutters and severed the first steel band, which sprang backward and lay in a semirigid curve. Two wooden boxes were now accessible. Delving his hand into his pocket, he retrieved a small key on a string, the same lock for every box, supplied by Gerry. They had sent another onward to Southampton by airmail.

He slid the key into the nearest keyhole. He turned. It jammed. He thought for a moment, applied pressure again, and it rotated with a reassuring clunk, snapping the latch satisfyingly free. Billy rested his palms on the lid and slowly lifted, revealing two stacks of three gold bars, each gleaming like a resplendent sun, separated from its neighbor by a thick piece of paper. The bars gleamed with a creamy iridescence, like bleached buttercups, and the whole deep tank now radiated a soft, but odd, yellow light consuming everything within. He breathed slowly out through pursed lips. *Oh! My Goodness. This is really it*, and he smiled thinking of Peter; "That's the ticket."

Reaching in, he clumsily sought to clutch the first gold bar, but it failed to move, causing him to believe, momentarily, that it was somehow tethered. He tested again and it wouldn't move. Taken aback, it appeared unseeingly fastened. He tried again and realized it was the ungainly shape, but most of all, the spectacular weight that baffled his retina-scorched mind. Finally, he clumsily held it in the clasp of two hands and measured the ridiculous, unfathomable heaviness. *So, this is the real thing?* He studied the bar's broader face, with the markings "1963," "Rand Refinery," "99.99" (reflecting its purity), and a unique serial number. So special, so exceptional. Billy held it to his body and its proximity warmed him. There was no aroma, as if it were inert. He spent a few moments just handling the bizarre, alien artifact, becoming more familiar with its heft and other worldliness. Returning to reality, he set to arranging and sorting the equipment. He wanted a plan that would keep the bars moving. He knew, naturally, that progress would hasten if he prepared properly from the outset.

Some time later, after much head-scratching and readjustment to the shear legs, he was ready for his first bullion lift. Controlling the switch, the winch began a too-quick hoist, which he slowed, hauling up two gold bars in a cylindrical canvas linesman's bag with one bar exposed at the top. Content with the rate of climb, he watched it slowly rising, then stared alarmingly as it caught on the manway edge, tilt and dislodge. Billy released the electric switch, nimbly bent and athletically reached down, clasping the lustrous, slippery ingot in his grip. But his hand did not possess sufficient strength and the gold bar plummeted back into the tank, colliding in a loud, clanging reverberation below. He froze, listening to the thump of his heart, feeling his collar tighten. He waited and pondered. Dropped objects have been an issue since the force of gravity has existed. Negligence and careless behavior he did not need. He sat down and breathed out slowly, hearing the reverberation slowly dissipate about him in the gloom. Would anyone hearing the abrupt, metallic resonance judge it remarkable or in need of attention? He sat and thought it through. It was a singular noise—once! Seafarers disliked repetitive, irritating noises. There was just the very slightest action of the ship, side to side. They expected the odd noise and they would dismiss it.

Removing the surviving gold bar from the canvas bag, he placed it on the steel deck. He mentally required an adjustment to recognize how something so compact could weigh so much. He had initially considered preserving a sense of orderliness in his darkened realm, but now he knew that could not be. John Russell had assured him they would not open the hatch, so he proceeded on that premise. It didn't matter if a few errant gold bars lay around. He lowered the bag, climbed down and refilled it with two more. He now used a chisel to slip under the edge so he could more easily grasp them. Today was a day for learning. *Slowly, Billy, let's get this right. Plenty of time, no more accidents.*

The rest of the day he spent lifting the gold by electric winch. Up and down he climbed and made a mental note to move deliberately. He was unseen and unknown by anyone on the ship. They say once you have been alone; you are ready for the company of others. Loneliness is something to be learned, its burden never being easy to overcome. As a seafarer, Billy had already seized the sensation, and he understood the risk. What would happen if he stumbled and injured himself? Would anyone hear his calls for help? The ship motored on, out of sight, out of mind to the world beyond. The universe wouldn't care, and they'd find his emaciated body lying in this anonymous tween deck on arrival in England. The sea swallows everything, then forgets.

By late afternoon he had hoisted twelve bars and lay them carefully on the tween deck floor. No sudden heavy roll could move them, he supposed, especially since he stood so near the ship's center of gravity. What really surprises the first time someone sees the ocean is the enormity of the place. To understand that feeling of vastness, you need to feel its strength. And Billy had known that sensation. He felt comfortable. He suspended activity and closed the lights, hiding his existence from the lookout, the hatch being directly in front of the bridge house. It was, perhaps, an overabundance of caution, but everybody associated in the planned work believed that—except for unforeseen circumstances—he should have ample time to accomplish his tasks.

By the day's end, although Billy didn't know it, the *Aphrodite May* was still in South African waters and had not yet reached Cape Town. He had settled down. His dwelling was modest, confined and surrounded by equipment, packages and tins of food. The Rowntree's fruit gums he had been so insistent on adding to the box in Woolwich now seemed bland and humdrum. He had fresh fruit from South Africa, and he relished the juicy contents of watermelon, mangoes, bananas, cantaloupe, and strawberries. He had brought on board two bags, which he felt would last at least a week. The fresh food changed his viewpoint of the world without noticing. If he consumed it all, he had tinned alternatives.

Awaking the following dawn, he needed to defecate and urinate. He'd been fretting about the situation, but the result met expectations. "Now, here's the problem young man, but I think I have it sorted," Razor had declared. They had never tested it, but now was as good a time as any. His body told him it was necessary. Fiberglass was not yet mainstream, but Razor had gathered together a half dozen US Army

Metal Insulated Food Containers made by Landers, Frary & Clark. "The Seals are good. The hinges are sturdy and snap nicely, the rubber seal is good and closes properly. The Americans have some marvelous plastic stuff now, but I couldn't get my hands on any."

Each container measured twenty inches by sixteen inches by nine inches. He had designed the canister to slide under a small stand with a wooden toilet seat forming the top. After use, Billy tossed in a few handfuls of sawdust and a scoop of lye, refastening the container until the next time. It performed as he might have wished, and for the next seventeen days he handled the containers like pieces of antique china.

Nibbling on something as exotic as watermelon, it brought to mind the obstacles and deprivation of insufficient food resources. Three years before his birth, the British government introduced food rationing with the noble goal of ensuring fair shares for all at a time of national scarcity. They gave every man, woman and child a ration book with coupons. As shortages amplified, long queues became commonplace. They never rationed fruit and vegetables, but they were often in short supply. After six years of suffering and privation, it was not until the early 1950s that most commodities came "off the ration." Meat was the last item to be derationed in 1954. He didn't know it, but Billy and his generation had grown up smaller than they should have because of those shortages. During his early years at school, he had gone to bed too many times on an empty stomach. Billy knew, only too well, what it meant to be hungry.

The War had been frequently hard for Londoners. Bombing caused fear, suffering, death and ruin, and they often separated families during evacuations. The citizens had learned to live with skepticism and peril, where dried and tinned food became common replacements as fresh meat and fish were in short supply. They encouraged families to "make do and mend" for their clothes to last longer. Over eighty thousand Londoners were killed or seriously injured during those years, one in ten of all deaths occurring to children. War had taught them to cherish the present as the future may never come. Rationing, and the meagre variety of ingredients and flavorings, would prevent even the best of cooks—like Billy's mother—from creating anything but standard fare; luncheon meat and boiled vegetables. There were no supermarkets, no frozen food or freezers to store meagre supplies, and the only takeaway remained the fish and chip shop, his favorite being Cyril's on Battersea Bridge Road. But the price of fish meant they specialized in "scratchings," the stray fragments of batter remaining after frying. There wasn't enough optimism in Battersea, and that's a deficiency that can only exist so long. It instilled the people with a need to improve or get out, which, ultimately, was how Billy came to this clandestine place. "Meat and two veg" remained the staple diet for most people after the War. The average family rarely, if ever, ate out, except at the pub. There, they could eat potato crisps (three flavors; plain or salted—until Golden Wonder launched "cheese and onion" in 1962), a pickled egg to go on top, and perhaps a pasty or some cockles and whelks from the seafood man on a Friday or Saturday evening. These were luxuries in the Tumbler family.

The three of them; Billy, Gerry and Razor had provisioned the box with ample stores, at first in Woolwich and later in Durban. The provisions comprised tins of Heinz Baked Beans, Libby's milk, Heinz oxtail soup, Smedley's mushy peas, Lyon's tea, Kellogg's Corn Flakes, tinned OXO cubes (which he didn't know how to use), Crunchie bars, Smedley sliced green beans, two dozen eggs, bacon, Saxa salt, bottles of Tizer (Russell had explicitly forbid alcohol), Nabisco Premium saltine crackers, Lyles Golden Syrup, Kraft Old English cheese, Bassett's Liquorice Allsorts, cans of Hormel's Spam, Libby's tinned pineapple, dried sausages, potatoes and twenty jerrycans of potable water.

They consider a survival ration one quart of water per day. Billy had much more. The jerrycans, made from pressed steel, had been filled with fresh water two days before departing Durban. Designed in Germany in the 1930s, the military world unanimously agreed they were first class, and readily available everywhere. For cleaning he had a box of Sunlight soap bars, a small can of Swarfega, Bronco toilet paper, rolls of kitchen towels, toothbrushes and a container of Vim scouring powder. His hidden life was temporarily profligate compared to his childhood.

The following day, Billy returned to work. He had undertaken some calculations after eating the previous night. If there were three hundred bars of gold, then that would require—at a minimum—forty movements of bars each day; gold coming up and into the Engine, while gold-painted lead had to return to the deep tank. He considered that workable, barring any unforeseen events. He had food; he had water; he had electricity and somewhere to deposit waste. He could focus on the work at hand.

He wore gloves outside the box. That had been impressed upon him by Mr. Russell; it might only require one fingerprint, "and you're on record now, Billy." He brought up more gold bars and spread them on the steel tween deck. He had thought through his plan and realized that he required to clear all the pallets first. It was just not practical to move anything around in the deep tank. He emptied each box individually, the gold bars removed and laid on the tween deck before he could begin withdrawing the gold-painted lead bars from the floor of his home to replace them.

Once the first layer of pallets had been emptied, he sat for a while and practiced shining the torch in the darkness, reducing its light with his hand, just to see them shimmering, making a weird, artificial soup of bright colors in the semi-dark. The gold lay still, as cold as a corpse. It had taken roughly three days to sit and watch the dazzling display, and it prompted curiosity and reflection. Gold was the truth. "Here's the truth about the truth," Daniel had said, "It hurts. So we lie." More money sat before him than he could ever fathom. He giggled to himself at the insanity of it all; sitting here with all this money while men of his ilk—his previous brothers—went about their cleaning and painting above. All that gold made it momentarily difficult to recall who he was. Then, coming to his senses, he thought, *I'm Billy Tumbler. Don't open that hatch!*

He began extracting the lead bars from the floor of the Engine, moving them to the deep tank, lowering them, arranging the first pallet and first layer of boxes. There was no chance of confusing the gold and lead bars. They were different colors, but the weight was the discerning factor. He repacked the boxes with lead, closed and locked each one in two neat layers of six. Once he judged he had replaced them in the correct position, he used a Standard BAND-IT C-169 tool supplied by Razor, based on the information sent by Gerry. He pulled the steel tight—as tight as he could—and cut the band, leaving it much as before.

The calendar, upon which he had been dutifully striking off the days, suggested the voyage had been half accomplished. He rested that day and reflected. "Our business is not yet completed," Mr. Russell would have said. He cleaned his clothes the best he could and hung them near the ventilators, where he could breathe the air, freshly brined by the sea. He had pulled out all the gold now and had only to replace with the lead bars and arrange his vanishing act. Sitting on an empty jerry can, he relaxed and glanced at the work so far. He felt satisfied. There was more to do, but he had broken its back. His tiny, one-bedroom flat he boasted all to himself, a small kingdom to clean each day, without too much exertion. Later, sitting on the edge of his camp bed, Billy reconciled his feelings as one of privilege. For such a poor man, that was difficult to understand, but the more he considered it, the truer it was. He had, all to himself, this tiny domain, his own secret sovereign realm. It was his to cook the food he wanted. No one ever using the toilet or the bath (a large flat dish upon which he stood and sponged himself down). He could take mighty handfuls of paper rolls instead of newspaper squares and, using as much water as he liked, along with a bar of soap, wash himself down and dry. As long as he kept all evidence in the box, he could do as he wished for nearly eighteen days.

One quiet night, he ruminated on the recent past. When his father worked only intermittently, he couldn't see how he—Billy—could ever gain anything from life. Ambition and hope became an enigma to him, regardless of how well his teachers thought of him. His mother believed God had cursed the family. The silence of the night reminded him of his long, lost innocence. Billy couldn't remember many days too well, but it had been a cheerful childhood, filled with affection. Life was carefree, or terribly painful; always one or the other, never comfortable. His mother's funeral had been the last time he had seen so many distant family and friends. They had all stared at the stigmatized young man, and he had never felt so alone in his life. For sure the onlookers blamed him for her demise, and the chasm between him and them became too considerable to be bridged. He would be an outcast for the rest of his life. Sally's voice occasionally came to him in support, but he still despaired for what he had done to his mother.

He noticed that his senses had heightened because of the darkness, perhaps. Or was it the solitude? He missed Sally's touch so much. "Billy, we need to talk," and he smiled. He felt the soreness of his legs with all the hauling and climbing, but in some fashion, it felt good to use his body; he could feel everything in this senseless world. He experienced the ache of his limbs, and the natural, gentle roll of this fine ship. He occasionally heard the work of the sailors above, their faint voices through the ventilators. It had taken ten days, but for the first time in his life he believed he would rise from the lowly station that his father, or God, or just life had given him. Everyone knew the son should be better than the father; that was what they called progress. He knew from an early age once he had figured out that whatever his father's problem—which he would never understand—he would have to support himself. With your mentors and heroes, the best he could do was to rise to their level. But his father had walked out creating a profound psychological scar. Once a life on the river evaporated, where would that leave him? Following in the steps of the muffin man, the salt seller or the knife sharpener, living on the street? His mentors and heroes were someone else now. And he so wanted to be free somewhere; Australia, perhaps, so far away from the cruel life of Battersea. And he would be with Sally forever.

Three days from Southampton, as best as he could determine—there had been no foul weather—the entire palleted contents of the deep tank were returned in place, except that the gold now lay on the floor of the Engine and the pallets contained three hundred gold-painted lead bars. The BAND-IT tool had performed well in Woolwich, but down here in the deep tank, constrained for space, he had found it challenging to tie the boxes to the desired (original) tension. The winch, the wire, the shear legs had all been returned to safe stowage in the crate. After a splendid meal of fried spam and mushy peas, followed by a can of peaches and Lyles Golden Syrup, the next morning he set to throwing the mail bags back into the deep tank.

He stood and shone his torch. He didn't expect he'd disregarded anything. So, he sat, and then he lay down, and thought through every stage of the entire enterprise. He could think of no flaw, so laying there, boredom became his worst enemy. The following day he cleaned the studs of the manway, replaced the steel opening, reattached the nuts and painted the entire area with a fresh coat of white paint.

Billy believed he had become "one of us." And they were Billy. He thought about all the failures and blunders and how to face them. At the outset of his life, he was sure he was one type of man, only to fall into these circumstances and discover he was another man all together. In discovering who he now was, he felt that he might develop into the son he always wanted to be. If he fell shy of that ambition, he could fall back on the recognition he was, after all, only a human. The word "adventure" seemed a little cheap.

The next day he heard the crew of the ship opening the dogs that secured the steel hatch covers. He heard the *Aphrodite May*'s engine changing its tone. Billy returned to inside his aluminum and wooden house, closing the door tightly behind him. They were arriving to

Southampton. He was carrying the pot of gold at the end of the rainbow, and nobody had seen Billy Tumbler coming.

THE BOAT

Second-hand gold is as good as new.

- Ken Alstad

March 08, 1963 - Battersea

ON THE SAME DAY THE *Aphrodite May* left Durban, in the Prince Albert snug, Peter Badger sat and stared suspiciously at the two men sitting opposite. Something was plainly coming his way, which he would ordinarily take in his stride, but this felt somehow strange.

"We really appreciate this, Peter," said John Russell. Then, taking a gulp of his Bass Ale, he added, "Bag of crisps?"

"On the house, Peter, the new cheese-and-onion flavor. Just in," avowed Daniel Geddes.

On their visit to Wrigglesworth's demonstration, Russell and Geddes had both quickly come to the same conclusion, once they recognized there was a canal running past his property. On the return ride in the Aston Martin, they had run the scenario through in conversation without understanding if the idea was credible. Neither had any notion how the canal system worked. They waited until after the meeting with the entire crew before sitting down a few days later for an amicable chat. After a few minutes of explanation, Peter grasped the idea, and its inventiveness surprised him.

"No need to bribe me, lads," stuffing his hand into the bag of strangely-seasoned crisps, quickly becoming acquainted with the flavor. "Stow the gold on my boat? I want this to work as much as anyone. It's a...interesting idea," he frowned in deep thought, or was he just savoring the innovative taste? He remained quiet for a minute as the other two gazed on hopefully. "I'm just thinking it through. The narrowboat will have to keep moving—cruising, we call it—otherwise it won't work. We can't just park my boat at Biggles's place. The law is bound to turn up sooner or later and rummage around."

"Right, but the boats have engines, yeah? We figured you could just drive it around for a few months," Russell suggested, but Peter grimaced at the suggestion. "It'll be like a holiday. Take the missus," he coaxed.

Peter shook his head slowly and explained his position: "Well, that's where the idea falls down, don't it? The law will come looking for me, we can assume. How do we explain that I'm not at home with Maria? You know she's always got something going on with her charity stuff. For that matter, we're all known, so they're gonna be stopping round everyone's place asking questions, flashing warrants, including Biggles's probably."

The three of them sat scrutinizing the options and sipping beer. Why had they not resolved this matter months ago? They had mulled over so much, but assumed they would just bury the gold at Wrigglesworth's place, or stash it in a lockup somewhere. Now those options no longer seemed adequate, but they just might have to revert to an unknown garage in North London. Nobody wanted to leave the gold unattended anywhere.

"Hold on, are we stupid?" exclaimed Daniel. "One of us is not even known to the police!"

"Billy?" questioned Russell.

"Exactly. As far as anyone knows, he's gone to sea for a year. He's perfect," confirmed Daniel with a strong sense of triumph.

"And I assume he can steer a boat too—that's a bonus," said Peter, dryly. But he had to admit, that was another good idea.

That evening at home, Peter dragged out his bundle of maps and studied the route from Watford (where his narrowboat sat out of the water) to Napton on the Hill. It was a long way. He had never really ventured on such voyages before. Traveling with Maria, they would set out on a morning, or sometimes not, and just appreciate wherever they finished for the day. If they encountered a quiet place to tie up the boat by lunchtime, it wasn't unusual to remain there, and if they moored nearby a village with a pub, so much the better.

After an hour studying and smoking cigarettes, he determined that it would probably take him a week to drive the boat to somewhere remote, but safe, near Napton. To do so single-handedly, however, might pose a challenge. The more he contemplated and smoked, the surer he believed he required another hand. He advised the other two, confidently, that another member of the gang would have to assist, but the timing was not good. They had surveillance commitments in Southampton; there really wasn't anyone available, and John Russell was reluctant to bring another professional in. That would cost money and add another hole to the possibility of leaking.

For the profit of everyone, the answer revealed itself to Peter early the following morning while he lay in bed with Maria. He waited until after breakfast, then called his sister on Canvey Island in Essex, about thirty miles east of London. Mary had a teenage son named Davy— along with three daughters—who had already shown interest in Peter's boat. Without revealing the ultimate intention, Peter suggested Davy might assist him in moving his boat to Warwickshire for a stipend of twenty pounds. Mary knew of Peter's illegal activities, but this offer didn't raise any suspicions. He then called John Russell and disclosed the move would not be an issue after getting the new engine installed and refloating the narrowboat.

* * * *

The British canal system in 1963 remained a legacy of the industrial revolution, but was recovering, slowly, from the lowest of times. Narrowboats were once the working transport of the preceding three centuries, a highway laid with water, hauling cargoes from one place to another; coal, fresh produce, cement, finished goods, everything. They were the innovative transport system of their day, outcompeting the horse and cart on furrowed lanes.

As commerce developed without standardization, many realized the chaos that might ensue, until the Trent & Mersey Canal Company established locks (used to ascend or descend uneven terrain) capable of holding a boat seven feet wide and seventy feet long. The proportions, although seemingly picked from thin air, were considerably narrower than vessels using nearby rivers. But, by necessity, they chose the dimensions because of a requirement to build a tunnel under Harecastle Hill; the thin proportions were an expediency. This matured into the standard size on all subsequent canals of The Midlands, the nucleus of industrial Britain, as the country manufactured the goods for a waiting empire of commerce.

Customarily, earlier on, families lived together on a boat drawn by a horse on a towpath, while working as unpaid crew. Generations were born and lived in the tiny interior space of the narrowboat, surrounded by decorative brass work, ornate china and that distinctive, flowery script for ornamentation. Sometimes the horse-drawn boat towed a second dumb barge called a "butty." As time passed, the economic conditions inevitably shifted with competition from the railways. Towards the end of the nineteenth century some companies introduced boats powered by steam engines, working nonstop day and night. The disadvantage of this method being that the engine, boiler and coal needed for each trip consumed much of the cargo space, and the additional crew required ruined any economic advantage. Only the introduction of the diesel engine sustained the industry.

In 1948, after years of neglect, and then war damage, they nationalized the waterways, creating the British Transport Commission. But traffic had sunk to an all-time low trying to compete with the roads and railways. Despite some attempts at revitalization, by the early 1960s too many working boats were surplus to demand, so the Commission—which changed its name to British Waterways in 1962—discontinued most of its narrowboat carrying activities. Many boats had been frozen in during the terrible winter, left to decay in lonely, unused canal arms. From afar, the history of the canals appears charming, quaint and photogenic, but it doesn't pay to look too closely. The existence of child labor, substandard conditions and a marginalized roaming people living unorthodox lifestyles encouraged the spread of negative judgement upon boatpeople across the country.

There had been rumors of closing the canals as the country rushed headlong into a modern age of speeding transport on diesel trains and electrified rails, along with the introduction of high-speed motorways. It was difficult to make the argument for cargoes moving at three miles per hour, other than freedom of choice and the pure joy of it. It didn't transpire in one glorious moment, but slowly the public recognized they could use the enchanting canal routes for pleasure craft as the commercial traffic dwindled. Not surprisingly, entrepreneurs produced many early pleasure boats from ex-working examples. Peter, with his own dubious background, already exhibited an unspoken affinity for those inhabiting the vagabond life of the waterways, with their own customs, traditions and colloquialisms. He had acquired his boat from boatbuilders in Bumble Hole, just west of Birmingham, that had recently expanded into the pleasure construction business. Fortunately, they didn't close the canals, surrendering them to a splendid second life, and destiny, in the recreation business.

People and businesses began building purpose-built narrow beam pleasure boats, based on the old design, for which they had established the entire system anyway. In 1963 there were still a few thousand miles of inviting, navigable canals and rivers throughout the nation, with one continuous system stretching from Bath in the South West to Ripon in North Yorkshire, along with detours south to London. There were suddenly sixty hire companies operating on the canals. People enjoy narrowboats, if not as a source of income, primarily because the pace of life is slower than their daily routine, and they transport them into closer contact with nature. Like parks, canals serve as green lungs for the cities and are home to a tremendous diversity of wildlife. Boaters took much pleasure from the sound of gently lapping water and the nearness of the ubiquitous ducks and swans. When alongside in rural areas, the word "tranquility" came to mind, which they considered a major enticement for city-dwellers, amongst the peaceful world of landscapes. But make no mistake, the entire system needed repairs, maintenance and investment.

There was a robust understanding of community on the water, since canal living is idyllic, but occasionally strenuous. There were on-going repairs, maintenance and other demands to keep the boats operational, so canal dwellers generally supported each other. Most people one met were just nice, although sometimes eccentric. The nomadic character of canal folk helped connect different communities along the waterways. It was a rustic way of life too, which meant fresh air and exercise, creating a curious, but often hidden existence.

**   *   *   ***

Now, by early March, the weather had improved considerably. It wasn't hot, but there were some fine and sunny days. Peter took the phone call from Watford confirming his narrowboat was back in the water with a refurbished twenty-two horsepower Armstrong Siddeley diesel engine installed for £120. "I got taken care of," he advised anyone who might listen. He had sought to apply much of his schedule to the work, but other interests had intervened which, a few weeks earlier, would never have questioned his time. Peter thought with all the work and the use of his boat, then maybe he—Peter—merited a second share. He considered proposing the idea to Russell and Geddes. Then he thought again.

On March 12, Peter was nearly ready to move. The night before he had completed painting the new name, without using the word "gold", on John Russell's instructions. He accumulated a week's supply of food for the journey. He admired the boat and wanted soon to complete the refurbishment when it would be fully ready for his beloved Maria. The next day, he picked up his nephew Davy from Fenchurch Street railway station in the City and drove to the west of Watford. The large town lies just northwest of London on the Metropolitan Line of the London Underground, but he took the car anyway. Bridgewater was a minor place in the suburbs of West Watford, where the River Gade runs close to the Grand Union Canal Main Line. The small boatyard lay on the east bank of the canal just north of Croxley Green railway station and just south of the Underground branch line that terminated nearby. It was one of those maintenance places where people worked on their boats intermittently, sold diesel, propane, and tried to supply anything else the burgeoning industry might require.

Peter devoted an hour talking to the boatyard manager on the ins and outs of the new engine (refurbished). Upon returning to his waiting nephew he stated emphatically, "Can't really complain, but I will." Davy stood and listened, but wanted to begin the voyage. One benefit of living on a narrowboat is its convenience. Peter conducted a few housekeeping chores before moving, doing his best to explain his endeavors. He liked the young man. His relationship with the extended family did, sometimes, feel strained. Although he could not admit it, his own illegal activities caused the stress, with which he did not wish to be confronted.

He never minded clambering down into the engine bay and getting his hands dirty. He reviewed the level and cleanliness of the oil, then turned the greaser tap marginally to pressure the stern gland. He opened the rectangular weed hatch above the propeller to ensure it was free of obstructions. Then he turned the key, appraising the control panel lights: engine battery indicator, domestic battery indicator, temperature and oil pressure. He allowed the engine to idle for a few minutes, while he gave Davy some instructions. He could digest more details over the next few days. People like narrowboating because it's straightforward. "I'll give ya a bit of a demo," he said before letting his nephew do anything.

Davy stepped ashore, taking the center line with him, letting go the bow and stern lines. He pushed the boat—weighing some twelve tons—a few feet out into the canal. At the last moment he athletically stepped back aboard, and shimmied along the gunwale, while Peter slicked the gear lever forward. He might have wished Maria was along for the ride, but there was always something exciting about setting off; the sense that the scenery, traffic and weather were always changing. Life on the canals never felt routine, and he could see himself owning a boat—a better one—into older age. They had begun their low-speed, casual adventure to Napton, a place Davy had never heard of. Peter had visited Wrigglesworth's estate to facilitate setting up the gold transformation process, but had not seen the canal. It was well into the morning on a crisp spring day, so Peter expected a delightful ride heading north and northwest. He had in the cockpit with him a map, and Davy on call to make tea and a cheese sandwich when required.

The first day, although time-condensed, fairly characterized the next seven. When piloting from one place to another, the distance is, naturally, of first consideration. But when proceeding by narrowboat, perhaps the foremost issue is how high you have to ascend, or how low you have to descend. To achieve either in a narrowboat required the handling of locks, the distinguishing feature being a fixed chamber in which one can vary the water level. Water navigation locks work on an uncomplicated process which dates back over a thousand years. This added some physical activity and time, but was generally fun work, breaking up the uniformity of dawdling along. If all worked well, a fortunate boater might dismiss a lock in fifteen to twenty minutes, but if the lock were busy and queues occurred, they could easily lose an hour. Peter had assumed a journey of seventy-eight miles and seventy-nine locks from Bridgewater to Napton Junction, and he relished the trip.

Some boats have a steering wheel and vaguely act on similar principles to directing a car. Peter's boat had the more traditional tiller, an idea that has existed since man first took fallen trees onto the water, and they are more responsive than wheels. The slightest alteration of the tiller will cause the craft's bow to turn left or right, which is beneficial because it enabled Peter to visualize and sense the movements; that innate ability to understand the result of your brain's instructions. Pushing a tiller to the left causes the boat to turn right, and vice versa. It can unsettle when first attempted, but the point to remember is that narrowboats pivot about their center; if the bow turns right, the stern goes left. Couple this with the circumstance of Peter standing at the stern of his sixty-foot craft, with a woeful field of vision, and it requires a great deal of good sense. But the process is mostly uncomplicated, aided by the reality he traveled so slowly. The key is to anticipate what's ahead and correct in small, gentle actions. The essence of narrowboating is leisureliness. Peter acknowledged this and resolved to operate as it pleased him, at his own pace, remembering he was the owner and master of his vessel. Lacking brakes, he needed to give himself sufficient time to arrest forward motion. Therefore, judicious use of the reversing gear would be essential. Boating should never be a contact sport.

Beginning north under the conclusion of the Metropolitan Line, they quickly came across Cassiobridge lock. Like all locks on this stage of the Grand Union, it was double-sized, made to accept wide-beamed boats, or a narrowboat and its butty breasted up together. Peter shouted Davy's instructions, and he responded enthusiastically, checking the lock's readiness and opening the two downstream gates. Peter chugged the boat inside and threw a line up to his nephew who secured it. He then closed the gates and opened the upstream sluices to fill the lock chamber. This was where the second hand became essential; a lone boater being nearly unable to control his craft in a gushing lock, along with the difficulty of climbing out of a deep, wet-sided chamber. And anyway, Peter liked Davy and thought better of inviting him to become involved in his other business. They departed the lock successfully and set out through a green park appearing lusciously agreeable in the spring sunshine, the snow piles slowly dissolving, revealing life underneath.

There were a few accepted problems of narrowboating. One is being knocked overboard if the tiller caught on an unseen obstruction. Peter stood ahead of the tiller to steer in the plentifully open cruiser stern, looking straight along the roof of the boat, finding it easier to navigate through bridges and into locks without bumping the sides. A second well-understood drawback for boaters, when descending in a lock, is to avoid the physical structure of the sill, a narrow horizontal ledge protruding a short way into the chamber from below the upper gates. As the water goes down, the boat descends along with it, and those on the boat must ensure the rudder doesn't catch. Otherwise, the essence of a pleasant cruise is to remain in the canal center and avoid other boats. Peter readily settled into a casual, yet observant, routine, glad of the gentle breeze in his face and that delicious feeling of freedom.

In the pleasant Home County of Hertfordshire, the River Gade runs alongside the canal occasionally, but at Rounton, just north of Watford, the canal makes a few abrupt turns and, after the Hunton Bridge locks, heads out into the agreeable, suburban countryside of Metro-land, filled with its idyllic Tudor Revival houses for the successful commuters of North London.

Trial and error are incomparable educators. Peter, although he cherished his new boat, confessed not to be the nation's greatest boat handler, and accepted he had to allow Davy some time at the tiller. Blunders are the cornerstone of learning, and he soon recognized that his nephew's proficiency was improving. He kept his wits about him, fully aware of his surroundings, never drifting in to sloppy gaffes. For Peter, he delighted in the entire enterprise of boating, the capacity to overlook the burdens of another world, to even forget the purpose of the journey. What did it matter for these brief early days of spring? This was a safe journey through water only three- or four-feet deep; nothing to worry about, and nothing like what he imagined young Billy would currently be undergoing. When John Russell had explained to the listening professionals the enterprise that Billy would undertake, Peter, like the rest of them, was impressed. He shook his hand, enthralled by the courage of the young man to undertake such duties. He quickly became Billy's friend and mentor. Once they completed the caper, he, like the others, could see the resolution of one life and the creation of another.

Just north of Nashmills they turned northwest. Peter missed his Maria, but this was work, sort of. Soon it would all be over and he could let go of all the built-up pressures and resentments. He envisaged where they might live one day, as he moved through the farmland, slowly becoming the new town of Hemel Hempstead, growing to house the slum-and-bombsite-inhabitants of London.

They chugged slowly along through open fields, turning green as the snow finally disappeared. He traveled through green tunnels of overhanging fresh-leafed trees, passed pretty, scenic cottages and oddly incurious cattle. The first signs of spring were a welcome sight after the bitter days of this winter, signaled by the sound of birds, and the sight of buds on trees and early spring snowdrop flowers. Peter might not have known the names, but he was gladdened enough to see skylarks, song thrushes, and blackbirds. Passing the odd copse and hedgerow, their once-bare branches were beginning to bloom. There were an occasional, fleeting, fabulous burst of cherry blossom heralding a signal for nature to generally yield what it had in its underground store for the season's arrival.

The Grand Union Main Line occasionally runs alongside a railway, the West Coast Main Line from Euston to Glasgow, with the canal forming its prominent predecessor. Its primary line starts in London and ends in Birmingham, stretching for 137 miles. It has arms to other towns, including Leicester, Slough, Wendover, Aylesbury and Northampton. It was, and remains, the nation's longest canal. As the pace of life trended slower the further from the capital he piloted, it took him into closer contact with the awakening nature of the landscape and it felt somehow noble. Turning west, Peter halted for the night before the Boxmoor bottom lock, right near the Fishery Inn, close to the River Bulbourne and the A41 trunk road. Before dinner and drinks, Peter quickly assessed the day's workload; fourteen locks dispatched, and they'd raised the boat nearly ninety-four feet—a good start on the climb to the Chiltern watershed. He was glad he'd bought Davy along.

A week later, they drove the narrowboat south on the Oxford Canal, ambling away from Napton. It's a charming village on a hill, from which the locals can see seven counties on a clear day. They dispatched nine miles and ascended nine locks.

They found a reasonably safe mooring about a mile short of Griffins Bridge near open fields with a good towpath. Peter doubled the mooring for safety. They disembarked, and as they walked to the Banbury Road, carrying their bags, Davy conveyed his thanks to his uncle. They hitched a ride back into Napton and phoned for a ride to London while they drank in their shared familial experience at the King's Head public house. Peter knew it had been a week's work, but he had enjoyed the company of his nephew. Having said that, he anticipated the welcoming arms of his Latina maiden tonight.

* * * *

A week or so later in Southampton, on March 27, Peter had jumped onto the flat bed of the Atkinson Mk 1 lorry, squeezed inside the Engine and came back out holding—precariously because of its frighteningly, implausible weight—an eleven inch solid bar of glistening bright gold! "He's got 'em, he's really got 'em," and carelessly tossed the brick to Geddes, who too, was astonished by its heft.

He passed it to the still smiling John Russell, who weighed the bar in his palms, shook his head slowly, then passed it to Arthur, whose response summed up the consensus in that understated English manner they all understood, "Sterling work, young man."

"Okay, let's get this lorry dressed up and out of here," ordered Russell. They stopped celebrating and rolled up their sleeves. Early in the planning, they had decided Arthur would continue driving the lorry north, accompanied by Razor. He would, naturally, transform his identity before embarking on the added, longer, run. Second, Daniel would drive to Battersea to pick up a young lady.

They set to work on the Atkinson, disposing of the hubcaps to alter the wheel color from red to black. Razor climbed atop the cab with his screwdriver in hand and began clearing away the "Robinson" sign. Three of them draped a large green canvas over the wooden crate, with the expression "Smith's Grocery" on each face. They discarded the license plates and replaced them. Geddes, Russell and Arthur walked towards a fifty-gallon oil drum out on the open river side of the building. They removed their outer clothing, hats, makeup and tossed them in, pouring in a small dose of petroleum and setting it alight. Billy strode to the riverside, stretching out his arms and bouncing about, heady with a job well done, venting all that pent-up reckless energy, inhaling the sweet smell of fresh air, the bright sunlight and space to move. He was alive again.

It was a quick, rough-and-ready conversion, but they needed to return the lorry to the road quickly, while modifying its general color and shape. It wasn't much, and it wouldn't pass close muster. If there were roadblocks, it wouldn't help at all, but the priority was to move. Arthur returned to the cab as a cockney driver with a full set of black hair and absconded north.

Last, John Russell, with a new Jaguar Mark X, would take Billy and Peter as quickly as possible to the unnamed towpath of the Oxford

Canal near Napton on the Hill, where Peter had left the boat a few days earlier. In the large boot of the car, he carried five newly acquired, genuine London Good Delivery gold bars. They pulled out of the warehouse and took the A335 towards Eastleigh where, early the following morning, British Railways scheduled the steam locomotive *Wadebridge* to pass through. They were about twelve hours ahead of George Smith.

* * * *

In Battersea, the young Sally Dawkins had grown up within a stone's throw of Clapham Junction. Her only house move had put her even closer; so close that the regular rattling of passing trains had become, somehow, comforting to her. When recently she had lain in bed alone, the darkness swirled around her curled form as she endeavoring to understand where her Billy had gone and when he might return. Only the reassuring irregular noise made her feel safe and secure, like she had her own smoking, breathing industrial ogre outside protecting her.

She thought of Battersea as a strange part of London. The enormous, coughing, rattling, smelly junction was where you stood and looked into the city, not quite a part of it, because Battersea didn't have an Underground Station. How could they have missed that? The borough with the largest, busiest station in the country lacked a connection on the Tube. This infrastructural anomaly had played a mighty part in creating the community of Battersea. Yes, it was south of the river. Yes, many thousand commuters passed through every day, but somehow the city thought of them as outside, or inferior. The people of Battersea—deservedly proud in their own village—had taken that upon themselves and crafted their own idiosyncratic, and hardy, modest world.

Although it was true hers and Billy's families had moved on, and many friends were escaping the rapid bulldozing of the Victorian terraces, Sally still had a network of acquaintances. When not cleaning the mansions of Chelsea, or assisting at the "Antiviv," she worked for the Royal Voluntary Service, which everyone called the Women's Voluntary Services, or more likely, the "WVS." The organization had developed to help isolated and lonely people, particularly the elderly. After a day's service, she returned to embroil in the fraying lives of her neighbors, or she walked out with her friends Joany, Mags and Kitty to Maggie Brown's Pie and Mash Shop on Battersea High Street. They had grown up together and remembered picking up fruit and vegetable scraps behind the barrows on Northcote Road, helping to feed their families. Now she had the money (from Daniel), to buy the best servings. No more scratchings from the Fish & Chip shop. Sally lacked guile and complexity. What you saw was what you got. She was the beating heart of any group, but she wasn't a raw extrovert, and had a softer, more comforting side to her. Although never religious, she had, in her quieter moments, always maintained a noble dignity based on her humanistic belief in people. She supposed everyone was good at heart, except John Russell. She disliked her friend's occasional racist remarks aimed at the new West Indian immigrants. Sally saw them for what they were, just poor like them, trying to get on. She didn't judge people, but abhorred the English history with all its guns and wars.

It was a time when homosexuality and abortion remained illegal. Joany had become pregnant before her seventeenth birthday with a man from Putney, who everyone disliked. She was intent on avoiding what she believed, more and more, to be a dead-end marriage. Mags hung onto an unfaithful husband because the alternative meant going on National Assistance and starving. Kitty announced that her brother had a young tart up the spout. It was a time of casual sex and casual violence. The youth-driven cultural revolution was just about to arrive, but Battersea was solidly working class, and would begin swinging a little later than the West End. These young friends did what they had to do to keep going. They had few expectations other than keeping a job, so the nights out were an escape; gossiping, dancing, and drinking; never wondering further afield than the Junction area.

Sally felt privileged. She had her Billy, and committed to always sympathetically judge the less fortunate rather than enviously staring up at the monied class. Her mind sometimes drifted, worried that all this talk of money might come between her and Billy, and that made her sadder than anything else.

Sally had purchased a black dress three weeks ago for her work at the WVS. She enjoyed the liberation of the shorter dresses, but thought it inappropriate for voluntary service. She had, against her better judgement, bought it from a tallyman on the "never-never." In their world of survival, many acquisitions were on hire purchase and the tallyman visited every week to collect the payments. It was the slippery, "wide boy" Harry Lewis from Brixton, a man living in a prior existence, the archetypical predatory male of the species, with a fondness for misquoting Shakespeare. He drove around in an Austin ½ ton van, but compensated with his elegant, though loud mix of Teddy Boy-and-spiv dress sense which he thought made him appealing to the ladies, young and old. In the back, the small-time crook carried his specialized goods; plastic-wrapped dresses, lingerie, makeup and premium orders. He made good money selling to people too confused by the mathematics of hire purchase, installments, and interest. He sought, in particular, the new arrivals from the West Indies because they struggled with the concept. His modus operandi was to keep returning, receiving a never-ending supply of interest, long after they had settled the debt, confusing customers as to exactly what they were paying for. But Harry's hidden side, along with no morals and no backbone, was he enjoyed taking advantage of a situation, regardless of who caused it. Life was there for taking the best of the moment, typically during the day when women were alone. Sally didn't like his quick-talking, superficial manner based on greed and materialism, nor his tactic of viewing women voraciously, nor the threat he implied when people couldn't pay.

He stood at her door on Grant Road in his rakish trilby hat, drape-shaped jacket and bright pink tie "C'mon Sally, you need to pay me 'ten-bob'." He stood there confident, animated and cocksure because he thought it looked manly. "Is your Billy away again, Sal?"

"Yeah, but I got the money. 'Ow much total do I owe ya?" she asked.

"There's no rush with the money, Sal. Maybe I can keep ya warm on these frosty nights," he said as he leaned closer, stepping inside the open door.

His brazenness surprised her. "I got my Billy, Harry Lewis, and I'll have none of that talk." But the young, uncompromising man saw the situation from his own, sociopathic point of view. Here was a young, cute woman, all alone for months and he would make sure, eventually, she recognized him as a provider of all things pretty. And she would keep the bed warm at nights.

Standing too close to Sally, he made ready to make his next move as she stepped back, when the dull outside light from the doorway darkened slightly. His oily, smiling face turned slowly to find a gray-suited man standing three steps below on the pavement. "Who are you, grandad?" The man, staggeringly self-assured, then slowly climbed the three steps and filled the doorway, a clear head higher than most people Harry had seen. He wasn't lanky either; there were muscles on him.

"It's all right, Mr. Geddes, 'Arry was just leaving," said Sally.

"Geddes?" muttered Harry, turning pale and shrunken, "Daniel Geddes?"

"I have one question," the man in the doorway declared.

"Look, I don't want no trouble. Me and Sally are an item. Aren't we Sal?" he announced, trying hard to work out why this known criminal was standing in her doorway.

"Like I said, I have one question," said Daniel Geddes.

"What?" replied Harry Lewis, reaching slowly into his pocket for a knife.

The monumental man smiled contemptuously. "How the fuck are you gonna get outta this hallway," said Geddes, with that deep, unequivocal, slashing voice that intimidated so many.

Sally Dawkins, viewing the two men dripping masculinity, a cocktail of urgency and menace hanging in the air, stepping between them, stood, hands on hips, and said in a brash voice, "Daniel Geddes, just you behave yourself!"

* * * *

On the drive north in the Jaguar, the three men chatted, for once Peter being out-talked by someone else. John Russell began: "Well, for good or bad, you're one of us now, Billy." Loyalty was human, natural and likeable, and Billy, indeed, felt as if he were now one of them.

"I never really belonged until now," Billy answered surprisingly.

He then recounted again and again every element of his adventure, finding more detail and significance with each retelling. For a change, Peter enjoyed listening and became slightly envious. John Russell sat mostly in silence, especially when Peter began the army stories from Malaya, and thought to himself, the passing miles acting like a swinging clock, closing out the nearby talking and concentrating his mind. We've done it, but now it gets harder. Somewhere in his mind he must have believed they would not succeed. He understood that the gold could never be an event by itself, isolated and complete. Is it too much?

* * * *

Briefly before Arthur's arrival near Napton in the Atkinson, Russell appeared in his Jaguar at The Grange a few miles away and dropped off the five gold bars. He and Wrigglesworth fleetingly discussed whether to fire up the melting process right then. Readily, they agreed that it would be worth handling them immediately, which would be easy to disguise, quick to move and uncomplicated to display for certain friendly dealers in Hatton Garden and beyond.

* * * *

There were six hundred thousand lorries in 1963 handling half the nation's freight, the rest being carried by rail and coastal shipping. A tiny portion still moved by barges on the canals. Arthur, although tired, became more and more comfortable in his new role, and he enjoyed chatting with Razor. They skirted Winchester, then proceeded north past Sutton Scotney and into the picturesque English countryside near Newbury, to a realm of green curves beyond the straight gray lines and sharp angles of London. Russell in his Jaguar had left him by now, but Arthur had practiced the route three times. After Abingdon, he passed west of Oxford, and turned onto the A44. After a few miles he swung right near Shipton-on-Cherwell, the route becoming the A423 after Bodicott or, as they knew it locally, the Banbury Road North. Near the village of Fenny Compton in Warwickshire, there is a turning towards the east where the short, country road leads to a remote, disused farm, passing over a long curve of the Oxford Canal. Arthur slowed and swung right into the narrow lane between green hedges and a few oak trees just beginning to bud. The lane led slightly uphill as it crossed the canal. On the far side, Arthur and Razor's arrival shattered the evening's calm. He halted the Atkinson, turned around, and backed it towards the bow of the newly-arrived narrowboat moored nearby.

Peter and Billy stood on the cruiser stern, having just moved the mile from where he left it. It was another step, one that some might not have believed could occur, but there they all were together again, just as planned. There were precious wasted minutes with more congratulations, until Peter announced, "Let's get our hands dirty."

John Russell arrived in the Jaguar and shouted, "Put your gloves on."

They began transferring the gold from the rear of the Atkinson to the bow of the narrowboat, taking the bars inside through the two swinging front doors. They removed the floorboards, and lifted out the six-pound ballast stones and supplanted them with gold bullion bars, so as not to sink the boat too deep in the water with the added weight. They neatly lined up the ballast stones alongside the canal in some high grass where they might be reused, replacing bullion bars consumed in the furnace's heat.

They couldn't secrete all the gold beneath the floorboards, so they laid the surplus along the floor with some rough cuts of plywood pinned on top. Peter lay down a few mats to make it easier to walk upon them, but there was no intention of admitting anyone other than the boat residents. Lights were lit inside to facilitate the work. Outside, as twilight began consuming the day, they used flashlights, but they were now in a rush to complete their endeavors.

As the last bars were being handed over, Geddes drove up in his Ford Zodiac with Sally sitting beside him, her face hardly visible above the dashboard. She jumped out, and embraced Billy for the first time in three weeks. She had been nervous and unbelieving on the journey north, but she had to leave with him if only some of what he was saying were true. She was one of life's smilers, and everyone could see that. The obviousness of their affection was clear for all those in attendance to witness. She wanted to be the laughing soul of their endeavors, but in Billy's arms she began sobbing. She brought the emotion on by holding Billy, naturally, but also because of the life-transforming events overtaking her. It had been an enormous struggle for Sally to quit London, to travel north of the river, for goodness' sake, to the shabby beyond. Her personality of the game heroine with Geddes had now grown into an emotion she couldn't keep inside. Arthur turned to Razor and proclaimed, as if an independent authority on the subject of women, "She's a real gem. One of a kind."

The Atkinson grumbled back onto the Banbury Road, paused, then lurched and shuddered away and, accompanied by the Jaguar and the Ford, set off into the distance; everyone heading south to substantiate alibis. Razor would take care of the lorry tomorrow in a large disposal dump near Croydon. The mechanical noises slowly withered away, leaving behind Billy, Sally and Peter alone on some unknown towpath in the blackness, where only the owls and mice stirred. The two sweethearts went down inside, hand in hand, confronted by the claustrophobia of it all. The boat amounted to four hundred and fifty square feet of space for the bedroom, the kitchen, and a small living area. Capacity was limited, but then the possessions of Billy and Sally had never amounted to much either. She had all she needed; the man she would marry. There were hidden closets and spaces that had more than one role, and a wood-fired stove to keep everyone warm. For convenience, Peter had installed a new Elsan chemical toilet. Even with the lack of space, the boat seemed homely. Peter had freshly painted the cabin cream. It felt open and bright. He was still adding Victorian frills and other fancy features, but there was running water, and plenty in the tank.

He came down into the cabin and declared the plan for the night; "The bedroom's at the front for you young lovers. I'll doss on the floor here tonight, and tomorrow we can start moving."

Billy had not said enough to everyone in the commotion and sentiment of the moment, so he said it for both of them to the only one remaining: "Thank you, Peter."

THE SEARCHERS

Governments lie; bankers lie; even auditors lie sometimes: gold tells the truth.

- William Rees Mogg

March 28, 1963 - New Scotland Yard

DETECTIVE INSPECTOR TOM HALLIWELL sat silent and alone at the large, brown table sipping yet another cup of tea. Physically, he felt well. Waking up early to the shrill cry of the telephone was no longer the jolting shock it used to be. But this day, he knew, would drag on and on. He didn't expect to return home while his wife remained awake, but that had become the pattern recently. He was forty-eight now and he thought again of asking for a transfer to more suitable work, like the Fraud Squad, perhaps. First, Tom, he thought to himself, with the splinters of age and wisdom growing about his eyes, let me put Russell and Geddes away. This time for a lengthy term, not a long weekend like the last stretch they did. He cherished the challenge of understanding, using his intelligence to discern what had transpired. Sometimes it was unmistakable, sometimes it took an extra effort, but he prided himself on getting there, eventually. Put the fragments of the puzzle together and seek out the result, walk the perpetrators into court and let the legal people do their business. Putting a felon in prison made all the long nights acceptable. Or at least they had until now.

The chief inspector burst into the room, an immense bundle of wide-awake energy, "Tell me everything, Tom. And where's everybody else?" as he strode purposely towards his chair at the head of the table, beneath the portrait of the Queen.

Halliwell brightened slightly from his dour thoughts, "Morning, Guvnor. Short and sweet, it looks like…and I emphasize 'looks like'… there was a robbery of *one*," again he stressed, "of two Security Express vans last night in Mayfair. Park Lane. The second van was untouched. The first one took off—we're guessing the driver was an inside man— took a corner too fast, hit a working maintenance hole in the road, rolled over and spilled its load of gold bars. Four villains apprehended, rather fortunately I have to say, but collared anyway."

That should have been it, end of story and satisfying too, but the chief had known Tom Halliwell a long time and read on his face the report had not yet concluded, nor was it as cheery as it first appeared. "And the bad news I feel must be coming?" he asked, frowning, wanting the truth quickly.

Almost painfully, Halliwell continued, "You genuinely won't like this. The three hundred bars of gold, in the two vans, are…all fake." The chief inspector stared intently, as if he somehow misunderstood Halliwell. He grimaced enquiringly. So Tom Halliwell underlined his recap, "Gold painted lead bars."

Finally, raising his tone noticeably, "You have got to be bloody joking!" Halliwell slowly shook his head, while the chief reconfirmed, "We tugged four criminals?"

"Oh, yes, some big ones, including David Walker and Brian Spicer. I forgot the other two, but I didn't know them. The detective on site confirmed they're from the same outfit; George Smith's men." Halliwell laid out the details.

"That bit sounds good…but I'm still not understanding. Did we know about this gold movement?" Tom slowly shook his head, but the chief inspector continued, "And you're telling me George Smith held up a van for nothing? I'm at a loss, Tom." Just then the door opened and two more squad leaders walked in. They used the room every morning to discuss ongoing cases. A brief "good morning" from everyone and Halliwell recapped the story. It wasn't much of a story, but the chief inspector was glad to hear it again, as if he might have missed something.

The door opened once more, and another detective stepped half inside, "S'cuse me Chief. I've got the ship, Tom."

"Go ahead," he told him.

"Ship called the *Aphrodite May* came into Southampton yesterday. Unloaded three hundred bars of gold for the Johnson Matthey refinery in Wembley, and a few hundred mail bags, all from Durban in South Africa," explained the detective.

"That's it," said Halliwell, slapping the table. Turning to the chief, "we've been watching the Union-Castle ships going to the Bank of England, and this is some…private sale, I s'pose. Might be industrial, I'm guessing."

"Shall we…" someone said, but the chief inspector held up his hand.

Finally, "I'm just trying to get my mind around this. Where is the crime here?"

"Well…" began Halliwell after a few moments of awkward silence, "either on the Security Express convoy, or the train, or…the ship?" He finished the sentence as if it might be a query. The room's tension exposed the need of the three junior officers to say something, to get outside and begin their work, but the chief was still running it through his head, probably horrified by the jurisdictional entanglements involved, but he headed the one group of detectives—the Flying Squad—that had some kind of freedom to range across political and geographical boundaries. Once he had that firmly established, and he had decided, he began;

"Brian," glaring at the younger, tall, blond-haired detective, "take three squad and get over to West End Central. Find the detective first onsite and go through the entire scene again, including getting up to Wembley and talking to Johnson Matthey. I'm afraid to say I'm not sure what you're looking for. I'll talk to West End Central, let them know you're coming." Turning to the middle-aged, balding detective to his right, "George. Take a day out on the trains. Talk to the driver, the guard, any passengers, people who work on the platforms, I don't know. That train sounds too suspicious for me. I'll call the Transport Police CID… and the Post Office Investigation Branch. They will want to get involved. It's a lot of work. And Tom," turning back to Halliwell, "take your chaps down to Southampton. Hopefully that ship is still there. Talk to the captain, the dockmaster, customs, everyone. Search the dock sheds and the ship. Find out what happened. I'll call ahead, including the Southampton constabulary. Work with them."

"I'd like to chat with Russell and Geddes, Sir," said Halliwell.

"So would I, but we have very little to go on, Tom, except supposition for now. We need more information first. Everyone gets back to me by late afternoon and we'll probably schedule another meeting same time tomorrow. Gentlemen, we need to know what happened here!"

Then, after a moment of intense reflection, much louder to the whole room, "Find that bloody gold!"

The police were up against the clock concerning the gathering of evidence, both from a legal point of view and from the well-accepted notion that evidence trails deteriorated as time went by. They were also short of money to fight the underworld, so suspicious practices had become more common with the overwhelming fight against hardcore project crimes. The program (unofficially) lent itself to presuppose who had committed the offence and then fabricating evidence. "Verballing" was the well-recognized process of concocting suspect statements from those arrested. Once in court it led to a dispute between who were more trustworthy; the police or the known criminal. The police had become frustrated at the legal arrangement, or just believed a criminal required diminution occasionally. This led to dubious confessions and the occasional planting of evidence, which begat corruption in the Metropolitan Police Force as a whole. Undoubtedly, some police income derived from crime, but not Tom Halliwell. He believed he was just smarter than the average thief, and would unerringly arrive at the truth. The more time and investment required to create these crimes, the more satisfaction he derived from their solving. He wasn't at the point of fitting up anyone yet with false statements or untrustworthy evidence.

And that was the start for the Flying Squad, glad to be out doing something. By the end of the day they had learned much, but nowhere near enough to solve the puzzle. They could reach no more resolution from Johnson Matthey other than their legitimate purchase of three hundred gold bars from the Rand Refinery in Johannesburg, South Africa. Their primary concern was, naturally, where did the liability for the missing gold lie? They needed to begin insurance claim procedures or to sue someone. Security Express was a different matter. Both drivers and, possibly, their co-drivers were under suspicion. They were being interviewed, except for the driver of the crashed van who had died on the scene. His partner was in hospital, seriously injured. They interviewed Detective Sergeant Alan Humble—who had an exemplary record and reputation—along with the uniformed officers in the convoy. Even at this early stage the Flying Squad could see not a chink in the story suggesting it might have happened other than the way it appeared. There was no evidence to back up the suggestion of a second car ready to assault the second van. They brought in George Smith for questioning and he remained in the cells at the West End Central Station overnight. They could keep him for forty-eight hours without charging, but how could they accuse someone of a crime without knowing how it had taken place?

The investigation concerning the train had progressed slower. Initial enquiries had begun at each stop along the route, but nothing more than cursory. The Post Office had joined in the investigation at Waterloo.

The General Post Office in the United Kingdom was a department of state, and asserted a special status. Mail in transit was, technically, the property of the Queen. It was the Royal Mail. They had legal powers to load her mail onto any train they deemed appropriate. These were called "Post Office Controlled Trains," and generally ran at night, with timing patterns set to ensure connections between trains for the purposes of the mail. British Railways could add any carriages they deemed appropriate, but ultimately those coaches were the responsibility of the railway and the Royal Mail had absolute responsibility for letters (as opposed to parcels).

They had not interviewed the driver of *Wadebridge* that night; he was taking a few days holiday and had disappeared, and the guard raised obvious suspicions, but again, he could not yet be interviewed. They would need more time to run down everyone involved.

Detective Inspector Halliwell was fairly disappointed in being dissuaded from confronting Russell and Geddes. He had asked C11 to monitor them while he led his squad on a trip down to the south coast, to the Port of Southampton. The chief had advised the city constabulary, the British Transport Police and Her Majesty's Customs and Excise that the "Heavy Mob" were coming.

They entered the docks just before lunch and the convoy of vehicles drove over all the railway lines and onto 26 Berth. As they did so, they saw before them the gray and beige hulk of the *Aphrodite May*, some hatches open, and two electric dock cranes hauling out goods from deep inside. Naturally, this was a politically charged convoy of law enforcement with some conflicted interests. Halliwell hoped his chief had laid out the perceived jurisdiction the way he saw it. Alighting from the Wolseley, he made it clear. "Please have them stop working cargo." Then he decided, initially, to lead a small group of himself, his best man, Sergeant Green and one Customs man aboard the ship to make the initial enquiries. He said it would be brief and then, ultimately, they would probably have to search the entire vessel.

The ship's officer of the watch led him to the captain's office at the highest point of the accommodation; a small, but well-kept room next to his own living quarters. Here, he met Captain Minghella and introduced himself and the others. The captain invited them to sit, and offered them alcoholic drinks, which all three declined.

"Captain," began Halliwell, "can you verify you have just brought a cargo of gold bullion from Durban?" Minghella readily confirmed the question he had been awaiting. He sat there in his comfortably worn, leather chair wearing his rarely used, dark blue full uniform because of the cold weather. It restricted his movement, and he felt clumsy. He disliked it enormously, and yearned to complete the cargo work and set to sea, heading for the Mediterranean where he could feel the familiar warmth again, heading back to Singapore and retirement. This was the vague and third responsibility he bore for accepting the ten thousand pounds. He had five thousand pounds safely hidden away, and he expected the second installment before sailing, having handled any official enquiries. He thought back to the negotiations with the so-called agent, Gerry Jansen, and almost smiled to himself. Who could imagine it would come to this? But he also felt comfortable that any questions could be answered truthfully, for the most part.

"Captain, forgive these ponderous questions. Did you personally witness the gold coming on board and being stowed on your ship?" added Halliwell.

"Indeed, I did. Signed a bill of lading accordingly. I have an original here for my files." He leaned back to his left and reverted with some papers, "As you can see, it's 'Accomplished'," meaning the receiver had taken possession and responsibility for the goods. His manner struck Halliwell as strange. He had asked a simple question, but here he was providing documentation straight away. But maybe it was just the display of law enforcement sitting before him.

"Do you keep documentation for every piece of cargo, Captain?" Halliwell pushed.

"Yes, I do, Inspector. We've delivered nearly fifty pieces so far from Durban." At that moment, Halliwell realized they were too late. What was the point of suspending cargo operations now, while they had already put dozens of pieces on the docks and they had disappeared the length and breadth of the country?

"But just to be clear," Halliwell went on, "you saw the gold actually coming onto your ship in Durban."

Minghella frowned and clarified, "No, not quite, Inspector. I and my chief mate witnessed the boxes 'said to contain' gold bullion." For emphasis, he showed the detail on the bill of lading. "Did we open the boxes and touch the gold? No. How would I know what gold looks like?" And that was the problem. Carriers never sign bills of lading corroborating the contents of packages. The document described four consignments (each of one pallet) containing so many boxes stated to contain so many gold bars. There was some scribbling on the bill of lading where someone—maybe the chief officer—had counted and confirmed the number of boxes. This is the manner in which ships carry goods. It would be unmanageable for anyone on the ship to verify the contents were gold of a certain standard, just as it would be unreasonable to confirm a cargo of oil was exactly as the name proclaimed on the chemical assay. Maritime lore did not expect ship's personnel to do this.

Back on the dock discussing the goods delivered so far, it was also obvious that nobody proposed the dock manager and the shed manager scrutinize each gold bar. They witnessed the pallets and boxes said to contain gold bullion being put on the dock. That was all.

Halliwell, learning this information, and not liking what he heard, then politely ordered—and they gave him—a thorough search of the shed and the *Aphrodite May*, adding "see if there's any gold paint." Captain Minghella had pointed out that delays cost money. The ship might face a claim for excess berth occupancy, and the shipowner might claim demurrage. Halliwell said he didn't know the answer to these problems, but he would organize a search anyway. After interviewing the captain more fully, along with the chief mate, the bosun and a handful of others, Halliwell returned to dockside and leaned against the car discussing with Sergeant Green their thoughts on the situation.

Green offered: "Guvnor, they can search that ship for six hours—they won't find anything. I was quite impressed with the security and, unless everyone on board is in a conspiracy, I don't see how it could have been done on the ship. I've two bets"—he always liked a wager, but it was just his way of clearing his head, Halliwell knew—"either they took the gold from the train, or it never went on the ship in the first place."

"I'm coming to the same conclusion, Fred," believed Halliwell, but he also knew they were missing something. Something disassembled and stowed away in a hopeless corner of his mind, where it was bound to rot.

They remained in Southampton until he felt the dead certainty that he was completely lost and it was getting dark. The Customs had gone through the documents for all goods discharged at the port and found nothing suspicious. Another department of HM Customs and Excise, the Waterguard—dark blue uniformed members who specialized in the rummaging of arriving ships seeking illicit contraband—felt that after nearly six hours they were confident that three tons of gold bullion had not remained on the *Aphrodite May*.

The following morning at 8:00 a.m., the three squad leaders met again with the chief inspector at New Scotland Yard, where a sense of frustration and disappointment hung heavy upon the air. This, they all knew, was not the way the business was supposed to transpire. The feeling of gloom was all-pervasive. Everyone knew they needed a break fairly quickly, and the arrest of George Smith and his minions only seemed to point in the wrong direction. Eventually, the chief inspector said it for all of them, "Someone is being very, very clever. I don't like it, and it's not the way the game is played. Or at least it never has been. This is becoming an embarrassment to Scotland Yard, and that is unacceptable. Am I missing something? Can we be sure the theft even occurred in the UK or the thieves were British?" he completed, his voice louder than normal. There was no answer, other than to knuckle down and hope for a break. The chief sent them out with the order, "Gentlemen, crack some heads today."

The questions plagued Halliwell. He didn't need a new theory because he hadn't had a first one. Perhaps he was looking at this all wrong. Maybe it wasn't how the crime was committed, but when.

He saw no point in returning to Southampton, so he sent Sergeant Green. Meanwhile, he put out feelers to his informants, including Charlie Riddle. He caught up on paperwork and, as soon as opening time came around, headed southwest, across the river, to Battersea. It was a journey he had taken many times; along Millbank, along

Grosvenor Road, keeping the river to their left, along the Chelsea Embankment, then crossing on the Albert Bridge. He needed to confront the two of them, develop some sense by their mannerisms as to their involvement. It wasn't a precise science, but he felt he could read the mind of the average thief.

The driver dropped him and waited outside the Prince Albert. He'd known these two men for many years, seen them enter his purview of serious crimes and grow in stature. He'd seen John Russell in his expensive shirts from Frank Foster, his quality cigars, the nights in Ronnie Scotts and the holidays in Cannes, all to give him a mock, polished and refined presence. London was an exciting city if you had money to spend, and these two always did. He'd also seen the results of their work for anyone who got in the way. Could you imagine being punched by an angry Daniel Geddes? To gaze into his viscously intense eyes when in a black mood demanded you look away. They were characteristic and interesting people, but prepared to cudgel anyone over the head who got in their way. Although the brains of this crew, Halliwell knew neither were afraid to get their hands dirty.

Stepping into the saloon bar, he found it empty, having just opened. Moving towards the bar, the barmaid appeared, "Good morning, Swoozie," he hailed.

"What can I get you, Inspector?" she asked, wearily, neither happy nor unhappy. He wondered how much she knew, but saw no point in asking. She'd seen him before. She behaved as if she'd seen everything before.

"Not right now, dear. Are Daniel and John round the back?" he asked. Disappointedly, she waved him in the office's direction, which he took to mean they were expecting him. C11 had already advised they had seen them for some considerable time in the pub the day before, and the evening before that. He knocked and entered the office.

"Good morning, gents. Expecting me?" They sat beside that old, broken down desk, as usual, drinking tea. The room was clean, but disheveled, and unspeakably dreary.

They greeted him amicably, then Russell added, in that superior manner of his, "How's the detecting going, Tom?"

"What do you know of last night's events in Mayfair?" asked Halliwell, pulling up a wooden chair.

"More than you, apparently. We read the papers, Tom." Geddes showed him the Daily Express; "Sensational Failed Bullion Heist in Mayfair." The police had not released the information concerning the lead bars and the Post Office insisted the details remain undisclosed for now until they had completed their enquiries. As far as anyone knew, it was a gold heist gone bad.

"There goes the neighborhood," smiled Russell.

"I've come to arrest the two of you," Halliwell offered, to stir a reaction. It was a low, ineffective play in such company, but he was still struggling to wrap his mind around recent events. Profiling had changed detective work, emphasizing the criminal rather than the crime. The known criminal had become the center of attention. Halliwell believed he knew who committed the crime, but as yet he could see no manner in making the case against them.

"They teaching comedy now at Hendon?" retorted Russell, and the two crooks laughed out loud. "You can't accuse the normally guilty-but-innocent-this-time, you know?"

"Word on the street is you're involved," baited Halliwell further. What was the matter with him this morning? He felt he was acting like his first day at work.

Geddes didn't take the bait, "The street's wrong, as usual."

"Suspicion of aiding and abetting an armed robbery and aiding in a criminal conspiracy. It's a serious offence to rob the Royal Mail." He continued fishing, but the two oversized men were not about to bite.

He admired their placidity and decried his own ineptitude inside. The two of them sat, implacable. Geddes took another sip of tea and scoffed at the idea, "Bit short of big hats to arrest us, aren't you, Tom?" Geddes liked Halliwell, as much as he liked any policeman. There was no milage in making enemies of the police, but best not to let him get ahead of himself.

"Who did they tug at the scene?" asked Reardon.

"I think you know David Walker and Brian Spicer?" answered Halliwell.

"Well, I'm buggered. Stand up man Walker is, but hardly nature's last word," pronounced Russell.

"Yeah, Dave's a bit heavy footed," added Geddes.

"You have alibis for two nights ago?" asked Halliwell.

Russell and Geddes smiled and slowly nodded, confident in their position. He regretting now beginning the entire conversation, as if they would crack. These men, he knew, would never bend for anyone. A few minutes later, angry at himself for his blundering ineptitude, Halliwell left. Could he possibly be wrong about them? He imagined he could hear the two of them laughing as he made his way outside to the car. Another useless day completed in the great annals of pointlessness.

Once he had gone, John Russell and Daniel Geddes sat quietly and pensive for a few minutes. Swoozie Popkin cracked open the door and said; "He's gone out the front."

Russell nodded and turned to Geddes, "Well, we survived first contact with the enemy."

"He'll be back. He seemed a little off form," replied Geddes after a few moments.

"Because he has absolutely no bloody idea, Daniel." John Russell overexaggerated his confidence, perhaps. He recognized where The Sweeney would go looking. Sooner or later the Fraud Squad would track down every box that came off the *Aphrodite May* and discover de Havilland had not received any jet engines. The narrowboat was a time bomb of evidence, but he could not envisage how Halliwell would ever find that. There were no witnesses and no fingerprints. And no one knew anything about Billy Tumbler. He felt they would have to hold their breath for a few months while Biggles went about his business, but so far, he was surprised at their success. And he could wait.

Outside, Halliwell was angry. These two were always guilty, even when they weren't. He slapped the car roof in frustration. This case was driving him mad. He knew, somehow, he just knew, that those two were involved, even though there were many firms working in London. The detective needs facts and Halliwell could see none here. How could they prove who stole the gold if they didn't know how they did it? He decided that not knowing was suddenly the worst feeling in the world. Having lost the illusory concept of control, a strange sinking feeling gnawed away in his belly.

God, they needed a break, just a crack in the case. He needed to retune his brain and wait for the concert to begin again. Just when Halliwell thought the day could not get better, the car window opened, and the driver poked his face out, "Radio call for you, Inspector."

They drove back across the river at high speed. The call had been good, but without details. Back at New Scotland Yard, he rushed to find Sergeant White at his disheveled desk, two down from his own, "What have you got?" he asked him.

"Five years ago, guess who served time in Durham with one John Russell?" replied White.

Halliwell stared back quizzically, "Who?"

"Gonville Wrigglesworth," he replied with some satisfaction.

Halliwell had decided as soon as the news of the crime broke that the gang—whoever they were—would need to melt the gold. They had a list of about a dozen possible smelters in and around the Greater London area. "Get the squad together, Chalky. I'll get the chief on board."

The United Kingdom did not possess a police force directed by the national government. Historically, they had about fifty separate constabularies, each geographically accountable to the local government. Once he found him, the chief liked the idea—because it was one of the few they had—and promised to call the chief constable of Warwickshire, "Peter Brodie, I think..." he murmured to himself while Halliwell went racing out the door, ready to head north from the city.

* * * *

The two black Wolseley police cars drew to a gentle stop in front of three local constabulary cars at an unidentified crossroads, as far as Halliwell was concerned, in the middle of nowhere. He alighted from the car and met a tall, young, uniformed Sergeant Tommy Morris.

"Good afternoon, Sir, I have the warrant from the magistrate. We're here to assist you."

They shook hands, "I'm Halliwell. Can I get you up to speed, Sergeant?"

"I assume it's the attempted bullion robbery yesterday?" he responded.

"Indeed, it is. Wrigglesworth has been on our screens for some time now. He's known to have made contact with a South London face called John Russell," explained Halliwell.

"And Geddes, Sir?" Morris added.

"You know them?" queried Halliwell with some surprise.

"I try to keep up with the national crime scene, Sir," declared Sergeant Morris, without cynicism.

"Excellent. We'll follow you," replied Halliwell, already impressed with the young police sergeant.

Five minutes later all five cars were pulling into The Grange, home of Gonville Wrigglesworth, who was not in residence. The Flying Squad began enquiries to see where he might have gone, while Halliwell followed Morris after breaking in the front door. Sergeant Morris had seven men with him, plus the Flying Squad. They searched the entire house and outbuildings. They found miniscule scraps of what appeared to be gold on the steel floor of the foundry room, but no lead and no gold paint. It was suspicious, but would that be enough? Halliwell set them out onto the grounds, seeking any recently disturbed terrain. They tested the few places they found with long, slim steel rods. They found nothing of interest.

And for Halliwell, the frustration grew, gnawing inside of him. He had never felt so lost on a case before. It was as if someone were shouting at him, and the gods were laughing. He wanted to chase somewhere. He wanted to corner some villains and handcuff them. He wanted…but in the back of his mind, the sight of those two Battersea criminals sneering at him, joking at his impotence as they planned what to do with all the money.

It was a desultory drive back to London, and they became trapped in traffic. Halliwell's mind whirled with different scenarios as he gazed out the window, but they just didn't add up. Sergeant "Chalky" White had rarely seen him like this before. It was recognized that Tom Halliwell rarely became involved with the more physical demands of the Flying Squad because that wasn't the best use of his talents. They needed him for occasions like this. He would work it out in his mind, then the more aggressive officers could begin breaking down doors.

"Something is bothering me, Guvnor."

Halliwell, returning his mind from another time and place, smiled contemptuously tired, and thought, *yes, I'm bothered too, Chalky.* He seemed haggard and strangely older all of a sudden.

Sergeant White rather hoped he wasn't asking something laughable, but it was on his mind. "Whoever took the gold bars, Guvnor…why did they paint the lead with gold paint?" Halliwell gazed back at him incredulously. "I mean, you spotted them straight away in Mayfair, and they sure wouldn't fool anyone at Johnson Matthey."

As he said the words, Halliwell's mind turned from disbelieving of the question to thoughtfully digesting the statement. Eventually, with acceptance of the puzzle, he said, "Yes. Why…did they do that?"

The following morning, back at New Scotland Yard, each squad leader was in attendance as the chief began; "I've been talking to Commander Jones over at Special Branch. He has some good contacts in

South Africa. I suppose we have to cover the assumption that the gold never actually made it onto the ship, although that seems somewhat of a stretch." Shaking his head in disbelief and angry that nothing seemed to elicit any evidence, he continued, "I think our best bet are your informants. Somebody will have to talk, they always do sooner or later."

Halliwell jumped in quickly, "So, we're saying the crime didn't even occur in the UK?"

The chief corrected the impression he'd made. "No, but we've got to cover all angles, Tom. I think you've got something with this Wrigglesworth chap. If he's out of the country, we'll pick him up on his return and see what we get. Perhaps it's time to visit any other smelters we know of? We still have more to do with the train, which must be the center of suspicion here. I read the report on the train driver. Didn't like him, nor the guard." To conclude the meeting, the chief knew that the jackals and vultures would be sniffing around for a slice of the spoils. "Gents, get your contacts and snitches working!"

"It's Russell and Geddes, I know it..." murmured Halliwell. The chief heard him.

"Tom! We need evidence. We need a lead! How the bloody hell did they do it?"

THE GOOD DELIVERY

Love is the only gold.

- Alfred Lord Tennyson

April, 1963 - Warwickshire, England

FIVE DAYS LATER, JOHN RUSSELL and Daniel Geddes sat in the snug of the Prince Albert. For a few minutes now they had not spoken. Inwardly, Russell felt enormously proud of himself and the men who had worked with him. There had, perhaps, always been the thought that the caper might fail, but there would be scant evidence pointing back to him. But Billy had come through, so now, for the nine of them, no more years of hard work just to end up poor at the end of it. Now, he had the immense satisfaction of being a major component of a plan—complicated and detailed—that had actually worked. He was drained, but he kept imagining, what happens now? Time dragged like it wasn't real. They had all worked hard. He was even satisfied with Henry Hale, who had prevailed, and performed as promised. Russell could not have asked for more. He never realized how intense the paradox could be of having nothing to do while worrying so much about the gold, floating around in the middle of England on a nomadic boat. Emily and the baby were healthy. She had read the newspaper headlines every day, like the rest of the nation, stunned by the news and not knowing. She hadn't explicitly asked him, but her eyes had pierced deep into his mind. The Metropolitan Police and the General Post Office had finally revealed the full story the day after Halliwell met the two villains in the pub, causing much uproar across the nation, which the press eagerly fed upon.

The gang were eagerly awaiting the inflows of money into their new Swiss bank accounts, and dissatisfaction concerning cash shortages were remarkably subdued. Geddes had preempted any anarchy by visiting each in turn offering small cash injections if required. There were outstanding debts still to be settled, the largest of which was repayment of the loan from George Smith. This was now a serious problem. Smith had sat in prison for the first night smug that he had an airtight alibi for the duration of the Park Lane fiasco, but since then the news had broken that he'd been made a fool of, if somehow vicariously. He sat in Fulham simmering about something he couldn't quite wrap his mind around. His own work had been usurped by someone, and he wanted to know who.

The government had been seriously mocked and ridiculed, which had not gone down well. The Prime Minister, Harold Macmillan, had leaned heavily on Scotland Yard. There were plenty of theories as to how the robbery had taken place, but without evidence, it remained possible, if not likely, the gold had disappeared while in the custody of a train operated by the state-owned British Railways, or, as some had asserted, while on a train engaged in the business of Her Majesty's Royal Mail. Either of these scenarios pointed to serious banditry aimed directly at the two vital public services. The robbers had to be apprehended and others had to be deterred.

The South African authorities had completed, what they termed, a "very thorough" investigation and concluded, without doubt, the gold had been safely delivered to the British ship, RMMV *Aphrodite May*. The British press continued their, usually, front page stories of "Bullion Heist" and "Gold Robbery," but they had fewer ideas than the police, so they sullied the Met. The press did, however, promoted the £20,000 reward offered by the insurers. The Royal Mail, or British Railways might have added more, but as John Russell predicted, they still didn't know where the robbery occurred.

In London, mighty wheels began to turn due to the apparent scale of the crime. After an emergency meeting of the interested parties at the GPO Headquarters on Newgate Street, the Metropolitan Police set up a special team of investigators headed by a detective chief superintendent. He chose ten good detectives, including Halliwell, but increased that to thirty when New Scotland Yard were soon overwhelmed with a deluge of information. The snitches and contacts were rapidly coming up with information and names, including Russell, Geddes and Peter Badger. This frustrated Halliwell because he recognized the informants were just producing the typical names one would associate with this category of crime.

The Post Office finally withdrew from the investigation, satisfied that the mail had been, was and would be, secure.

Wrigglesworth had been held and extensively interviewed. And he had talked incessantly, but the detectives couldn't draw him away from the fact that he engaged in smelting—legally. Like all the UK's ruling class, he had connections on the periphery of the military, politics and intelligence. Not one piece of information suggested how the crime had been committed, or where the gold was hidden. The Flying Squad had been breaking down doors all over London, presenting dozens of search warrants on some days, creating an unforeseen benefit of lowering the serious crime rate. In the now, daily meeting, Halliwell, against all his instincts began to suggest they would need an informant or a stroke of luck; the crime was making mincemeat of any logical interpretations. He also said they should revisit the possibility of the gold not being loaded onto the ship.

* * * *

Billy and Sally reveled in their first relaxing week on the English canals. Although occasionally chilly overnight, the days were becoming bright, sunny and full of the life of spring. The intensity of being safely together in the fresh air among the green, gently rolling hillsides, fulfilled something that had been missing, or they had never experienced. Sally fretted initially about Lady Someone and Mrs. Somebody else, the guilt soaking into her subconscious for not cleaning their mansions—the awful power of childhood conditioning. But even that dissipated as they motored slowly along, the putt-putting, soothing rhythmic engine somehow foiling all her terrible dreams. At night they returned occasionally, but again she had her sweetheart to hold, feeling secure and content in his arms as they warmed each other's body under the blankets on a cool country evening. They giggled together at the new prospects, then hushed themselves in fear of disturbing the nearby wildlife; a category of existence they were unfamiliar with. They began contemplating, however tentatively, a lifestyle where they didn't need to mend and make do.

Despite Peter's worries, it had not taken Billy long to accomplish the technique of steering a narrowboat; all the training, all those hours at sea, could now be put to good use. Billy fully understood the innate, temperate technique of anticipation, and now Sally was learning too.

At regular speeds, the boat could accept a nudge against a hard canal side, with little, or merely superficial damage. The boat would bounce back. At walking pace, the narrowboat, whose hull they constructed wholly of steel, could doubtless accept a glancing collision with another boat. The abruptness of the impact might cause some damage inside as objects fell to the floor, but almost surely, the hull would survive without serious impairment. The art of narrowboating encouraged the helmsman to slow down while passing other boats tied up alongside, but scrapes and dents were common come the time for a fresh coat of paint.

The issue with Napton on the Hill, as its name implies, is that it lay atop a hill. The Oxford Canal, predominantly, was laid to follow the contours of the countryside by winding around hills and valleys. But only when prudently possible. Frequently, the canal had to use locks to shorten the length, lifting the narrowboat trade over a hill, or down a valley. Just to the south of Napton, where the boat had been loaded with bullion, at a place called Griffins Bridge, Billy took the boat north. Peter stayed aboard for the first day, helping him with the locks near Napton—there were nine of them. The canal, as ever, twisted east and west. While chugging along or when taking a break, Peter explained the daily chores: checking the engine oil, checking the weed hatch, tightening the stern seal. Billy learned how to fill the fresh water, where to dispose of the chemical toilet, where to obtain coal for the fire, and he explained how he could pick up dry wood on route. "Oh, and be careful of…it's gone completely out of my mind. You can get the gist of what I'm saying." Like any conversation with Peter, it would suffice.

The young lovers soon settled down. Once the initial astonishment had dissipated, they enjoyed the cozy confines of the boat. At the aft end, just forward of the open cruiser stern above the engine, sat a small galley, with a Calor gas stove that aided heating the interior. Forward of that were two comfortable armchairs, and a table for eating. Peter's upgrading had been temporarily suspended. There were myriad cardboard boxes stashed with pictures and knickknacks ready to be installed. When Billy made fast the boat in some quiet countryside they could sit inside during the evening and chat about their plans. Sally had come to the recognition that their past had, in one quick instant of closing the door of Daniel's car, disappeared. True, they had nothing to keep them in Battersea; almost no family, other than Billy's Uncle, who they disliked. Sally had relatives too, but they had escaped for Blackheath and Tooting, where it was now difficult to keep in touch. They might not know Sally had gone for a long time. What they had now were themselves, the circumstance they had both wanted more than anything since the age of fourteen.

But it was the alacrity of the change of circumstances that now lay before them. In the next few weeks, as Billy explained, having now lost any traces of boyhood, sums of money would begin being deposited in their own Swiss bank account. And the prospective amounts were just unimaginable. In a country where a truly good wage might be two thousand pounds a year, they were awaiting an eventual payday of £160,000. Just a few more months, they would be gone, never to return. As they sat alone in the evening, or if they secured near a village, perhaps in the cozy bar of the local pub, Billy would narrate his stories. They were stories of a jet airplane, his work in the Engine, of Australia and South Africa, of the delights of the sun, of wide-open spaces, of blue seas and clear, breathable air. Sally listened, shocked that he had flown, not understanding his work on the *Aphrodite May*, all the while envisaging a future with a baby or two playing in the garden, rather than the street.

The only inconvenience for Billy and Sally was not knowing how far they could travel between deliveries of gold. They remained, as best they could, within a ten- to fifteen-mile circle from Watford Gap in the Northeast to Napton in the southwest, encompassing the Grand Union Main Line, Grand Union Leicester Line, the Oxford North and Oxford South canals, all situated around what is commonly considered the focus of the British canal system, the town of Braunston. Billy soon considered the boat his new comfortable home, all perilous work completed. He was on holiday.

John Russell had delivered the first five gold bars from his car. The melting had gone smoothly, and Wrigglesworth had disappeared for a few days fencing the gold. After his long conversation with the Metropolitan Police, the next delivery had been directly from the narrowboat, coming alongside the soft grass at the bottom of Wrigglesworth's estate. Billy had thrown out a gangplank and made fast with two ropes, one around a small tree and the other round a peg in the ground. Peter had driven up to be on hand assisting with carrying the five bars of bullion to the workshop, along with measuring the quantity for financial purposes, and generally helping with his evident handyman skills. When completed, Wrigglesworth expected to be traveling for a week. And the gang had realized that, in the cautious atmosphere created by the police watching everywhere, it was far more prudent to move gold out, as well as in, by the narrowboat.

For Billy and Sally, it was not their concern. As speedily as the last gold bar was in Peter's possession, Billy gunned the engine and off they journeyed farther, for at least five days. He tried to call into the Prince Albert every second or third day, but they had recognized the police might be listening, so they used an elaborate code. For now, they remained in the Napton and Braunston area, hidden in the heart of England. It was a normally busy area, with a few remaining work-boats moving about, along with a growing number of holiday makers beginning to show interest in the expanding leisure industry, combining epic countryside views along with that spirit of being in charge of your own destiny, like a self-driving holiday home without pressure. And the weather was improving every day, and the snow retreated as spring fluttered her eyes awake.

* * * *

The clouds that early morning drew back, revealing the sun rising like gold through the trees. Billy and Sally were returning north to Napton, descending the locks, for a planned consignment on April 9, the Easter weekend. Billy steered towards one of their favorite areas just southwest of the village where nearby the Napton Bottom Lock No. 8 stood the Bull & Butcher pub, which they both enjoyed. It included a public phone from which Billy could call the Prince Albert, or more likely, John Russell's sister-in-law. They planned to step down the locks, then moor for the evening. Sally had begun cooking a beef stew dinner to which Billy's expectancy was high. After eating, they would doubtless take a short stroll along the towpath together before retiring for the night in the countryside's silence. Billy was navigating single-handed, with Sally busy inside. This technique he had mastered on the second day—it was a common enough practice on the canals—and Sally helped on occasions.

Billy drove the narrowboat gently close to the single, upper gate, with a tender nudge. Slipping the engine into neutral, he shimmied along the gunwale to the bow, stepped off and swung the gate open. He paced back down the gunwale to the stern, slipped the engine into forward gear and slowly squeezed the narrowboat inside. The lock was ten feet deep, seven feet wide and seventy feet long; it was average. He had sufficient room. Rather than opening the down-lock sluices and allowing the boat to descend, he took the boat's center-line rope and loosely coiled it around a bollard midway along the lock. He then headed towards the waiting pub, to purchase two carryout beers to consume with dinner.

Billy was unaware, however, of the developing leak in the bottom gates. They had postponed much maintenance throughout the canal system during the years of neglect since the War. Towpaths had over-grown; canal sides had sometimes fallen into the water and many gates had sprung leaks. As promptly as Billy had closed the upstream gate and made fast the rope—knowing he would quickly return—water began draining from the lock into the downstream pound, like a sink with an open drain. The outflow was slower than opening the lower sluices, but draining the lock was. Without attendance, the boat slowly dropped as the waterline descended, the center-line rope tight-ened, restraining the boat adjacent to the upper gate. She continued down, drawn inexorably by the force of gravity, inch by inch as forty-thousand gallons of water gushed from the lower gates. Gently, with no one knowing, the stern set onto the upstream sill.

Sally did not, initially, feel the boat silently descending, even though she was aware of Billy navigating into the lock and his inten-tion of buying beer. Then she felt the bow dropping and the equilibrium of the vessel slowly changing. This was a phenomenon she had not experienced before—scarce people had on the canals. The stern of the twelve-ton boat settled on the sill, the leak continued to empty the lock and the bow, still buoyant, continued its slow downward slide. Sally's feet, enclosed in canvas slippers, felt the floor losing its symmetry. Her mind, having sensed no boat movement in her life, struggled to comprehend. The bow continued down, while the stern remained fast. Once, and quickly realizing the change of attitude, she screamed—more in ignorance than fear—and scrambled for the aft door of the boat, slipping on the floor, becoming more anxious, struggling as the incline increased. She reached the aft hatch, heard the stew pot go crashing forward, and pulled herself up. She shouting out for Billy as she escaped onto the open stern, the relentless and unassailable force of gravity attempting to pull her back within the dark tube of the boat. She screamed the only word she could, "Billy!"

Hugging the sloping stern, hanging on in desperation, she looked to see the bow slowly dropping into the dirty lock. Fifteen degrees, twenty degrees. She screamed out for Billy again. Inside the pub, Billy misunderstood the first cry as something unknown, then he heard his distant lover again. Abandoning his business with alacrity, he rushed outside to be confronted by the hideous spectacle of the boat's bow disappearing in the lock. Uncomprehending of such an incongruous sight, he rushed to the stern and the shouts of Sally. Flinging himself to the dock edge, he held out his hand, and she climbed up the moss and lichen covered lock wall, slipping and struggling. She desperately grasped Billy's hand. Then she climbed over his body to safety. A bystander from the pub arrived to assist the last few steps, pulling her upright.

Billy recovered to his feet and took in the scene's alarming calamity. Dashing forward, he saw the bow, having lost its buoyancy, had entered the canal surface water. At the same moment as he stood there staring, a heavy object relocated noisily inside and exploded through the front swing doors; a twenty-seven-pound, solid gold bar splashed into the water and lay shimmering submerged inside the bow.

A few others had now stepped from the pub and gathered to watch, while one man advised, "I saw this before up at Rugby. You'll need to call the Waterways, but all might not be lost, young lad." The situation, however, devastated Billy, teetering on the edge of the abyss. He wanted to scream out for help. What could he do? Sally held him, and with her warm embrace strove to wrench his mind from the calamity of the circumstances before them.

He hugged her tight, "Are you all right, Sally?"

"I'm good, but this don't look like it should, Billy," she replied. "'ow could it 'ave 'appened?" Billy shook his head, still in shock at the dilemma.

"There's a phone inside lad. Can you call someone?" Yes, he could. This is where he habitually called the men in Battersea, and there was no more vital time than now.

Another man standing near the bow called out from the lock side, "What's that in the bow, under the water?"

Billy knew all too well what was lying conspicuously in the dirty water. He ran into the bar towards the telephone at the end of a short hallway, near the toilets. He made a reverse charge call to Battersea, to the Prince Albert, all secrecy and security lost. Hesitantly at first, then with more panic, raising his voice, he relayed the dilemma to Daniel Geddes.

Police Sergeant Tommy Morris was off duty, relaxing, relishing his black, stout beer sat at the bar, chatting with the landlord, believing it unnecessary to walk outside and engage in a situation that did not involve him. Then he heard the agitated young man on the phone use the words, "Mister Russell," and his eyes widened, and his hand hesitated before the glass. He changed his mind about the scene outside, advising the proprietor he had better investigate and make sure there were no injuries or anything untoward. "I think I'd better get interested now."

Outside, in the dying afternoon sun, he walked over to the boat, now drying, wedged at an acute angle in the lock. Tommy Morris overheard the two youngsters back together chatting. South London accents? Mr. Russell? And then Sergeant Morris's eyes fell upon the name of the boat just forward of the cruiser stern, and the incredible enormity of the state of affairs before him permeated his mind. A bystander drew his scrutiny to the glistening bar under the water, which merely went to confirm his growing suspicions. The magnitude of what he witnessed invaded his mind. Then he turned to the youngsters, "Is this your boat, lad?"

Billy nodded silently, while Sergeant Morris returned to the bar and made two telephone calls, one local, and the other to Whitehall 1212. Sally pleaded with her man, "Billy, I've never saw you like this. You look scared. This man said we can get it pumped out!"

Billy embraced her again, kissed her cheek and then a long kiss on the lips. Then he whispered conspiratorially, "One of the gold bars has fallen through the front doors, Sal. It's there, under the water, in the bow." Then he kissed her again, and she grew fearful of his manner. "Sweet'eart, you 'ave to go, quickly. I'm sure he's a copper. That means more coming. Please go now…"

Sally stared back incredulously. She knew Battersea, she didn't know this place, the countryside, where people 'talked funny'! "'Ow? Where?" She shook her head in ignorance. He passed her his wallet. "Please go, Sally. 'Ead for Battersea. Find Daniel Geddes at the Prince Albert."

"No, I love you. We gotta stay together, Billy" she said as her tears flowed.

"We'll be together ag'in. But you have to go now, Sal. Before ev'rything goes arse over tit 'ere. Go, please." She kissed him, her eyes welling up in understanding, and they briefly hugged in happiness before the future closed in around them. All her wit, resourcefulness and confidence seem to drain from her exquisite, brokenhearted face. Sally turned and walked away in fear and fragility, like the doomed heroine she was. Tears surged in Billy's eyes understanding he had just lost the love of his life, his freedom and all the dreams he'd ever had. He couldn't watch Sally departing, but the return of the policeman from the pub brought his mind back to the then and now, to the hellish paradigm, the brain-scraping disaster tormenting his soul.

The policeman walked over to two men standing nearby and said something to them. Then approaching Billy again, he said, "I'm a policeman, son, what's your name?" Billy shook his head in silence, so Tommy Morris slipped his arm under Billy's and held him powerfully, guiding him back into the bar, sitting him alone in the corner.

"Where's the girl you were with?" Billy remained silent. Within five minutes two police constables arrived, one of which handcuffed Billy and sat with him in the bar, allowing Sergeant Morris to step back outside to reconnoiter the situation.

The police constable spoke to Billy. "You're in trouble, son. Do you want to talk?" Billy shook his head and stared at the older man directly, his eyes glassy.

"Please?" said Billy, his bottom lip trembling.

"Tell me your name, lad," responded the constable.

"It don't matter anymore, does it?" responded Billy, the guilt, loneliness and impotence contorting his face in grief, as the lingering emotional repercussion finally arrived, turning his dreams into a trap. Billy closed his eyes and dreamed of Sally, the streetwise urchin—joyful, radiant and effervescent—dancing in the street.

* * * *

The scene remained calm for nearly two hours, needing a jolt of energy to bring some kind of conclusion. The blue Ford Zodiac quietly crept into the gate opening of the field and pulled to a stop. The two large men alighted and looked towards the scene near the Bull & Butcher. They saw the freshly rigged lights and the people milling about. Daniel took his binoculars and surveyed in the scene's direction, seeing the boat trapped at a strange angle in the lock. Russell took the glasses when offered and saw the same. "Daniel, we gotta get up there and see what we can do for Billy."

"That's not a good idea, John. We're too late," responded Geddes.

"Never too late, Daniel," said Russell, trying to instill some energy in his friend, just like the old days. One more chance to take. "There's not many. If we need to offer up some aggro…"

"Hold it, John, there's a car arriving," declared Geddes. "Police."

"I don't care, we have a duty to the kid…" responded Russell.

"It's the Sweeney. Halliwell." Again, Russell pleaded with his friend to come and assist, but Daniel rationalized, "They're carrying, John! We're not."

Tom Halliwell stepped from the Jaguar, slammed the door and entered the glare of the lights. Initially looking around in confusion, his eyes then settled upon the hatless Sergeant Morris who, for a few seconds, he didn't identify. He stepped over and stretched out his hand, "Good evening, Sergeant, nice to see you again," he smiled. "Now, what's all the calamity about. Have you really found the gold?"

"Pretty sure, Inspector. Come over and have a look."

"Is this normal?" said Halliwell as Sergeant Morris led him over to the bow of the narrowboat, still under water and pointed to the gold brick glinting beneath the waterline in the lights. There was a long ladder now secured with rope at the top, jammed into the narrowboat's bow. "I've been down, Sir. Pretty sure it's gold, and I can see more inside lying on the floor. No warrant, of course, so I didn't enter."

"Well, I'll be damned," expressed Halliwell both with wonder and a hint of admiration. "They hid the bullion on a boat and just kept driving it around?"

"Looks like it," responded Morris.

"Anyone on board?" asked Halliwell.

"A young lad, maybe twenty, I think. He's in the pub with one of my men," was the response.

"All by himself?" asked Halliwell.

"There was a girl—same age—but she's disappeared, I'm afraid. The lad's got a South London accent, but he's not answering questions."

"Goodness. It's brilliant, isn't it?" Halliwell admired. "We still don't know how they did it, you know."

"They didn't take it from the train, Sir?" asked Morris.

Halliwell stood contemplating, while gently shaking his head. "What gave the game away?"

"Two things, Sir. I heard the lad making a reverse charge call to a 'Mr. Russell'." Halliwell smiled with content, "And the name of the boat, of course."

Halliwell turned his head and frowned, "The name of the boat?"

"Yes Sir, come and take a look." Morris led him to the stern of the boat where on the side, freshly painted by Peter in a refined Victorian script, was the name, *The Good Delivery*.

GLOSSARY

Understanding that much of the story is based on a particular time, place and profession—and that I've tried to reflect how the characters might have communicated with each other—I suspect a small number of words or phrases might confuse a few readers. In an attempt to keep my goal of authenticity, here follows a short glossary in chronological order.

Pro	'Moolah', money.
1	'fag'; cigarette
	'MV'; motor vessel.
2	'Sweeney'; rhyming slang (Sweeney Todd), the Flying Squad.
	'Hendon'; Metropolitan Police Training School.
	'aggro'; violent behavior.
3	'pavement artist'; outdoor robber.
	'Jimmy Riddle'; to urinate.
4	'conkers'; traditional children's game using the seeds of the horse chestnut tree.
	'singling up'; a ship getting ready to depart.
	'sweets'; candy.
	'off-license'; shop selling alcohol for consumption elsewhere.
	'knock down ginger'; street game involving door knocking and running away.
	'tallyman'; a man selling door to door merchandise on credit.
5	'tiddlywinks'; game played by children using small discs and a pot.
6	'borstal'; youth detention center.
	'clobber'; clothing and accessories.
	'quid'; £1 sterling.
	'Barclay's Bank'; masturbation.
	'cheeky sod'; mild pejorative.
	'welly'; force or effort.
	'George the fifth'; King George V Dock, London.
	'Put a tiger in your tank'; ESSO commercial jingle.
	'The pools'; a betting pool predicting the outcome of soccer games.

8	'plimsolls'; simple design and manufacture of athletic shoe.
	'eleven-plus'; exam taken at age 11 to decide the high school attended.
	'poppy'; money.
	'Arding & Hobbs'; large department store.
	'long-firm fraud'; opening fake companies to borrow money.
	'flop'; distribution of the money.
9	'toff'; derogatory name for upper-class person.
10	'the six-foot'; the nominal distance between adjacent railway lines.
13	'crisps'; chips.
	'wide boy'; a man who lives by his wits.
	'ten-bob'; half of £1 sterling.
14	'big hats'; uniformed police.
15	'GPO'; General Post Office, The Royal Mail.
	'Calor Gas'; British supplier of liquid petroleum gas.

VOYAGES to *Serendip*

Strap yourself in. John Smith's life is about to change in a manner he never envisioned.

As a non-conformist schoolboy, he has a burning need to escape the comfort of southeast London suburbia, escape the industrial hemorrhaging of a post empire Britain, escape the zombies of death.

This dazzling memoir, written in beautiful, confident prose begins in 1977 with England in a state of despair. How does a boy become a man? It's a question as old as life itself. He decides to travel in a different world, experience life, women, poverty and the fear of war in a vivid account through a young man's eyes.

His adventures at sea and on land teach him who he is and what he truly wants from life. He visits the dazzling lights of New York, Cape Town and Hong Kong, but also the numbing blandness of Suez and Halul, the rigidity of religious Arabia and the poverty of West Africa. Along the way, John has time to reflect on some philosophical aspects of life.

What begins as an escape becomes a search for something else, something hidden awaiting to be found. Immerse yourself in *Voyages to Serendip*, a story about recognizing where you come from and the random, struggle to find a way forward revealed in fate.

Written with candor and self-deprecating humor, this memoir will literally take you round the world to find a better place. *Voyages to Serendip* tells the age-old tale of growing up, but in a very different style.